HEAVENLY SCENT

HEAVENLY SCENT

FAY SMITH

Fay Smith

I

Eve

Eve hefted the full pot of coffee and wheeled around the counter to check on her tables. The dinner rush had already come and gone, so the diner was only half-full of patrons still eating, chatting, or stalling for time. The diner was old with fifties-style Formica tables, with chrome around the edges, which showed a lot of wear. The plastic-coated booth benches, which looked like the bench seats out of an old car, had been patched and were ragged. Those seats caused your legs to sweat in the summer and then stuck to you like duct tape when you rose too quickly to leave, leaving a throbbing burn on your thighs. This was like her second home, everything worn and familiar. She looked over her side of the dining area and counter and headed for the few individuals still drinking coffee to top them off.

She was working the night shift with Becky, the usual Sunday night routine. Becky was nice enough... but Eve just couldn't connect with her as a friend, just like she couldn't connect with most people. She had lived in this small Oklahoma town her whole life, yet she felt like an outsider and was just different. While the town didn't feel like home, the diner was comfortable and familiar.

With all her tables checked and happy, Eve had only to wait, lost in her thoughts, until a customer would summon her again. This left her a lot of time to think. Too much time. Was she unhappy? No. She was, however, lonely. Her gaze swept over the room, taking in the small groups of friends and families conversing over their food.

Eve had lived in the small rural town all of her twenty-five years. She had graduated high school, gotten some online college courses, and worked a dead-end job at this old diner. This was the sum total of her short life. She had never been popular, always... different from other people her age. She couldn't say how; besides her naturally indigo hair, she always felt odd. It was like she was on a different wavelength, which other people didn't understand or want to.

She didn't really have friends, not the way she saw other people with their friends. She had grown up without girlfriends to confide in or gossip with, and she wasn't invited to parties or sleepovers. She learned early to enjoy her own company, so as an adult, she preferred the company of an interesting book to a boring local who only saw as far ahead as the next party on the weekend.

Her dating life had been just as deficient, which was not a hardship, as she was in no hurry to land a husband and start pumping out babies. Not before she had even really lived yet. She had dated a few of the guys in her town, but relationships never lasted long. The dating pool was small and stagnant. Sure, guys wanted to fuck her, but they didn't want to bring her home to meet Mom; in some ways, that was ok with her. It's not that she wanted a white-picket fence relationship... but it would have been nice to have someone see her that way.

She had dreams of leaving this tiny town one day. She had no idea where she would go or what she would do, but it had to be better than this. She glanced over the diner again, and one thing was for sure: there was no future here for her.

Damn these slow nights.

Eve blew her bangs out of her eyes in frustration. She was about to start cleaning behind the counter when the bell over the door announced another customer. Eve looked to the door and caught her breath. In walked three of the most drop-dead gorgeous men she had ever seen in this middle-of-nowhere town.

They were movie-star gorgeous. Panty-creaming. Hell, they might be angels if she believed in such things. They were... perfect. They were tall, with tight shirts spanned over muscular, toned, but not grotesquely huge, arms and chests. Equally impressive thighs and, dare she add asses, filled out their jeans very nicely as they moved into the room. They had rugged square jawlines, piercing eyes with unlawfully long lashes. Each had his own coloring, hairstyle, and differences, but as a whole, they were other-worldly. She realized she was staring but couldn't drag her eyes away. She was stunned into inaction, frozen in place. She shook her head to clear it, finally moving her eyes away from the masculine walls of sex.

Her eyes flicked to Becky, who was unabashedly staring at them, wide-eyed, mouth open like a carp. This seemed to break the spell for Eve, who chuckled under her breath as the three newcomers headed to a booth in Becky's section.

Oh well... Can't win'em all.

Eve cursed under her breath and went back to collecting silverware and salt and pepper shakers; there was still work to do. Taking the lids off the salt shakers, she tried to focus on what she was cleaning, but her curiosity kept getting the better of her. This small backroads town didn't get a lot of visitors, and certainly none who looked like those three.

She could imagine herself on a Hollywood movie set with them, sprawled in satin sheets while their hot-oiled bodies prowled around her... They were the fodder of fantasies.

She glanced over the top of the counter where she worked to see Becky already at their table, laying the flirt on thick as she placed menus and silverware, all but pouring herself onto the table with them. Eyelashes batted. Cheeks flushed. Becky made it a point to bend over low to point out the specials on the menu, showcasing her cleavage barely restrained in a red lacy bra, threatening to burst out of her low-cut shirt.

Eve chuckled at Becky's antics until she noticed that one of the men facing her was looking right at her with a smirk. His eyes were... intense. And then it seemed like she was locked in his gaze, and nothing else existed. His smoldering looks took her in, and she felt vulnerable, exposed. Her former Hollywood fantasy rose to the forefront of her mind. It felt like... minutes? Seconds? She couldn't tell. It was awkward and felt highly personal.

As the noise of the surroundings came rushing back, her cheeks flamed hot as if she had been caught doing something naughty, and she noted that Mr. Intense was still locked on her. She looked back down at her salt shaker, now filled to overflowing. Luckily it was behind the counter, where the stud-muffin couldn't have seen it. She took a shaky breath as she began scooping salt, trying to distract herself and not look back at him. Even without looking, she could feel his eyes boring into her.

Really, Eve, are you a teenager? It's not like you've never seen a good-looking guy!

Eve turned to clean her sponge in the sink and jumped, startled, when Becky was standing in the previously empty spot, practically on top of her. Throwing her hand over her charging heart, Eve laughed and started apologizing but trailed off as she noticed Becky was not quite right. Sure, she was still smiling, still perky, but her eyes... her eyes were wrong. She had a million-mile stare like she was sedated and just happy to be in her own world.

"Becky, you ok?" Eve ran her hand in front of Becky's face.

"Yeah. Of course.... I'm fine." Becky slowly brought her unfocused gaze to Eve's face. "I think you should wait on eighteen."

Becky reached past Eve, picked up the coffee pot, and headed back to the far side of her section, away from the newcomers, at table eighteen.

Alright, what the hell just happened?

It was not like Becky to give away a table; she needed her tips too. But to give up a table of three Greek Gods for NO reason?... No. Clearly, something was said, and Eve was not going to put up with it. She didn't care if they were gods; no one harassed the staff. Working to keep her simmering rage from boiling over, Eve headed straight for the table in question. Three perfect masculine faces smiled up to receive her.

She got only a few steps away before she pulled to a sudden stop, confused.

Wait. Had she said god-like? Because up close they were, well, they were still good-looking, but not with the initial 'stop traffic' kind of looks she had thought they had. They were very handsome, but she wasn't sure why she had reacted that way earlier, and she had only been a few feet away from them.

She looked from one to the next, confused, like she had just come to her senses.

And how had she not noticed their HAIR? Mr. Intense had dark purple hair, another had bright flaming red and another dark green. How had she missed THAT? Her own Indigo blue hair was the talk of the town; she was the only one that usually stood out.

They were still buff and beyond mouth-watering, but it was no longer like a scene out of a movie where heavenly light showered down over them, making the world stop at their appearance. Eve shook her head again to clear her distraction; she latched eyes with the man who had caught her attention earlier, Mr. Intense.

"What did you say to Becky?" She put enough growl into her voice to let them know she was not to be toyed with but not enough roar to bring the whole diner into a melee.

"We didn't say anything, Darlin-" Before the man on her right even got the words out, Eve repeated herself to Mr. Intense, whose eyes she had never left.

"WHAT.DID.YOU.SAY.TO.BECKY?!"

His lips never moved, but the muscles around his eyes tensed for a moment, carrying some hint of emotion like confusion. It was quickly gone, replaced with the warm greeting eyes she had been met with at the table, like a mask falling back into place.

"I think I understand..." he spoke to her slowly, intentionally, like she was a feral animal about to attack. "We didn't say anything offensive, I swear. We just told her you should wait on us. That's all."

He put both hands up in surrender, his big slate blue-gray eyes twinkling up at her innocently.

"You expect me to believe--"

"I don't expect anything. But it's the truth. Ask her."

As it happened, Becky was walking behind Eve at that moment, and the man on Eve's right called her over and asked her to verify what Mr. Intense had said.

"Yeah. That's what happened." She smiled vacantly and skittered off.

"Then why is she acting stoned?" Eve fired back after Becky was out of earshot.

"You'd have to ask her about that, Love. Now, could we get some coffee?"

Mr. Intense smiled in what was probably supposed to appear a sweet way, but it only came across as gloating, his eyes laughing.

Why does this shit always happen on MY shift?

2

Tark

Tark spoke with his companions in their own language to be sure they weren't being listened to. His glamor had done just what he expected; to everyone present, they appeared to be normal, if not highly virile, humans. Becky had been eating out of their hands. The plain waitress would have rubbed her crotch on them like a cat if she could have done so inconspicuously. Tark chuckled under his breath.

He watched the conversation between the waitresses from the corner of his eye. Eve: her name was Eve. Becky had given them that, although to be fair, she hadn't had any choice. The added compulsion made humans do whatever they suggested, in addition to their altered appearance.

He eyed the women as they talked. Eve had the right features: the indigo blue hair that he was pretty sure was not dyed that color, sharp cheekbones, wide eyes that made her look very young, and a feline way of moving. And while she had the Fae litheness, she was definitely more curvy than your average Fae.

Not that he was complaining.

Those curves look good on her, and not everyone wants to fuck a twig.

Humans thought women should be rail-thin. Tark frowned; he could tell them they were wrong. He lived with fae women built like ballerinas, and it got old fast.

He'd love the opportunity to sink his fingers into lush hips, pull that full bottom against his hard length, and run his hands up that ribcage until he hefted the weight of each globe of a breast in his palms...

He had to subtly adjust his jeans and change his line of thinking, or he would be too distracted. He never got distracted by females, but she was really tempting him.

Get it together, Tark! You're not an adolescent!

After a quick exchange of words, Becky swung the coffee away, and Eve headed toward their table with murder in her eyes. He tapped his fingers on the table to alert the others that she was on her way. It was all coming together.

They all turned to her, smiling in a friendly, human way. Tark waited for the glamor to affect her; instead, she appeared confused and distracted, looking from one of them to the other until finally bringing her heated gaze back to Tark with intention.

"What did you say to Becky?"

She was angry. A few patrons of the diner stopped, their heads swiveling to take in the conversation. Tark was taken aback, expecting the compulsion to bring her into submission. But he kept his features schooled.

Before he could answer, Lamn spoke up. "We didn't say anything, Darlin-"

"WHAT.DID.YOU.SAY.TO.BECKY?!"

Her eyes never left Tark's, and her words rolled with energy.

Definitely not just human. Also, the glamor wasn't working on her: interesting.

"I think I understand..."

He quickly glanced at his companions, Lamn and Skiff, letting them know he would handle it. He turned his full attention back to the waitress, Eve.

"We didn't say anything offensive, I swear. We just told her you should wait on us. That's all." He spoke clearly and calmly, hoping to regain control of the conversation.

She clearly didn't believe him. Her arms were crossed over her chest, with her hip popped out to the side as she glared at him. He saw Becky headed back towards their side of the room and suggested asking her as Lamn reached out, summoning her over. And just as he knew she would, she verified everything he had said. Again, not like she had a choice in the matter.

Humans are so frail-minded.

From the corner of his eye, Tark saw Lamn's green tresses fall subtly as he leaned in ever so subtly toward Eve and inhaled. Instantly Lamn tensed, his eyes widening and nostrils flaring. Tark noted it but said nothing, not until they were alone. She was still glaring at Tark and hadn't noticed.

Eve was clearly stuck. With Becky backing the story, she would be rude to insist anything else had happened, but she clearly wasn't ready to let it go. Tark closed the conversation quickly by ordering coffee for the three of them and then watched her head back to the counter, looking over her shoulder to scowl. He then switched to their native Faeish.

"Clearly not just human. The compulsion and glamor didn't phase her, not even with the three of us powering it. I'm wondering if any of it worked." Tark looked between his companions.

"No, she's otherworldly, alright. Fae, and... something else." Lamn's eyebrows were knitted, and his fingers drummed the table. "I've smelt it a few times before, but very few. And I don't know just what it is, but it's rare. Of course, it's hard to scent anything over soap, shampoo, conditioner, body wash, powder, deodorant, cooking grease, dishrags... oh, AND perfume. I don't understand why human females feel the need to smell like a field of flowers and toxic chemicals."

Tark and Skiff laughed in agreement as Eve returned with three cups of coffee, setting them down almost violently on the Formica.

"Would you like to order anything else?" She asked coldly, staring at her notepad.

Tark smiled, enjoying her frustration with them.

She's so adorable when she's angry.

"How about three apple crisps?"

"Ice cream?" She growled.

"Sure." Tark tried his hardest to repress a chuckle; he knew it wouldn't help his cause. But she was absolutely delicious when her brows knit together, and her eyes narrowed in anger. He was willing to bet she'd be ferocious in bed.

She was off again without a backward glance, and they resumed their conversation. Their informant from a few weeks prior was correct; she was a hybrid. They just didn't know what kind yet. Still, it was fortunate their scouts found her first. There really weren't many hybrids. They'd have to move quickly and get her to safety before she attracted more unwanted attention.

If Tark could find her, so could the Unseelie of the Winter Court, which would not end well for Eve.

3

Eve

Eve watched as the men at table eighteen drank their coffee and ordered desserts, and within forty-five minutes finished, paid, and left. Eve swooped in to clear the table immediately as if she could erase their presence from her mind. They left a ridiculously huge tip of $100 on a twenty-four dollar check for Eve, which she then split with Becky because it *should* have been Becky's table. She would want Becky to do that for her... but then again, *she* never would have given up a table when the diner was so slow.

Becky seemed ambivalent: acknowledging the money, but still staring off into the distance.

A fifty-dollar tip and she doesn't care?!

Eve watched as Becky cleaned absently, almost poured coffee on one patron's hand, and just seemed out of it. Becky never seemed to snap out of whatever daze she was in. As closing approached Eve called Becky's loser boyfriend to pick her up and take her home; she honestly didn't want her driving in that state. Not surprisingly, Becky didn't argue. Eve didn't know what they had done to her, but she was sure those guys at table eighteen had done *something*.

Smug bastards. They think they're so damned hot. I'll bet girls just drop their panties for them. Well, not THIS girl. I see through their little act.

Eve ran the dishes through the dishwasher, having already wiped down all the booths, tables, and counters. Her side-work was done, and she was helping Eddie in the kitchen so that they could close for the night. Secretly, she also wanted to be sure she left at the same time as he did, so she wasn't walking out alone, not after those weirdos. They could have doped Becky up, drugged her in some way, and Eve wouldn't be their next victim. This was a small town, but bigger cities had designer drugs she knew nothing about.

Why do guys who look like that feel the need to drug women? Or is it just an entitlement thing?

As Eve gathered her purse her cell phone started to ring, the chorus of "You're So Vain" by Carly Simon spiking her pulse. She had set that ringtone as a warning, and looking at the screen she confirmed, it was Richard Royce... her ex. She groaned out loud.

What part of never contact me again do you NOT understand?

This night just keeps getting better and better.

It had been two years. *TWO YEARS.* Why was he calling her now? While their relationship hadn't been very long, he had broken her heart and humiliated her, and it had taken everything she had to put him in the past. And here he was ringing her phone like they were good friends. Just seeing his name brought back the rage and made her cheeks flush hot.

Apparently, dating her hadn't been enough for him. He had kept their relationship a secret from everyone, stating that he "liked his privacy," even though he had no such privacy qualms with previous girlfriends. Of course, this need for privacy was very convenient for him when he reached out through social media to a naive girl in China, almost young enough to be his daughter, and started grooming her to be his next girlfriend.

CHINA?! I mean seriously, she barely spoke English! Who DOES that?!

His passive-aggressive bullshit had been bad enough, but it was the way she found out he had cheated and lied. When he suddenly no longer valued his privacy, he metaphorically slapped Eve in the face with a post of his new-found "one true love," his Chinese *fiance*, all over social media; this after having treated Eve like she was some shameful whore that he couldn't be seen with in public. And of course, he had no idea why Eve was upset about any of this. His last words to her were, "You should be happy for me."

Carly was still belting out the tune as Eve 'noped out' on taking the call, hitting silence. She had zero fucks for Richard and his Chinese Social Media bride, after the night she'd already had. Maybe he'd take a hint... but knowing him, she highly doubted it. He never was that smart.

She grabbed her purse and headed for the door.

Eve's feet were aching as she and Eddie walked out of the diner, locking the door behind them. They said their goodnights before they each got into their cars. Eve made her way out of the parking lot, ready to head home and put the night behind her. Almost.

Eve only had a twenty-minute drive home from the diner, which meant that she had to drive all the way across town and back again to drag it out to a forty-five-minute drive. As tired as she was, there was no point in getting home before midnight; not that it was her home anyway.

Eve had never known her biological mother. Instead, she lived with her grandmother, Nancy, who was really the only family she had ever known. Her relationship with Nancy was complicated. Nancy believed herself a self-appointed representative of God. The fact that she was a raging alcoholic was irrelevant. She was the judge of who and what met the standard. And Eve had never met the standard. Never.

When Eve's mother had shown up at the hospital ready to give birth, after having disappeared over a year prior, the police recognized her from the missing person posters. It was Nancy who came. And when Eve's mother left the hospital, and her hours-old newborn daughter who had not even been named, it was Nancy who took that baby in... begrudgingly.

Eve never met her mother, found out what she had done to piss Nancy off, or even why she had run away. Nancy never talked about her, except to say she was a whore of Satan, and the like. Eve figured out fast that Nancy was batshit crazy, as well as being a drunk. For the most part, she raised herself.

She could have moved out long ago, she was twenty-five and had saved. She just never did.

Still, she wasn't getting home before midnight, on the off chance that Nancy was still not passed out after her bender. Eve didn't need to hear the "Sunday is the LORD'S Day" lecture again.

As luck would have it, when Eve tiptoed through the side door of the ancient crumbling ranch, she could hear Nancy snoring like a chainsaw from her chair in the living room. Grateful for the peace, she snuck into her own room and quietly closed the door.

Watching from across the street, a deer stepped from his hiding space in the woodline and raced away.

4

Eve

The next afternoon Eve pulled into the parking lot of Eddie's Diner, ready for her shift. So far it had been a good day, Nancy was still sleeping off her Lord's Day celebration, so Eve had been able to get ready with peace and quiet. Mondays ranged from fairly quiet to nearly dead. Becky opted for the turn-around morning shift to catch any breakfast or lunch crowds. Eve was not a morning person and was happy enough to relieve Becky and take whatever she got in the afternoon to evening. There was less money, but sleeping in was worth it. Eve expected a slow afternoon and evening and hoped she'd get a chance to talk to Becky before she headed out at the end of her shift.

The small Oklahoma town didn't offer a lot by way of industry, or tourism, which worked both for and against the old diner. While there was not a huge flow of people passing through, there was also almost no competition in the area.

If people wanted to meet to discuss business over lunch, it was the diner. If people didn't want to eat at home, it was the diner. If people just wanted to hang out and chat over coffee, it was the diner. So while it wasn't very large or impressive, and it definitely showed its age in its worn paint and chrome, the diner was THE local meeting point.

Eve hung her sweater up in the employee closet and put on her apron. She tapped Becky on the shoulder, startling her out of her thoughts. Becky's cheeks were suddenly blushing as her eyes shifted nervously, and Eve wondered what she had been thinking about. She knew Becky had opinions about her, opinions she never spoke of to Eve directly. Eddie had told Eve he had caught her sneaking to look at the employee files. When she was asked why, she stated that she believed Eve was too young to work and had a fake ID. But Becky never said anything to Eve. She never did.

"Hey, Becky, how are you feeling today? I wanted to ask you something about last night."

Becky instantly stiffened defensively. "What about it?" She tried to pull off nonchalant, but couldn't keep the annoyance out of her voice.

"Uh... you remember those three guys, the ones at table eighteen? Why did you agree with those guys to let me take them? I'm just curious."

"Agree with them? It was my idea," she spoke as if it should be clear that the conversation was over.

At this Eve blanched. The guys had told her they had suggested it, and she had agreed: and then she had corroborated the story. Now, she was telling a different story.

"But why? I mean, was it because of the hair color?"

Becky's brows furrowed in confusion or annoyance, a small frown pinching her lips tight, as she rubbed a hand over her temple like she was getting a headache.

"Hair color? What are you even talking about?!" Becky's voice went up an octave. Defensiveness was definitely up a notch and recruited a side of pissed.

Eve sighed and tried to word it in such a way that made her look curious, and not judgmental. "You know... because MY hair is blue... and theirs were funky colors? Did you think we'd just get along? Or did they want to meet me?"

Becky stopped.

Full annoyance achieved.

"Eve, I have NO idea what you're talking about. What funky colors?! YOU are the only one here with funky hair color. I told you, I just suggested it. What's the big deal? Look- I need to get going."

She was loud and clearly upset. Moving quickly, she dropped her apron on the counter, grabbed her purse from behind it, and bolted for the door before Eve could even get a status on the dining room. Eve had no idea what the hell had just happened. She had asked politely, kindly even. Becky was normally sweet and mousy. Why was Becky acting so out of character?

And Becky hadn't noticed that Mr. Intense had deep purple hair? Or that the guy across from him had dark green hair? And their friend: red? She just... missed that? How is that possible?!

But hadn't Eve herself missed it at first? All she saw was three god-like guys coming in. It wasn't until she went to their table that she suddenly noticed their hair color and that they didn't look so god-like after all. It was as if she was seeing through an illusion. But how is THAT possible?

Ugggh... This is too much weirdness. Let it go, Eve.

She grabbed the coffee pot and headed out for the first round of warm-ups.

As predicted, the afternoon dragged by with only the occasional patron. With a half-hour left till closing, and all the side work already done; only Edgar, a lonely local, was seated at the counter reading a paper and drinking his coffee. Eve was getting ready to dump the half pot of burnt coffee when the bells over the door rang. When she looked up, she saw Mr. Intense looking right back at her: this time, alone.

Just.fucking.peachy.

He walked to the other end of the counter, away from Edgar, slowly slid his jacket down his muscular arms, and sat down, the whole time keeping eye contact with her. His dark purple hair was mussed in a way that said he did it on purpose, and his t-shirt stretched over hard pecs as he rested his elbows on the counter, biceps bulging. Snorting a frustrated breath, she retrieved her notepad and headed his way. It didn't improve her mood that he was trying hard to repress a chuckle.

"You're back. Lucky me. What can I get for you?" She deadpanned.

"Coffee... and a moment for me to apologize?" He smiled up at her sweetly under his lashes.

But see?... Right there! There's laughter in his eyes: he's mocking. His apology isn't sincere, it's just a foothold to a conversation, and I see RIGHT through it.

Eve narrowed her eyes at him.

"I can get you a coffee. But if you're going to pretend and give me some bullshit apology you don't really mean, then save us both the aggravation."

She turned on her heel to the coffee pot, grabbed the half pot of burnt coffee, and poured him a cup.

5

Lamn

Lamn walked the Divide Between the Worlds carefully. He had not told Tark and Skiff where he was going, only that he had to pursue a lead. Having met the hybrid, Eve, at the diner, he now had a theory about her origins, and he had to know for sure. He could get his answers here if he was lucky.

While it was a sort of neutral zone, open to all other-worlders, it also had its own set of rules. It was not wise to stay for too long, and chance offending a more powerful other-worlder if it could be avoided. Unfortunately, today, it could not be avoided. Answers were needed, and time was of the essence. Still, he moved cautiously, aware of his surroundings.

He made his way through the trees, accompanied only by an eerie, unnatural, silence. The forest was vast, with rises and gullies. Sunshine streamed through the canopy overhead, making his dark green hair shine like the leaves around it. There was no real path to follow, more small trails through the underbrush that you had to know to find. No birds sang. No frisky critters ran to and fro.

As the sun climbed high overhead, he found what he was looking for. It was a simple stone pillar, nothing remarkable to look at. The glyphs which had been carved in it were a very ancient language that only a few still spoke. In fact, Lamn did not, but he had been told what to look for. It was a marker of the Grigori, the "Watchers," and if he was lucky he could summon one.

No one had told him what would happen if he was unlucky. Maybe he was about to find out. Putting aside all doubt, and firming his focus and intention, he placed his hand on top of the stone, and spoke loudly and clearly.

"Grigori... Grigori, if you watch even now, I have come to ask you for your assistance."

Lamn could feel the atmosphere becoming more dense around him as if the air pressure were squeezing him gently, getting a feel for him. But after several heartbeats, nothing else happened. He huffed out a breath in frustration.

"Grigori... I need to know what manner of other-worlder is Eve Sherman. It is a matter of life and death."

It was a risk putting all his cards on the table, but he didn't have time to play games. His gamble paid off. As soon as he spoke the name the winds picked up into a small gale, thrashing branches, leaves, and debris around in a whirlwind. The density in the air gripped him again, and a feeling of dread filled his heart. Forest debris whipped by him and lashed his dark green hair away from his face. A booming voice filled the air, seeming to come from all sides.

"What right have you to disturb me, to ask favors; Lamn, Son of the Summer Court?"

Lamn turned to see the tall imposing figure standing behind him. The Grigori, or Watcher, was a force of nature. His robes were white linen, his features fair, but those were the only thing one could consider 'ordinary' about him. He stood head and shoulders taller than Lamn, who was tall by human standards. He didn't need to appear overly muscular, or ornate. The Watcher was massive, immovable, radiating divine power. His wings were arched, ready. His sword and shield were also ready, although Lamn knew he wouldn't stand a chance, even if the Watcher was bare-handed. While he knew this Grigori, Armoniel, was letting him see his full divine aspect with his unearthly glow, it didn't make it any less spectacular, or less frightening. Grigori were not to be tampered with, as they were among the most powerful of other-worlders, the most dramatic, and moody, when they wanted to be.

"Armoniel, please forgive my intrusion. I would not disturb you if I did not believe it absolutely necessary." Lamn bowed low in a show of respect. Every court has its own etiquette, and the Grigori also had their own. Manners never hurt.

"Rise, Lamn, Son of the Summer Court. Why do you need know of Eve Sherman? If you give me sufficient cause, I will answer your questions. If not, I will banish you from this place."

Lamn, still bowed, tried not to roll his eyes in frustration. He didn't want to have to lay out the entire situation for the Watcher; although, likely, the Watcher already knew and was just testing him. Watchers despised deception and treachery, and let's face it, the Fae thrived on it.

"Armoniel, we have only just become aware of Eve as an other-worlder. You know the situation of the Fae, you know why we are looking for other-worlders? I am certain you do, you see much."

A little stroking of the ego can't hurt, right?

"We have discovered Eve, but she contains more than Fae blood; we don't know what we are dealing with. We don't want to chance intro-ducing more demon blood into the world if we can avoid it. I was won-dering if you knew her true nature, and would share it? Time is of the essence, as the Winter Court can't be far behind. If they find her, they will not care what blood she carries, nor if she is willing to share it."

Armoniel stiffened a little, his already annoyed appearance becom-ing more hostile.

"And what of the Summer Court? If she carries demon blood, would you dispatch her?"

Lamn had to tread very carefully here, as he felt there was more behind the Watcher's question than he was aware of. It felt like a trick question, and if he answered wrong he would get nothing.

"What right have we to take her life, for a blood that is no choice of her own? No, we would not condone ending her life. However, to leave her with the mortals is to tempt the Winter Court to snatch her for their own devices, and they would do much, much worse. Perhaps the safest course for her is to offer her sanctuary among the Summer Court? I would value your input on this issue."

Again, a little boost to the ego couldn't hurt, right? The Grigori were a proud race.

"There, I have laid out my quandary before you, Armoniel. I have answered your questions justly. Will you tell me what manner of other-worlder is Eve Sherman?"

Armoniel seemed to roll the information around in his head for a few moments, which stretched in the silence, before meeting Lamn's eyes in a decision. He allowed his appearance to shrink back, matching the Fae in height and stature, and with less illumination. Gone were the sword and shield, and his wings folded comfortably at his back, in a more relaxed posture. He sighed in acceptance. When he spoke his voice was more conversational and less booming.

"Sit, Fae. We have much to discuss."

6

Armoniel

Armoniel was fatigued. Not from this short interaction with the Fae, but of his own existence... of always watching and knowing... and maybe of his own failings. He knew this time would come, sooner or later, and he would have to stand and atone for his role. That was the curse of the Grigori: to watch over this world, but never be OF this world... to watch, but never have.

Well,... almost never.

Armoniel took a seat on a fallen log and gestured to Lamn to join him. Seated, Armoniel turned to Lamn to begin the tale.

"You have already guessed her paternity. You know the fae blood she carries."

Lamn's eyes went wide, and he opened his mouth as if to dispute it, but Armoniel carried on.

"What you do NOT know is the paternity of her grand-sire. And for that, I must tell you the story of Nancy."

The Story of Nancy

Born to the wife of the fundamentalist preacher Pastor Sherman, was the small babe named Nancy. Both the mother and father were pleased with their precious girl child, and she was brought into the world with love. Her early years were unremarkable, being raised as babes are.

But shortly after her sixth year, a terrible drought took their small farming community. Crops were ravaged, animal herds suffered, and there was lack and frustration throughout the community. The Grigori watched and wept at their suffering.

The preacher doubled his efforts, appealing to God, and damning his community for their human failings: their lack of faith. His Book told him that if the community suffered, they did so because of God's wrath: because they took part in wickedness. And so it must be.

He delivered the verdict to them: repent, or suffer.

The drought continued, first one season, then two, then three. Many in the community had no choice but to give up all they had and move away, in hopes of surviving. But the preacher's ego would not allow him the same. He felt the betrayal of each family which left him, left God, for their own selfish means. He saw them as fickle and wicked: too weak to prostrate themselves before God. He became angry, bitter, and enraged.

He was always angry. He began shouting at his wife to take out his frustrations, and eventually, he would strike her, working out all the self-righteous anger he had been storing for so long. His wife, a pious woman, had always done what was right by him and God, but after a few years of taking his beatings, she was defeated, and couldn't take it any longer. And so she crept away in the middle of the night to find a new life for herself, leaving Nancy and her husband behind.

If the preacher had been angry before, his rage knew no bounds when he found his wife gone in the morning. This last betrayal was the worst, and his mind formed the idea that his Book was right, that women were the root of all evil in the world. They were the portal through which Evil entered into this world to tempt the minds, hearts, and bodies of good men. His fervor took on new life. He was a man possessed.

That was the day he began beating his own child; telling her that she was a worthless whore, like all women, sent to earth just to tempt men and then break them with their sex. And this treatment continued for years. He no longer preached to the community, because there was almost no community left; no, now he preached to Nancy.

Day in and day out he assaulted her with his fists and his words; fire and brimstone to burn away her sinful flesh and wonton desires, of which she had none. When she came of age, ripe for the downfall of mankind, he knew what he had to do. He would 'test her.' He would lure her to explore him in inappropriate ways, offering her the love and approval she had been seeking from him for so long; only to turn it back on her, calling her a demon vixen, cursing her vile seductive body, and beating her to chase the succubus from her. She was tormented daily.

And so, Nancy grew, broken and unloved.

Now it happened in her eighteenth year that a few of the girls, whom she considered friends from church, invited her out on a Saturday night for a bonfire in the fields. It was a secret, only they knew. These were good girls, and good friends to her, although she didn't have much access to them. She could certainly never confide in them what happened behind closed doors at home, she could never tell them how she really got the bruises and cuts. Still, they didn't push her, and accepted her for who she was.

While she was afraid of the punishment she would surely get if she went out with them; she did not want to miss the opportunity to get away from her father and be in the safety of her friends, if only for a few hours. She longed to be like other girls. She was always doing what she should, always the good girl; she just wanted ONE night to go out and be a 'normal' girl with friends.

So she waited until the house was silent, and she knew her father would be asleep. She held her breath in terror, afraid her breathing alone would give her away, as she snuck out of the ranch-style house. She crept slowly and as quietly as she could, still somehow sure that her father would see her, would catch her. But as she put distance between herself and the house, she gathered her courage and ran the rest of the way through the cornfields to where her friends were waiting. She had done it!

The fire was already blazing. One of the girls had stolen alcohol from her father's liquor cabinet, and they were mixing it with punch. The girls drank, talked, and laughed into the night with their transistor radio playing music in the background. As they were not used to drinking, they became sloppy, and uninhibited, even with little alcohol. In the heat of the summer night, one of them pulled her clothing off, which set the others to laughter and then to pull their own off. Not to be left out, Nancy pulled off her blouse, and then her skirt. Why not? There were no boys here to see. There was no one but the three of them: FREE. The three of them danced around the fire to the music, laughing, and singing, in their own private world.

But it wasn't private. Nothing is private from the Watchers.

Armoniel saw the beautiful young lady, her arms swaying over her head, her auburn hair flowing around her shoulders, her pert breasts bouncing with the rhythm, her tight stomach and rounded hips swaying, and the sweet firmness of her backside flexing with every step. She was enchanting as she reveled in her freedom, all of her despair flooding from her fingertips, her feet stomping in a rage for all of the women who had come before her. The light of the fire cast a warm glow on her curves as she moved. Her porcelain white skin was marred with the lumps and bruises of her daily beatings, and her broken body waved as a banner for the rights of all women and children, all of the vulnerable ones who are hurt by unfeeling monsters.

But it wasn't just her body that tempted him. He saw the purity of her soul. He saw her suffering, and how she remained kind to others. He saw how she took the beatings but held no malice against the man who should have been protecting her. She was a rare gift to humanity.

God help him he couldn't resist.

The girls eventually drifted into a drunken sleep, and he went to her. He placed his hands reverently on her skin, healing the bruises, lumps, and scars. Tears rolled down his cheeks as he considered the abuse she had suffered. He wished he had the authority to intervene, to do more for this child of Grace.

Before he could finish, her eyes fluttered open wide as she took him in. He couldn't imagine what he must look like to her. She reached a thumb to brush away his tears in a movement so tender... so generous.

It had never been his intention...

But, their eyes met, and... they were lost in them. She wanted. She wished... Just once, she wanted to be loved, to be valued, to feel it with her heart and her body. She was a virgin, too afraid of any man to allow herself to be open. But he was no man, he was an angel, and with him... She wanted him to show her what it was to be loved thoroughly, cherished, and valued. And, *God forgive him*, he wanted that too.

And so he gave her what she wanted.

In the privacy of the cornfield, he laid her down and worshiped her, every part of her, piece by piece. He explored her, asked nothing of her, and adored her. He paid attention to every part of her, laving each with love and attention. He brought her to pleasure many times over, and in many ways; sometimes gently with butterfly touches, others, at her request, with animal carnality thrusting in and out of her warm soft body as she wrapped it around him snugly. Her moans and sighs were prayers to his ears. He existed only to bring her to rapture again and again.

For hours they explored, kissed, rolled, touched, sighed... until finally exhaustion overtook her mortal body, and she slept. Armoniel watched her sleeping in peace. Such a pure soul, who had known only cruelty her whole life.

And then Armoniel knew what he must do. He would not stand by and merely watch any longer.

Leaving her in the safety of the field, Armoniel appeared at the bedside of the preacher. It was still very early in the morning, and the sky was still dark with night.

"WHY?!" he demanded of the sleeping figure.

The preacher woke with a start, and fell out of the bed, tangled in the blankets. It seemed an angel of the Lord appeared beside him, and he didn't know what to do with himself, having given up on God long ago. He was afraid.

As he should be.

"WHY?!" Armoniel repeated, louder.

"I don't understand! Why.... what?" the man groveled from the floor, his forehead on the floorboards prostrate. His voice cracked and his body shook.

"Why did you hurt her?!" Armoniel clarified.

"H-h-her... Oh!... Nancy?... Oh,... er... well, because she is mine to do with as I please. She is wicked. The Book says–"

His screams cut off the end of his sentence and rang out into the night as Armoniel took out his wrath upon him.

The sun had risen, and it was mid-morning before the girls all awoke from their drunken stupor. Through their hangovers, they dressed and all rushed to get back to their homes, and whatever consequences awaited them. Nancy ran as far as the border to the field, and then stopped.

She didn't want to go home.

She didn't want to face her father's rage.

She wanted her dream lover back, the angel who had laid her down on corn stalks and worshiped her body. Even if he wasn't real, she still didn't want to let her father put his filthy hands on her again. She had seen what it meant to be precious to someone, even in a dream. She couldn't go back. She worried her bottom lip between her teeth; she knew what she SHOULD do, what she was told to do. But her heart staunchly refused.

Sirens in the distance caught her attention, she followed the line of the ambulance down the dirt road, toward her house, and wondered what was going on. Fear rushed through her body, her muscles suddenly tense and ready to move. She resumed her run, full speed toward the house, all other thoughts forgotten.

The police told her that Mr. Henry had stopped by that morning to work in her father's field, and when her father didn't answer the door, Mr. Henry had worried something had happened, and let himself in. They thought her father had suffered an aneurysm. He was gone.

Shock held Nancy in place.

He was gone.

She would never have to suffer him again! No more lectures! No more beatings! No more looking over her shoulder! She was FREE!!! FREE!!! Her heart swelled with joy and tears leaked from her eyes.

And as suddenly as the thought hit her, she was leveled with another feeling like a sledgehammer to the gut.

GUILT.

Acid rose in the back of her throat, as her stomach threatened to bring back all of the alcohol she had drunk the night before.

He was her FATHER. How could she stand there and celebrate when her FATHER was DEAD?! While she was out drinking and whoring as he'd always predicted she would, he was there alone and suffering. Hadn't he always told her she'd turn out just this way? Was she the reason he was dead now? Had she killed him?! She was selfish. Just like her whore mother, running off to have a good time while he suffered. In the end, she had proven him right. She was nothing. Worthless.

Nancy collapsed to the floor, inconsolable. In the end, paramedics had to sedate her to get her to calm down. She would never be the same again.

She lived her life full of regret and guilt, turning away from anything that would bring her happiness. That included the lovely baby girl that she gave birth to nine months later. Her baby, Ruth, was her reminder from God that she was sinful and weak.

Armoniel watched... she had rejected him in the aftermath of what had happened, something he had never expected. Her mind had been broken by what he had done for her.

He had hoped...

What had he hoped?! That a human could love him? Want him, and not just what he represented? No. He was meant to watch, not to have. He had broken the commandment, and made them both suffer.

And so he watched over Ruth as she grew. He visited her often, remaining invisible. He shared his magic of protection from enchantments with her. In his own way, he loved her from afar.

He saw when she finally left home, tired of Nancy's religious tirades. He was proud that she became a healer, helping the poor and sick. Even though Nancy could never love her, she gave her love freely in healing anyone who needed it.

He saw when she met the handsome fae lord who was injured, and she nursed him back to health in secret. She never judged him for not being human. He saw the love in her heart for him. And if not for the fact that he knew she couldn't be enchanted, he would have ripped the fae to pieces for daring to touch her. She loved this fae, and so he let it be. The fae took her from the earthly realm he watched to the Summer Court, and out of his sight. He was glad she had found family of her own making.

So he was surprised when he saw her return to the Earth realm full with child, fear consuming her, a year later. He did not know what had happened to her to bring her to this, he had not watched the Summer Court, assuming she was safe with her lover. But she returned alone and terrified. She gave birth to a beautiful baby girl, and not hours later, he watched as she silently snuck out of the hospital and into the night with tears streaming down her cheeks.

It fell to Nancy, her only living relative, to take in the newborn, whom she later named Eve. And Armoniel watched over them both.

7

Lamn

Armoniel went quiet and then turned his gaze back to Lamn.

"So Ruth is Nephila, half-human, and half-angelic, and you were her sire. Nephila are exceedingly rare...And that makes you Eve's grandsire. "

It was a statement, not a question. Lamn had spoken it, more to break the shock of his own mind at discovering it, than to clarify.

"Yes, and her divine Grigori blood supersedes that of her human. The other Grigori do not know of her, and I would keep it that way." Armoniel looked at Lamn pointedly, "Some of them may see her as an abomination, and work to eradicate her." It was spoken as a command, not up for negotiation. Armoniel looked away again.

"That explains the scent!" Lamn hadn't meant to say that out loud, but as Armoniel swung his head back to him he explained. "There is a scent of something like ozone around Eve. I know the fae scent of her, but the other was what we couldn't identify. It is very seductive to the fae, powerful, like a pheromone." His eyes widened with realization of what he had just acknowledged. "It's not safe for her there anymore."

Armoniel stood. "Then you know what you must do." Again, it was stated, not asked.

Lamn shook his head in acknowledgment and got up to leave when Armoniel reached out and held his arm, stopping him.

"I should... like to make a bargain with you, Lamn of the Summer Court."

Lamn raised an eyebrow. This was highly uncharacteristic for a Grigori. They did not participate in fae bargains; they did not usually need to. Lamn nodded nervously.

"I should like you to locate Ruth as well. Make sure she is protected. Vow this, and I will do what I can to assist you."

Lamn nodded again, the air shifting with a heavier density as the magical weight of the vow accepted between them took hold, snapping against their skins, and then he hurried back the way he had come. He had no time to waste.

8

Eve

Eve put the bitter cup of coffee in front of Mr. Intense.

"Anything else." She eyed him with thinly veiled hostility.

"Tark", He smiled.

"Excuse me, what?"

"Tark. My name is Tark. Pleased to meet you." He held his hand out for her to shake, but she just stared at it like it was poison.

She swung her finger between them, back and forth. "Yeah, no. We're not doing this. We're not friends. I don't want to know you, *Tark*. Just drink your coffee, order food if you want to, and move along. OK?" She held her glare.

He smirked! The bastard actually smirked.

"C'mon, you must have questions?" Again, he smiled up at her non-threateningly.

"You know what? Fine. I do have questions, *Tark*. What did you do to Becky yesterday?! Tell me THAT if you're so keen on talking with me." She crossed her arms in front of her chest in challenge and raised an eyebrow at him. When he seemed to be thinking it over she started to walk away.

"Yeah, I thought so–"

"It's called a glamor." He was no longer smiling sheepishly or smirking, and she could *feel* more than see that he was telling the truth.

She stopped and turned to him.

"A 'glamor?' And just what is that? Some sort of hypnosis?" Her arms were still crossed over her chest defensively.

"I guess you could think of it like that. Some people are highly suggestible, so I just suggested you should wait on us. She accepted the suggestion and then acted on it. It doesn't hurt her, honestly. Look, I really am sorry to have upset you. This isn't how I wanted us to meet."

"You're sorry? You're sorry you mind-fucked Becky? Or you're sorry that I'm mad at you because of it?"

Tark cringed. *She was going to be a difficult one.*

"If I'm being fully honest? I use glamor all the time to protect myself and those I care about; so I can't say I'm sorry to use it on anyone if it keeps people safe. That being said, you are one of the people I'm trying to protect. So while I'm sorry I hurt your feelings, I would... how did you call it?... 'Mind-fuck' Becky every day of the week if it meant keeping you out of harm's way. Honest enough?"

Eve felt his words. *Truth.*

She huffed out a laugh. "You're trying to protect ME?" She smirked at him skeptically. "... from WHAT exactly? Dude, I'm not exactly in mortal peril here. This is rural Oklahoma. Nothing dangerous happens HERE." She swept her arms out.

It was as if the Gods of Old had heard her words because even as they left her lips the sound of exploding glass punctured her reality. Eve saw it all happening as if in slow motion. Her head turned as the building rumbled. The window glass fractured into lightning. A thousand jagged shards exploded. Tiny glass fractals surged into the diner. Suddenly, a dark shadow flew past, blocking her view.

She found herself in the kitchen, as the glass blasted through the tiny window opening between the kitchen and the diner. She spun in a circle, dazed and confused. How had she gotten into the kitchen?! She had been at the counter! There was glass and debris everywhere, and Eve's ears rang from the force of the explosion.

Eddie appeared at her side with a shotgun in hand, a look of terror on his face. Luckily, he had been in the supply closet, otherwise, he would be shredded to ribbons in front of the tiny serving window. Stopping only to make sure she was ok, he headed into the dining room.

The dining room!

TARK!

She ran after Eddie into the dining room, where glass shards covered every surface. Menus, napkins, and other debris were everywhere. It looked like someone had taken a shotgun the size of a cannon and fired it right into the diner. The internal wall was pock-marked with millions of tiny slashes. Seeing no remaining threat, Eddie started sweeping up glass.

Tark was nowhere to be seen. She wondered how badly he was injured, he was only feet from the window! But there was no blood any-where... none of it made sense! He should be suffering from a thousand cuts shredding through his body. There should be blood everywhere. His mangled body should be slumped over the counter. But there was no sign that he had been there at all.

Eve could feel hysteria pulling at her mind. How did she get into the kitchen? Where was Tark? Who had bombed the diner?! Who would even WANT to bomb the diner?

Her eyes scanned the area in a panic as if she would see the answers she was missing, but it only left her with more questions. She wrapped her arms around herself, as a cold chill swept through her. She did not feel safe here. She didn't know if she ever would again.

The sirens made their way into the parking lot, suddenly loud. Two police cars and an ambulance pulled to a stop. The officers made their way in; she knew Steve Gulman and Eric Rainier. They were frequent patrons of the diner, getting their coffee and sweets to take out on the road with them. They asked Eddie what happened, and he told them I was talking with a patron, 'no he couldn't hear the conversation, the guy looked to be in his late twenties, with dark hair, a navy t-shirt, and roughly 6'2" tall.'

Eve froze. Why hadn't Eddie mentioned the purple hair? That was a pretty identifying characteristic... then again, Becky hadn't noticed that either the first time she saw him. Had his 'glamor' kept them from seeing it? And if so, why didn't it affect her? This was insane!

When the police got around to asking her what she saw, she mirrored Eddie's story. She didn't know why she was protecting Tark, or maybe she wasn't. Maybe they couldn't see his purple hair either. Maybe she was protecting herself from ridicule. At any rate, for all she knew he was dead. Nothing could have survived that blast, with glass like a million tiny knives.

But where was his body?... And the blood?

After twenty minutes of sniffing around, walking the perimeter of the diner, and coming back in again, the officers didn't seem to have any idea what had happened to cause the explosion. There was no sign of explosives, no burn debris, no accelerants... it was as if the glass just imploded on itself. Which was crazy.

Eve hung her head. Eddie walked up beside her, and putting his arm around her shoulders, he told her to head home. She wanted to stay and help clean up, but the look of sorrow on his face told her he just really wanted to be alone. This diner was all he had left, it was his baby. It looked like a tornado had swept through the small building, and it was going to take a while to put it back together. After much debate Eve agreed to go but told him that she would be back to help clean up the next day.

She didn't want him dealing with this alone. While he wasn't her friend, per se, Eddie had always looked out for her. She could do that for him. He gave her a hug and whispered he was glad she wasn't hurt, he knew 'stuff' could be replaced, but people can't. This was a side of Eddie she had never seen before. She hugged him back and told him likewise. His vulnerability tugged at her heartstrings.

Reluctantly, grabbing her coat and keys, she headed home for the night.

9

Armoniel

Armoniel watched, invisible, as Eve got into her car and drove away from the diner, its window frames open maws with a thin trail of jagged glass teeth. He had watched the purple-haired fae protect her.

So Lamn hadn't been lying: they weren't here to kill her.

Still invisible, he willed himself to the wooded ravine where the purple-haired fae stood, pulling his sword out of the last burning husk of a body, while the red-haired fae made sure there were no others. The demon minions were dead, the last one turning to ash at the feet of his slayer. They would never go after Eve again.

Armoniel made himself visible. The fae turned in surprise to see a Grigori approaching them, and the one with purple hair raised his sword to protect them if necessary.

Unwise.

Armoniel only waved his hand toward Tark, and he was swept off of his feet, smashing into a thick tree trunk ten feet off the ground, and held there, sword still in hand.

"I have no fight with you, Tark, Fae of the Summer Court. I came to tell you that she has left, and there are others. You must not let them get her first."

He flicked his wrist again and Tark dropped to the ground, landing unsteadily on his feet.

"If you know this, why aren't you protecting her?" Skiff demanded, his red hair sticking to his sweaty brow. "Why come tell us?"

Armoniel sighed wearily. "You know I am not meant to interfere."

"And telling us isn't interfering?" Tark quirked an eyebrow.

"No, it is not. What you do with the information is not my doing." He smirked at them before he allowed himself to dissolve into the wind, to go find her, watch over her himself.

Both of the fae stared at each other, wondering what the hell had just happened to bring a Grigori to them, and how he knew what they were after, but they would have to discuss it later. Eve was on the move, and so, it appeared, was the Winter Court.

Eve

Eve had the window down and the radio blasting as she sang loudly to shake the memories of what had happened at the diner. Moonlight danced over the dark tree-lined road ahead of her, with no other headlights to brighten the drive. There was just too much crazy over the last few days, and she couldn't allow herself to get sucked back into the hamster wheel in her head, spinning, spinning, spinning, but never getting anywhere. She needed to get her head on straight before she got home to face Nancy and all of HER drama.

She was just a few miles away from her street when something large shot out of the treeline and across the road in front of her. She screamed as she threw the wheel to the right. The car slid. The tires screeched. Her heart pounded. A loud THUMP reverberated off of the hood before the car lurched to a standstill.

For a moment all Eve could do was hyperventilate and stare at the hood.

What the hell had she hit?! It moved so fast! She never even got a look at it!

Finally, she raised her shaking hands to unclasp the seatbelt; unfortunately, the tremors stopped her from being able to accomplish this on the first, or even second, try. Finally, the belt sprang from her hip to slide over her shoulder.

She gingerly opened the car door, and slowly moved to put first one foot, and then the next on the pavement. Her body was shaking so violently that she had to lean against the car as she got out, in case her legs wouldn't hold her. Leaning on the door, and then the hood, she made her way around the car, trying to mentally prepare herself for whatever blood-bath awaited her. Tears welled in her eyes.

She inched around the bumper, steeling herself, to see...

Nothing.

There was nothing there! There should be a body, blood, gore... She could feel the acid churning in her stomach. Twice in one day... this couldn't be happening!

She continued her trek around the front bumper, to the passenger side of the car. Again: nothing. NOTHING!

She knew she should be relieved, but at that moment she just wanted to sob, as the fear and panic crept up her throat. She was tired of the roller coaster of emotion and adrenaline shocking her body, only to dump her back down. She was on the edge of just losing it.

She looked around in shocked disbelief. She inspected the hood: no dent. *So what the hell had happened?!* She was left with a feeling of over-whelm, and no way to account for it. She couldn't have just imagined that THUMP on the hood! She had SEEN something run out! She had FELT something slam into the front of the car! BUT THERE WAS NOTHING!

Eve suddenly felt an impulse to jump to her right. Before she could even question it, she was moving, just as an arm came down into the space she had been standing in. The man was huge, built like a line-backer, and he had those same tell-tale looks of Tark and his friends from the diner. There was no doubt he was one of them, all muscle and sharp features. So why was he trying to grab her?

He swung to grab her again, and again she moved ahead of him as if she knew he was going to attack. Her body seemed to be on autopilot. She moved as he launched, in some twisted dance for dominance.

She never even had a chance to come down from the panic of the 'accident,' and now her blood was flowing and her heart was pumping for its survival. Her breath came in fast shallow pants. She had no clue who this guy was, but he obviously wanted to hurt her. She felt, more than saw, the aggression radiating off of him like violence. Another swing, another precarious step away, this time barely missing his fingertips. She couldn't keep this up forever, she had to get away from him before he got his hands on her.

A blinding streak of lightning overhead and a deafening boom of thunder distracted her for just an instant, and that was all the time he needed. She found herself wrapped tightly, with his arms like steel bands binding hers to her sides. He lifted her off of the ground as if she were weightless. She kicked and flailed, genuine panic starting to build in her. She screamed and kicked, but it didn't seem to affect him at all. He turned, still hauling her in the cage of his arms, to carry her away. Her mind screamed that she had to find a way to free herself. She couldn't let him take her away where no one could find her.

PAIN.

And then they were both on the ground in a crash that forced all the air out of her lungs. She was free of his hold but had everything she could do to get air in her lungs again, gasping like a fish out of water. She rolled her head on the pavement to see fighting. She recognized Tark and his friends from the diner. They were fighting some other guys who looked pretty similar in build, among them the one who had tried to snatch her.

They moved incredibly fast, sometimes blurring and then appearing somewhere else. They shouted at each other in another language, and they fought with swords. Who the hell fights with swords? It was brutal and bloody.

Internally her mind steamed. She had to move! She had to get up! This was insane!

No, what was insane was that there was an angel... a motherfucking ANGEL... making his way over to her. Norse God looks, flowing blond hair, muscular, white robes, huge WINGS spread out, glowy aura...

WINGS!!!

ANGEL?!

WHAT.IN.THE.EVERLOVING.FUCK?!

Eve could do nothing but lay on the pavement in stunned silence with her mouth hanging open.

I O

Eve

I have lost it. I have officially lost my mind.

Eve watched as the huge man with wings skirted the melee. His eyes were full of concern and never left hers, even as he flung bodies out of his way with a careless wave of his hand. He was focused on her.

Eve's stomach was in her throat.

As he got closer she scrambled upright, and then crab-crawled away from him over the pavement as fast as she could move, until she ran into the side of the car. He must have seen the terror in her eyes, as he slowed to a stop a few feet away from her as if she was a frightened animal.

He spoke calmly, his voice deep and full of power. "Eve, get into the car. Leave here. I will make sure you get home safely."

Eve just stared at him. She couldn't seem to move, it was like she was paralyzed.

An angel was talking to her. AN ANGEL!!!!

"EVE. GO." This time the power his words conveyed rippled through her with a slight shock. He didn't appear angry. He seemed deeply concerned for her safety.

And, I mean, that's what angels are supposed to do, right? Look out for people?

I have lost it!

Eve shook her head, to clear it, and still watching the Angel-Man out of the corner of her eye, she jumped up and darted for the driver's door. Jumping inside quickly, she jerked the key forward, threw it in gear, and pressed the gas with all of her strength. Tires squealed as her tiny beat-up Honda Civic tried its hardest to be a sports car and scream away into the night, spewing gravel and smoke in her wake.

In her rearview mirror, she saw that there were still two or three men fighting in the road, the others lay on the ground, not moving. She didn't know if it was Tark's buddies still standing, and she wasn't waiting to find out. She kept the pedal to the floor until they were long out of sight.

She saw the man in the white robes spread his snowy white wings wide, and launch into the air. Her jaw fell, and she had a hard time bringing her attention to the road in front of her. There was no denying it was an angel, fakes can't FLY.

Once she had reached the safety of her home, she jumped from the car, ran to the door, yanked it open while falling inside, and immediately slammed it shut and locked all of the bolts. For once she was grateful for Nancy's paranoia and multiple bolt locks. She fell back against the door, completely exhausted, nerves frayed.

She was crazy. She had to be.

People didn't disappear from explosion scenes. She knew she had hit something, even if there was nothing there. And angels weren't real! None of this was real! She must be delusional! What if that Tark guy had drugged HER?! It was the only rational explanation!

She was afraid to move, afraid that if she did, she would upset the peace, and some other form of craziness would pop out to get her.

As Eve leaned against the door, clutching her purse to her chest, she realized she had just stormed into the house like a hurricane and had likely roused Nancy from her inner sanctum. She had to move fast.

SHIT! SHIT! SHIT!

Cautiously, she tiptoed down the hall. Her bedroom was in sight, just a few more feet...

And that was the moment that Carly Simon, again, started singing loudly from her purse.

SHIT! SHIT! SHIT!

She cursed as she rushed for the safety of her bedroom, while simultaneously rummaging her hand through her purse to silence Richard's ringtone on her friggin phone- too late.

The door next to her flew open, and Nancy appeared from the doorway of her own bedroom, still clad in her nightgown, which she had probably been wearing all day, rage written on her pale bloated face.

"What the hell is all that racket? Are you trying to raise the dead?!"

Her eyes were bloodshot, and her hair was obviously unbrushed, as it stuck out in all directions. There was also no mistaking the stale smell of alcohol and body odor that wafted around her.

Eve finally got the phone silenced. "Sorry, Nancy," she offered briskly.

Stepping around the woman, she bee-lined for her room, before the inevitable lecture could begin, and shut the door firmly behind her, locking it. Undaunted, Nancy launched her tirade in the hallway to the now-closed door. As Nancy's rant about Eve's inconsiderate and ungrateful nature and her unholy and treacherous lifestyle reached a crescendo, Eve plopped down on her bed, just trying to make sense of the day.

And then it hit her: Nancy!

Super, ultra-religious Nancy!

Eve jumped off of the bed and threw the door open, much to Nancy's astonishment. The woman stopped mid-sentence in surprise.

"What do you know about angels?" Eve blurted.

Nancy gave Eve the side-eye as if this was some trick question.

"If you were a good and moral person who read the Book now and again, you would know, wouldn't you? Angels are the messengers of God, as his countenance is far too divine for the eyes of mortal men and–"

"Yes, yes... but have you ever SEEN one?"

Again, Nancy paused before resuming. "It is not for sinners to presume that they should know the mind of the Heavenly Father–"

"Yes, yes,... I know all that. Have you ever MET an angel, Nancy?"

At this all of the color drained out of Nancy's face, and if she had looked pale before she seemed absolutely sickly now. Nancy's eyes widened in horror, and she began to shuffle back, away from Eve, her hands held out in front of her as if she was a vision from her nightmares. Her eyes reflected nothing but absolute terror.

"No... NO...NO... NO... I will not have that abomination, that corruption of all that is holy, near me or my house! NO, NO, NO... If you cavort with Satan and his minions you can just get out now! In the name of God, I compel thee, demon! Heavenly Father, give me strength! I will not host the legions of evil in my home! Our Father, Who art in Heaven–"

With that she scampered into her own room, slamming her door, and Eve could hear the wailing of prayers of protection directed at the Father, Son, and Holy Ghost, as well as her Lord and Savior Jesus Christ, Mother Mary, Saint Michael, and a few others she had never heard of before.

Eve stood staring at the cheap splintered brown door which had been slammed inches from her nose, before turning down the dank hallway for her own room.

Well now, that was not the response I was expecting.

11

Eve

Eve considered what to do next. She didn't have any answers for all of the craziness she had experienced. She was exhausted. It was all just too much for her sanity, never mind her nervous system. She considered getting something to eat, but the very thought made her stomach curdle.

Instead, she opted for a hot shower, lingering under the spray and allowing it to loosen her muscles until the water ran warm and too quickly cold. She dried off and went through her nightly bedtime rituals: drying her hair, removing her makeup, and brushing her teeth. She couldn't help but notice, again, how sad and neglected the bathroom was. The whole house was if she was truthful.

Half of the light fixtures didn't work anymore, so the house was perpetually in shadow. Nancy kept the window shades down during the day anyway, so there was never sunlight. The shag carpet was ancient and gross. Who knew what color it was originally? The dated and peeling wallpaper, the chipped Formica of the counters, the loose and peeling linoleum of the floors... It was as if the stains, dirt, grime, and darkness had taken hold, never to be released again.

How had Eve stayed here this long? How had she not opted to move somewhere else, anywhere else? Somewhere clean. Somewhere bright. Was it really the money that kept her here? Or was she just another depressed feature of this sad house and its ghosts of the past?

Back in her room she threw on clean pajamas and climbed into her bed. At least her room was clean and bright. She couldn't keep up with Nancy's drunken 'redecorating;' endless bottles, vomit stains, and broken furniture. But she could create her own sanctuary in her tiny room.

It was small: big enough for a twin-sized bed, her small desk from high school, and a chair. It was really more appropriate for a teenager. Still, it was hers. It was all she needed, really. Her eyelids were heavy as she took in the details, and soon she couldn't keep them open any longer.

"Eve... Eve... We need to talk."

Tark was in her dream, all smiles, and hotness. And his smell! He smelled delicious, all masculine and sexy! Eve sighed, and rolled over with a gentle smile, imagining nuzzling her head into the crook of his neck and inhaling. She imagined running her hands down washboard abs...

The sudden brightness made her throw her arm over her eyes with a frown, as sleep tried to drag her back down into the depths of her dream. Tark was there in her dream, wanting to talk to her, she wanted to see him again. She wanted to know he was alright. She wanted to smell–

"Eve." This time it was louder.

Eve pulled her arm off of her face, her eyes flashing open. Her mind swam through the confusion of one who was startled awake. She tried to focus on what had woken her, even as her dream swam around her like a fog.

Where?... What?... His presence was thick around her, as was his smell.

She sat up groggily. The lights were on in her room, effectively blinding her, and it took a few seconds for her eyes to adjust.

Why were her lights on? She had shut them off! Is this a dream? What?...

Eve sucked in what would have been a scream, as her eyes finally came to land on the form sitting in the chair near the end of her bed.

NOT a dream!

Tark smiled, and waived a few fingers at her, sitting casually and waiting for her to pull herself together.

As her mind struggled to catch up and understand what was going on, she launched questions like machine gun fire.

"HOW did you get in here?! What are you doing here? How did you get out of the diner? HOW ARE YOU ALIVE RIGHT NOW?!" Eve whispered, nearly hysterical, her arms flailing out to her sides.

"It takes more than locks to keep me out. I came to talk to you. I have ways of getting out of danger. And why wouldn't I be alive right now?" The corner of his lip quirked upward, and there was genuine warmth in his eyes. "How are *you* feeling?"

Where he was calm, Eve couldn't seem to put a coherent sentence together. She flailed her arm toward Tark, then the locked door, then the lamp, then back in her lap, then back to Tark, finally throwing them up in defeat. Her head whipped from one direction to another, as if to follow the chain of events.

It was then that she realized that she was sitting in her bed, in her skimpy lavender unicorn pajamas, having a conversation with a very hot, but unknown, guy.

Eve ripped the comforter up to her shoulders with horror before starting again.

"What are you doing in MY BEDROOM?!"

Eve's mind was already running overtime, trying to anticipate where she would move if he tried to pounce on her. Damnit! She didn't keep any weapons close to the bed! She needed to keep a knife under her pillow! She had no way to defend herself! Her face paled as she considered what a vulnerable position she was in. Her breathing grew shallow and rapid, as her heartbeat only slammed at a faster pace in her ribcage.

Tark chuckled under his breath at her obvious distress. While she was crazed, he was as cool as a cucumber.

"Well, it was either this or the living room, and I didn't think you wanted Nancy to join us. So the bedroom seemed safest." He was using the voice he reserved for frightened children and animals.

"Safest for WHOM?!" Her eyes were wide, still darting all over the room, trying to find the magic escape route. Her heartbeat cranked up another notch.

"Eve, I'm not here to hurt you. If I was, why would I have woken you up? I could have just killed you in your sleep."

Eve froze.

He pinched the bridge of his nose between his thumb and forefinger. "No, no, no... ugh. (sigh) That's not what I meant. Look, please hear me out. I promise I will not move out of this chair."

"Promise?" Eve gave him the side-eye. This might buy her time... If she could keep him talking, maybe she could maneuver to the door, or talk him into leaving peacefully.

"Promise." He waited for her to nod in agreement, and then continued. "I know you have a lot of questions. I'm here to answer them. I would have waited for a better time, but you're not safe anymore. I have no choice but to explain now—"

"How are you not dead?" Eve didn't like the way her voice cracked, nor the sting of tears that threatened to bloom in her eyes. "I saw the explosion, all that glass. How did you get out?" She was overwhelmed with the impossibility of him being alive, never mind in her room. Her own vulnerability was suddenly forgotten, with her relief at realizing he had survived.

Tark took a deep breath, contemplating. "Remember how I told you about glamors? Well, there's a lot more to me than that. I know you might find this a little hard to believe, but again, please hear me out..." He paused, looking unsure. "I'm not exactly human. I'm a fae. We have certain... abilities."

Tark eyed her nervously.

Eve just stared at him with an eyebrow cocked. She didn't know what she expected to hear, but that wasn't it. She was overloaded with all of the things she had seen and felt over the last few days: outrage, shock, fear, relief... so she just continued to stare at him, until he got it all out. She felt a numbness spread through her body that came with feeling too much.

When she didn't respond, didn't even move, Eve could see the look in his eyes that said he didn't know what to do next. Clearly, he had expected some sort of response from her. She waited. She could feel his unease from where she sat.

"Ummm... right, so... Wow. You're taking this a lot better than I thought you would. Uhhm... So, here's the thing, uh... So fae belong to one of two allegiances: I'm with what's called the Summer Court, but there's also the Winter Court.

"The Summer Court respects life, and is peaceful by nature, but the Winter Court tends to be pretty cruel. The bombing tonight: that was the Winter Court. The attack on the road, also the Winter Court.

"I wanted to offer you sanctuary with the Summer Court because the Winter Court will hurt or kill you if they get their hands on you."

Eve continued staring at him.

"That's it in a nutshell." Tark dropped his hands into his lap. Eve still said nothing.

"Uhh... so, this would be where you ask me about anything you don't understand..." Tark fidgeted, his formerly confident posture slumping. His eyes darted around the room.

Eve brought her knees up to her chest under the comforter and wrapped her arms around them. She tilted her head to the side as she rolled his words over in her mind, trying to make sense of it all. The emotional numbness gave her a kind of clarity and objectivity.

I mean, it was batshit crazy. But then again, so is seeing an angel. In some ways, it was better to believe this, than to believe that she was just losing her mind. Every time her consciousness balked, she just saw those wings spread in her rear-view mirror.

Maybe, if she had been more awake, she might have called him a fucking liar, thrown him out, screamed. But at that particular moment, after days of crazy unexplainable shit, explosions, car accidents that weren't, and a big ass fucking angel... If it wasn't for the angel... she might have been able to reject the whole situation.

Was it crazy? Yes. But what HADN'T been crazy over the last few days?

Tark was really starting to look uncomfortable the longer she sat and mulled it all over. Worry set into his eyes.

Eve smirked.

My, how the tables have turned.

That made Tark look even more uncomfortable as he squirmed nervously in his seat. Eve could sense him bracing for a violent response. But she didn't have one, and it didn't come.

"Let's just say I believe that you're a... fae. Wait, Is that like a fairy? Cause you don't look like a fairy."

"We prefer fae, but yes, I think some of your mythology refers to us as..." he curled his lip in distaste, "fairies.... And how do you know what fairies look like? How many have you seen?"

He had her there.

"Well... I haven't seen any. But I have read books, and fairies were always small, with butterfly or dragonfly wings. And they have pointed ears."

"Your books were probably referring to pixies, who are in fact tiny, and have insect-like wings, so I can't help you there. The ears, however,..."

He pulled his purple hair back to reveal one beautifully pointed ear.

Eve wanted to touch that ear to see how he reacted when another thought suddenly hijacked her train of consciousness.

"Why are the fae... Why is this 'Winter Court', or the 'Summer Court' for that matter, interested in me? Why ME? I'm just a plain old human."

"Good question."

Tark seemed to breathe a little easier, assuming she was coming around to understanding and accepting.

"Well, it would seem you are not a 'plain old human' at all. You have fae blood in you. So you're a mix, or a hybrid, with both. And, well, the fae like to have their kind in their own world. Fae don't belong on the Earth Plane. It's just never a good fit. Your skills and instincts are far better than humans'. Hybrids tend to be loners and outcasts when living among humans. They suffer high rates of depression.

"Our scouts just found you recently, and I guess the Winter Court was right behind them. That's why we're having this discussion right now. I wish I had more time to break it to you gently or offer you more proof, but I don't.

"The Winter Court sees hybrids as 'less-than' fae. They hunt them down and enslave them. So, teams like mine search the Earth Plane for the hybrids to find them before the Winter Court does. If the Winter court found you, they would simply kidnap you, and force you to leave as their slave. We give hybrids the option to come with us for their own protection, and none have refused yet.

"In the Summer Court they are received as equals, and they are taught to use all of their special skills and abilities. Haven't you felt alone here, Eve? I'd like to take you away from this, to offer you a better life where you would fit in."

"And if I refuse?" Eve remained even-keeled, her face flat and emotionless.

Tark blew out a frustrated breath.

"Well, if it was up to the Summer Court, that would be fine. We wouldn't force you. However, as I've said, the Winter Court doesn't really give a shit what you want. They would grab you and take you against your will. That's what they were trying to do tonight."

"So I'm going to have to fight assholes like that all the time if I just want to stay and live my life here?" The anger was starting to rise in her voice, the calm facade slipping away.

He had the decency to look apologetic as he answered.

"Um, no... actually, uh, because you can't win against them. As I've said, the fae have... abilities. You do too, but you've never learned to use them. You'd be no match for them. If we hadn't gotten there when we did, you'd already be gone. And once there, you'd have no way to get back without help. And, Eve, NO ONE there would help you."

"I'm not going anywhere." She stated stubbornly.

"I'm sorry to be the bearer of bad news, I really am, but I don't think you understand the full scope of what they can and will do to you. That diner? Child's play. They can destroy any building, anywhere you go. They can kill your friends and your family. There is nothing they won't do to get you. They will not stop. They have no respect for life whatsoever, yours or anyone else's. They will hurt or kill anyone around you to get to you. They don't fight fair. They are what you call 'evil.'"

Eve almost told Tark that there was nothing they could do to her; she HAD no friends, no family... but even as the words formed on her tongue she thought of Eddie... of Becky...

Just because the people of this town weren't her friends didn't mean she wanted them all caught in the crossfire. Eddie could fix his place... this time. Next time it might be destroyed. That look of pain in his eyes as he surveyed the damage haunted her. As much as she really didn't like Nancy, she wouldn't wish her dead. Or Becky... or anyone else in her small town.

Tark looked like he could see her coming to terms with it, so he continued. "And Eve, if they get you, and they WILL get you, you are a half-breed; you will be their plaything. They will torture you, rape you, share you around... you can't even imagine. When I said I wanted to protect you, I meant it. Your life would be a living hell with them." His eyes were pleading with her to understand, he exuded protectiveness.

"And there's no way to just get them to stop? There's no... I don't know... fae police?"

Tark gave her a small smile that didn't reach his eyes. "No, there's no way they will stop. Not voluntarily. And their court will support them in taking you. I guess I'm the closest thing you have to police: but I can't fight an entire court, even with Skiff and Lamn, the guys with me yesterday. And if the Summer Court stepped in to intervene, it would mean war. And they won't do that, not for a half–" Tark quickly censored himself. "Not for hybrids."

Eve narrowed her eyes and shot daggers with her stare.

"So, what?! I just give up and leave with you? Leave my life? For how long? I don't even know you! Where, exactly, are you suggesting we go? How do I know YOU aren't the bad guys? Isn't this what the bad guys would say?! And WHO was the angel?!"

Tark shook his head sadly. "I know this was a lot for a human to take in, but time is not on our side. Eve, I understand this is hard; it's a lot of change, very quickly. We only just found you, or I would have more time to explain. The Winter Court was right on our heels. It's not safe for you here anymore. And it won't be safe anywhere except the Summer Court, where they can't get you.

"Please come with us. I promise, if you feel we are mistreating you, I will personally bring you back to the Earth Realm. Fae cannot lie." He looked into her eyes and hoped that she saw his sincerity. Eve felt an electrical snapping against the surface of her skin, and then it was gone.

She met his look, the original Mr. Intense himself. She was skeptical. She wanted to laugh in his face and tell him that everyone lies. But she felt the warmth from the energy of his words in her gut, she felt the truth in what he was saying. She didn't understand how, but she *knew* he was telling the truth. And if she was honest, there was something about him that made her feel safe, made her want to trust him.

"Let me think about it." She conceded quietly.

"Eve, we don't have time. It could be hours, it could be minutes before they find you. If they don't get you, they will come back with more reinforcements. They will be back tomorrow, and the next day, and the next... if they're not here already."

Eve felt the truth in that as well. But it was overwhelming. It was too much to ask her to make that kind of decision impulsively. Normally, she would balk. She would not be pushed or manipulated into rushing an important decision. But this time, she knew... she just knew that what he was saying was true. She couldn't risk taking too much time to move on this.

She couldn't just pick up and leave her life, could she?! She couldn't be expected to just walk away.

Or could she?...

She looked around her tiny teenager's room. *Everything she owned, except her shitbox car, fit in this room. She had no friends. Nancy was her only relative. Wasn't she just dreaming about moving away?... Getting out of this town? Here was her all-expense-paid trip with a bunch of hot guys, and a promise of a return ticket if it didn't work out. This might be her best chance, as well as her only hope.*

But she still wanted to tie loose ends.

"Tark, I can't just walk out of my life right now. Look, let me help Eddie clean up the diner in the morning, and then I will go with you."

"You can't go back to the diner! They've placed you there! You might as well give yourself up to them." Anger flashed in his eyes. Or was it protectiveness?

"I can't leave without helping the only person who's ever given a damn about me! That's my deal, take it or leave it."

"A bargain, eh? And here I didn't think you understood fae." Tark muttered quietly, suddenly very serious. "Alright, here are MY conditions: we go with you to the diner to protect you. If the Winter Court arrives, we leave immediately, no questions asked, no argument. 'Morning' ends at noon, finished or not."

The look on his face and his arms crossed over his chest told Eve he was not happy about making this concession. But she felt that she had to get some small decision in this whole situation that was hers to make, some small choice that was her own.

"Deal."

The air grew dense around them and between them, and again there was an electrical 'snap' against her skin, before returning back to normal. Eve was about to ask what happened but Tark cut her off.

"If we're going to do this, you should get some sleep. I'll stay and guard you tonight."

"In my bedroom?" She asked, horrified.

"Well, that's where you are, so..."

Tark slowly got out of the chair and reached to turn the lamp off.

Eve's head was, again, swimming. It was too much. It was all just too much. She laid back down, wrapping her comforter around her like a safety blanket.

"You never told me who the angel was." She whispered.

"The Grigori?... Yes, I suppose you call them angels... I have no idea who he is."

12

Eve

"Rise and Shine, Princess."

Eve jumped, still half asleep, hearing the voice beside her ear.

Her heart was pounding in her chest until the memory of the last night slowly flooded into her brain. She could see the sunlight just starting to illuminate the edges of her window around the shade. It must still be early.

Tark. He was still there.

She turned to face him, and lost her breath at seeing his unearthly beautiful face so close to her, haloed in dark purple locks.

Not god-like, he was still damned good-looking. She wouldn't kick him out of bed for eating crackers.

His smile broadened.

And he knows it.

Eve's cheeks flushed, and she gave him a glare that she hoped conveyed that she hated getting up early, as if it had nothing to do with the way she went all warm and gooey whenever she was close to him. He smelled amazing, and she had to resist the urge to lean in and just sniff him deeply. With a frustrated groan Eve disentangled herself from her sheets and comforter. She realized she was still in her pajamas, but after everything she had been through, and the lack of sleep, she really didn't give a fuck. Tark pushed up and headed to the door.

"I have coffee ready. Try and be quick, the sooner we finish, the sooner we get you to safety." He looked over his shoulder before pulling the door open.

"WAIT! Nancy!" Eve had her hand up as if she could stop him from across the room.

Tark looked back at her with a sad smirk like she was a naive child. "Not to worry. She will be asleep for *quite* a while."

He continued through the door and away down the hall. Eve didn't quite know what to make of that. Had he drugged her? Used his 'special abilities?' Or did he just guess she'd drunk herself into a blackout again? Regardless, Eve had to get moving, and at least Nancy wouldn't slow her down. For just a moment she felt a pang of guilt, leaving Nancy to her own devices.

But, she argued with herself, *staying would put Nancy in danger, so...*

She groaned as she hauled herself out of the warmth of her bed.

Eve rushed through a quick shower, pulled her wet blue hair up into a messy bun, grabbed her toiletries and a few changes of clothes to pack, and dressed in jeans and a t-shirt that she could get dirty. She chose her work boots but slipped her old worn sneakers into her small worn overnight bag. She still didn't know if, or when, she would be back, but she really didn't own much of value to bring with her.

As she slipped out of the room, bag in hand, she reached back one last time to grab the picture frame from the shelf by the door. It was a picture of the mother she had never known, which she had stolen from Nancy before Nancy could destroy them all. Eve didn't know what made her want to bring it, but she suddenly very much wished she had a mom she could talk to. This would have to do.

She closed the door behind her without looking back.

Twenty minutes later Eve and Tark arrived at the diner. Eve could see Eddie inside, already putting things to order, and Tark's two buddies sitting outside waiting for them.

She killed the engine and reached for her seatbelt when her phone started vibrating in her purse in the back seat. She twisted, trying to reach for it, and Tark, seeing her struggle, reached back and fished her phone out of her purse to hand to her.

She saw the caller ID as he extended the phone toward her. Her eyes widened as she flailed her hands to try to stop him as if she could push the phone away from her, but Tark was already putting the phone in her hand, and accidentally hitting the button to receive the call.

"Hello?" Richard's voice filled the car.

Eve just stared at the phone, rolled her eyes, and groaned. Then she shot Tark a death glare.

Tark's eyebrows quirked in confusion as he shrugged his hands up in the 'oops' position. He had no idea why she was upset.

"Helloooo? Eve?" Richard's singsong voice held the faintest whiff of impatience.

Eve moved the phone, reluctantly, to her ear. "Richard." She stated it like a curse as she held the death glare on Tark.

"Heeeeeey! EVE! So good to hear your voice!--"

"What do you want?" She was angry at herself for how soft and whiney it came out, she wanted to sound badass. She wanted to sound like "leave me the fuck alone."

"I don't want anything, Sweetheart! I was just calling to see how you are!" His voice dripped charisma.

"I'm great. Okay, bye now."

"WAIT– wait," Richard chuckled like it was a cute joke between them, "I wanted to let you know I've moved back. Isn't that great?! I'd love to see you and catch up!" He was oblivious to her completely hostile tone, he never was one to pick up on social cues.

"Uhhh, yeah, I'm gonna hafta say NO to that. I have a lot of work to do with Eddie, and–"

"You're at Eddie's?! Fantastic, I'll stop over! See you soon!"

The line went dead in her hand. Eve let out an exasperated noise somewhere between a shout and a grunt as she dug her fingers into her hair like she would tug it out.

"Who was that?" Tark's expression was surprisingly gentle. Maybe he could sense the pain she still felt stabbing her in the heart? If not, he certainly saw the epic tantrum she was trying to suppress. Eve closed her eyes and blew out a breath, and then took another deep breath to clear her head.

No looking back. Moving on. I won't give him another fucking ounce of my energy, she swore to herself silently.

She looked at Tark and said, "Nothing, I mean nobody... I mean, he's my ex. I just never want to speak to him again. That's all. Come on." She pushed the door open violently, to find Tark's two friends already standing by the car waiting on them.

Tark rounded the car and made introductions: Lamn was the one with the green hair, Skiff the one with the fiery red. His friends didn't seem particularly happy to be there. While they greeted her warmly, their eyes repeatedly scanned the area for any signs of movement. So far, there was nothing to see. A part of her wanted to ask them about the fight the night before, the melee on the road on the way home from work, but Tark quickly put his hand on the small of her back and gently guided her toward the diner door.

This was her farewell gift to her old life.

13

Eve

Eve's eyes had teared up when she walked into the diner. Eddie had swept up the glass and debris, but the walls and counters were scarred as if they'd been sandblasted with daggers.

And they had been, hadn't they?

The diner was always old and worn, but it had been comfortable, homey. Now it looked vandalized. Eddie did what he always did, he put his nose to the grindstone and worked harder. Without a word, Eve started righting the napkin holders, salt and pepper shakers, and other staples of the diner. She took the shattered coffee pots and threw them away. She salvaged what she could and disposed of the rest. No one spoke. Tark chipped in, but she noticed that his buddies, Lamn and Skiff, remained outside.

Probably keeping watch.

When Eve and Tark were alone together, she would ask him about where he came from, and what it was like. His eyes seemed to sparkle when he described the Summer Court, and he made it sound as magical as she imagined it would be. She found herself leaning in, listening to him talk. Yes, he was amazingly hot, but he also seemed kind and intelligent. She found him interesting.

About forty minutes later Eve heard music outside, through the gaping hole where the windows used to be. Getting louder, the sound of tires on the road approached. She looked up from her latest batch of broken glassware to see Richard pulling up, his head thrown back, singing loudly to his own music, playing on his sound system. He pulled in at the corner of the diner, screeching to a halt.

Richard fancied himself a musician, and he'd be the first to tell you he was better than most. He had made his own CDs and given them out to anyone who would take one, most of whom discarded them discreetly as they left. Eve had always supported his music while she was with him, but hearing it now made her cringe. He was a sad, balding, bloated little man still stuck thirty years in the past. He was a legend in his own mind.

How had she ever found that attractive?

As he made his way to the door, Skiff and Lamn intercepted him. Eve's heart began to beat harder, and she could feel herself sweating as she mentally faced having to talk to Richard again. She ran her palms down her jeans. He had always had a way of making her feel small, of making everything her fault. Her stomach started rolling with anxiety, the same anxiety that had always surfaced whenever she faced Richard.

It would be so much easier to hide in the back.

She watched as Richard gave Lamn and Skiff the side-eye, right before he switched into 'charming' mode. As Eve watched Richard try to schmooze them, she realized that this would be the last time she ever saw Richard. She was leaving soon. This was her last chance to say what was on her mind, to set the record straight. This was her chance to speak and be heard. Straightening her back, she headed for the door.

On the steps, Lamn and Skiff blocked Richard, who was trying really hard to connect with them like they were bros. Richard was, of course, oblivious to the disinterest their bodies conveyed. The guys were solid, arms crossed over bulging chests, an immovable wall of solid muscle. Richard saw her coming out and started waving around the guys for her attention like a patron in line waiting to get past the bouncers into the hottest club.

"Eve! Eve! Hey, Eve! Hey, can we chat for a minute?"

She eyed him warily, one brow raised. "So talk."

She took the same arms-crossed stance the men in front of her had, standing on the stair above them so she could see over their heads. Richard looked very put out, and openly pouted. She could see the anger in the clenching of his jaw, and the draw of his eyebrows. Richard did NOT like not getting his own way.

"Can't I talk to you ALONE?" he sulked like a petulant child, and there was a touch of hostility in his voice.

Eve felt Tark's fingertips gently touching her lower back, his breath warmed her ear as he leaned in and asked, "Is everything ok?"

"For Chrissakes, I just wanna talk to her! Eve?!" He looked at her imploringly.

Eve sighed. "Yes, everything's fine. Just... give us a minute."

She turned to look at Tark. He held her look for a moment, and a look of indecision crossed over his features. He looked at Richard, and back at her, before finally tapping the others on the shoulder to get them to stand down.

"We'll be right over here." Tark was looking directly at Richard when he announced this.

Eve moved down the stairs to Richard, who immediately backed up to where he'd parked his car at the corner of the diner, away from the door. Eve knew Richard, she knew he was no physical threat to her, none whatsoever. If push came to shove, she knew she could hand him his ass in a fight. He had tried to be violent with her once and she had laughed at him. It wasn't violence that made her keep her distance from him.

"Eve, I'm so glad you're talking to me. Look, I know I made a lot of mistakes–"

"Like cheating on me and lying to me?"

She saw the flash of anger in his eyes at the confrontation, but he quickly went back to playing the repentant lover.

"It wasn't like that, Eve–"

"Which part? The part where you looked for a new girlfriend on social media WHILE you were fucking me? Or the part where you groomed her to take my place? Or the part where you denied all of this? Or the part where you and she lied to everyone, saying you'd known each other for years when you literally hadn't met in person yet? You can't rewrite history, Richard, I was there too, remember?"

Eve stood straight, taking her pound of flesh, even as her heart squeezed at having to admit that he had hurt her so deeply, that she had ever cared for him. Because she had. No matter how badly he had treated her, she had let him. Her own shame clenched at her heart as well.

Truth be told, when he first wanted to meet her, she suspected he was still in a relationship, and she had confronted him. Little did she know she was the side piece that later replaced the main squeeze, only to be replaced by the next side piece, later to become the main squeeze... etc.

Richard was starting to flush red with anger, huffing and trying to put together a sentence. Eve knew Richard HATED to be contradicted. He had to be right. She watched as he battled down the anger, again going for the repentant ploy he probably felt was more effective for getting whatever it is he wanted.

"I'm sorry Eve, I didn't realize I hurt you that badly... I... I didn't know how you felt. Wow, I really am a shit. I don't want to be that person. I know I was wrong. If it makes you feel any better, I'm working with a therapist now, to help me to be a better person." He looked down as if trying to express just how deeply sorry he was, how vulnerable he was allowing himself to be with her.

Eve resisted the urge to laugh out loud. She had no doubt in her mind that his marriage wasn't working out, and his whole reason for wanting to 'catch up' was to get his fragile ego stroked, as she had always done when they dated. He would bring her around when he was low, and disappear once he felt better. And she would bet her last paycheck he was not working with anyone 'to become a better person.' He had always been so transparent, she just never let on she saw him for what he was. This was another of his 'alternate truths' he would use to get what he wanted, nothing more.

He disgusted her, but more than that she felt pity for him. He would always look for validation outside of himself, leaving relationships as soon as they weren't new and shiny anymore. She realized that he would spend most of his life alone.

She was done with this, and him.

Before she could say anything he suddenly became animated, his eyes lighting up.

"Oh, Eve, I have something for you! I found this after I unpacked! It's yours, and I knew you'd want it!" He bustled around to the other side of the car, farthest from the diner door.

"Just keep it." Eve turned to walk back to the diner.

"NO. WAIT! You'll want this! It's...It's... It's your mom's." He looked terror-stricken that she would leave him, trying desperately to buy himself a few more minutes.

Sad and desperate.

And there it was, that pity for him that always softened her to him during their relationship. She rolled her eyes and cursed herself, even as she turned to round the trunk.

As the old saying goes, "No good deed ever goes unpunished." She never saw it coming.

<h1 style="text-align:center">14</h1>

Eve

Eve felt something crash into her, and then she was falling and trying not to vomit. It felt like her entire digestive system wanted to crawl up her throat. She managed to land crouched on the ground, her arms around her middle. She looked expectantly for Tark to come running over, but she wasn't at the diner.

Richard's car was gone, the diner was gone, and the guys were gone. She was in the woods, who knew where. She whipped her head around, in confusion.

"Sorry about that, Love. It takes some getting used to."

Eve jumped to the side, her intestines protesting.

Standing next to her was another otherworldly beautiful man, she was guessing a fae. He was tall, well muscled, with jet black hair that ran down to his shoulders, one lock held back by a pointed friggin ear. *So they really did have pointed ears.* He was dressed all in black, like some tactical operative. And as Tark wasn't there with her, she was guessing this guy was one of the Winter Court fae.

This was bad. This was really bad.

She looked around her, trying to assess her situation, but it didn't take long to see she was well and truly screwed.

"How did I get here?!" She put on her bravest face, no point in letting him see she was scared to death.

"Ah, Love, That's not important. What's important is where we're going next!" He smiled a toothy grin, and bounced his eyebrows at her.

He turned to the right suddenly. "Ah, that'll be them, then. Come on." He started walking through the trees and down a small gulley.

Eve just stared at his back. There was no way she was going anywhere with him. He must have felt her hang back, because he called over his shoulder as he walked, "I'd suggest you keep up, Love. There are a lot more of us, and I KNOW they would love a good hunt. Unless you want them all chasin' after you, hunting you down, you'd best do as you're told. You don't want to know what they do with their prey, once caught."

He never even stopped to look back. Eve considered his words, and quickly started after him, but left a good distance between them. They hadn't gone very far when a fae woman appeared in a clearing, and with her was a human male. Eve felt the blood drain out of her face.

He looked a little green, and Eve guessed that however they were transported had something to do with it. He was bent over, his hands on his knees, breathing deeply. It took her a second to realize it was Richard.

Holy shit! He doesn't know about them! I've gotten him fucking kidnapped! Goddamn it, of all the people WHY him?!!!

Guilt hit Eve like a tidal wave, and she felt another bout of nausea rise in her throat. She despised him, but she would never put him at risk like this. She had to figure out a way to get them both out of this. Richard finally looked up, and finally noticed her standing behind the male fae.

"Richard, RUN!" She yelled, throwing her arm wide, hoping that for once he would just listen to her. He looked shocked. But he didn't run.

Instead he smiled.

He fucking SMILED.

The male and female fae both turned to look at Eve, who was still on the verge of a panic attack, and then back to each other. And then, to Eve's great dismay, they threw their heads back and laughed. And fucking Richard joined in.

Oh, I get it now. You're all in on this together, and as usual, I'm the last to figure it out. Fucking Richard!

Richard was still chuckling as he strolled over to the female fae.

"Eve, I never knew you could be so dramatic!"

He was still chuckling as he threw his arm around the buxom female. Dressed all in black, the fae woman had dark mahogany hair which spilled down to her waist in thick shining waves. She was tall, and like the men well toned, but she didn't look masculine at all. She had huge breasts, and a tiny waist, which accentuated muscular hips and thighs. She didn't wear a lot of makeup, but she didn't have to. She had thick eyelashes, large almond-shaped eyes, and full lips. Like the guys, her features were fine and sharp.

She stood a good six inches taller than Richard, so he had to put his arm around her waist, he couldn't comfortably put it around her shoulders. If Eve hadn't been so entirely pissed off, she would have laughed. It was like seeing a supermodel with a troll.

Richard tried to pull her into him, but she looked down her nose at him before rolling out of his reach and heading to the other fae. Richard crossed his arms nonchalantly like it hadn't happened.

"Let's get moving. Can't stay here too long." The male looked around, and then at each member of the party. He turned and plowed into the brush. The female waited for Richard and Eve to follow. The male called back over his shoulder, "Unless you want to be hunted?..." Eve felt the frustration rise in her. She didn't know what to do.

Why hadn't Tark told her more, prepared her, just in case? Was she willingly marching off to her own doom? Or would it be worse if she tried to stay? She couldn't even say where she was, but she could hope that if she could delay them Tark and the guys could track the Winter fae, somehow. The female fae was staring at her, an impatient look on her face. Richard seemed quite content, waiting for her to go first.

Fucking coward.

They had been walking a while and Eve could see the movement of the sun overhead through gaps in the tree canopy, it was her only way of knowing how much time was passing. She cursed herself for leaving her cell phone in her purse in the diner.

Richard had hung back to talk with the female fae. He flirted and joked, and she giggled at his stories.

It was gross, really.

"So what did they give you to hand me over?" She looked pointedly at Richard.

"Give me? Oh, Honey, I did this for free." He chuckled as if it was hilarious. "See my NEW girlfriend here, she told me how much their people need us. And I'd do anything for this wonderful lady of mine." He turned to her, pulled her closer to him, and reached up to kiss her on the cheek. She played the coquette.

"Wow... what a 'coincidence' that they happened to run into my ex, huh?" Eve shot him a death glare for good measure.

"I know, right?! But it gets better! Apparently, they hold some sway with the court system: I'm going to get a title out of this! I am going to be Sir Richard!... no, wait... Lord Richard!"

"Seriously, Richard? What's next? Is an Ethiopian Prince going to wire you a million dollars?"

"You will not talk to your superiors that way, half-breed." The female fae was suddenly dead serious, none of the tittering and blushing from moments before. Eve swore to God that she saw Richard cream his pants at that.

"Where are you taking me?" Eve had to change the subject. Winter fae were dangerous, and Richard was delusional, she'd get no help here.

"To the Winter Court, of course. Pretty little half-breed like you will be very valuable for breeding. I'll bet you bring in a lot of silver at auction." The female fae practically purred.

Eve stopped in her tracks. "In English, please? What the hell are you even talking about?"

Richard pulled lovingly on the fae's arm. "May I?" He seemed positively gleeful.

"Yes, of course, my Darling, whatever makes you happy!" She made kissy faces at him as she rubbed noses with him.

(supermodel / troll = shudder)

"So, apparently, the fae are dying out. For whatever reason, they can't make as many babies as they used to; however, they have found that if they have sex with half-breeds, like you and me, their birth rate is higher! So guess, what? I'm a sex god! And unlike when I was with you, she'll even bring a friend!" He smiled smugly from ear to ear, so proud of himself.

Eve had to process the information in chunks.

They can't reproduce.

They need half-breeds to reproduce.

THEY NEED HALF-BREEDS TO REPRODUCE! WHA–... THEY PLAN TO...

Wait, did he say he's a sex god?!

Are you fucking kidding me?

ARE YOU FUCKING KIDDING ME?!!!

SERIOUSLY?!!!

He could never keep it up!

Worst case of limp dick I have ever seen!! I spent our entire relationship frustrated!

Well, I guess that's THEIR problem now.

At this Eve did giggle out loud.

Hope you're not expecting HIM to father any babies... unless you have magic to take the deflate off of his dick.

With her attitude adjusted, Eve considered the sobering ramifications of this situation; she was a broodmare, nothing more. She had to get herself out of here, had to find Tark and the others because living as a sex slave for these fae was NOT an option for her. She'd have to come up with a plan. She watched her surroundings, trying to see an escape.

The male fae kept walking, and Richard and Kissy-Face were too busy flirting to pay much attention to her.

$$15$$

Eve

Why did I wear work boots?

They had been walking for hours, by Eve's estimates, based on the movement of the sun. She knew she had blisters on her feet and was limping along, moving more slowly as time passed. The fae female had tried to get her to up her pace, but it was no use. Eve was tired and sore, and it was in her best interest to stall them as long as she could. The male finally noticed them lagging behind and rejoined them.

"We'll take a ten-minute break, have water, and then we move." He looked at Eve as he made the announcement.

Eve groaned and flopped on the forest floor. Richard followed suit, sweat dripping off of his face, and Eve was silently thrilled to see that he was in much worse physical shape than she was. He was breathing hard, and his face was red from their walk.

"Hey, how come you can't just transport us to wherever we're going like you did from the diner?" Richard griped. Eve wanted to strangle him and shot him a death glare. He was going to ruin her chance of escaping or being found.

The male didn't even face him to answer him, so Eve could see his face while Richard could not.

"It doesn't work like that. Phasing takes a lot of energy, and can only be used for short distances. Lara and I won't have recovered enough to phase again until we're closer to our destination. You're stuck walking."

Richard huffed and whined.

Eve could see the look of disgust on the male fae's face; clearly, he wasn't a fan of Richard, either. The female fae (Lara?) dropped down gracefully beside Richard and gave him a canteen of water, which he took without looking at her as if she were a servant. Eve chuckled in her mind, *he thinks he's punishing her by withholding affection. Some things never change.*

"Richard, Love, half-breeds have strong fae blood within them. They can draw on that energy to keep going." She was smirking at him as she comforted him like a spoiled child.

Something wasn't adding up to Eve. Richard was the only one who seemed completely spent. It was clear the male didn't like him, and the female... well, she played the role of being on his side, but Eve could see a condescending gleam in her eye. They had used him, they did not consider him an equal, the way he saw himself in this equation. Knowing Richard the way Eve did, she knew she was going to have to get herself out of this mess before he pushed the issue and got them both killed.

Running wasn't an option.

Eve sat the farthest from the others, and behind her back, she drew an arrow in the soil with a stick, representing the way they were walking. She had to hope it would be a clue for those who would look for her, and she had to believe they would look for her. When the fae announced that their break was over, Eve quickly got up to join them, so that no one could inspect the area where she had been sitting.

She continued this every time she acted tired, saying she needed a break. At each stop, she left an arrow. She even managed to leave a bracelet on a branch as she walked by, the male was ahead of her, and Kissy-fae was too absorbed in stroking Richard's wounded ego to notice.

It would have to be enough.

Tark

It had been hours. Tark was furious at himself. He had seen the moment the Winter Court fae had materialized on the other side of the car; he moved to materialize beside them and block them from escape, but it was no use. The fae had taken Eve and Richard and phased immediately out of the area. There was no way of knowing in which direction they went.

The only good news was that they couldn't have gone far. Phasing on the Earth plane took a hell of a lot more energy than it did on the Fae plane, so they had to be close. It didn't help much, though, because they still didn't know where to begin their search.

Luckily, Armodiel had been able to locate their landing point about an hour after they had left. Tark, Skiff, and Lamn had taken a vehicle to the state forest after them because if they phased now, they would not be able to phase again to follow the Winter Court Unseelie if *they* phased again in the near future. It was costing them time, but tactically it was their best option.

Still, Tark was furious with himself for not having foreseen the abduction, to begin with. He couldn't lose Eve now, not when they were so close to getting her to safety. Beyond just her being a hybrid, he had talked with her and gotten to know her. He genuinely liked her. She was easy to talk to, and not overly dramatic. And the way she smelled made him long for her body in a way no female ever had.

At first, they had split up to find the trail, once they had it they were rushing to follow as quickly as they could. There was the very real fear that their adversaries would arrive wherever they were headed, and have transportation waiting, or simply phase to a fae portal and leave the plane and they couldn't let that happen. If they got off of the Earth plane it would be infinitely more difficult to get Eve back.

But they couldn't just phase ahead, either, not knowing where the others had gone. To speed up the process, Skiff offered to phase ahead in small bursts, requiring less energy usage, until he was close enough to let the others know exactly where they were. That's when Tark noticed the arrow on the ground. He had seen one other and dismissed it, but there was no mistaking now.

Clever girl! She left us a trail!

They were on the right track. He pointed it out to Skiff and sent him ahead.

Tark and Lamn still continued on foot, and if Tark was furious with himself, Lamn seemed devastated that Eve was taken. He hardly said a word, but Tark knew his friend well, and Lamn's eyes spoke of sorrow and desperation. Lamn was never this emotional about a hybrid. Tark opened his mouth to ask what had Lamn so upset, when suddenly Skiff was back, holding up a small piece of sparkly jewelry, Eve's jewelry: her bracelet.

Tark felt relief flood his system, and closed his eyes in a brief prayer of gratitude to the Old Gods, but was careful to keep a neutral mask on in front of his brothers. He did notice the urgency with which Lamn forged forward, he was renewed in his purpose as Skiff once again phased ahead, blipping out of sight for recon.

Tark and Lamn were about to continue on the trail when the Grigori returned to them.

"They are reaching the portal. You are almost out of time!" And with that, Armoniel trickled away into the air like dust.

Not.Helpful.

Eve

For what seemed like the millionth time Eve flopped heavily on the ground. Her legs ached, and her feet were hamburger. At least she wasn't as bad as Richard, who was an absolute mess. He was having a complete meltdown, whining and crying about how unfair this all was, and that this was not what he had signed up for, or was expecting. He had a full adult tantrum, yelling and flailing. He demanded respect, to be treated better, to have transportation, and lastly: a foot rub, or a blow job, either way.

This was what Eve had known was coming, knowing Richard as she did. Even on the ground, she put distance between them.

The male fae got right in Richard's red splotchy face and all but spit on him.

"You know what, 'LORD Richard?'" the male asked snidely, "I have had just about enough of your attitude for one excursion, so let me be clear with you. When we said there are some half-fae hybrids here, we never said that you were one of them. You just assumed, and we never corrected you. So when we bargained for you to assist us in apprehending Eve, and we told you we would ensure that you received the full lifestyle and respect of 'your kind', we were, in fact, referring to your *human* kind. And as a human, your life is worth less to us than dog shit."

Richard froze mid-tantrum. The color leached out of his face.

As dawning slowly crept into his brain, his eyes registered fear. He looked to Lara, who openly smirked, and then to Eve. The warning in her eyes must have made him rethink his retort. The male fae continued without pause, turning to Lara, "He is really of no further use to us, we have the hybrid." She shrugged as if to say she couldn't care less. The fae turned his glare back onto Richard.

"If it was not for the fact that we also promised to bring you back to the Winter Court with us, I would kill you where you stand, and be done with you. However, I am a fae of my word. I cannot WAIT to see what torture awaits you at the Winter Court. And so, *Richard Royce, you will continue walking with us, without comment, without complaint, and you will respect your status as our PET befitting a human such as you are.*" The last sentence was spoken with an energy that seemed to suck all of the oxygen out of the air, and Eve could only watch as Richard folded on himself, curling into the fetal position on the ground, whimpering quietly.

The male fae then turned to Eve, "And you, *Eve Sherman, you will continue walking without complaint or stopping until I say we have reached our destination. No more delays.*"

Eve let her body rise and stood waiting to leave, her eyes on the ground.

A compulsion: that's what Tark had told her this was when he helped her clean up the diner. He had explained glamours and compulsions in detail. One was to hide them, the other was to get people to do as they wished, like Becky in the diner.

And she also knew that, for unknown reasons, they didn't work on her. This was her chance. She waited for the male to start their trek again, and she could only hope that he assumed he had control of her. If she could just get him preoccupied with something else, she would have her chance to run, unguarded. Although her feet might never forgive her, she had no choice but to play along.

16

Eve

Eve scanned the greenery as the group trudged on. She had given up keeping track of time, or of trying to engage the fae in conversation to get any information. They had walked in relative silence, disturbed only by Richard's heavy breathing as he tried to keep up with them.

He had a sad and beaten air about him, like a kicked dog, as he tried to shuffle along with the group. She wanted to say it served him right, but at that moment he just looked so dejected and pathetic, that she couldn't bring herself to do it.

Her legs now ached, and her feet felt like solid hooves. There was only pain from the hips down. It was through sheer willpower alone that she kept lifting one foot and putting it in front of the other, she had to appear to be under the fae's power if she was to have any hope of somehow getting away. She just hoped her legs would still work when the time came.

Movement ahead got her attention.

There! Behind a small group of trees, she could see... something moving. She just couldn't see what it was. She looked down at her feet again and saw a single downy white feather. Cautiously, she slowly lifted her head as if she was bored, again letting her eyes float to the trees: movement! A tip of a large feathered wing gently flexed back and forth, ever so slightly. Eve caught her breath, and quickly tried to school her expression to one of pain and boredom, as she nonchalantly snuck a peak at the others. The fae were both focused on their destination, and Richard had his eyes downcast, seeing only the brutal future ahead of him. She gently made a nodding motion, and resumed her walk, tense and ready. She didn't have long to wait.

Suddenly, a wind from nowhere howled through the trees like a freight train, grabbing leaves and small stones from the ground and pelting the party. The male turned back to his traveling companions, and looking to Eve and Richard he shouted, "*Stay here until we return,*" to be heard over the screaming winds and crashing debris around them.

Richard curled in a ball on the ground, but Eve remained standing, ready. Lara and the male both pulled swords out of sheaths attached to their belts, and set out further to find the source of the attack. There was no doubt that this WAS an attack on them.

Eve watched as a tree swayed unnaturally under the force of the wind, and then suddenly bent, and released, catching Lara and flinging her into the air to land several feet away with a scream. The male ran in circles, never going too far from his captives, trying to locate their assailant. Eve watched as the male turned, just as a large rock was flying toward his head; and before he could adjust he was struck right between the eyes. The cracking noise was loud, even with the howling wind, and his body dropped like a sack.

This was her chance!

Eve didn't wait to see if he got back up, she launched her body as fast as it would go; which in truth, wasn't more than a slow jog. She heaved her legs away from the fae, not even caring where she was going, as long as she put distance between them. She pumped her legs forward, even though it felt like lifting logs, and took the scratches of the branches on her face and arms as she plowed through them. She threw everything she had into getting away, heaving breaths, throwing her feet in front of her. She had no reserves left to worry about being graceful, or even cautious: this was her ONE opportunity.

As she ran on she could see Tark ahead of her, Lamn behind him. She just desperately wanted to get to their safety. She saw their eyes light up when they saw her, filled with joy, and then they morphed into looks of terror. Tark screamed and pointed to her, but she couldn't hear him over the wind and the sound of her blood pounding in her ears.

Suddenly Tark was gone. And then he was in front of her, reaching to grab her, just as hands closed around her waist and pulled her backward and off her feet. She saw the panic in Tark's wide eyes, and his grim resolve as he launched toward her, arms still outstretched to snatch her back.

She was hauled away from him as if she were being carried on the wind itself, too exhausted to be able to fight out of the iron arms around her waist. She screamed as tears of frustration ran down her cheeks. Tark on his knees reaching for her was the last thing she saw before the world exploded in light and colors.

The world seemed to turn inside out, again. It was as if she was floating, being pulled by some vacuum through a field of light, color, and energy. Her skin buzzed, and she still felt the arms securely fastened around her waist, but she couldn't see herself. It was as if her consciousness was outside of her body somewhere.

And then they hit the ground. She was at the edge of a forest, with a lush meadow stretching out before her, which extended into rolling hills. She rolled, and her captor rolled with her, not willing to let go of his prize. She turned her head, to watch a male fae slowly moving to rise, but before he did he looked her in the eyes pointedly and said, "*Eve Sherman, you will stay with me and obey my commands at all times.*" Again she felt all the oxygen getting sucked out of the air.

"Who ARE you, you fucking asshole?!" she shouted at him, as he took his time getting up and dusting himself off. "I need to go BACK!"

He gave her a bemused smile with a slight head tilt that said, "Isn't the human adorable?"

"How rude of me," he bowed low, sweeping one arm in front of him and the other out to the side dramatically, "I am Vane. I am to be your caretaker here in the Fae plane until we meet your new master." He stood up tall, clearly proud of himself for having snatched this hybrid treasure up from both of the groups of fae that were no doubt still fighting over her, wherever she had left them.

"I need to go BACK," she repeated loudly, ignoring the nonsense he had just spewed at her.

"Oh, no, no, my dear. That is simply not possible," he stated, still smiling at her as if she were mentally deficient.

"And WHY is it not possible? You brought me here, YOU can take me back." She glared at him openly as she slowly picked herself off of the ground in a most unladylike and less than graceful way. Her legs still ached, but not nearly as much as they had.

"Ah yes, that's true, I *can*," he stated it as a fact, and turned and started walking away into the meadow. "Come along." He called over his shoulder.

"But you WON'T," she finished. Not moving from where she stood, still wincing with the pain in her feet as feeling slowly returned to them.

"There, you see?" He turned to look at her, "The more you resist my commands, the more it will hurt you. I suggest you keep up. I don't want to deliver damaged goods, but he never did specify in what condition he wanted you, and I'll not be inconvenienced. Hup Hup. Let's go." He smirked arrogantly as he turned and continued walking away.

Eve was livid. Even Nancy had never treated her like this, like a possession, a *thing*. And if he was from the Winter Court, she was pretty sure it would only get worse from here. If she stayed by what she must assume was a doorway or wormhole between Earth and the Winter Court, he would realize that he didn't have control of her, and then he would force control by other means.

Not a good option.

If she followed him, she'd be farther away from the door, but as she didn't know how to use it herself, anyway, that wasn't as big of a loss. Logically, it made sense to go with him, and try to find another way to escape. Again.

Fuck my life.

Groaning out loud, she hobbled after him as quickly as her mangled feet would carry her.

Already her legs were recovering and she didn't understand that.

Her feet no longer felt like compacted hooves; sure, there was still plenty of pain, but it felt like it was healing. Was this one of the fae 'abilities' Tark had alluded to?

Tark.

She had lost him again. Part of her was pissed at him for not being able to protect her as he said he would, and part of her knew it was her own damned fault for letting Richard manipulate her. She didn't know how she felt about Tark, she hardly knew him. But he had seemed genuine back at Eddie's as they cleaned up the mess. He had seemed like he might be a friend one day. Maybe more?

If she didn't already know Richard was going to suffer for his part in all of this, she would threaten to rip his balls off if she ever saw him again. She really hoped that Lara put a leash around his dick to drag him around with.

Eve stayed several feet behind Vane (*appropriate name*) as they walked, and took her first real look around. She nearly stopped in her tracks. Sure, there was grass, trees, sky, clouds... birds and creatures... but it was all... *extra*. There was an intensity in the colors, density, feeling... she couldn't put words to it. The grasses were greener, lusher, softer, and more vibrant... she could feel the life in the grass. It didn't glow... but it had a weird energetic *feel*. Everything did. It was overwhelming to her senses. It was like she was somehow connected to it all. Somehow it was all very multidimensional, like walking through a cloud of things, rather than over them, or between them. Her language just didn't have words to fully define it.

She looked up, to see Vane's back walking ahead of her. Even he had the weird energy signature. She could feel his smug glee and arrogance, she could also feel indecision and worry, and most concerning, she could feel his desire. As if reading her mind, he looked back over his shoulder and their eyes met. Yes, he wanted her to believe that he was her temporary lord and master, but she saw the hunger in his eyes. She saw the way they trailed her body, stopping on her chest, before meeting her eyes again. He quickly turned his head forward with a broad smile that he didn't even try to hide, and kept walking.

17

Eve

Haven't these people ever heard of transportation? A taxi, a wagon, a carriage, hell, even a horse?

Eve grumbled under her breath. By her reckoning, she had been walking most of the day. She was no longer sore, but she was tired. Specifically, she was tired of walking.

"Hey, Vain, how the hell much longer are we going to be hiking?" She called ahead of her, where he was still walking along like he didn't have a care in the world.

He turned to look at her over his shoulder. "It's Vane." He corrected, and she wondered how he knew she had meant the other spelling.

"Ah, poor human-hybrid. Don't worry, it won't be long now." Although he smiled broadly at her discomfort, his words dripped sarcasm.

"I need to rest." She demanded.

"No, you don't. Here in the Winter Court, your body will recover much faster, even if you are a half-breed." The last part of his sentence was uttered with disgust and his body shuddered as if responding to the filth of the idea itself.

"I still need water." She was reaching for straws, hoping to find something to poke beneath his armor of arrogance.

"Indeed." Was all he said. He tossed a canteen over his shoulder, which she fumbled and finally caught in her fingertips. "Drink while you walk." He never even turned around.

She twisted the cap off and sniffed the liquid suspiciously. Weren't there fairy tales warning not to eat or drink anything in the Faerie Kingdom? But would she be better off weakened from dehydration?

She put the canteen to her lips and drank deeply, letting the water slice over the edges of her lips and run down her cheeks and onto her shirt. When she finished she wiped her mouth on the back of her arm.

Fuck dainty, at this point.

Sure enough, it was only another few minutes before they crested yet another hill, and she could see a town ahead of them surrounded by forest. It was like she had stepped back in time. The houses were all of wood or stone construction, like something out of the middle ages. The houses were painted in bright gingerbread style around the edges, with flower boxes and tiny gardens in tidy yards. The roads appeared to be dirt, but further in the town she could see cobblestone. The houses changed the farther as well, giving way to businesses in buildings which were side by side with plate glass windows. She could see signs with scissors, shoes, meat, and a tankard, indicating what was inside. It would have been a very quaint little village, if she weren't worried about being used as a sex slave as soon as she met her new "master."

Is this where he lives?

She almost stopped walking as she noticed the 'people' of the town. Her jaw dropped as she watched what looked like a lizard in clothing, walking on two legs, strolling down the street. There was also a centaur walking in the other direction, with a tunic over his human torso, but his horse body left unclothed. There were several creatures buzzing around that looked like humans, except for their tiny sizes and brightly colored skin, not to mention their wings. *Were those pixies?*

"This way."

Vane veered off their course and headed for the backs of the houses on the outskirts of the town. Eve could feel the discomfort rolling off of him in waves. Something had him spooked, and that did not bode well for her. He continued around the outskirts, keeping them hidden within the tree line, until they came to a large building smelling of horses, behind another large building which appeared to be a large house, or an inn, facing the road.

Vane turned to Eve, all smug smiles gone from his face.

"Eve Sherman, you will remain here and do your best to remain undetected. You will not leave this place until I return." He looked at her, waiting for her to acknowledge that she understood. She nodded at him.

He continued to stare at her, and she felt his indecision. He looked to the house, and then back at her, before finally making the decision and leaving her hidden among the trees. However, he looked over his shoulder several times before rounding the corner of the building to use the front door.

Eve knew this could be a trap. She was alone, she could run. But where? And if she left too quickly, he could change his mind, and return to find that he hadn't really had control of her. She didn't want to be tied to him. She also didn't know how long he was going to be, so she couldn't deliberate too long. She counted to thirty slowly, and then planned to make a run for it. She only reached twenty five when she heard a voice nearby.

"Hey, who's out there?... I can see you miss. Come out and make yourself known." The voice was not speaking the lordly arrogant talk that Vane used, this sounded like someone who was more common. But would he help her? There was so much at risk.

The man walked toward her, but not in a threatening way. He appeared to be human, but Eve saw the tip of a pointed ear poking out of his bushy hair.

"Miss, the sun is setting soon, it will be chilly out here. And there are wolves in these parts. Why don't you come in and have a pint of ale?" He smiled warmly as he approached.

"Please!" she began, "I need to get out of here. It's not safe for me." She was praying that he was someone who would help her, and not someone who would use her as Tark had warned.

The man stopped a few feet away. "You're the hybrid, the one with Vane?"

She froze. *He knew too much. Oh God, had she sealed her fate with her big mouth? Why didn't she run when she had the chance?!*

At seeing her expression his eyes softened into something like pity. "No, Dearie, I'm not working with that ass. I've been looking for 'ye. Tark sent me with a message: he's on his way. Just stay safe, is all."

"Tark?!"

Eve's heart squeezed tightly. He was coming for her!

She felt the tears rising in her eyes when shouting from the building interrupted their conversation. Vane was running toward them now, shouting at the man to get away from her, and that she was his property. He was making threats and drawing his sword as he got closer.

The man turned back to Eve and winked at her before turning back to Vane, who had arrived and was quickly pushing Eve behind him and away from the stranger.

"Oy, Sir, Tha's a lovely little dove 'ye got there. She smells delicious! How much for an hour with the lass, eh?" The man leered at Vane, and Eve noticed his accent was much thicker, and he slurred quite a bit as well, he hadn't sounded like that with her.

"You'll not have any time with this one, old man." Vane was radiating anger, but underneath it Eve felt his fear, fear of losing his prize. "She's with me." He tried shuffling Eve away and into the woods.

"You?! An 'ow is it YOU come by such a pretty little thing, smelling so sweetly? I'm sure your Lords at the Court would want to be hearin' about the likes o'her! Come now, tell me who it is ye' serve so's I can petition HIM for some time with the fair tail! He'll tire o'her soon enough, and I know he'll be auctioning her out for all the coin she'll bring. She's a fair one. My money's as good as theirs!" He was openly ogling Eve now, and palming a bag which made the tell-tale noise of coins jingling together, making a good show of his interest.

"What Lord Jef–... What her Lord and Master decides for her is no concern of yours. We're leaving." Vane grabbed Eve's arm roughly and yanked her along his side, as he quickly made his way back into the tree line, and continued on the outskirts of the town toward the far end.

Eve looked back over their shoulder as Vane marched them further on. The stranger smiled and offered her a small salute with his hand, before turning and heading into the town himself.

"I specifically told you to remain undetected!" Vane sneered between gritted teeth.

"He must have seen us arrive. He already knew I was there. You ordered me to stay there, so I couldn't hide myself." She knew she should be frightened, but she was privately delighted at his anguish.

"You were not to be seen! You have endangered us BOTH." He was clearly furious, and by the feel of it VERY afraid, as he clutched her arm painfully with a death grip and all but dragged her through the trees.

Eve stopped listening as he ranted on. She had enough experience with Nancy to know that there was no reasoning with him, so she let him spew his verbal venom, threats, and other nastiness.

None of that mattered. Tark was coming for her!

<h1 style="text-align:center">18</h1>

Tark

Tark swore loudly and pounded his fists on the ground. *He'd almost HAD her! He was so close!* He climbed to his feet to go after the two fae who had transported them, when a fist collided with his jaw, sending his head arching backward with the force of the blow. He stumbled back a step, and put up a defensive posture, only to drop it again when he saw it was Lamn standing in front of him.

What the hell?!

Lamn hit him again, this time in the nose. There was a sickening crunch as his nose broke, and blood ran like a waterfall from his nostrils, even as his eyes teared up with the impact.

"What in the faerie realm is WRONG with you?!" Tark demanded as he cupped his injured nose in his hands.

Damn it hurt.

"YOU LET THEM TAKE HER!" Lamn was out of control. His eyes were wild, his hands balled in fists, as if ready to strike again. Tark had never seen him like this.

Skiff rushed over to put his body between them.

"Easy Lamn, there was nothing he could do. We did everything we could." Skiff held his hands up, as if to stop them from going at each other again, but Tark hadn't wanted to fight Lamn in the first place, and was still completely dumbfounded by his friend and Commander's behavior.

Skiff turned to Tark, "I got the male, but the female and Richard got away. Probably phased to the next portal."

Lamn was clenching and unclenching his fists, pacing in circles, completely oblivious to the conversations, and clearly distressed. Technically, Lamn was his superior, but Tark knew there was something he was missing here.

"Lamn.... LAMN!"

Tark's voice seemed to pull Lamn out of whatever anguished scenario was playing out in his head. He turned to Skiff and Tark, genuinely surprised to see Tark's bloody and bruised face. His anger evaporated. He stared for a moment, opened his mouth to speak, thought better of it, and shut it again, only to open it a moment later. He looked at his feet as he addressed his brothers-in-arms with shame in his voice.

"I guess I owe you an explanation... and an apology." He didn't meet their eyes, as they waited quietly for him to continue. Lamn sighed deeply, closing his eyes against the confession.

"She's my daughter."

Tark and Skiff both jerked with a shocked gasp. Neither had expected this.

"I only just found out. Her mother was my mate... she was taken from me. I could never find her. I didn't know she was with child."

Lamn finally looked up to meet their eyes. There was no judgment in them, only sorrow.

"Lamn, I–"

"Wait, there's more. Much more." Lamn cut Tark off. "She is Nephila, as was her mother. I had wanted to tell Eve of her parentage before I told you. It just didn't work out that way. One of the Grigori fathered my Mate, Ruth, that's why a Grigori is helping us. I made a vow that we would keep this information secret. I made a deal with the Grigori to help find Ruth and keep her safe, as well as keep Eve safe, and I have failed at both."

Lamn stopped, clearly having trouble getting the words out. When he did speak, his voice cracked with emotion. "I can't lose Eve. Not after having lost Ruth... Not again."

His body was rigid as he tried to hold back the emotional tidal waves that were so close to breaching his wall of control.

Tark walked the few steps between them and put his arms around Lamn. Yes, they were the most feared and powerful fae among the Summer Court, but every fae had his limits, and Lamn had just met his. There was no shame in comfort between them.

"We'll get them back, Lamn. We need a strategy, let's go." Lamn held Tark's look for a moment, swimming in gratitude. Finally, Lamn mentally and emotionally pulled himself together. He was the best damned strategic leader the Summer Court had, he was going to have to draw on his many centuries of knowledge to make this work. Tark was right, they needed a plan. He made eye contact with each, nodding in acknowledgement, and then they were moving.

The three fae phased to the vehicle and drove back to diner to retrieve Eve's purse, and grab a few provisions. The locked doors didn't stop them for a moment, and they were soon back at their safe house. Tark's heart still hitched when he saw Eve's travel bag in the backseat of the car, where she had left it.

He understood why Lamn was so emotionally attached, as shocking as it had been, but Tark had no excuse for why he himself seemed too attached. She was supposed to be just another job, another hybrid. She was supposed to be just another life to save, and just another chance to save the fae from extinction. It wasn't supposed to feel personal. He would probably never see her again, *even if* he did manage to get her to the safety of the Summer Court.

And even if he could, would he want that for her? His life was dangerous, he was often away on missions. With her new-found lineage, she could marry into the most noble families in court and live the life of a princess. Why would she ever want to settle for someone of his stature? What did he have to offer her? It would be selfish to want anything more from her.

He told himself all of these things, but his heart still hurt at the thought of letting her go.

Well, you can't let her go until you find her, idiot.

Lamn, Skiff, and Tark settled in for a long strategy session. They would need to call on every favor, every contact, every sympathizer they knew... and bribe a few they didn't, if they were going to pull this off. And they WOULD pull this off.

Eve

AGAIN, WITH THE WALKING!

Eve was over this. She was hungry, tired, and quite frankly, pissed off at being tied at the hip with Lord Smug, as she now called Vane... well, in her mind, at least.

The sun had finally set, and the cold was setting in as the stranger had predicted. Luckily, there had been no signs of wolves or other predatory animals, but she really didn't want to give any the opportunity to find them... unless they would eat Lord Smug, and leave her alone. She was about to complain, again, when he finally stopped walking.

"We're here." was all he said, as he turned and headed through the trees.

Eve followed, and in the darkness she could barely make out a small cottage with a thatched roof, hidden behind a stand of trees. If he had not pointed it out, she never would have seen it.

He made his way to the door, and pulled a stone out of a pocket; she watched as he waved the stone over the door handle. The stone glowed blue, and there was an audible 'click,' before the door swung open.

A key! I'll have to relieve him of that.

Eve watched him intently, as he slipped the stone back into the right side pocket of his pants. Without a word, Vane ushered her into the house, and closed the door behind them and barred it from the inside. He crossed to the hearth and waved his arms over it. A cheery fire sprang from nothing, setting the logs to crackling. Likewise he waved his hands over a few sconces, and they ignited instantly, casting the room in a warm subdued glow.

"Where are we?"

Eve took in the cottage. It was absolutely adorable: one main living area, a small kitchen off to one side, and a staircase that led up to more rooms. The furniture was very rustic, rough hewn wood with hand-sewn cushions. The table was also hand-worked and sturdy, with a few sturdy chairs around it.

"We'll be safe here tonight." Vane informed her without fanfare. "The doors and windows are spelled, so you can't escape. Don't bother trying. There are sleeping rooms upstairs, and there are provisions in the kitchen. There are bathing chambers in each of the sleeping rooms. I suggest you take a bath while here." He looked at her pointedly, and curled his lip as if to suggest that she smelled like an animal.

"I'll be resting. Do not disturb me," he finished.

With that, he turned and headed up the staircase. Eve noticed he entered the second door at the top of the stairs, closing it firmly behind him.

Immediately she rushed to the door as quietly as she could and gently tried the handle. It turned! She quietly pulled the door open, and with a last look over her shoulder she rushed to get outside. Unfortunately she ran headfirst into some sort of invisible barrier, and with the force of her momentum she wound up on her ass on the floor, rubbing the throbbing goose egg on her forehead.

"Are you DAFT? I told you it was spelled." Vane's muffled voice filtered down the staircase and into the living area.

So much for that idea.

She went to the kitchen next, as she hadn't eaten all day. While there was no refrigerator, she did find bread, and a cold storage with cheese and preserved meat. Not her favorite things, but at this point food was food. She even found a bowl of fruit, some she recognized, others not, that she grabbed to take with her.

She ate while standing, not wanting to get too comfortable in case Vane showed back up. It was then that she noticed what was missing. There was no technology. There had been nothing mechanical on the streets of the town they had visited, and there was nothing mechanical or electronic here, either. She scoured the room, and then the living room.

Why rely on technology, when you have magic?

After a quick meal, and a long bath (how they had hot water she really couldn't fathom), she climbed into the bed. It was much larger than her twin at Nancy's and surprisingly comfortable for a straw mattress.

She had barely just laid down before sleep overtook her.

19

Eve

Eve woke with the sunlight spilling between the sheer curtains like a spotlight on her face. She groaned and rolled over before the realization hit her.

Sunlight?! I'm not at home!

With that, she hurled her body upward into a sitting position, heaving in panicked breaths, trying to assess where she was. With the rough-hewn furniture and wooden floor and walls, her memory flooded into her brain.

Richard, Lara, Vane... the town... the cottage... endless walking. She flopped back down onto the bed.

Oh God, Please tell me we're not going to walk all over this... country? Court? Whatever it is!

She contemplated laying back down and trying to go back to sleep as if it could postpone the inevitable hours of walking, when she heard muffled voices downstairs. One of them was Lord Smug, she could tell by the haughty air of authority in his speech. The other was male, but she didn't recognize him. She threw her legs over the bed and gently rested them on the floor. Surprisingly, all of the pain and blisters she knew she had been cultivating were absent: her feet looked perfect and felt fine.

Rising slowly to stand, she gingerly put one foot in front of the other, freezing whenever a floorboard made a gentle groan under her weight. She stopped, and listened, but the voices downstairs continued undisturbed. There was no loud pounding on her door, demanding the day's death march, and she was infinitely grateful.

Slowly and painstakingly she made her way to a small wardrobe, curious as to who the cottage belonged to, and more importantly, wondering if there were any clean clothes she could wear. The practical outfit she had arrived in was filthy, soaked in sweat, dirt, and most of the forest floor. Inside the wardrobe she found some nondescript peasant shirts, and drawstring pants. The shirts were baggy on her, and the pants were a little too short, but they would do. She also found some leather shoes, nothing like she had ever seen at home. They were a pretty good fit as well, and surprisingly comfortable.

She hated to leave her own clothes behind, maybe she could wash them in the tub and let them dry if there was time. She didn't want to give up any connection to her home. She also decided that if they were going to be marching all over the land, she wanted to bring spare clothing to change into. Who knew when she would get her next shower or clean change? She found a burlap satchel in the bottom of the wardrobe and loaded it with several shirts and pants. Unfortunately, there was only the one pair of shoes. It would have to do.

Eve cleaned up quickly, and made her way to the door of her room. It opened, and she gently pushed her hand through the doorway to avoid another head-on collision. When her hand moved through the space easily, she put the satchel strap around her neck, crossbody, and crept toward the railing to better hear the conversation below.

"And how do you know Lord Jeffers ISN'T aware you have her?" the new voice said.

"Truthfully, I don't. But I would suspect that if his Lordship thought for a moment this hybrid was in the Winter Court, surely he would have sent reinforcements to guarantee her delivery? He sent many teams to recover her, and it was still not easy." Eve could imagine Lord Smug's nose in the air.

"I don't know, Vane. This is tricky business. If I get caught–"

"If WE get caught. Yes, Rodolfo, I know what would happen, you don't need to tell ME. But we WON'T get caught. I just need some time to hide her away, to let them think she evaded capture. Once enough time passes, they will lose interest and set their sights on another hybrid, and we will be free to capitalize on what is ours."

"That's a huge gamble, Vane. I can smell her scent from here, and she is clearly of mixed descent beyond just fae! You don't even know what you are dealing with."

"Yes, her scent... She is unique. Just think of all the coin we will earn with that alone. And she's not as plain or damaged as some of the other hybrids, dare I say, she's almost attractive. She has lots of fea qualities shining through that ugly human husk. I guarantee we will be living like kings with her as our main offering. And any offspring she may produce... well, we will have generations of income. We may never need to work again! You just need to buy us some TIME, Rodolfo."

Eve slowly crept away from the railing and back to the wall, until she slid down to the floor. She was horrified to hear them discussing her potential 'offspring' as if she were a cow. The reality of the situation hit her hard. She was going to be prostituted, just another sex slave. And as a hybrid she would have no rights, no voice. Just because nothing truly terrible had happened up until now didn't mean it *wouldn't*. She HAD to find a way out of here.

The conversation downstairs lapsed, and then stopped altogether. She could hear the men moving around the space, doing God knows what. She had no desire to go downstairs and... *what? Meet them? Confront them?* There was no point. Neither would be open to helping her in any way.

Not for the first time, Eve wished she was like some badass heroine from a storybook, and not just some small town girl with no survival skills.

Deciding that hiding wasn't serving her any better, Eve made her way down the stairs to try to determine what Vane's plans for her were. At least if she knew then maybe... maybe... she could find a hole in them that she could exploit. She reached the bottom of the stairs just as a man was getting ready to walk out the door. He must be the mystery man that was speaking with Vane. Eve couldn't help but notice that the man had two tiny horns on his head, nor that his capri-length pants displayed thin furry legs, ending in cloven hooves.

"Come, come, now, it's rude to stare. Surely even humans know of Satyrs?!" Vane was giving her a disapproving look, his mouth in a scowl.

The man at the door stopped, and Eve looked from Vane to Rodolfo, unclear what she should do. Luckily, she didn't need to do anything. Vane turned back to face the leaving Satyr.

"Full moon. Be ready."

Rodolpho tore his eyes away from Eve, where he himself had been staring, and nodded in understanding to Vane before glancing one last time at Eve. With that, he was stepping through the door and closing it behind him.

"I see you took my advice and bathed. Excellent. Clean clothes as well. Very good."

At his words of praise, Eve suddenly wished she could put her dirty clothing back on, perhaps if she stank no one would want to buy her services.

"We are leaving at dusk for the next portion of our trip. Make yourself ready to travel. I need to leave to secure provisions for us, but I will leave the spells in place. Please don't damage yourself again trying to escape; I find it irksome and disrespectful, and I do not wish to have to discipline you. I will be back before dusk."

Vane picked up his coat and headed to the door, and in a breath, he was out and the door was closed behind him.

Eve stood in stunned silence for a moment. She didn't know whether to be outraged at his 'discipline' comment or fearful of where they were going. It seemed obvious to her that Vane was not taking her to Lord Jeffers, whom she assumed was his boss. But what did that mean?

She made her way into the kitchen, pulling out anything she felt she could stomach, and wrapping whatever she felt would travel well. She couldn't even have time to feel guilty about robbing the owners of the cottage, given her desperate situation.

If Vane was double-crossing his boss, would that work out better or worse for her? She had heard the stranger in town say that this Lord would tire of her, and then pimp her out. But Vane had said as much for himself. Sure, she might be able to get Vane in trouble, but that still didn't help HER, unless she could use that information to her advantage, as leverage. There was just too much she didn't know, but she was pretty sure that as a hybrid she wouldn't have any rights no matter who she was with.

A noise in the living area got her attention. She had never heard the door open, nor had Vane announced himself. She quickly flattened against the nearest wall, and crept toward the door to the living area. She steeled herself as she cautiously peeked around the corner. There in the center of the room, taking it all in, was the angel!

Well, maybe not THE angel, I mean, I haven't seen that many... they might all look alike.

As if feeling her eyes on him, he turned and caught her just as she was trying to duck her head back into the kitchen.

"EVE! Oh, thank goodness you're alright!"

The angel closed the distance between them with large purposeful strides. Eve was frozen in place, not knowing what to say.

I mean, how does one address an angel?

"Uh... who are you?" Was all her foggy mind could come up with, and she mentally kicked herself.

"Dearest Eve, I am called Armoniel. I am helping the Summer Court Fae to find you and recover you. I cannot tell you how happy I am to see you, alive and well!"

She wasn't sure she was 'well,' but thought better than to argue with an angel.

Eve remembered him from the car 'accident,' and then later...

"You were in the forest when those other two fae had Richard and me, that was YOU with the windstorm."

Armoniel only smiled and nodded. Eve felt there was something so familiar about him, as if she had known him before, or seen him when she was younger, but there is no way she'd forget the wings!

It must just be that he looked like someone else...

"Well, this is great, Armoniel! Since you are here, you can just get me out of here and we can be on our way!" Eve grabbed her bag of food and headed for the door, for the first time she was truly hopeful.

"Ah, yes, about that... You see, I have no power here, in this realm. I cannot undo what has been done. I can only work with the natural forces, I cannot counter magic. I can't release you from the containment spell." Armoniel had the decency to look apologetic, as he couldn't quite look Eve in the eyes.

"Wait, you WHAT? If you can't help me then why are you HERE?"

Eve felt like her last shred of hope burned in the wind. She could feel the tears rising to her eyes, and she wasn't sure if it was anger or hopelessness. The angel wrapped his arms around her in a hug, oddly enough Eve didn't feel the need to object. He felt so familiar to her, so safe, and after all, he WAS an angel.

He spoke to her as he held her. "Eve, I am so sorry. I have failed you in so many ways, and I hope that you can forgive me someday. I came here today in hopes of just determining your location, so I can make the others aware. We are planning to come for you, we just needed to know where to find you. The fae already had a report that you were seen at a town not far from here. I've been searching the area ever since."

Eve was humbled into silence, and wrapped her arms around the angel, hugging him back. Remembering Vane's earlier conversation, she pulled away from Armoniel and looked him in the eye.

"Wait. I won't be here long. Vane, the fae who took me, he works for some 'Lord Jeffers.' I guess he was supposed to deliver me to him. But now he's decided that he wants to keep me all to himself, well, himself and Rodolfo, who's half goat. They want to rent me out, to make a living off of my 'offspring'..." Eve couldn't say anymore as the sobs choked off her words.

"Eve," Armoniel touched his hand to the side of her face, cupping her cheek gently, "Do you know where he's taking you?" His touch was oddly comforting. Eve felt a warm relaxation settle into her body, she felt peaceful, even if she still felt fear.

"I don't know. All he said was that we leave tonight at dusk."

Armoniel seemed to consider this for a moment, and then gently released Eve.

"I must go back and alert the others. Do not fear, my Eve, we ARE coming for you." Eve could tell that the angel seemed to be struggling with leaving her alone, and the need to report back. His eyes were haunted as if he were to blame for her situation.

"I trust you. Go. Get Tark and the others." She put her bravest face on. He considered for only a moment more, and then he was gone.

In the silence of the room, alone, Eve was free to let the tears fall.

20

Eve

There is nothing worse than dreading something but having to WAIT for that something to happen.

Eve had washed her clothing and laid it out to dry, which they did surprisingly quickly. She had packed, and she was ready. She paced in the living area because she had literally nothing else to do, and the anxiety was eating her alive. Hours passed. She sat, she paced, and she ate. Finally, the door opened and Vane stepped into the cottage.

He dropped his coat on a chair and headed up the staircase and into his room. Not wishing to rush their departure, Eve sat quietly and watched. Moments later he was descending the stairs with a bag of his own, and gathering up his coat. He opened the door and stood by it waiting. When Eve didn't move he finally turned to look at her.

"We haven't got all night," he remarked dryly, but it lacked the venom he usually reserved for her. Eve noticed he looked tired, with dark circles under his eyes. His usually immaculate shirt and pants were wrinkled and unkempt, as if he had either been sleeping in them or wrestled in them.

Eve silently gathered her things and headed out the door, with Vane hot on her heels. He was still giving off a sort of desperate-fearful energy. Outside the cottage, the sun was just about to set, and the last of its golden glow fell over the woods and three horses tied to a branch. One had bags and packs tied to it, the other two were clearly for riding.

Thank you, GOD!

Eve stopped beside one horse to run her hands over its soft shoulder when she suddenly felt two vicelike hands grab her hips and launch her up onto the horse. She had all she could do to stay on top of it, and not slide off the other side from the momentum. After much-undignified squirming and heaving, she was on the horse's back firmly. She noticed Vane was already in his saddle, and that he held the reigns to her horse in his hand. She shot him a glare to let him know how much she appreciated his less-than-gentle help and the fact that she wasn't even trusted to guide her own horse.

First chance I get, I'm kicking you in the nuts.

Vane only smirked at her, then turned his horse and began it walking at a brisk pace through the trees. Eve's horse and the pack horse followed along behind it complacently.

The journey seemed endless. They traveled through the dark forest, or if they had to cross a field they would stay on the outskirts and work around it, to keep the cover of the trees. Time seemed to stand still in the silent darkness. Eve couldn't tell how long they had been riding, only that her ass hurt her in ways that she was sure wasn't natural. She kept her eyes open, hoping to catch a glimpse of Tark and the others, or even of Armoniel. But all she saw was darkness and shadow.

Once she did catch sight of a small deer near a stream, but it quickly ran as they approached. The longer she rode, the more the hope of rescue seemed less likely. She was fighting fatigue, trying to watch for movement, a sign, anything. But there was only the soft rhythmic beat of the hooves on the earth.

"We're here."

The words, spoken far too loudly, startled Eve out of deep sleep. She jumped, and as she started to slide, she realized she was still on the horse. It was too late to regain her balance, as she grasped and windmilled, looking for anything to keep her upright. Her body rolled off of the horse like molasses and plopped her on the ground unceremoniously. The horse had the gall to turn its head back and stare at her, a puddle of limbs at its feet.

Vane was laughing, full-on, doubled over, belly laughing. His face was turning red from laughing so hard, and he couldn't seem to catch his breath. Eve was on the verge of making a sharp comment along the lines of *"Let's see who's laughing when Lord Jeffers finds out you've stolen his prize."* Only to realize that while it might be true HE wouldn't be laughing, SHE probably wouldn't be either. There was no point in poking the bear. She'd have to swallow her humiliation for now.

She dragged her aching body off the ground, and for the first time noticed the stone building behind Vane. She guessed it was a huge residence: there was a door, and she could see windows, but it was an oddly shaped building that was tall and narrow. There were small towers at the four corners. Vane was still chuckling as he pulled the key stone out of his pants pocket and waved it over the door handle. With a click, he pushed it open and ushered Eve inside.

Eve was shocked by the interior, which was richly decorated. Just inside the door was a small reception desk, empty. Artwork hung on walls, a soft carpet lined the floor, and soft couches lined both sides of the hall, positioned between the many doors. It was not the rustic chic she had seen thus far. There was a chandelier overhead that spoke of money, even if it held candles and not electrical bulbs.

Eve didn't get a chance to investigate any further, as Vane's hand at her lower back urged her down the hall. The place seemed completely empty, although that could have been due to the late hour that they had arrived. Every now and then one of the doorways in the hall would be open, and she could just make out sitting rooms or parlors. Most of the doors, however, were closed.

The hall ended at a door, which Vane opened into a dark kitchen; he then resumed pushing Eve through, and to a door on the far side. This door opened to a stone spiral staircase and he indicated that she should go up.

When she just looked at him with an eyebrow raised his face contorted with anger, and he grabbed Eve by the arm and hauled her up the stairs after him. There wasn't much she could do, he was much stronger than she was, and her body was still stiff from the hours on horseback. The endless stairs finally leveled out at yet another door. Vane waved his key stone over the handle, and when the door was open he launched Eve inside by her arm and swung the door shut behind her. The telltale 'click' of the lock told her all she needed to know.

As the day bloomed it was murky at best, with the overcast sky holding back the sunlight that wanted to warm the land below. Eve looked out of the small window, one of three in the room. The clouds threatened rain, and painted the scene below in muted browns and grays. That pretty much summed up how Eve was feeling as well.

She had woken up in the tower room, and the chill of the stone seemed to seep into her bones. She had lit a fire in the small fireplace with supplied wood and matches, but unless she sat right at the edge of the hearth, there seemed to be no warmth at all. Vane had clearly already been there, because her bags waited for her on the floor.

For all of the nice and expensive furnishings that she had passed in the hallway downstairs, this room left a lot to be desired. The mattress, if you could call it that, was made of straw, and covered with the cheapest, roughest blankets you could find. Many had holes in them. There was no carpet, nothing to insulate against the cold of the stone floor or walls. Other than the bed, the room held a small wooden chair and a small writing desk with nothing on it.

There was a bathing room attached, but it was not much more than a toilet, the world's tiniest sink, and a 'bathtub' that she would have to stand in. Turning the taps confirmed that there was no hot water. They had left one motheaten towel and rag for her, and a bar of soap.

Eve looked around her new room, and it occurred to her that in many ways it was better than her room at Nancy's. She didn't have her personal stuff, but she did have a view. She also had privacy, as she would be able to hear anytime someone was approaching on the stone steps.

It became clear that the building was not empty. With the first light of morning came the smells of food cooking in the kitchens far below.

About an hour later a note was slid under her door, which told her that the dumbwaiter within the wall, beside her door, would have her meals delivered and that she should simply put her empty dishes back on to be washed. She found the wooden door and opened it, to find a cold breakfast waiting for her, something that was probably supposed to be oatmeal, and a glass of water.

Eve could also make out the noise of movement from below, but the stone muffled most of it. She had managed to see people approaching the building, as her tower at the back ran parallel to the road in the distance. She noticed many riders on horseback coming and going. Correction, she noticed many MEN on horseback, coming and going. She had a pretty good idea of what kind of establishment she was staying in.

21

Eve

Eve sat alone in her tower room all day. Other than food deliveries, she had zero interaction with the outside world, which suited her just fine. The day consisted of hours and hours of hours and hours. With nothing to do she rotated between pacing or looking out the window, it felt endless. The room seemed to be shrinking around her. She hadn't heard from Vane at all, and she didn't know if she should be grateful, or worried.

And Tark! How would he find her here? The anxiety in her gut kept churning, but there was nothing happening to change it in any way. She just looped in this endless cycle of worry. Night finally fell, and with no light source but the fireplace and a candle, she went to bed early.

The next day was much like the previous. There was still no word from Vane and no sign of Tark. Anxiety gave way to boredom, and Eve spent most of the day laying on the uncomfortable bed lost in thought. Night fell without fanfare. Boredom gave way to hopelessness.

Day three started much the same, but after Eve had finished breakfast there were slow and steady footsteps on the stairs, followed by a knock. At this point, Eve didn't care if Satan himself was on the other side of that door, she wanted the hell out of her room. She rushed to the door as it unlocked and opened. (*Silly girl, you don't have the key, remember?*) A bored looking fae stood at the door with a garment over his arm. When Eve didn't say anything, he launched into his purpose.

"Lady Silver is expecting you for an audience. I have brought you suitable attire. You will get dressed now, and I shall accompany you downstairs. Should you refuse, or in any way disrespect her Ladyship by misbehaving, you will be disciplined severely." With that he extended his arm to her, with a dress draped over it.

Eve took the dress begrudgingly and stepped into her bathing chamber to change. The dress was nothing special: not fine, but also not the moth eaten cloth she had been living with. It was black, modest, and practical, covering her from her neckline to almost her ankles. Her brown shoes didn't go with it at all, but Eve really didn't give a shit. If she was going to meet her pimp, she didn't care if she was fashionable.

The butler fae led her down the spiral staircase and into the kitchen, which was now bustling with several people working at several stations preparing food. Many of them tried to sneak a peek at her as she went by, while still appearing busy with their work. No one said a word. The only sound was the cooking of food and the cutting of vegetables. It struck Eve as eerie; every kitchen she had ever been in had been alive with conversation.

She was led back down the main hallway, past sofas and lamps, when the butler stopped in front of a door and knocked. A voice within granted them access, so he pulled the door open to present Eve, and then stepped into the background.

Eve stood before a striking fae woman dressed elegantly in a long silver satin dress with a deep neckline that showcased her cleavage. Her blond hair was done up stylishly, and the jewelry on her fingers, wrist, neck, and ears contained stones which caught the light and sparkled like stars. Like most of the fae her facial features were sharp: high cheekbones, rugged jawline. However, on her they looked severe and cruel. Her expertly made up eyes were narrowed in judgment. Her brows were knit, as if she were displeased, and her full lips were pulled ever so slightly into a disapproving frown. She took Eve in from top to bottom and back to top, and if her expression was any indication, she found Eve lacking.

Lady Silver lowered herself gracefully into her overstuffed chair. Eve noticed that there was no other chair in the room, setting the tone for this meeting. The Lady wasted no time getting to business.

"You are to be staying with us for an undetermined amount of time. While I am always sympathetic to my fae associates, I am not in the habit of providing charity. While you are here you will work to earn your keep. For the *luxury* of a private room, the clothing we will provide, and the food for you to eat, I expect for you to contribute to the well-being of this establishment. Drek will be your handler." She indicated the fae standing behind Eve. "He will be given a list of duties for you to perform, and he will inspect your work. I will not tolerate any insolence or disrespect while you are here. Remember, my Dear, that while my associate wants you kept alive, he never stated that you had to have all of your body parts intact. You begin immediately. Go." With that she picked up some paperwork from her desk, effectively dismissing Eve and Drek.

Eve stood in stunned silence until Drek took her by the arm and pulled her bodily out of the room before she could make a scene. He brought her back through the kitchen and into a side room filled with cleaning supplies.

Eve was still playing back everything she had just heard in her mind. Lady Silver had made it seem like this wasn't forever, she just had to get through it without losing any body parts. She was pretty sure she could do that. And at least they weren't expecting her to have sex with the clients, at least not yet, so there was that.

"I have your list of duties. Please don't fuck this up, because if you do, they don't just beat you, they beat me too, and if there is some perverse bastard client in residence, they may even beat or torture most of the staff for their entertainment and make you watch. They are just looking for a reason. Don't give them one." With that, Drek pulled a sheet of paper out of his pocket and unfolded it for her.

"In the morning before breakfast, you will collect all of the laundry and linens and take them out back, wash and hang them. You will take the clean linens from the closet and replace the dirty linens and make up the rooms. I have outlined all of the rooms you will service. I will show you the servants' entrances and hallways.

"You are never to use the clients' hallway.

"After that, you will help in the stables: mucking stalls and cleaning the horses.

"You will only use the back door of the building to access the stables.

"You are NEVER to be seen by the clients, nor to be alone with any of them, for any reason. Her Ladyship is deadly serious about removing body parts. You are to have minimal to no contact with staff, other than myself. Do you understand all of this?"

Eve stared at him with wide eyes. She couldn't believe what she was hearing, she couldn't believe that this was her life now. She realized Drek was waiting for an answer, and she nodded her head mutely.

"Good. Let me show you the rooms so you can get started on the laundry."

With that, Drek turned on his heel and went to the other side of the kitchen, into another room containing shelves loaded with linens. Eve immediately noticed that the sheets and blankets were soft and of fine quality, completely unlike what she herself was expected to use. Drek showed her a door at the back of the room: it opened into a dark narrow hallway that had access doors to all of the rooms she would clean. She was responsible for thirty 'client guest rooms,' those were the rooms in which clients would be 'entertained' by the ladies, and even a few men, on staff. They never stayed all night. The rooms were slated to be cleaned first thing in the morning so that they would be remade and fresh for the day's upcoming clients. Eve was horrified when Drek repeatedly told her where to find the cleaning solution to remove blood, and other stains from the linens and carpets, and how to dispose of body parts.

These fae must really have a fetish for dismemberment or something.

Next, he showed her where she would wash the linens. A small exterior room at the back of the building offered wash basins, water, soap, and scrubbers. Eve very nearly did cry when she realized that there were no 'washing machines.' She was it. She turned to Drek, overwhelmed.

"This will take me–"

"With washing, hanging, and resetting rooms, at least six to eight hours, yes. I wouldn't dawdle, if it takes longer than that, the House Manager, Rog, will come nosing around to see what's keeping you. He often dispenses discipline whether it's called for or not."

"But if this takes me eight hours, how will I have time for the stables?"

"Oh, you will. But you won't have a lot of time for sleeping. And don't get caught napping on the job. Rog especially loves to make an example of those who do."

With that, Drek left Eve with her first load of linens to begin her new life.

2 2

Tark

Tark was beside himself, and Lamn was losing his ever-loving mind. Skiff, unfortunately, had to mediate their broody or angry outbursts, calm them when they started arguments, and generally keep them fed and sane. They wanted nothing but to stare at the map as if it would magically give up Eve's location, and start fights when it didn't.

Their spy had reported seeing Eve by a small town near the Winter/Summer border in the Winter Court, but then she was lost again. It felt like time was slipping away from them. Every hour that passed felt like it could be her last, and the pressure to rescue her only got worse. That pressure was building on itself, and sooner or later, it would explode.

As much as they wanted to, they couldn't just storm in after her and take her by force with just the three of them and a Grigori. They would be easy targets, and the Winter Court would have no issues with just killing them where they found them. And then there was the little problem of not knowing just where she was.

Instead, Armoniel had offered to travel within the Winter Court realm to see if he could find her. It was outside of his jurisdiction, so he was completely unfamiliar with the geography, but that didn't stop him. It took him a day, but he reported back with her location, and the news that she was being moved. At least there was a starting point.

The fae sent Armoniel back, to see if he could track them or find their destination, while they plotted reasonable traveling distances, nearby towns, and other potential stopping points. Skiff could see that it was killing Lamn to sit and wait, he had always been a fea of action. While he had never been impulsive before, both Skiff and Tark had needed to hold him back several times from just going off and raiding the Winter Court half-cocked.

Tark looked up from the map, working it all out verbally. "So we know Vane reports to Lord Jeffers. But he's clearly decided to keep Eve for himself. But why? If he got caught stealing from his Lord, death would be a blessing. The nobles of the Court don't fuck around."

Skiff nodded. "Sounds like greed, my friend. He's wagering that he can make Lord Jeffers believe that he never acquired Eve, that she's still missing. He's playing a waiting game until he can use her for his own benefit." Skiff jumped back as an enraged Lamn launched at him for his choice of words, but Tark intercepted Lamn and got him back into his seat with a little coaxing.

Tark turned back to Skiff, "Still, that's a huge gamble. And she's pretty rare, even among hybrids. He'd have a hard time advertising ..." Tark looked down at Lamn and back, "... what he was offering... without bringing Lord Jeffers right on top of him."

Lamn bounced up out of his seat anxiously, dragging his fingers through his hair as he had been doing all afternoon. "That is all irrelevant. She has to be somewhere NOW. Do we have spies at Court? Can we see if Vane has her with him? I mean, it would be exceptionally foolish to bring her anywhere NEAR Court, but he's not the brightest fae."

"Already on it." Tark nodded. "I assume she's not with him, but we had to know for sure. I also have spies who know Jeffers. I'm waiting to hear back from both so that we can move on a plan."

Lamn groaned deeply and started pacing beside the wall.

Tark felt for him, his anxiety and guilt were eating him alive. Truth be told, Tark only held it together for the sake of the others, at night, in the privacy of his room, he broke down and cried with the fear of losing Eve, what it would do to Lamn, and him as well.

He knew the Winter Court, and he didn't want to imagine any of the unholy tortures she may be subjected to. Time was not on their side; if it took too long, then while they may still be able to find her alive... would she still be herself?

Tark's cell phone buzzed in his pocket, pulling him out of his thoughts, and he rushed to answer it so quickly he nearly dropped it. Putting the phone to his ear, he listened as his spies gave him the information he had been waiting for. He nodded his head, forgetting the caller couldn't see him, and finally ended the call with instructions to just keep watching and report any change in status. When he turned, Lamn and Skiff were on their feet anxiously waiting to hear.

"So apparently the female fae who took Richard made it back to Court. She had only seen us, and assumed that the Summer Court took Eve. On the upside, Vane will think he got away with it, and that no one is watching him. On the downside, it won't be long before spies in the Summer Court don't confirm the story. Luckily, my guy knows one of the Nobles on the Summer Court, and he has agreed to start spreading rumors about his 'new hybrid,' and that he's very jealous of her, due to her uniqueness. That will give the appearance of her being at the Summer Court, and the fact that no one is being allowed to see her.

"Eve is not with Vane, which we figured. He must have stashed her as he made his way back to Lord Jeffers. There are only two small settlements between where we last saw her and the Court itself, but I doubt he would bring her to either. Chances are much higher that he's stashed her at a brothel, here." Tark pointed to a remote pass in the mountains, deep in the forest, on his map.

"Here's what I'm thinking: what if we get to Vane before he gets to Court, tell him he's been made, and that Jeffers wants Eve? I have a fae from the Winter Court I can trust, but this is going to cost us, BIG time. He can act as Jeffer's representative, and have an armed guard, put the fear of the Old Gods into Vane. Then we can make sure they stop for the night somewhere that we can get to easily. It's still a risk, we'll have to fight to get her out, but it will look believable. We'll need Armoniel to create a portal for a quick exit, but we will have to walk in. We can't risk using a portal twice, it will draw too much attention. Plus, a Grigori portal will leave them wondering who really has her, and may throw off trying to recover her once we're back in the Summer Court."

Skiff nodded in agreement, but Lamn held his chin in his hand as he considered.

"Armoniel won't like this, he wanted Grigori involvement kept under wraps."

Tark rolled his eyes. "I know that, but I don't see a better way of getting her back. The longer we leave her there–"

"I know. I know." Lamn nodded. "I'm just making you aware. He will not like it."

Armoniel

Two weeks. He had been searching for two weeks, and nothing! Armoniel flew over the forest again. His invisibility ensured that he wouldn't be seen, but that was the least of his concerns. He had never disliked trees so much in all of his long existence. He couldn't see much through them, so finding trails was almost impossible. And tracking on the ground was too time consuming. He knew the fae had taken Eve in this direction, so they couldn't have gone too far. He flexed his fists in frustration as he circled to look again.

This time he soared to the other side of the mountain, farther away from his previous attempts. He saw a smaller road which wound around the base of the mountain, but there were no towns, no Inns, no signs of civilization. After another half hour of following the road he turned to make his way back, when something shining on the ground caught his eye. He wheeled around in a circle and descended to get a better look. As he flew into the foothills he saw a large building, previously hidden by the outcroppings of rocks at the base of the mountain. The light reflected to him again near the back, and he cautiously flew a circle around the perimeter of the building. Chances were the fae could not detect his presence, but it was best not to take any chances.

He saw a small outroom at the back of the imposing stone building. There were tubs of water reflecting the rays of the dying sun, that was what he had seen. And when Eve stepped out of the building he nearly fell out of the sky! He had found her!

He dove quickly, no longer caring if he could be detected, and landed a few feet from her. She looked up from the pile of linens in her hand, clearly stunned to see him. His heart broke. She seemed frail, afraid, with dark circles under her eyes. Her cheeks were sunken and her hair had been pulled up hastily into a messy bun, sticking out in all directions as it fell back out.

At seeing him her eyes grew large and wide with terror. She looked around in a panic to be sure no one else was watching as she whispered to him.

"Armoniel! What are you doing here? I'll get in trouble if they see you here!" Tears rolled down her cheeks, leaving pink streaks in the dirt that marked her face.

He wished he could grab her and fly away with her. He wished that he could pull out his sword and slaughter every last being in the building for keeping her. But Watchers were never supposed to interfere. He had broken that commandment once, and now he was paying the consequence.

"Oh My Eve, they cannot see me. I am visible only to you. But I shall not endanger you. I will let the others know where you are. They will be here soon."

Eve brought the linens up to her face to muffle a sob, as she ran to Armoniel and flung her arms around him. She buried her face in his chest and cried, releasing all of the pain and fear she had been holding. Armoniel rested his hand on her shoulder, and she felt peace descend on her.

"I must go now, but I will be back. I will come to tell you how to prepare yourself for leaving. Do not lose faith, little one. I will never abandon you."

"Don't go! Wait! Don't leave–" But he was already dissolving in Eve's arms.

23

Eve

She felt like she would never get out of there. At night she dreamed of Eddie's Diner, even of her room at Nancy's. She missed talking to people, even though she hadn't had friends she missed the social aspects of her life. She missed Betty's smile while she poured coffee, and she missed Becky complaining about her boyfriend. Most of all, she missed the freedom to live her life the way she wanted to.

How long had she been a prisoner here? Ten days? Fifteen? She hadn't thought to count. Had she considered herself tough, growing up without a mother, and with an alcoholic? She laughed at that now. She was now expected to get up before the sun was up and clean out all of the rooms, and she was disgusted at what some people considered 'entertainment.' Bodily waste was one thing, but on more than one occasion she had needed to find Drek to deal with the animals left behind, and their mess.

She didn't have a mealtime per se, any time she stopped to eat was time she wasn't finishing her duties, and she was disciplined. She often had to grab food out of the kitchen and stuff it into her mouth as she ran to do the next job, that's if there was food to be had. She went up and down the stairs a million times a day gathering, cleaning, restocking. And then she was in the washing area.

As she scrubbed the sheets by hand over the washboard the sun would beat down on her. There was no shade. Her hands were permanently pruned, and as soon as they dried they would crack and split from overwashing. She had to work really hard to keep from getting blood on the sheets: the House Manager, Rog, had already beaten her with a cane for that. Once washed, the sheets seemed to weigh a hundred pounds. She would have to ring them of excess water, and then hang them all on the many lines behind the washroom to dry. It never seemed to rain, so they were always ready the next morning. The washing and cleaning alone left her drained and exhausted, and the lack of food didn't help, but her day was far from over.

Once the wash was finished, and it seemed Rog was always right there when it was, she made her way to the stable. Several hours of shoveling horse shit, sweeping, and then washing and brushing the horses followed. At least the Stable Master seemed kind, there were a few days that he told her that only a few of the horses needed washing, and she could leave 'early.'

'Early' was rarely before midnight. She was lucky if she got four to five hours of sleep a night, which left her tired and forgetful the next day. Rog took great delight in snapping his cane out and whacking her on the shin, or the forearm, to "help her remember things." She was covered in bruises. The beatings she could endure, but hearing the screams of the other house tenants searing into her brain as she worked in the washroom or stables was almost more than she could take.

As Eve walked through the kitchen with her last load of linens she could hear two of the kitchen girls talking quietly, which was very unusual. She stopped just outside the door so she could hear them.

"I don't know either! But business is booming! We've even had guests come back several days in a row! I think they'd stay the night if the Lady would allow!"

"I could see if one or two came back so soon, but so many? Why? The girls hasn't changed none."

"See, that's what I don't know! Even the Lady seems surprised, though she ain't complaining. Oh! An' that's the other thing! They all want the west wing! Everybody's requesting rooms in the west wing! I swear, if we could clean'em out fast enough, we could see two or three guests per room, per night, instead o'just one! Some of the guests were really unhappy being told the wing was booked for the night, and maybe the following too!"

Eve saw movement out of the corner of her eye and hurried away from the door, in case Rog was around. She piled her linens with the other dirty laundry and pondered what she had heard. She cleaned the west wing, although the laundry from the east wing was brought for her to wash as well. Where she had thirty rooms, the east wing was the VIP area, largely parlors and only three entertainment rooms. She just never got into those rooms. Did this have something to do with her?

Eve realized she had forgotten a pile of sheets and headed back into the corridor to retrieve them. As she stepped back into the washing area a blur of light appeared ahead of her and was quickly replaced with the angel.

Armoniel. He had found her!

She realized quickly they could be seen by anyone, and her head whipped to both sides to make sure the coast was clear. Rog would draw blood if he saw her talking to anyone. She was still limping from his last beating, she didn't need to lose a toe.

"Armoniel! What are you doing here? I'll get in trouble if they see you here!" Tears rolled down her face that she couldn't stop. She was simultaneously so grateful to see him, and terrified that he was here and couldn't help her escape.

"Oh My Eve, they cannot see me. I am visible only to you. But I shall not endanger you. I will let the others know where you are. They will be here soon." There was a deep sorrow in his eyes, like he shared her pain. It looked like he wanted to say more, but couldn't.

Eve lost it. The fear of being forgotten, of living out her life in this hell, knowing it would only get worse... and then seeing her angel; the tsunami of emotion overtook her. She brought the sheets to her face to muffle the sound of the sob as it tore out of her chest. She was running to him before she was even aware of it, and throwing her arms around him like he was her father, and there to protect her.

She burrowed her face into his chest and let the tears flow freely.

For the first time since she had come to this place she felt a moment of safety. She was aware of his hand on her shoulder, and a feeling of peace came over her. She knew she would be okay.

"I must go now, but I will be back. I will come to tell you how to prepare yourself for leaving. Do not lose faith, little one. I will never abandon you."

He was leaving?!

She pulled her head up with terror.

He couldn't leave her!

"Don't go! Wait! Don't leave--" But he was already dissolving in her arms. She looked around her for some sign of him, but she knew he was gone. She wiped the tears from her face and got back to work before someone accused her of resting.

At least she had hope, but she wondered how long she could hold out for them.

24

Vane

Vane sat in his armchair by the window, enjoying the breeze. He sipped his coffee and considered his itinerary for the day. He had to make sure he was seen around court, but not *in* court, he was just hoping that Lord Jeffers would not summon him.

He had gotten word that Lord Fen's underling, Lara, had returned with a human, her mission to retrieve the hybrid, a failure. He also heard that she had told the Court that the Summer Fae had stolen the hybrid out from under them.

But talk flowed easily when stakes were high.

He didn't know if it was believed that the Summer Fae had his trophy, it could be a political ruse designed to drive him out of the grass. It wouldn't be the first time false intelligence had been circulated. Until he knew for sure that Lord Jeffers had given up on the hybrid he needed to act casual, business as usual. And he had to hope that Lord Jeffers didn't summon him to give his accounting of the details of his mission. His forced allegiance would make concealing his betrayal hard to hide, harder even if Jeffers tortured him, or compelled him. That would be his end.

His favorite slave appeared by his side with a plate of pastries, and he nodded at the table beside him. She was dainty, with dark brown curls pulled under a cap, and a uniform that showcased her spectacular breasts. Yes, she was a hybrid, they all were, but he could overlook that.

As she put the plate down he reached behind her and squeezed her ass cheek in his full hand. She started but didn't make a sound, to her credit. She turned to him, slightly, and smiled, but he could see she had to work at it. He had been too rough with her the day before. He was sure if he gave her another day or two she would be healed enough for a little more fun.

Not to worry, there are plenty of others.

A knock sounded from his study door, followed by the entrance of his personal butler in his formal suit, eyes straight ahead. He stood by the door until Vane acknowledged him, and then approached the chair with a parchment, eyes still straight ahead of him, obediently.

Vane took the parchment roll from him and noticed Lord Jeffers seal, he opened it immediately, as a sense of dread grounded his belly like an anchor.

"Lord Vane,

It has come to my attention that the matter which we discussed has not yet been completed, I find myself without what is rightfully mine. Worse, there is word among courtiers that fae who should be loyal to me, are, in fact, stealing from me. This causes me great concern, as my status as a noble has not been called into question in centuries.

I need not tell you how angry I would become if I found myself humiliated with betrayal in truth, and not merely in gossip. I daresay, there would be no end to the punishment I would be forced to execute to redeem my social standing among the nobility. Death would be a mercy to any who would dare take what is mine.

I am having my trusted advisor, Melrick, visit your office this after-noon at the two o'clock hour. You are to report to him, assist him in any way possible to close our previous business, and deliver to me what is mine. Should you fail in any part of this,… well, let us hope for your sake you do not.

Lord Jeffers"

Vane's hands were trembling as he dropped the parchment onto the table beside him. He could feel the blood draining from his face, and he was suddenly very dizzy. Getting a breath was becoming difficult like his ribs were squeezing the air out of his lungs. Realizing his butler was still standing by, he waved his hand in dismissal, before he did something foolish, and embarrassing, like fainting in front of him.

How did he find out?! Who betrayed his secret?!

His fear quickly morphed to anger. There was NO way he could have known! There were no witnesses except the Summer Fae, and Lord Jeffers wouldn't entertain them. Had Rodolfo broken under the pressure?

He always was such a weasly fae, no backbone.

Regardless, he had to meet this Melrick at two, so he needed to put affairs in order. He needed to calm down and compose himself.

"Sera!" He barked the name like an order.

The slave skittered into the room with wide eyes, a dark brown curl bouncing from her cap, and obediently came to stand at his side. He unbuckled his leather belt and slid it from the loops around his waist, weighing it in his palm. Whether she was ready or not, he had needs to be met right that moment.

Tark

"I told you he wouldn't like it." Lamn looked pointedly at Tark. Everyone was talking over one another, trying to come up with a solid extraction plan, and it was getting nowhere.

"ENOUGH!" Tark slammed his hand down on the table and stood. Oddly enough, everyone shut up.

Tark turned to Armoniel. "I'm sorry, can you explain to me again why you can't just portal us out of there?"

Armoniel sighed deeply, and repeated his story. "I am bound by certain restrictions. My purpose is to witness: I am forbidden from tampering."

Tark waved his arm, pointing to everyone in the room. "And THIS is not tampering? What you're doing here with us?" He was trying really hard not to lose his shit on the Grigori, partially because, of the two of them, the Grigori would win.

Armoniel supported his head in his hand. "I am unused to having so many conflicting experiences at once. My duty is to witness. But my duty is also to protect Eve. It may have been through the... breaking of an oath... that we find ourselves in this situation today. How do I know that my actions today will not create further problems we cannot foresee? Yet, how can I refuse to act? I am so unclear on what is right."

Tark clapped a hand on his shoulder, "Armoniel, Buddy, now is not the time for an existential meltdown."

Armoniel looked up at Tark, but before he could respond Lamn stood and addressed him. "Armoniel, you have jurisdiction over the Earth Plane, correct?"

"Yes." Stupid question.

"So, you have no jurisdiction in either of the Fae Courts?"

"No, of course I do not. Why–"

"So if I asked you to create a portal from one court to another court, you would not be breaking your oath within your jurisdiction, am I correct?" The corners of Lamn's lips crept up into a subtle smile as Armoniel blinked in shock.

Armoniel's eyes widened at the realization. He had spent his entire existence upholding the commandments and he had never seen the loophole, he had never even looked for it. He groaned loudly and dropped his head into his hands.

"Brother, it's ok. This is good right?" Tark patted him on the shoulder lightly to cheer him up.

"No. This is NOT good!" Armoniel's voice came out with some of the energy of force that his kind were known for, deep enough to shake the room like a mild earthquake. He picked his head up and looked at the fae, the tears in his eyes spoke of agony.

"I HAD her! I HAD her and I COULD have saved her! Right then and THERE!"

With that he pushed out of his chair and left the room. Tark moved to follow him, but Lamn held him back and shook his head gently. He deserved a moment to process.

A half an hour later Lamn stepped out onto the porch where Armoniel was still sitting, staring at the stars. He approached slowly, and when the Grigori made no acknowledgement he took the seat beside him.

Lamn looked at Armoniel. "I'm glad you didn't."

Armoniel swung his head to Lamn with fire blazing in his eyes.

"Because if you had taken her, they would have known the Grigori were involved. A representative would have gone to the Grigori Council to demand reparations, and then the Grigori would have looked to the Earth Plane and found Eve.

"If you took her, the Grigori would have killed her in the end. She has to be ported from one Court to the other, BOTH out of Grigori jurisdiction. This way she gets to live, even if we do feel the burden of guilt for it now. And for what it's worth: I'll still do whatever I can to keep your involvement in this secret."

Armoniel seemed to be contemplating this as he looked back to the stars. His next words seemed to come out of nowhere.

"I'm glad Ruth found you. You are an honorable fae. I had hoped she found love and happiness with you. I am happy to have found Eve,... And you."

He looked back at Lamn, and there were no more words that needed to be spoken between them. They understood each other.

25

Vane

At exactly two o'clock there was a knock at the door to Vane's office. He straightened his waistcoat, and checked his reflection in his desk mirror, before voicing permission to enter. He stood behind his desk, to appear more important. He would not be bullied or cowed in his own office.

He was a high-ranking Lord, after all.

Head held high, he met the eyes of Melrick, standing just outside his door... with four armed guards.

Who brings armed guards to a business meeting?! It's vulgar and rude!

Already, Vane did not like this Melrick. Although, truthfully, he had decided that he didn't like him before he even arrived.

Melrick moved into the room as if he owned it, head high, expression bored. He ignored Vane's narrowed eyes, his sneer, and his clenching fists at his sides. Melrick moved casually, noting the decor, and finally moved to sit in a comfortable chair opposite the desk without being asked. Vane's nostrils flared with insult, and his eyebrows were about to arch themselves right up and over his face.

"*Pleeeease*, have a seat." Vane bit out between clenched teeth, as he took his own chair. His mouth smiled pleasantly, but his eyes spoke rage.

"Vane, I'll get to the point. Jeffers knows you have his hybrid." He said it casually like he was talking about the weather.

Vane was aware of this, but to hear it so directly made him swallow, lest he choke on the sudden dryness in his throat. He tried to keep his chin up, his face impassive, but even he could tell that his anxiety was leaking into his features without his permission, which just made him more angry.

Melrick went on, "He simply wants the hybrid in his possession. You can tell him whatever you want, that you were hiding her from other poachers, that you were ensuring you got her to Court safely… I could give a rat's ass WHAT you tell him. Give him the hybrid, and all will be forgotten."

At this Vane paused, he had a moment of hope for his future.

"However, refuse to deliver…" Melrick didn't need to spell it out.

If he didn't bring Eve to Jeffers, his life, as he knew it, was over. Everything he'd worked for would be stripped from him: his title, his land, his slaves. He would be common, a prisoner. Worthless… no better than a slave really. Shudders wracked his shoulders as a chill moved down his spine.

Melrick stood up suddenly, looking expectantly at Vane. Vane could only stare at him blankly; he had absolutely no idea what it was Melrick was expecting. He didn't have the hybrid WITH him. Gods, that would be foolish indeed, with her pervasive scent.

Melrick spelled it out for him.

"Let us be off then, to retrieve the hybrid." He looked at Vane expectantly, as Vane started to stutter and mumble, clearly ready to give excuses as to why they could not leave immediately. The look in Melrick's eyes left no room for argument, even Vane could see that. Conceding defeat, Vane stood up with his shoulders slumped and allowed himself to be marched out to retrieve the prize he had so hoped to keep.

Eve

The brothel household was in turmoil. Eve kept herself in the background, in hidden hallways and dark corners, but even she could see the upheaval. At first, clients were rushing back, eager for more services, but now it was not enough for them. They were like drug addicts who had developed a tolerance and suddenly needed more to get their high. First, there was disagreement, then anger, and within days violence had broken out as some clients claimed that others were getting something 'better' than they were. Money was no object, and blood was spilled.

No one could put their finger on what that 'something better' was, but everyone seemed convinced that there was some new slave, some ultra-seductress, dispensing immeasurable pleasures, and they wanted in. They DEMANDED in. The problem was, there WAS no new slave. The entertainment slaves had not changed in months. The only new slave was...

Eve froze.

It couldn't be *her*, could it? She didn't entertain. They never even SAW her.

She remembered the stranger on the outskirts of the small town that first day, he had said she smelled delicious. And Rodolfo said he could smell her from the living area. What if the fae have heightened smell, and they were catching her scent from when she cleaned the rooms?! It seemed unlikely to her, but what other explanation was there? She was the only differentiating factor.

OH GOD! She had to keep them from figuring it out! If they thought it was her, they might start leasing her to clients! This wasn't just prostitution, these clients 'owned' bodies for the evening, and could do whatever they wanted, as her fae side would heal her quickly. Short of death, there was no limitation on what they could do to the entertainers. The tortured screams heard from the rooms made clear that these clients took full advantage.

She carried on her duties of washing and hanging, trying to act normal, as she formulated a plan.

Early the next morning Eve headed down to begin her day, earlier than usual, as she hadn't been able to sleep all night for fear. She crept through the dark kitchen, and seeing no one around, she made her way to the servant's entrance to the east wing, instead of the west. She cautiously made her way up the stairs and down the halls, certain that at any moment someone would jump out and catch her. Luck was with her, as the wing seemed to be empty, after the previous night's frivolities. She silently cracked open the first door, and seeing no one in the room, she walked in, shutting the door behind her.

Now what? Was it enough to BE in the room? What should she do? How does one get their scent in a room?

She thought of peeing on the carpet but decided against it. Not having any better ideas, she just winged it, rubbing the curtain fabric on her neck and her armpits, rolling on her back on the carpet or sofas... She couldn't do much to the bed linens, she would be washing those later.

THE BED LINENS!

A wicked idea occurred to her. She would take the clean linens, and sleep on them herself to get her sweat into them, and then remake the beds throughout. That way her scent would be in every room, and not just the west wing. It would be harder to point right at her... although it all began after she arrived, there was nothing she could do about that. It was gross: but it was worth a shot.

For good measure, though, she still rubbed herself in the fine draperies in the east wing before leaving.

26

Tark

Everything was ready. They had gone over the plan again and again. It wasn't a sure thing, but their odds were pretty good. They would have to make it work.

Tark picked up Eve's bag with a heavy heart, dropped it on the table, and promptly heard a loud cracking noise. Terrified he'd broken something of hers, he gently unzipped the bag and saw the picture frame tucked into a side, its glass now cracked down the middle. He groaned as he picked the frame out of the bag like it was a delicate child, it had meant something to Eve and he had carelessly broken it. He looked at the picture of the woman, she looked like Eve, but with beautiful strawberry blond hair. She had the same smile Eve had. His heart squeezed in his chest again.

Lamn's face appeared over his shoulder, "What are–", he froze, eyes glued to the picture.

"Ruth…"

It was whispered so softly that Tark could have missed it.

Tark could feel the waves of sorrow rolling out of Lamn, and he handed him the picture.

"I didn't mean to break it, I didn't know it was in there," was all he could say.

Lamn never took his eyes off of the photo as he brought his hand up to gently trace the outline of Ruth's face. His eyes reflected adoration, grief, longing.

The moment was shattered as Skiff marched through the door, all business, gathering up supplies and loading the vehicle. Tark and Lamn's eyes met in a shared moment, and then Lamn handed the frame back to Tark so he could replace it into Eve's bag. Tark could see it took everything in Lamn to give up the photo, and as soon as he had, he turned and buried himself in the preparations. Checking their watches, they headed out to the vehicle. They had someone from the Summer Court ready to bring Eve's belongings straight there, and her bag was handed off.

The three fae piled into their vehicle, Armoniel would meet them at the portal to the Winter Court. Sure, they could have Armoniel port them in, but then his involvement would be obvious if questioned by the Grigori. They wanted to use his abilities as little as possible, and preferably between the Courts, where he had plausible deniability. They were saving him for their exit.

As they knew that portals left a residue, their intrusion would be noted. To avoid conflict, which would slow them down, once inside the Winter Court Armoniel would port them close to the extraction point, where they would wait for Vane to bring Eve through on his way back to Lord Jeffers. They would grab her, fight their way out, run for the woods, and Armoniel would port them all to the Summer Court. No sweat. Tark knew they had done similar extractions hundreds of times, and they had their inside guy with Vane to keep the situation under control.

So why did his gut keep churning?

The wheels of the vehicle spewed rocks and debris as it climbed through the forest of the mountain pass. The portal was close.

Hang on, Eve! We're on our way! He prayed she somehow heard him.

Eve

Morning had just dawned, and the kitchen was full of activity as she passed. Eve made herself as invisible as she could as she went through the motions of the rest of her day, but she listened intently. It was a big house, with lots of staff, and no matter how much they threatened staff to be silent, there was always gossip whispered. She heard the best gossip when she stopped to listen on her way in from the stables late at night, outside the staff bunk rooms. Apparently, they didn't have the *luxury* of a private room like hers, and they were eager to chat amongst themselves, unsupervised.

She knew the situation was getting worse. One slave had been killed by a client, and another was severely maimed, as clients took out their rage for the perceived slight against them. It really was like they were on drugs. Of course, the staff was informed of none of this, but they all knew, regardless. Some clients had to be banned from the establishment, and Lady Silver had brought in extra security for the front entrance and front parlors, where guests socialized and waited.

With higher tension among clients, came higher tension among staff. Some slaves had rebelled, refusing to service clients. Others had tried to escape. Others had been unwilling to participate in whatever 'fun' their client had planned. Clients were suddenly outright hostile with slaves, as they couldn't get their 'fix' of whatever it was they needed, and the slaves were too afraid for their own lives to simply weather it. Discipline seemed the better option.

As a result, Rog was nowhere to be found lately, constantly chasing after one slave or another, or trying to keep the household running smoothly, despite staffing issues. Fear and rage ruled the day. Eve moved silently through her duties, attracting no attention.

It was mid-morning, not yet lunchtime in the kitchen, and Eve was diligently trying to remove stains from some sheets, when she heard panicked screaming and loud crashing noises from the house. In any other circumstance, she would have run inside to see what was happening, but not here. She would gladly wait from a safe distance for it to blow over.

But it didn't blow over. The shouting continued, sometimes punctuated by screaming. She heard glass shattering and more crashing, like large furniture hitting a wall or floor. Still, she stayed put.

Then, there was only screaming, never ending wails of terror. It was only when she smelled burning wood and saw and heard the roar of the flames licking out of the windows of both floors around the side of the building that she decided to move.

There were no windows on this side of the building, there was no one around. This was her chance!

With one last look to be sure she wasn't seen, she hiked up her dress and ran as fast as she could for the tree line ahead of her. The smell of smoke followed her, making it hard to breathe, but she kept running, knowing her life DID depend on it. She tried not to look over her shoulder, focused instead on where she was running, but for so long she had been conditioned to check, to make sure she was safe, it was hard to fight the urge. Lack of food and sleep made her weak, and she knew she was not running as fast as she needed to. Even as she ran, her breaths heaving and her legs pumping, she was sure there must be someone right behind her.

Any minute now they will reach out and grab me, pull me back, and then... then they will hurt me. Maybe cut off a foot so I can't run? Maybe cut out my tongue? Maybe slice my skin in thousands of places, knowing it will heal tomorrow and they can do it all again? These were the punishments she heard others got.

The terror of getting caught fueled her panicked sprint for freedom. She ran and ran and ran...time didn't exist for her. Her pace got slower and sloppier as she ran out of energy and air. Her foot snagged on a root, sending her tumbling headfirst into a ravine, gasping for air. She felt like she needed to throw up.

She tried to urge her body to get up quickly, to resume her flight, but it was no use; too many missed meals and too little sleep left her weak and uncoordinated. When she couldn't stand, she crawled, hand over hand, willing herself to just keep moving.

The sky was getting dark before she finally allowed herself to collapse on the forest floor. She had heard no sound of pursuit but was unwilling to believe it wasn't coming for her. She looked around for a place to rest, somewhere to hide. The best she could do was a hollowed-out tree trunk; it was tight, and it stank of wet wood and rot, but she wedged her sore body inside and piled leaves and pine needles around her to hide her. Exhaustion dragged her into unconsciousness soon after.

Melrick

Melrick smiled from the back of his horse. Behind him, Vane was pouting like a spoiled child: lower lip extended from a dramatic frown, eyes furrowed, arms crossed over his chest. It made Melrick want to laugh out loud, and he had all he could do to hide the chuckle that escaped. He peeked over his shoulder to see Vane shooting him a murderous glare. Melrick didn't care, he had dealt with pompous brats like Vane before. They were all bluster and no battle, and could only be strong when beating someone weaker than them. He would be easy to dispatch, should it become necessary, but he really hoped it wouldn't. He would rather enjoy seeing how creative Lord Jeffers could be with his punishment, especially after Melrick himself let Lord Jeffers know the extent that Vane had gone to, to steal from him and lie about it.

Melrick had been paid handsomely to perform this duty. He would never tell the fae of the Summer Court this, but he might have been willing to do it for free, just to see Vane finally get what he deserved. Yes, court life was cutthroat, but Vane was beyond ruthless, and cruel in a way that was un-fae. He took a little bit too much pleasure in the suffering of others, without ever experiencing even the slightest hardship himself. He was weak, and so he preyed on the weakest. There was not an ounce of compassion or empathy in him, he was a monster. It had been an easy decision to betray him to the Summer Court.

"WHAT–"

Melrick turned to see Vane upright in his saddle, staring openmouthed. He followed his line of vision to a burnt-out husk of a large stone building, smoke still filtering off of the charred remnants.

This had better not be where he stowed her.

Melrick kicked his horse into a gallop, and all of the horses behind him followed suit. Within fifteen minutes, they were entering the courtyard of the destroyed building. He dismounted his still-moving horse and moved to the front of the house to see if there was anyone still left alive. The door was charred through and wouldn't budge. He turned to Vane.

"You left her HERE?"

That seemed to break Vane out of his shock. He started wailing like a girl, tears running down his face, and still in the saddle, Melrick saw a stream of water flowing down the saddle from blooming wetness in Vane's pants. Melrick cursed and ordered his men to take Vane into custody, he couldn't chance him trying to make a run for it, as cowards were prone to do.

Melrick ordered his men to search the remains, but he already knew she was gone. Either she fled, was taken, or was dead. He'd have nothing to offer the Summer Fae... unless he gave them Vane... but who'd want *him*?! Still, he'd ruined Vane's life, one way or another, so ...*Success!*

27

Eve

Eve yawned and tried to stretch, but found she was held completely immobile. Her eyes snapped open, fighting the afternoon sunlight to focus. She soon realized she was stuck in a tree trunk. She didn't remember getting into a tree trunk, and wondered how she had come to be there. Spitting and swatting away the leaves that covered her, she slowly pressed her body out of the snug wood. She was healing faster than she ever would have back home, and yet every part of her ached, her back, her limbs, her lungs...

Awareness caught up with her, and she quickly scanned the area to see if anyone was nearby. She still couldn't shake the fear that at any moment Rog or Lady Silver would pop out from behind a tree, laughing arrogantly, and drag her back. But she didn't see or hear anything, other than birds.

What now?

She had no idea where she was or where to go. There was no one she could trust. She couldn't remember which direction she had come from, and she didn't want to wander back to the brothel by accident.

But at least she was no longer a slave.

She sat down and recounted everything she knew: she had run up the hillside, away from the brothel. At some point, going uphill was too tedious, and she shot sideways, across the hill. Then, she had fallen in the ravine, part way back down the hill. So, as long as she didn't go further down the hill, she wouldn't run into the brothel. She looked around for signs of which direction she had come from, and finally found a few broken branches, which she assumed she had caused. She turned in the opposite direction and started walking.

Melrick

Melrick sat on a large rock at the back of the building. The plan had gone to hell. He had no way of contacting the Summer Fae, other than meeting them at the rendezvous point. He got up and prepared to gather his men for the return trip when a flash of light stopped him mid-step and a Grigori stood before him. The Watcher addressed him immediately.

"You are Melrick, of the Winter Fae?" His presence loomed large, making the shell of the stone building appear more modest.

"Depends who is asking, Grigori." Melrick knew to be cautious. He had never seen a Grigori in the Fae Plane before, but they were powerful and moody, and not to be messed with.

"I believe we have associates in common, Fae. We are all working to recover the same prize, am I not correct?" Armoniel cast him a knowing look.

So the Grigori were working with the Summer Fae now? Interesting indeed.

"It would appear we are, Watcher. As to what happened here, that, I cannot tell you. We arrived a few hours ago and found it thus. We have searched as much as we dare, but there is no way of knowing if any of those poor souls who perished are our prize."

Armoniel turned to the building, closed his eyes, and raised his arms to shoulder height. The soft glow around him intensified into a much brighter ball of light, which slowly grew larger and larger. He stood like that for several seconds before dropping his arms and dimming the light. Turning, he faced Melrick.

"No. She was not here. She lives, I can feel her life force. I will track her. Keep your meeting with the others, I will bring her there."

Melrick nodded in understanding, as Armoniel dissolved into the air.

A few minutes later, Melrick had his men loaded up and ready to go. Vane was still crying, tied to his horse. There was also an additional cart at the back being pulled along behind them, containing Melrick's backup plan.

Eve

Eve walked for hours. She had found a stream for water and a few berry bushes, but nothing more substantial. She was tired and dizzy but kept her feet moving. It was probably her malnourished state that had her walk right into the snare trap without seeing it. By the time she heard the whoosh and zzzzip, she was already suspended by one foot, upside down above the forest floor. She groaned and tried furiously to fold herself in half to reach the rope at her feet, but her body had given up anything strenuous long before then.

She really just wanted to cry at that point. If this was Lady Silver's doing, she was a goner. She tried to muffle her cries as all hope of escape leaked out of her.

"Well, well, well... what do we have HERE?" Eve swung her head to the sound of the voice to see a very happy-looking Lara, smiling up at her.

Fucking great. Not you again.

"And here I had hoped for a tasty critter for dinner. Instead, I get the grand prize!" Her eyes glinted cruelly, as she stood back, enjoying Eve's discomfort.

"Has anyone ever told you that you talk too much? If not, let me be the first." Eve bit out. Her head was really starting to hurt with all of the blood flowing to it.

Lara's response was immediate, the butt of her knife to the back of Eve's head.

"I've already warned you about how to address your superiors, *half-breed*." All playfulness was gone from her eyes.

Eve held the back of her throbbing head, and suddenly she was falling and then colliding with the ground painfully. She just lay motionless for a moment, trying to get air in her lungs, when Lara let out a loud whistle. As Eve was finally standing, she could hear others approaching them through the trees. She turned and groaned out loud as she saw a very tired and rough-looking Richard, leading a group of three slaves from the brothel, bound and tied in a row.

"Ah yes," Lara crowed, "You two are acquainted!" She flashed her wicked smile.

Tark

Tark, Lamn, and Skiff were all waiting inside the small stable Melrick had indicated for them. There was a larger house nearby, where Melrick would stop his group and meet with them behind the stable for the exchange. The appointed time was growing close, and all three fae were getting antsy. They had expected Armoniel to return with a status by now, they had sent him to warn Eve, and hadn't seen him since. Tark's stomach churned with anxiety.

Skiff tapped Lamn and Tark silently to indicate movement, and the three of them watched as Armoniel appeared outside the stable and made his way to them. There was a collective breath of relief until Armoniel opened his mouth.

"There's been a complication."

Tark could feel the blood draining from his face, he turned to Lamn to see he looked no better.

"Somehow, the brothel burnt down before the envoy got there. Don't worry, Eve is fine... or at least she's still alive. I wanted to update you before I go and search for her. The envoy will still meet you here as planned. I will port Eve here to you."

The three fae looked between themselves, no one liked it, but what choice did they have at that point?

"Go." Lamn ordered, and the Watcher disappeared from sight.

Eve

Lara shoved Eve toward the other slaves.

"This will be too easy. *Eve Sherman, you will come with us willingly and offer no resistance.*" She smiled smugly at Eve.

Compulsion!

Eve wasn't sure what it felt like to really be under a compulsion, so she acted angry, making a show of glaring at Lara, as she dragged her feet toward the slaves and Richard.

"Can you make her have sex with me?" Richard asked hopefully.

"Silence, pet! We both know you can't get it up anyway, so don't waste any more of my time with ridiculous requests. Perhaps I shall make YOU pleasure all of us instead, and get nothing in return, it's only fair, considering your dismal performances. Thank the Old Gods our survival does not depend upon your cock."

Lara practically pushed him out of the way as she headed back into the forest. Richard hung his head dejectedly and followed after her, pulling the rope of slaves with him. Eve walked behind them... for now.

It was late afternoon before Lara ended their woodland hike in a clearing. She ordered Richard to tie the slaves to a tree, and then to make camp for her for the night while she hunted. She looked at Eve pointedly. "I won't be far away. But run if you can, I'd love a good hunt." Eve knew that, in her condition, she'd never make it far, and she'd never stand a chance against Lara when caught. Instead, she sat down with her back against a tree and rested.

Richard was a good little pet and got Lara's tent up, gathered rocks and sticks for a fire, and got everything ready for Lara's return. When he walked closer to Eve, looking for more kindling, she broke the silence.

"So, Richard, Fae life turning out like you'd hoped?" She meant it to be a cruel barb, but it still came out a little flat.

He stopped and turned to her with all the dignity he could muster, "Clearly not what I signed up for, but you know what, I'm making the most of it. I may not be a Lord, but I'm still very important. Lara *needs* me. She *appreciates* everything I do for her!"

At this, the slaves started to giggle.

"Richard, you do realize you are a *slave*... right?!" Eve was stupefied. Before anything else could be said, Lara appeared with some rabbits to be cooked. Eve turned a little green at seeing their small, dead, furry bodies, but her traitorous stomach growled all the same.

Richard ran right over like a lap dog to do as much for her as he could, and anytime she praised him he would shoot a smug grin at Eve.

God help him, he really thinks he's winning here, doesn't he? Eve shook her head. *He always did live in his own little world, and in it, he was always 'the best.'*

While Richard put together a meal, Eve took in their surroundings. It's not like there was anything helpful, any place markers or landmarks she could use, but she couldn't just sit by helplessly. The sun had set, and it was getting darker by the minute. The fire crackled warmly in the center of the clearing, where Lara's good little sycophant happily sauteed vegetables with her rabbit.

Eve caught movement out of the corner of her eye and slowly rolled her head that way nonchalantly, so as not to alert the others. She smelled him before she saw him: Armoniel! She hadn't even been aware that he had a smell before, somewhere between ozone and the salty air of the beach, but as soon as it hit her nostrils, she saw him in her mind's eye. Then, the telltale tip of his wing behind a tree. She slowly turned her head back toward the fire to see if anyone else had noticed, but luckily, the fire smoke was upwind of everyone else but her and Richard. A small smile played on her lips.

Seconds later, Lara exited her tent to fetch her meal, and Armoniel was bringing his sword down where she stood. She jumped back, pulled out her own sword, and met his next swing with her own. Richard scrambled away from the fighting and hid in the tent. Eve was on her feet. The sound of grunting and swords ringing and clashing filled the forest. Blow for blow, they danced around the clearing. Lara could defend, but couldn't seem to land any blows on Armoniel. He had managed to get quite a few shots in on Lara, and she was bleeding from several different cuts and favoring one leg.

Eve saw the moment that Lara realized that she was no match for the Watcher. Fear flashed over her eyes before she steeled herself, ducked, and rolled....

Right toward Eve.

Armoniel stopped short as Lara popped back up behind Eve, while

Eve tried to escape to her left. Lara had her right arm before she could move away. Eve met Armoniel's haunted eyes, horrified with his own helplessness, and then she looked to Lara, who was wearing her smug smile again like she knew she had won. Lara lifted her sword, and Armoniel lifted his as if to stop her, but then Lara placed the grip of the sword into Eve's right hand and spoke so Armoniel could hear her.

"Eve Sherman, you will kill the watcher!"

The air grew dense with the compulsion, the compulsion that would not affect Eve in the slightest. For a moment, Eve just stood there dumbfounded staring at Armoniel.

She CAN'T be that fucking stupid, can she? Yup. Apparently, she is. She and Richard make a great pair.

Lara gave Eve a little shove toward Armoniel, whose brows were raised in confusion. Eve knew he wouldn't hurt her, and she quickly formulated a plan. She faced Armoniel head-on so that Lara was behind her.

"I will kill you, Watcher!" She shouted vehemently, but she was smiling and winked at Armoniel. The slaves gasped, but Eve was counting on them not to rat her out. She raised her sword clumsily *(These things are HEAVY)*, and swung it far aside of Armoniel. He didn't even need to parry the attack. When he didn't move to engage, she winked at him again, twice this time. Finally, understanding lit behind his eyes. He smiled but quickly schooled his features to look tortured and anguished.

The next time she swung the sword, still very far from his body, he made it look as if he were taking it seriously and attempting to protect himself. Step-swing-crash. Step-swing-crash. They continued their dance of murder around the circle. She kept swinging to his right, so he kept adjusting to his left until finally, he was within striking distance of Lara, who was looking on with ghoulish glee.

"This ends NOW!" Eve shouted, largely because she was exhausted and didn't know how much longer she could keep lifting the heavy-ass steel sword and throwing it around. She made one last show of hoisting it over her head and aiming in Armoniel's direction, as he prepared his defense, bringing his sword up to block the downward blow, and then he turned suddenly on his heel and ran his blade straight through Lara's chest.

Surprised.

The bitch had the nerve to look surprised...

Right before she fell over and died.

2 8

Melrick

It was much later than the pre-arranged meeting time when Melrick finally saw the house ahead. He was grumpy, his ass was sore from riding, and fucking Vane would not be quiet. They had finally had to knock him out to shut him up. For a full-grown fae, he acted like a child when he didn't get what he wanted. Melrick hadn't broken the news that the hybrid still lived, and he was very much looking forward to seeing Vane break down all over again after losing her a second time.

He shouted loudly to his men in the back, "We're upon it now. Henk, you take the horses to the stable. Fren, you take Lord Pissy Pants into the stable as well. Make sure he is bound tightly." Fren groaned loudly. It was his signal to the Summer Fae that they had arrived, so they could vacate the stable.

At the house, they all dismounted. The horses were taken, and Lord Pissy Pants was dragged on the ground into the stable by his wrists. Once the horses were secured, Vane with them, he had all of his men turned in for the night to bathe and rest, with the exception of one to stand guard at the only door. Melrick excused himself to search the perimeter and told his men to stay put.

Once he was sure he was alone, Melrick walked to the back of the stables to meet the Summer Fae. Tark held out his forearm in welcome, and Melrick grasped it with his own near the elbow in return.

"We heard about the fire. Any news?" Tark opened.

Melrick sighed. "None. It was gone before we arrived. I had wondered if Vane had sent word to move her and destroy the evidence, but he's honestly not that clever, and his breakdown over the thought of having lost her seemed genuine."

"How can you be sure?

"There are very few Lords who would soil themselves to appear convincing," Melrick smirked. The other fae curled their lips in disgust.

A flash of light in the tree line alerted them to a portal opening, and they all ducked for cover. Armoniel's glow preceded him, Eve, at his side. Armoniel had someone slumped over his shoulder, and there were three females behind them as they all made their way to the stable.

Eve

Tark and the others stood, casting curious glances at Armoniel, who unceremoniously dumped an unconscious Richard on the ground in front of Tark.

"He would not come willingly," was his only comment.

Lamn rushed forward and grabbed Eve in a bear hug, squeezing her until she had to tap his shoulder to breathe. She looked stunned, confused, and clearly underfed, but otherwise unscathed. Tark was next to grab her into a hug. The shock had worn off, and a part of her said she shouldn't get so close to someone she didn't know, but it felt right to just hug him back and be glad.

Skiff just waived from where he stood. "It's good to see you again."

Armoniel filled them in on their little adventure and the death of Lara. He also explained that the slaves requested asylum in the Summer Court. As refugees, they would be subject to death, if they stayed and were caught. Richard was just a moron who couldn't be left alone in the Winter Court because he would get himself killed, and then, Eve would feel guilty.

Armoniel looked at Eve pointedly. "Let it be known, I voted that he be left here." Eve met his look and didn't back down.

Tark blew out a breath. His little party had just gotten a lot bigger.

Tark turned to Melrick. "How will you explain this to Jeffers?"

Melrick smiled broadly. "I will tell him that the building burnt and Vane planned to hide her elsewhere. I have two badly burnt bodies to bring back, one male, and one female, both unrecognizable. I will say we found them in her room, which we had to climb up to once the stairway had burnt away, leaving them no escape."

Tark looked confused. "But you cannot lie."

Melrick laughed. "How am I lying? The building burnt. Vane was planning on hiding her elsewhere, eventually. I did find those two bodies in what had been her room. I never said they were Vane and the hybrid."

At that, Tark smiled, and then a thought occurred to him.

"If you have two bodies, what will you do with Vane?"

"Ahhh, there is much I would do with Vane,… but he is rather inconvenient, isn't he? I could just give them the female's body, but I fear he would be compelled by Jeffers to tell the truth of the situation. It would be better if he were just to … say… disappear. Would you have any need of a new slave in the Summer Court?" Mirth glowed in his eyes as the corner of his mouth tipped up in the smallest of smirks.

Tark really did not want to take Vane with them, however, Melrick had gone above and beyond to help him get Eve back, and he would not appear ungrateful. Vane would only make trouble for Melrick.

With business settled, they all shook hands with Melrick in farewell. Tark carried Vane, while Skiff carried Richard. Lamn escorted Eve on his arm, and the slaves brought up the rear as Armoniel led the weary group of travelers into the tree line and opened the portal.

Eve's eyes met Tark's as they got ready to step through. He nodded to her encouragingly, and she smiled and nodded back.

She could almost hear him saying, "Welcome to your new life."

29

Eve

The group made their way through the portal, and again, Eve was subjected to being turned inside out on a psychedelic trip, before being spat on a lawn. It hadn't gotten any easier. Lamn caught her and righted her, and she was starting to feel a little annoyed that he was being so touchy-feely. Her time in the brothel had made her wary of fae. Tark, she somewhat knew, but this guy? She hardly knew him at all, and he couldn't seem to keep his hands off of her.

She gently pulled herself away from him, thanking him for his help, and stood on her own. He seemed reluctant to let her go, sad even, but respected her wishes, thankfully.

Armoniel turned to Tark. "This is where I must leave you for now. I still have my obligations to fulfill."

Then, he turned to Lamn. "I will visit. I will make everything clear in the end. I thank you for your help. Please do not forget my other request."

Addressing everyone, he said simply, "Farewell, for now." He gave one lingering glance to Eve, and she rushed to hug him before he disappeared. Tark noticed that the Grigori's face flushed pink before he could disintegrate into the air, and he chuckled to himself.

It was only a short walk until the group came upon the carriages that had been sent for them. Eve was thrilled, and squealed with glee, much to the fae's amusement. They rode for a few hours before coming to a large city. Eve perked up and noticed the smaller farms and homes at the outskirts, morphing into closer homes and shops, morphing into larger buildings of businesses side by side. Dirt paths became crushed stone, became paved packed stone or cobblestone. The further in you went, the denser it all became, just like back on Earth, only pre-technology.

Eve turned to Tark, he had been silent the entire ride.

"Where are we going now?" It had never occurred to her that she would have to go *somewhere* within the Summer Court, she wasn't just going to live out in the wild.

It's not like they had time to plan that far.

Tark looked a little sheepish and seemed to slip back into his 'business mode,' as she had first met him in the diner. "You'll stay at Lamn's estate until we can get an audience with the Court, and get you set up with your own citizenship; then you can move around freely." He stared straight ahead as he delivered it all matter-of-factly. She noticed he referenced her, only.

"And where will you be staying?" She asked quietly, sad at the thought of being separated when they had just been reunited. Next to Armoniel, she trusted Tark the most. She realized she had been looking forward to getting to know him better.

He seemed surprised by the question but quickly schooled his features back into 'business mode' before answering. "Well... uh... I have my own estate here." He seemed flustered, quickly adding, "But I'll probably be sent out on another mission soon. I travel a lot."

Eve wondered if that was somehow too personal a question to have asked. He had seemed so warm and friendly when they had talked on Earth; now that she was finally here, it was like he wanted to distance himself from her. His body language was aloof, he didn't look at her, didn't speak until questioned, and kept his physical distance. But she could feel sadness in him that he wasn't expressing. Did her presence make him sad? She just couldn't know and wasn't about to ask.

"Here we are!" Lamn lit up as he turned to the group, and extended his arm to the large gated mansion. His estate seemed to take up a whole city block itself. He smiled at Eve, and she suddenly didn't want to be staying with Lamn, even if the others were there.

She turned hastily to Tark as he started to climb out of the carriage. "Will you stay too?" Her eyes were pleading.

Tark was clearly taken by surprise, and when he looked at Lamn for direction, she could see that Lamn wasn't happy about potentially having Tark there as well. This interchange sealed it for Eve, she didn't want to be left alone with Lamn without knowing his motives.

She hurriedly added, "Please Tark, I know I don't know you well, but I know you more than anyone else here. After the... last place I stayed, I just want to feel safe for a little while."

She could feel her cheeks flushing. She hated making herself vulnerable, for all she knew, Tark might have ulterior motives too. And he had already made it clear he wanted to get away from her. This might just push him for good. Maybe he had planned to dump her with Lamn?

Still, what options did she have? She didn't want to go from being a slave at the Winter Court to being a slave in the Summer Court, and it was Tark who promised to return her if she didn't like it.

Tark was about to say something, the look in his eyes apologetic, when Lamn cut him off, "Of course, he can stay if he wants to. We want you to feel safe here, Eve." He shot Tark a pointed look, and Tark's eyes conceded.

"Of course we do." He said quietly, giving her a small smile that argued with the sadness in his eyes. A part of her felt guilt for manipulating the situation, but the practical side of her felt relieved.

Footmen met them at the bottom of the marble stairs, next to the large circular drive, surrounding a bubbling fountain. The air was heavy with the scent of the flowers in dramatic colors springing from the artful gardens, sprinkled around the fountain and stairs, and the sound of the water burbling made Eve think the water was giggling softly. With the imposing white marble columns and huge double doors at the top, it was an overload to her senses, which were already heightened. She extended her shaking hand to the hand ready to help her down.

Bags were taken in, and the group proceeded through the doors and into a massive front hall with high ceilings. To say it was opulent was an understatement. Eve had never seen a mansion before, but this is how she might have imagined a royal castle. Marble floors, heavily carved woods, huge painted portraits, plush area rugs, fine furniture, crystal chandeliers... it went on and on. It was the details, she decided: the crown molding, the carved railings, and the furniture.... Everything was meant to be a work of art, beyond its practical use. She felt like a tourist with her head craned back to take it all in as the others moved ahead of her. She heard Tark chuckle beside her, and turned to him quickly, while she had the chance.

"Look, I'm sorry. I didn't mean to force you to stay here with me. I... I just don't..(*trust*)... know Lamn that well, and..." She stared at her hands as she fidgeted, deeply uncomfortable with her admission.

Tark took her chin with two fingers and gently lifted it until she was looking him in the eye. There was a warmth and humor there, the Tark she had come to know in her bedroom, and cleaning the diner. Her Tark.

Her Tark?!

"It's okay. You didn't force me to do anything. We DO want you to be comfortable, Eve. I need for you to be able to tell us when you're not. Okay?"

Eve had to fight back the tears that wanted to spring to her eyes, as gratitude filled her heart to overflowing. She wanted to throw her arms around him and hug him but thought better of it, and just stood smiling at him, feeling awkward. Just a few minutes ago he was distant, she didn't want to read anything into this.

Tark broke the silence. "Let me show you to your room?" He swept his arm toward a curving marble staircase on the right, which half-circled the room and led to a balcony high overhead. Eve just nodded and headed for the staircase, their moment now passed.

Eve spent the next several hours exploring her suite. It was not a 'room' as she had been led to believe. First, there was a sitting room or small parlor, it was beautifully appointed with tasteful couches and chairs beside a huge fireplace hearth in pink marble, and most of the walls were built-in bookcases giving it a library feel.

The exterior wall was all grand windows, and a double glass-door exit, onto a marble patio, overlooking gardens and a pool.

Off of the sitting room was her bedroom, which was bigger than all of Nancy's ranch-style home. A huge king-sized four-poster bed made of intricately carved mahogany took up one wall. The linens were all in blush pinks and golds; and they looked so expensive that she was afraid to touch them, for fear of ruining them. Another set of double glass doors led out to another patio. There was a wardrobe with shelving, a dressing table, and comfortable chairs: and there was still enough room to hold a small rave.

Off of the bedroom was a bathroom, equally ridiculously large, in pink marble, with a walk-in soaker tub that could probably fit six comfortably, a multi-jet shower, and a private toilet area.

Also off of the bedroom was a room, bigger than her old bedroom, which was apparently the closet.

When she first walked in she squealed, feeling like a princess, but after Tark left her she suddenly felt small and out of place. She didn't know what to DO with all of this. She was used to bare-minimum, hand-me-down quality. What if she broke something? Stained something? She tried to touch as little as possible.

She found her own clothing folded and put into the wardrobe. It took only half of one shelf for all of her personal possessions. In the closet, she found her sneakers! She had never been so happy to see a worn-out pair of sneakers in her entire life. There were other clothes hanging in the closet, some she recognized from Earth, others she assumed to be local, and shoes as well. She didn't know who they belonged to, so she didn't touch them either.

Her anxiety ramped up a notch when she realized she was using someone else's room, and her fear of ruining something expensive sent her out to the patio, where there was nothing fine or delicate she could get dirty by accident.

She had been sitting in a wooden chair, which she pulled onto the patio, for about a half hour when there was a knock at the door. She swiftly moved to answer it and found Tark on the other side.

"All settled in?" His warm smile was back, and she grinned broadly.

"Yeah, I guess so. I don't have much."

Why did she have to point that out to him?! He knew she didn't have money. She could kick herself.

"Good. Uh... Lamn would like to have a talk with you if you're up to that." He was smiling, but she could feel nervousness rolling off of him.

Why is he nervous? Oh God! Is this when Lamn was going to tell me his plans of making me his slave? Is Tark in on this?! Is he OK with this?! Is that why he was leaving me here? What have I gotten myself into?!

Tark read her face, even though she hadn't said a word. "There's nothing to be afraid of, Eve. I promised you before you came that if you feel like you are being mistreated, I will return you, remember? It's just a talk." The nervousness was still there around him, but with it was a sense of protectiveness...

Was that fondness? Don't overthink this, Eve.

Right. Better get this talk over with, before I get too attached.

With resignation, she followed Tark out of her room, shutting the door to the fantasy room behind her.

30

Eve

The walk down the steps felt like another death march to Eve. She held the banister in one hand, while the other wrung the hem of her t-shirt. She had changed into her own clothing, and now, surrounded by the rich fabrics and colors around her, she felt like a redneck at a royal ball. She briefly considered going back and changing, and then remembered she had nothing better to change into.

This is as good as it gets, folks.

Tark led her through hallways, past a room with a huge piano and instruments, and another large room lined with bookcases (*a real library?*), before bringing her through a set of glass doors at the back of the house, and into an enclosed patio and greenhouse, if she had to guess. There were a lot of, what looked like, exotic flowers, and the smell was amazing.

In the center of the room, Lamn stood from the table where he had been sitting, and offered her a chair, even being a total gentleman and pushing it in for her. Of course, his being extra nice only made Eve more suspicious of him. He offered her coffee, which she accepted. She tried to keep her face neutral, but the old saying must have been written about her, "*If her mouth didn't say it, her face would.*"

Tark was excusing himself and turning to leave, but Lamn asked him to stay. Tark turned with an upraised brow; clearly, he hadn't expected to be included in today's "talk." Tark only nodded and took a seat next to Eve.

She didn't know why, but right then she had an overwhelming urge to reach over and grab his hand in hers. Then her cheeks began burning at the thought of touching him, like holding his hand would be too intimate. Then she had to peek at Tark to see if he had noticed she had that reaction and guessed what she was thinking, except he wasn't looking at her at all, until he noticed SHE was looking at him.

And then he DID look, and he saw her blushing fiercely, but he couldn't know why...

Unaware of Eve's internal dilemma, Lamn had been pacing, and chose that moment to begin "the talk."

"Eve, how much do you know about your mother?" He was standing behind a chair, holding the back of it as he looked at her.

WHAT?... Okay. This was unexpected.

"My.... mother?" She was eyeing him uncertainly. Of all of the things he could have said to her, her mother was the farthest from her mind that day.

Lamn just nodded, waiting for her.

"Uh, well, nothing, really. I know she was gone for a long time. Then she showed up ready to deliver me, and as soon as she did, she took off again. That's what Nancy told me. I've never met her." Eve waved her hand dismissively.

Was this some kind of attempt at mental torture? Because she'd come to terms with being abandoned a long time ago.

Lamn nodded. He grasped the chair firmly, then relaxed his grip, then grasped it again as if clenching his fists around it. She realized he was fidgeting, the same way she did when she was nervous.

And he WAS nervous!

This revelation surprised Eve and gave her a little more confidence.

"What I'm going to tell you... may be hard to believe... I just ask that you consider that fae cannot lie." He stopped and looked her in the eye, she could see he was struggling with whatever it was he needed to say.

But Eve was clueless as to what it could possibly be, especially involving her mother.

When she didn't interrupt, he continued.

"Eve, I am your father."

At that moment, all Eve could think of was a scene out of a science fiction movie, where the hero confronts the villain and the villain announces, "I AM YOUR FATHER" in a deep raspy voice. She couldn't help it: she burst out laughing uncontrollably.

Lamn and Tark stared at each other in confusion; this was not how they thought she would take the news.

She finally got her giddiness under control, and wiping tears from her eyes, she apologized, in a way that she hoped looked genuine. At least she felt better, the laughter had let all of the stress out of her body.

Lamn looked completely off-kilter, and not knowing what to do, he just continued with his story. "I met Ruth while I was on a mission. I had been injured on the Earth Plane, and she was the first one to find me. I couldn't heal as quickly as I do in the Summer Court, and she took care of me until I was well enough to travel back. I just couldn't leave without her. We fell in love, a rare and beautiful thing for a fae. She was beautiful and kind, just like you, Eve. You have her smile."

He smiled sadly at Eve, and she could see he was holding back tears. She was suddenly very serious.

"So what happened?"

"We had many happy years together. She lived here, with me. We were officially mated. I knew she was a hybrid, but I didn't know what kind."

"Wait. What do you mean you didn't know what kind? Was she part fae?" Eve was confused now. Hybrid had always meant part-fae, part-human to her.

Tark and Lamn shared a look, Lamn subtly shook 'no.'

"She had the blood of another being in her too, Eve. There are more here than fae and humans. I didn't know her genetic makeup, at the time. And I didn't care. I loved her more than life."

"So where is she now?"

Lamn sighed, and his breath caught. "We don't know. I was leaving for a mission, and she told me she had news to share upon my return, but when I came back from the mission I found her gone. The household staff told me she went to the portal to meet me, which she had done numerous times before, but she wasn't there when I returned.

"We searched and searched, and searched. She had no reason to run, I assumed she was taken. I called in every favor I had, even going to Earth and the Winter Court myself to try to find her. In the end, I couldn't. I have never given up hope of finding her.

"The day we met you in the diner... your scent... It is SO much like hers...

"And you have her smile, her face... but your hair is very different." At this, he smiled sadly at his own joke.

Eve felt her heart breaking open. She had never gotten to love her mother, or miss her: but here was a guy who was falling to pieces without her.

Is it weird that he's my father, but he looks my age?

The thought shocked her.

"Wait... how old are you?" *It was probably rude to just spit it out, but, well, what's done was done, so...*

Lamn laughed genuinely, "My Dear, fae age differently than humans. Once we reach maturity, we stay that way for a long time. We eventually get gray, yes, but it would take thousands of years. To answer your question, I am seven-hundred sixteen years old... And a half." He winked at her.

Wow. How do you respond to that?!

"You don't look a day over five hundred." She commented with a slight grin.

Tark still exuded nervousness, looking back and forth between Lamn and Eve. He finally chimed in carefully, "Again, I have to say, you're taking this awfully well, Eve."

"For a human, you mean?" She asked him, still grinning.

"No,... for a daughter." He said it gently, but it had the same impact.

She could joke around the topic all she wanted, but this wasn't about her missing mother, this was about her missing FATHER.

She suddenly didn't know what to think or how to feel, she knew logically that she had a father out there somewhere, but she had always just assumed it was a random one-night sperm-donor kinda deal. Now, here she was, face to face with a man claiming to be her dad.

She had his facial structure, his jawline. She had the same line on her forehead which wrinkled when she contemplated something. She could see it. She just didn't know what to DO with it. She couldn't pretend to miss a man she never knew, correction, fae. It was all very... sudden.

Lamn stepped in before she felt she had to fill the silence. "Look, I know this is unexpected for you, I want you to know I'm not expecting anything from you. I was just hoping that you'd... give me a chance to get to know you. My home is your home, for as long as you want to stay." For such a big guy, the last part came out very weak and quiet, almost a plea.

Eve smiled broadly. She dealt with hard feelings with humor.

Better he see it now.

She got out of her chair and rounded the table to hug him.

"Don't worry, Pops. After seeing your digs, I think you're stuck with me for a while. Well, actually, you're stuck with me for a while anyway, 'cause I have literally nowhere else to go." At this, they both chuckled.

"Yeah, I'm just relieved to find out I'm your daughter, and not going to be your next sex slave." She laughed, but Lamn went absolutely rigid and pulled her to arm's length.

"Is THAT what you thought?!" His eyes were wide, and she could feel guilt radiating off of him in waves.

"Lamn... er... Dad(?)... Ever since Armoniel brought me back, you've been super touchy-feely, hugging me, holding me, very hands-on. After my last experience–"

"OHMYGODS!" Lamn pulled her into a tight hug and then quickly pushed her back out when he realized he was doing just what she said, again. He was mortified.

"NO. Eve, NO. You will NEVER be a slave. You will NEVER be

disabused. NEVER AGAIN. I was just so relieved to see you alive. I was so afraid of losing you after I lost your mother. I'm so sorry. I didn't think." His voice cracked. Tears were rolling down his cheeks, no matter how quickly he tried to swat them away.

Eve genuinely felt horrible, she had totally misread the situation. She had never had a parent that cared about her, that worried about her. She had always had to take care of herself. He had tried to be her father, even when she didn't know who he was. She stepped back into Lamn and hugged him warmly before saying, "And how am I supposed to believe you can protect me when you go and get all girly on me? Tsk, Tsk...Cry baby. Big threat YOU are!" She looked up at him and smiled through teasing eyes.

It worked. Lamn laughed out loud, and hugged her back tightly. They stayed like that for a few minutes, just being there and holding space for each other. When they finally broke apart, Eve noticed Tark had left them to reunite alone. Eve and Lamn sat down at the table and told each other their histories, their passions, and their dreams as the afternoon dragged on, and the night fell. Eve didn't know how to deal with suddenly having a father, but she knew, on some level, she loved and accepted Lamn, and the rest would work itself out.

31

Tark

Tark walked down the hallway to his bedroom in his own estate. It was far smaller than Lamn's, rightfully so, as he was a lesser noble in the Court. Still, it was far bigger than any one fae needed, and it did have a lovely lakefront view to make up for the lack of sprawling grounds and gardens.

He dropped his jacket over the back of the chair and walked to the window to look at the lake. The water usually calmed him. It was quiet, as usual. Suddenly, too quiet. After so many weeks of spending time with Lamn and Skiff, and even Armoniel at times (*It still blew his mind they were on a first-name basis with a Grigori!*), suddenly being alone was... suffocating. But it wasn't even the lack of his friends if he was honest: it was the lack of Eve. There was just *something* about her. Something he missed.

It's her Nephilum scent. That's ALL it is. Don't overthink it.

He pulled away from the window and undressed, grabbing his robe as he headed for the bathing chamber. It was good to be home, in familiar surroundings, but tonight it felt lonely. This was new for him, he usually valued his time alone. He was never a needy or clingy sort of fae. He was the one who turned down invitations to go to the pub or the games with friends, preferring a good book by the fire.

So why was he so miserable?

He filled the tub with steaming hot water and added oils to soothe his muscles. As he climbed in and sat back he let his eyes drift shut, and just savored the warmth on his limbs. It had been a long and strenuous mission, and he was glad it was complete. They had recovered a hybrid, and Lamn had found a family in Eve.

Eve.

He sighed involuntarily, picturing her arguing with him, pushing out her lower lip while being stubborn, smiling up at him, touching him... He felt the arousal growing in him, raising his heart rate, and he scowled at himself.

Are you some adolescent, Tark? You're acting like you've never seen a pretty female before.

All thoughts of enjoying the bath were gone as he battled his own mind and body for control. He quickly washed and got out of the tub, releasing the water. He dried himself with efficient strokes of the towel, and dropped it on the floor, pulling the warm robe around his body.

He was angry at himself. He was getting too attached, and he was going to get his feelings hurt. He didn't have time for that.

She had all but admitted she thought we had brought her here to be a sex slave!

He shook his head.

She didn't trust him. She didn't care for him. He was reading too much into it... So why had she begged him to stay, to make her feel safe if she didn't trust him?

Females were confusing on the best of days. He'd get no answers tonight. He wished he could just stop thinking about her altogether. Maybe he should report to Court that he was ready for another mission, it might help take his mind off of... everything.

He started a fire in the fireplace, more for the ambiance than the heat. Dropping his robe at the end of the bed, he pulled back the sheets and climbed in naked, pulling them up to his chest. He tried to count inventory in his head, to keep himself occupied, but again and again, her laughter caught him off guard, he counted the swords in his arsenal, and saw her smile.

Fuck my life. Definitely need a mission.

After much tossing and turning, he finally fell into a deep sleep and dreamed about Eve.

Eve

Eve was comfortable in her new bed, moreso when she found out she was not sleeping in someone else's room. It had been a guest room and was now hers and hers alone. The clothing in the closet had been bought for her, courtesy of Lamn, so she would be more comfortable during her transition to the Summer Court. And Lamn had told her he would take her shopping in the town, Avenwhar, the next day.

At first, she slept deeply, with wonderful dreams about intense eyes and purple hair. But somewhere early in the morning, the dreams had become sinister. She woke with a start, and could only remember that she had been running from Rog: first through a fire, then in the forest. There had been blood, lots of blood, and there were fae all around, laughing at her distress. The windows were still dark with night, and she couldn't get her heartbeat to slow down. She was wide awake and knew there would be no more sleep.

She reached for her robe as she got up, and pulled it on over her nightgown. She had no slippers, but the floor wasn't cold.

Maybe a snack will calm my nerves?

The house was dark as she left her room and headed for the staircase. As she wandered down, she tried to remember which way to go to get to the kitchen. She had never been inside a house big enough to get lost in before. She was pretty sure it was to the right, as she left the staircase. She wandered down the hall and knew when she saw the formal dining room she couldn't be far. After two more doors, she finally saw the kitchen ahead.

Entering, she waved her hand over the sconce on the wall; Lamn had shown her how to turn on the lights. She still didn't understand it, but it worked. She went to the fae equivalent of a refrigerator: a cabinet on the outside, that stayed cold... somehow... on the inside, and pulled out some meat and cheese. She found a breadbox behind her and cut two slices of homemade bread for a sandwich.

She would have to teach Lamn how to make mayonnaise.

From the hallway she heard a sound, like something glass being struck gently to create a tinkling noise, and then nothing. She looked up for a moment, and then went back to her sandwich. A small thumping noise sounded next, followed by another, and then silence.

Eve wondered if Lamn couldn't sleep as well, and thought to invite him to join her for a sandwich and a cup of tea.

Like father, like daughter, right? Too soon?

She headed into the dark hallway and down the hall. She hadn't gone very far when a hand grabbed her mouth tightly, while another grabbed her around the waist from behind. Her body went rigid with panic instantly, the visions of Rog in her dreams still too close to her consciousness. She tried to swing her arms and kick her legs, but the man who had her was like a steel trap. He lifted her effortlessly and headed toward the front hall, and the door.

As they got closer, her mind snapped to attention, suddenly clear. She couldn't let him take her out of there. She struggled as hard as she could, but it made no difference. He was almost to the door.

As he tried to use the hand around her waist to grasp the knob simultaneously, there was a quiet knock at the door. The attacker froze. Eve continued to struggle, but he clamped his arm tighter around her, almost cutting off her air. The knock came again. The attacker didn't move.

Eve knew that if there was someone on the other side of that door, he or she may be her only hope. As a last resort, Eve bit down on her attacker's hand, HARD. She could feel and taste the blood filling her mouth.

He pulled his hand back reflexively as he cursed quietly, and Eve screamed as loudly as she could. She heard whoever was on the other side of the door trying to break it down, and then there was a blinding pain in her head. She heard the door blast open as she slipped into the blackness.

32

Eve

Eve woke up with the blush and gold comforter pulled up to her chin, the sun spilling through the curtains. Before she could begin to piece together where she was, a searing pain in the back of her head roared to the forefront. She brought both hands up to her head as if to hold the pain back.

"Hey! You ok?!"

She cracked her eyes open to see Tark's face in front of her, concern written all over it.

"No offense, Dude, but you look like shit."

He smiled warmly, but it didn't erase the pain in his eyes.

"Have you looked in a mirror lately?" He taunted back. She laughed and then winced.

"Tark, what happened?"

"I'm so sorry, Eve." He backed up and started pacing out of her line of sight, she couldn't turn her head to see him without the pain worsening. "I should have expected this. I KNEW better. It's all my fault."

"You hit me over the head?" She asked incredulously.

"What- NO. Vane did."

"VANE?!" She tried to sit up and was immediately jolted back down by a lightning bolt of pain in her skull. "Owww... How?..."

"Lamn had all of the other, uh, previous slaves taken to an Inn, to wait for their appointments with the Court. But he secured Vane downstairs in his… uh… jail cells."

"Wait. Lamn has jail cells?"

"The point is: I should have foreseen he'd try to escape and come after you, he was pretty obsessed with you. I'm still not sure how he got out, those doors are spelled really well."

"Key stone."

"What?"

Eve rotated her head slightly so she could look at Tark. "He has this stone in his right pocket which works like a key. I've seen him use it a few times. I meant to lift it from him, but never got the chance."

"Wait here, I'll be right back!"

And where, exactly, am I going to go?

Tark took off running out of the room, thumping heavily down the hall and stairs. Eve nursed her head, and a few minutes later she heard the telltale thumping of Tark returning as promised.

"Is this what you saw?" He held the small stone in front of her face.

"I think so. It glows blue when you pass it over a locked door." She squinted her eyes to look at it, but without seeing it in action, she couldn't be sure.

Tark sat on the edge of the bed and placed his hand on her cheek gently. "Well, just to be safe, we stripped him down in a cell with a physical lock, a spelled lock, AND an armed guard. You won't have to worry about him again. Eve, I am SO, so sorry this happened." He rubbed his thumb absently over her cheek.

Eve leaned into the warmth of his hand and breathed a deep breath of relief that had nothing to do with what he had just told her, and everything to do with his proximity. She let her eyelids close as she savored the feeling. She felt him shift closer, and she could feel the warmth of his breath on her cheek. She just wanted to rotate toward him, lift her mouth to his…

Heavy steps sounded in the hallway, and her cheek was suddenly cold as Tark whipped his hand away and stood quickly. He was two steps away from her when Lamn walked into the room and headed straight for her bed.

Lamn looked distraught again. "Eve, I am SOOO sorry!"

Eve saw movement and pulled her eyes away from Lamn to see Tark trying to slip out of the room.

"STOP!" Tark and Lamn both froze, eyes on Eve.

"Both of you: this is NOT your fault. This was Vane's action and Vane's alone. No more being mopey, hear me?" she looked from Lamn to Tark and back.

Tark's lips quirked up, and Lamn tried to put on a smile for her.

Lamn raised his hand to show her two tablets and a glass of water in his other hand, and she nodded. When she looked up again, Tark had slipped out and was gone. She blew out a frustrated sigh.

Lamn helped her to sit up, gave her the tablets and explained that they were fae painkillers, and helped her drink the water to get them down. Once she settled she looked at Lamn.

"Is Tark ok?" Something passed over his eyes, but the expression moved so quickly she couldn't pin it down. She could feel something like sadness in him.

"Yes, Tark is fine. He's just really busy. He has some obligations he needs to attend to. How are YOU feeling?"

Eve noticed the subject change, but let it go. If something was up with Tark, she'd take it up with Tark. Instead, she and Lamn had a very nice conversation while she waited for the painkillers to kick in.

Forty minutes later Eve was showered, dressed, and ready to go shopping.

Holy shit those painkillers were AMAZING!

She had joked with her dad... er... Lamn... *she still didn't know what to call him,...* about selling them on the black market on Earth, but he assured her that they only worked on someone with fae physiology. (*Bummer.*)

Lamn met her in the main hallway by the entrance, he was dressed like her, in jeans and a t-shirt with a pair of sneakers.

"Can we get sneakers here?" She asked hopefully.

"Unfortunately, no. But I can get them the next time I go to Earth for a mission." He smiled at her.

There was no mistaking the love and pride in his eyes, and Eve was willing to bet that if she were another kind of woman, she could have him wrapped around her finger if she wanted to. But she didn't. She was just happy to have a father at long last, his stuff wasn't important to her.

They walked out the front door, to the waiting carriage pulled by two chestnut mares. Eve looked around.

"Tark's not coming?" She tried not to pout.

"Uh, no. Obligations, remember?"

"Oh, yeah, right..." She absently climbed into the back of the carriage. They had just pulled away from the estate when it hit her. *Was 'obligations' a code for 'family?' Did Tark have a wife and kids?!*

Eve looked out the side of the carriage, trying to contain the burning in her cheeks and her sense of humiliation.

It all made sense! Tark had tried to distance himself once they got here! He had said he was going to HIS estate. He has 'obligations.' And here she was flirting away with him like a shameless homewrecker! Thank God Lamn didn't seem to be aware! She couldn't even imagine having THAT conversation with her newly found father and one of his best MARRIED friends!

Lamn noticed how interested she seemed to be looking out the carriage window, and so he started pointing out landmarks, shops, and other points of interest. Eve nodded, and "uh-huhh'ed" so as not to be rude, but all of the air had left her balloon.

Lamn brought her to buy clothing, candy, shoes, hats... it was like he was trying to make up for twenty-five years in one gala shopping spree. Eve was very minimalistic, so she had no trouble turning down most of the things he wanted to get for her, she did accept a cute hat, and some chocolate. She tried her best to smile for Lamn, and have a good time, and she did have a good time, but he noticed her enthusiasm was waning.

After a few hours, and some coffee at a local cafe, he suggested he take her back. "Don't want to overdo it with a head injury." She reluctantly agreed and was grateful for the cover story.

That's it. Head injury.

Until that day, she hadn't even been aware she was seeing Tark as boyfriend material, his 'obligations' had made it pretty clear to her how she was really feeling. Her cheeks would flush every time she thought of Tark, and what she'd almost done... what she wanted to do. She needed to lose him like a bad habit. This was her new life, her new chance.

But the entire ride back she battled with not wanting to let him go and needing to let him go. He wasn't hers, after all.

33

Tark

This just SUCKS.

Tark was in a foul mood as he walked through the back streets of Avenwhar. Lamn had told him that he and Eve would be in the shopping district, so he was avoiding that like the plague.

He had touched her face today. What the everlovingfuck was he thinking?! Lamn could have seen! What a fucking awkward conversation THAT would have been with his best friend about his best friend's DAUGHTER. Lamn would probably kick his ass for even THINKING about Eve. And rightfully so! If he wasn't careful, he was going to lose his job, his title, his friend... and for what? Like she should have to settle for what he could give her, after seeing Lamn's spacious accommodations. She'd probably laugh in his face... Right before Lamn punched him in it.

He picked up his pace to burn off the frustration and anger.

He had gone to the Court earlier, and they had a mission lined up for him in two days' time, all he had to do was get through the next two days without losing his mind.

Maybe he'd go get a drink, maybe that would help take his mind off of things... Probably not.

Eve

Eve wandered around the halls until she finally had some sense of direction. It helped that Lamn had put up little signposts in most of the intersections with arrows indicating which rooms were in which direction.

It was cute, really.

She found herself back in what she assumed was the music room, as there were instruments strewn throughout, and the biggest piano she had ever seen right in the center of the room under a ginormous chandelier. She found herself walking in and sitting down at the piano. She touched her fingers to the keys and listened to the crisp notes.

In school one of the nuns had noticed her interest in the small standup piano they had, and had given her lessons. At the time, Eve wasn't terribly interested in learning to play the piano, but she HAD been interested in something that would absorb hours of time, keeping her from going right back to Nancy after school. She kept it up the whole time she attended that school, even coming in on weekends to practice when Nancy was out of control, or just when she needed to get away. The piano was her refuge.

Placing both hands on the keys, she began to play in earnest. It had been years since she had played last, but the memory never left her fingers. Her favorite pieces had always been melancholy and seemed to sing to the broken hearts of the world. She let them flow. With each note, she was grieving the loss of something she never really had. A connection? A friend? Potentially more? She would play her song like a funeral dirge, and then she would consider it buried. Gone. She let the tears flow, and she said a silent goodbye.

Hours had passed, and after a quick dinner with Lamn, Eve sat in the greenhouse room, curled up in a large chair and reading a book she had pulled off of a shelf in the library. Lamn had told her it had been one of her mother's favorites, and Eve could see why. She was deep into the story when she heard shouting coming from the front hallway. Putting the book down, she warily scrambled inside to see what was going on.

Hiding behind a door, and just peeking around the corner, she could see two very official people holding a clearly drunk Tark between them. Had it been him shouting? Yes, it had definitely been him shouting as he started again, and tried to pull away from the two officials. Lamn held the bridge of his nose between his thumb and forefinger, shaking his head gently. Lamn finally ordered Tark to stand down, which seemed to spook him into obedience and told the officials he would take it from there.

Eve knew she really shouldn't eavesdrop, but she also couldn't seem to tear herself away.

Lamn was pacing.

"Tark, you know you can't just go starting fights without attracting the attention of the officials. What's all this about?"

Tark was swaying pretty well. "Lamn... (groan) Lamn... You just don't understand...."

Eve's guilt got the better of her, and she was just stepping to back up when she heard her name and stopped.

"I can't get away from Eve, damnit! I can't get any peace. No matter what I do, no matter where I go... I can't get away from her! She's always THERE."

Eve was frozen in place, trying to understand what he meant.

Had she been too demanding of him? Or did he want more from her? And with him having a family, which was worse? She never thought he had a drinking problem... but how would she have known?

Lamn was right in front of Tark now, no longer pacing.

"And is this how you wish to make your intentions known? Drunk off of your ass? Hauled in by officials? Stinking of God knows what?"

Apparently, that was the wrong thing to say, because Tark instantly went from drunk to enraged.

"Oh, is that how it is?! I can see now that I have overstepped! Clearly, I was wrong in thinking we were friends! Apparently a lower noble isn't good enough for you, now am I? Well, pardon me, My Lord Vassal! I'll just be on my way to the other side of town. You just call me when you need a dirty job done, and you don't want to get your own hands dirty then, eh?!" He was gesturing wildly, or maybe that was just his body swaying and pitching.

Lamn just shook his head and said nothing, clearly disgusted with his friend's behavior. When Tark had finally wound down, Lamn took him gently by the arm and escorted/carried him to a chair to sit, before he could fall over.

"I'll have my carriage take you home, and make sure you get to bed to sleep this off. We can discuss this in more depth tomorrow when you are sober and clean."

Eve could see the concern in Lamn's eyes, she knew they were close. Guilt nibbled at her insides, as she worried that maybe her coming here had not been the best idea. She didn't want to come between their friendship, or between Tark and his family.

Clearly, the latter is not an issue, he has made it abundantly clear he wants to get as far away from me as possible. How did I not see it? Was he just being polite? Did I really imagine his interest?...

Clearly.

Without staying to hear anymore, Eve quietly tiptoed to a back staircase to head back to her own room.

She had just gotten there. She had just found her father. She had finally found a place she could consider home and family! And now she was wondering if it wouldn't be best for everyone if she moved out as soon as she could, so they could have their lives back, undisturbed.

34

Tark

Tark woke in his own bed, feeling like he had just licked the pavement. His mouth was dry and gritty, with a terrible taste, and he had no memory of how it had gotten that way. There was a half glass of water on his nightstand, and a bottle of hangover tablets.

That answers one question.

He peeled himself out of bed, still fully clothed and filthy, and made his way to the bathing room. A look in the mirror confirmed that he looked as bad as he felt; although, he knew he should be feeling worse. His fae genetics had likely already cleaned out most of the toxins he had taken in... even if he didn't remember it.

He relieved himself, and then pulled the dirty clothing off of himself and heaped them on the floor, he might just get rid of them, they smelled so badly.

What HAD he been rolling in? He must have had a LOT to drink, if he was this blurry the next day.

A Shower, and his usual morning hygiene ritual, went a long way to making him feel fea again. He grabbed his briefcase, and tried to decide how to spend the day, as he would leave the next day on a mission for who knew how long? Although his body was detoxifying, he felt incredibly clear headed.

He needed to replenish some supplies. And he supposed he should inform Lamn he was leaving, as he reported to him. And it wouldn't be a bad idea to say goodbye to Eve. Chances were, by the time he got back, she may be a citizen. Who knew? She may meet someone, what with Lamn's large social circles...

He suddenly felt very nauseous.

The idea of returning, and finding her on the arm of some arrogant fae made him both murderous and desperately depressed. Tark flopped heavily in his chair, which groaned under his cannonball weight, and his briefcase hit the floor with a 'thwap.'

This is not working.

He had taken the mission to try to get her out of his system, but he now realized it might do the opposite and get him out of HER system. Not that he was sure he was ever IN her system... whatever. He may be giving up any chance of seeing if she ever did have any interest in him. Once she found someone, and undoubtedly she WOULD, he would be relegated to the 'friend zone.' As Lamn's friend, he would have to see her at parties and social gatherings, smiling at someone else. Holding on to someone else. Doing–

But that's what he wanted, wasn't it?... No. It honestly wasn't. And he couldn't even consider it without his stomach heaving. Yes, it was selfish of him to want her in his life, when she had so many better options she didn't even know about yet. But he couldn't stomach the alternative.

In a terrifying moment of clarity, he realized that he had to know if she had any interest in him, any at all. If not, well, that would make it easier (*and harder*) to just busy himself elsewhere. But if so–

Tark jumped out of the chair and grabbed his jacket as he raced for the door. He called to his housekeeper to ready a horse as he rounded the hallway and descended the stairs, heading for the stable. Accepted or rejected: he would tell Eve what he was thinking. This had to be resolved, one way or the other.

Eve

Lamn and Eve sat in the dining room, joined by Skiff, eating a light brunch. They had introduced Eve to a fae game of cards, similar to gin rummy from Earth, and were enjoying each other's company, even if they each seemed to be forcing a bright face, while they clearly each had a lot on their minds.

Eve appreciated the two fae spending time with her, while she was feeling so down. Of course, she couldn't tell them why she suddenly seemed so mellow. Luckily, Lamn seemed equally as pensive and distracted, and hadn't noticed... or at least he hadn't said anything. Eve wondered if it had to do with Tark's appearance the night before.

"SNARK! And that's GAME!" Skiff dropped his cards on the table with a flourish and a big smile, and sat back crossing his arms over his chest in victory. Eve realized she had been so lost in thought, she missed a key play that might have saved her.

Yeah, this isn't working.

Eve congratulated Skiff on winning the hand and excused herself. Lamn looked at her with curiosity but didn't ask any questions, for which she was grateful. She wandered the halls, lost in thought, wandering aimlessly, and before she knew it, she found herself back in the music room looking wistfully at the piano.

Hello, my old friend!

She sat down, eyes closed, and let the music leak out of her hands and onto the keys, the notes ringing and floating, building in density and emotion, as they swirled around her. As she played she allowed her thoughts to drift.

She remembered seeing Tark at the table in the diner with the others, all intensity and bravado. His infuriating smirk. The warmth in his eyes, and the way they crinkled at the corners when he truly laughed. His voice in her bedroom. His face next to hers when she woke up that morning at Nancy's. The morning he spent helping her clean the diner, and explaining about being fae. The way he hugged her strongly when Armoniel brought her back. His look of encouragement when she stepped through the portal...

Her fingers became aggressive, the music transitioning from whimsy to torrential.

She remembered arriving at the Summer Court: Tark keeping his distance, looking away, avoiding eye contact. The way he softened when she pleaded with him, damn that made her feel angry now. He had shown her he wanted nothing from her, and she had practically *begged* him to stay to get him to acknowledge her, when for all she had known he could have been selling her out. Literally.

In some ways, he reminded her of Richard putting her on a pedestal, acting interested, and building her up, only to ghost her. Making her the unknowing side piece while he decided if he wanted his old flame, or her, or both, or even a new one. She wasn't proud of herself for taking Richard back all those times when he mansplained how it was all a 'misunderstanding.' But she'd be damned if she started her new life that way.

The music roared from the piano, crashing into the walls like a tidal wave of emotion. The chandelier shook on the ceiling, the crystal chiming like trembling stars.

Last night had sealed it. He had made himself very clear. He wanted space.

He'd have it.

The room went silent.

35

Lamn

Lamn wasn't oblivious. Despite the fact that he had a lot on his mind, he could tell that something was bothering Eve. Ever since the night Vane attacked her, she had been sullen, quiet. He gave her space to work through it, but he hoped that she would come to him and let him help.

It was probably unreasonable, considering she had ONLY just found out he was her father. That's a lot to ask from a capable, independent woman.

After she excused herself, Skiff and Lamn continued their conversation, freer to discuss work matters, when suddenly beautiful music filled the house. Both fae froze as gooseflesh crawled up their arms, and both heads turned in unison in the direction of the music. It felt much like a compulsion but in the form of notes, rather than words. It seemed to grip their hearts and take them along a journey through innocence, joy, laughter... But soon the music abruptly changed, bringing them longing, fear, doubt, and lastly anger.

Both fae were on their feet and moving to the music room without a sound or glance. The last notes of the piano crashed like angry waves in a storm against a rocky shore, as they reached the door.

Eve sat at the piano, head bent, tears tracking down her cheeks.

Skiff nodded to Lamn, understanding this was a personal moment, and excused himself silently. Lamn was at Eve's side in a moment, and sitting beside her on the bench silently.

He really wasn't good at this sort of thing, he didn't know what to do. Ruth had always just told him what she needed. He felt helpless.

Eve finally spoke.

"I think it's best if I don't see Tark again." She said it quietly, still focused on her fingers on the keys. Lamn's mind jumped through the many possibilities of what she could mean, what would prompt her to say this.

Did she know he was there last night?! No... she couldn't have. Then why?

"You don't have to, if you don't want to... Is everything ok? Did he say something to you?... DO something?..." Lamn was starting to feel the anger rising, surprisingly protective so quickly.

But Tark would never hurt Eve... Would he?

Visions of Tark, drunk, swinging and swearing the night before swam behind his eyelids. Even though he had rarely seen Tark that out of control, in centuries between them, it still left the smallest window of doubt.

"No, he hasn't." She turned to meet Lamn's eyes. "I just don't think it's a good idea. He has obligations, and I need to get settled."

"But when you first came here, you asked him to stay too. You said you knew him better. I assumed he made you feel safer. Did something happen to change that?" He was searching her eyes, waiting for her to help him to understand what had happened.

He didn't like the unease growing in his stomach with the thought that Tark had somehow hurt her. He didn't want to jump to that conclusion, but she wasn't telling him what was hurting her, only that it had to do with him.

"You happened. I found out you are my father. I know you're not out to hurt me, and I feel safer now. So it's okay to let Tark go back to his obligations. I'm sure I'm going to have my hands full soon anyway."

Lamn looked unsure but nodded. Clearly, there was something happening between Eve and Tark, but neither seemed to want to confront it head-on.

Eve

Eve was trying to be the bigger person here, but Lamn wasn't making it easy for her. She couldn't very well say "Dad, I'm really not interested in being Tark's side piece, so could you tell him to just move on?" If she was talking to TARK, yeah, she'd totally say that to his face, but this was her father... who was also his best friend. She knew she would have to see Tark around sometimes, but she was looking forward to having new friends to hang out with, to make herself scarce.

Speaking of...

Eve perked up. "Hey, those sla--... hybrids we rescued from the Winter Court, do you mind if I visit with them? After Armoniel got rid of Lara, we actually had a chance to talk. They were really nice, and I'd like to see how they're getting along here."

Lamn watched as the tension eased out of her shoulders, and she seemed to come back to herself.

He cocked a brow at her. "You don't need my permission. You're a grown-ass adult."

They both threw their heads back and laughed, and she threw her arms around his shoulders. Even though he looked more like a big brother than her father, it actually felt very natural.

Tark

Tark pulled the reins back hard, and the horse made a rebellious noise, mouth frothing, before stopping short. Tark threw the reins toward the doorman as he rushed up the steps. As he reached the top he stopped to compose himself, straightening his jacket, he didn't want to look crazed when he entered.

The footman announced him as Lamn was coming down the staircase into the front hall.

"Feeling better, are you?" Lamn asked him shortly.

Tark was taken aback. Something was off.

Had he been there the night before? Impossible. He was on the other side of town...

"I am?..." He looked to Lamn, suddenly far less confident.

Lamn shook his head as he realized. "You don't remember." It was stated, not asked.

"Remember?... What, exactly?"

Now Tark was beginning to sweat. He had only been drunk enough to forget what happened a few times in his many centuries. He was silently praying that this was not one of those times.

But clearly, it was.

"Come." Lamn bit the order out, and turned on his heel to walk to his office, he would not have this conversation in front of the household. Tark responded to the order, straightening his back and following like a fae. No matter what he had done, he would face the consequences.

Make no mistake, Lamn was his friend, almost like a brother, but when it came to business Tark knew there was a fine line he had to walk. Lamn was his commander, his higher-up in his chain of command. He had never given Lamn any reason to need to pull rank with him before, this was uncharted territory. It was made all the more horrifying by the fact that he didn't know just what he had done to cause the trouble he was in.

"Shut the door." Tark did as ordered. After a few moments, he noticed that Lamn had not given him the order to sit down.

Shit... What the hell did I DO?

He maintained his posture, even if he felt his stomach eating itself.

Lamn leaned on the edge of his desk and sighed deeply, "Let me inform you about what happened last night."

Tark cringed inwardly, but his body did not move.

"I was summoned to the door by two officials who had to carry you and contain you because you were so drunk that you were causing fights in the street. You were argumentative, violent, and belligerent. Naturally, they found out you were in my unit, and so they deposited you here late into the evening."

Tark considered what Lamn had said.

It was probably true, he was a mean drunk, especially when he was drinking while depressed... but that would not usually warrant a closed-door meeting. That would normally result in demerits, maybe extra duties, and lashings if he had caused lasting damage. So why–

Lamn continued, "Then, beyond the drunken debauchery, there is the issue of what you said to ME."

Tark froze. His mind was spinning, but he couldn't think of anything he could possibly have said to upset Lamn so much. His posture remained solid, but he gulped.

Lamn brought his forehead to his hand and waved at the chair with his other hand. "Sit," he said simply.

Tark looked at the chair, and back at Lamn, and slowly lowered himself down to sit. His hands were white-knucked as he gripped the armrests and his heart was beating out at a frantic pace in his chest.

Had he destroyed their friendship, and not even remembered it?!

Lamn sighed again, and then stood with his back to Tark, looking out the window at the gardens.

"Tark, I'm speaking as your friend now, not as your Commander. I want to know what the hell is going on between you and Eve– don't interrupt!

"I want to know what's going on between you and Eve, and I want to know what I have ever done to you to make you feel that I see you as inferior because of your social standing in Court. I expect you to be honest with me."

Tark had immediately tried to answer, but shut his mouth again until Lamn was finished.

He was astonished.

What the hell had he said about Eve?! And what the hell had he said about his status?! He was still drawing a blank.

Now he put his own head in his hand and groaned. He felt like a complete idiot. Shame colored his face, and he couldn't meet Lamn's eyes. Clearly his drunken state had allowed him to voice all of his inner insecurity, and where there was no problem in their relationship before, he had just made one.

"Lamn... I..." Tark started tentatively, knowing there may be no getting back what they once had. The most he could do was lay himself bare, and hope that Lamn would understand that it was a moment of weakness. He knew it was asking a lot, even if they did have centuries of history. Small things like this could fester, and tear people apart. Clearly, they already had, thanks to him and his big mouth.

"I don't remember what I said. That's the truth. But I can tell you what I was feeling, what I was thinking about.

"I have developed an attachment to Eve. I really like her, and I can't stop thinking about her. I told myself that it wasn't fair to her, that this is already an adjustment to her. And I know I don't have anything to offer her. I tried to ignore it. I tried to put her out of my mind. But the more I did, the more crazy I felt. I just lost it.

"And it's weird now, because... you know... you're her FATHER and all, now... and I didn't know how to approach her, or you. And I know she probably doesn't even think about me that way. And I didn't want there to be this weirdness between us, so I tried to just ignore it. But every time I see you, she's there. And I just can't help it.

"Look, I know I'm a lesser noble. I don't have the income, or the estate that you do, and I probably never will. I really wanted to wish her well, and hope that she found some nice fae among the upper nobility. I wanted to... but I can't. When I think of her with someone else, it feels like a part of me just dies."

Lamn turned and stormed across the room. Tark hardly had time to lift his head, which he did, just in time to see the right hook connect with his face. Tark just took it, he didn't even attempt to protect himself. He felt like he deserved it, and more. Lamn was livid. He shook out his hand and then crossed his arms over his chest as he looked down at Tark.

"Tark, we have been friends for a long time. A LONG time. I love you like a brother, but right now I have to tell you that you are the most stupid fae I have ever met."

Annoyance wrankled Tark, but he didn't interrupt. Lamn threw his hands up, turned, and sat in the seat opposite Tark.

"Tark, I think she's fond of you too. I also think she heard you last night when you said you just wanted to get away from her and never see her again... or something to that effect. She is now adamant that she now needs to 'give you space' to deal with your 'obligations,' as she put it." Tark's head shot up, his eyes wide, his mouth open.

He hadn't!... OH GOD, he HAD!

"And here's the thing, Brother, I would have been delighted if you had told me you were interested in Eve, so long as she wanted the same. Yes, she's my daughter, but in her world she's seen as a full-grown adult. She would not have needed my permission to pursue a relationship with you. In fact, I would have told her that she could never have found a more loyal or selfless mate.

"I don't think your social standing means shit to Eve, and I know it means nothing to me, either. Who your parents were is irrelevant, you have always proven yourself in the field. You are my chosen family. I am mortified to think you see me as so shallow. That cuts me deeply." All of the anger drained out of his words, as he looked at Tark with new eyes, the betrayal still ringing in his ears.

Tark hadn't thought it was possible to feel any worse, but there it was. He wiped his hand down his face, and blew out a breath. "Lamn, you have never given me a reason to feel this way. You have never been anything other than genuine and up-front with me. This is all on me. I let my fear get the better of me, and twist my thoughts. For that, I am deeply, deeply sorry. I hope that you can forgive me one day."

Tark felt like his heart was breaking, all of his fears were being realized, and it was all his own doing. He was losing Eve, and he was losing his best friend. He realized that fear is like poison in the mind, and he drank it willingly. He stood to leave, there was nothing more he could say to defend his behavior. He was wrong, and he wouldn't blame Lamn for never talking to him, outside of their work. Lamn might even have him transferred, so as not to see him at all.

"And just where are you going?" Lamn had the faintest hint of a smile pulling the edge of his mouth.

Tark turned, confused. "I... uh... I'm sorry, is there more?" Again, he looked mortified.

Lamn smiled warmly, confusing the hell out of Tark, "If you leave now, how will we ever figure out a way for you and Eve to resolve this mess between you? Clearly, I can't leave YOU to do it."

36

Eve

Eve enjoyed the afternoon with the other female hybrids who had escaped with her. Two of them had been born in the Winter Court, and the other had been kidnapped when she was a child, so none of them remembered Earth as their first home as Eve did. Still, it was nice to have girlfriends, something she had never had before. Their shared experience made them more grateful for each other. Eve was sure they would be friends for a long time.

Lamn had been very generous with the refugees, getting them a suite at the Inn in town, and getting them new clothing and other necessities. They were already looking for paying jobs that didn't involve sex, and considering where they would live once they became citizens.

For Eve it was the first time in... well, ever, that she felt like a part of something. These females valued her, liked her, and didn't expect to get anything from her. They shared their stories openly, laughed at jokes, and shared their dreams for their new lives. She told them all about Vane's attack on her, and how he was now locked in a cell naked. The girls howled with laughter.

Now she finally understood why she could never seem to connect with the girls back home. There was just something so bonding in sharing their life-or-death experience. She had finally found her tribe.

Eve was glad to find that the Summer Court didn't hold the same bias as the Winter Court. She would have to ask Lamn more about it.

She couldn't make any sense out of it: the fae needed hybrid genetics to carry on the species, but the Winter Court saw the hybrids as inferior... so any children resulting from the hybrid-fae pairing would always be seen as lesser or slave stock. What was the point of prolonging the species, if they felt like they were watering it down anyway? Or maybe they just wanted more slaves?

Thankfully, that was all a thing of the past, now that they were in the Summer Court. Here they were just fae, didn't matter what percentage.

After several hours of laughter, comparing clothing, gossip, and planning, Eve finally had to call it a day with the girls to head home.

Not that she 'had' to... she wanted to.

She realized that she really should have opened up to Lamn sooner about how she was feeling, maybe she just hadn't trusted him enough yet. Yes, he was Tark's friend, but he was also family, and she was determined to foster healthy relationships as a part of her new life. Even if she had no idea what that looked like, or how the hell to do it. Like everything else, she would wing it.

It was a short carriage ride back to the estate, and she was soon bouncing up the front stairs feeling infinitely better than she had earlier. She had snacked with the girls, but she was getting really hungry for dinner.

She went to the dining room and found it empty, so she went back to the greenhouse, and found it empty too. One of the housekeepers was walking by, so Eve saved herself from searching the entire building (*it would take days*), and simply asked where Lamn was.

Apparently, he was in his office, right off of the main entrance, which she had passed when she first came in. A brief retracing of her steps had her back at the front entry hallway, and the door on the left she had never used. She walked up happily, knocking, and seeing it was cracked open she just pushed it further open and walked in.

To find Lamn and Tark deep in conversation.

Eve immediately apologized for interrupting, not listening to their protests, and turned on her heel, and walked out of the room, shutting the door behind her. Gone was the playful disposition. It only took seeing him to reduce her to a smoldering pile of goo. But she was determined to stick to her guns.

The door opened behind her, and Lamn called to her. She stopped but didn't turn around. Lamn was soon behind her.

"Everything OK? Look, I'm sorry, I didn't get a chance to warn you he was here. I know you don't want to see him, but we have business to discuss tonight. Would you mind if he joined us for dinner? I understand if you prefer not to, just say so. But I did want to hear about your day as well."

Eve turned to face him as Lamn smiled at her with his hand resting on her upper arm, she could feel his genuine concern for her. He was really taking this fatherhood role seriously, even if she was all grown up. She didn't want to put him in an awkward position. Tark still worked for him. This was going to be one of those times she would have to see him around. While she really wanted to beg off, and take a sandwich up to her room, she also wanted to be there for Lamn, he was trying so hard.

She smiled awkwardly. "That's fine. I get it. Work calls."

His eyes lit with relief. "Great! See you in the greenhouse in half an hour?"

"Yeah. See you there."

She did notice Tark peeking out of the office watching them before she turned and headed for her room.

You can just watch my ample ass as it saunters away, my friend. I am nobody's second choice.

Half an hour later, Eve was strolling into the greenhouse to join the others for dinner. She had gone back to her room and changed. If she was going to have to face Tark, she was going to look great doing it. She fixed her makeup and her hair, and chose her best outfit; it was nothing fancy, but it made her feel comfortable and sexy.

Kinda like a sexy security blanket.

Tark was already sitting, while Lamn put food on the table. They were both engrossed in conversation. Suddenly, Eve felt silly all dressed up. What did she care if he thought she looked good or not?

You didn't dress for him,... you dressed for YOU. Too late now, they've seen you.

She picked up her pace as she entered the room, trying to look unfazed. Tark stood, but Lamn beat him to pulling out Eve's chair, and she smiled up at him gratefully. Lamn put the last dish on the table and explained what all the dishes were to Eve. They were local favorites in this area, and he was excited for her to try them. Apparently, he had cooked! He had pulled Tark into the kitchen while he pulled everything together. She was impressed. Eve, herself, wasn't really a good cook unless you counted boxed Mac'n'Cheese.

They ate, and at first it was awkwardly quiet. Eve finally broke the silence, telling Lamn all about her visit with her new girlfriends. She shared what was appropriate about their search for employment and housing, and about all of the things she had learned from them.

Sometimes, it has to come from a girlfriend.

Lamn brought up a symphony that was playing in the city for the next week. He loved music and was the one who had set up the music room.

"So Eve, since you are such a good musician, I thought you might like to hear the symphony! They are amazing, so much better than human musicians. It's not a prejudice, it's a fact. Hear them and then tell me I'm wrong." He laughed, and she loved to see him so animated. He seemed genuinely in his element.

"Anyway, there is a performance tomorrow night. Would you like to go?"

Eve bounced in her chair like a child. She had NEVER been to see an orchestra, not even a professional concert. The most she had seen was the American Legion band in town, they were ok... but THIS?! This sounded incredible.

Eve's eyes met Tark's in passing, and he looked like he'd seen a ghost. She looked back to Lamn, trying not to think about Tark or his expression, but Lamn had seen it too.

"Tark, you ok?" Lamn leaned in.

Tark's face was then flaming pink, and he looked really uncomfortable. "Uh, yeah, but, uh... the reason I came here this afternoon before we got... sidetracked..., uh... I wanted to tell you... I'm scheduled for a mission... leaving tomorrow." Tark cast a quick glance at Eve, and she quickly looked away and pretended she hadn't seen it.

"How long?" Lamn asked.

Tark blew out a long breath. "Undetermined."

"Wow. You really don't do anything halfway, do you?" Lamn asked, chuckling.

Tark looked at his plate miserably.

"What does that mean?" Eve asked quietly, and then mentally kicked herself.

You don't care, REMEMBER?!

Lamn turned to her, "It means Tark has to go back to Earth for a job, and he doesn't know when he will be back. Hey, maybe he can grab you a pair of sneakers while he's there?" He looked at Tark, who immediately bobbed his head up and down at Eve.

"Oh, ... ok." She hated that she sounded disappointed.

YOU DON'T CARE!

Her mind was still screaming, but her heart wasn't listening.

Tark stood up suddenly and turned to a mortified Eve, "Look, Eve, I owe you a HUGE apology. I am so, SO sorry for the way I have acted toward you. I really like you, a lot actually. And I was really insecure about how you might feel about me, so I pushed you away. Which, I now realize was wrong. I feel awful about that, I really do. The truth is, I can't stop thinking about you. When I'm not with you, I miss you. And I can't help but wonder if you weren't feeling the same connection I was? Eve, if you'd let me, I'd really love the chance to get to know you and to make this up to you." His eyes were begging. She could feel the sense of desperate longing rolling off of him.

Eve looked uncomfortably at Lamn, who gave her a subtle nod.

She stood, dropping her napkin. "I'm sorry. No."

And with that, she turned and left the room.

37

Tark

Lamn seemed to sense Tark's need for a moment and excused him-self to run after Eve.

Tark fell into his chair.

She said no. Just like that. She really had no interest all along.

He held his head in his hands, trying his hardest to hold his heart together. Honestly, he couldn't understand how this was torturing him so deeply, he hardly KNEW her. But it felt like she was another half of him. He couldn't explain it, but it was killing him knowing she wanted nothing to do with him. It tore him apart. Knowing he was going to fall to pieces any minute, he left to head back to his own home, so he could crumble in privacy.

Eve

Lamn caught up with Eve just as she was reaching her room. She looked back at him with tears in her eyes. For a moment, they just saw each other, and then she was sobbing into his chest.

It was killing her, walking away from him. She felt like she had stabbed him in the heart, after that speech. And it took EVERY ounce of willpower she had to get up and walk away. But it still stabbed her own heart as well.

The only reason, ONLY reason, she had been able to do it, was that she remembered that somewhere he had a wife and children waiting for him. His 'obligations.' She honestly didn't know if having multiple wives, girlfriends, concubines, or whatever was a 'thing' for the Fae, but she wasn't having it. She was not going to, knowingly, allow herself to be someone's fun on the side. She had seen too many women in the diner talking about "when their boyfriend was going to divorce his wife and marry her." And it never happened.

She had just gotten here. She had a fresh start for a new life. She didn't want to be pining for someone who didn't want to keep and cherish her.

NEVER AGAIN.

Lamn just held her as the sobs wracked her body, her tears soaking his shirt. It felt like forever before the sobs subdued into crying, and the crying into muffled mewls. Lamn walked her into her room, and ran her a hot tub of water, adding in some of the floral oils he hoped would make her feel better. When she was all cried out he kissed her on her forehead and told her to soak in the bath.

"It always made Ruth feel better."

Lamn

He smiled gently at her. He would have a cup of soothing tea waiting by her bedside when she got out.

Once he had her tea in place he jogged back down the stairs to do damage control with Tark, but it was too late, and he was already gone. He stared at the table of half-eaten food.

How the hell did this go to shit so fast?

Eve

Eve woke with the soft blush and gold fabrics cradling her skin. She had slept very deeply for the first time in a long time. Stretching, she noticed the cup her tea had been in on the nightstand and wondered if Lark had slipped her something to help her. If he had, she was grateful.

The sun was blazing in the window, and she hauled herself up to meet the day, and whatever it may hold. Guilt gnawed at her. She still felt horrible shutting Tark down when he was all but begging her, especially after she had begged him to stay when they first got there, and he had agreed for her sake. She felt unnecessarily cruel, and she didn't like it.

Nope. No matter how bad he felt, she wouldn't be used, or become a homewrecker.

A shower and a half hour made a world of difference for Eve, as she walked into the sunny kitchen and made her way to the coffee pot. Lamn was already up and drinking coffee in a chair by the window, so she made her coffee and went to join him.

She hoped her rejection of Tark wouldn't interfere with their relationship. He had said she could do whatever she wanted. She knew he and Tark were friends and hated this weirdness between the three of them.

Lamn smiled up at her, "Good morning, Sunshine!"

"Morning! Say... what was in that tea you gave me last night?" She gave him a mischievous smile that told him she was onto him. He just laughed.

"I couldn't tell you, exactly. It's an herbal blend Ru– ... your mother used to use when she was upset or anxious. I couldn't believe I still had a box, after all this time." He smiled at her as he gently brushed her indigo hair out of her eyes and over her ear. Eve could tell he was seeing her mother. At that moment, it made her happy.

"Well thank you! I slept better than I have in weeks!" She grinned at him, and just enjoyed his presence beside her, and the hot cup of coffee in her hands while the sun warmed their faces.

This is what she pictured 'family' looked like. It was the perfect moment in time.

Lamn put his coffee cup down and turned to her. "Eve, I respect any decision you make, but I'm curious. Would you tell me why you don't want to see Tark? I thought you had feelings for him?"

He had asked very gently and conversationally, and it just felt like what Eve thought a normal family conversation might sound like between a father and his daughter; even if the father looked more like an older brother.

She sighed and then sipped her coffee before answering. "I do have feelings for him. It's killing me to send him away."

"Then why do it?" He asked, surprised.

"Because of his 'obligations.'" She made air quotes around her coffee cup with her fingers.

Lamn looked even more confused. "Eve, I'm just trying to understand, which obligations are you talking about? Specifically?" Again, he asked very gently and non-judgmentally.

She shot him a side-eye. "Are you really going to make me spell this out? Look, I don't know how things are done here in the Summer Court, whether people have multiple wives or families, or whatever. But I only ever want to be a one and only. I don't share. And I won't be a second choice or a side dish." She sipped her coffee and stared straight ahead.

At this, he turned and faced her fully.

"Eve, I have no idea what you are talking about. We don't have polygamous relationships here, as a norm, well, there are a few species of fae.... The point is, I don't see what any of that has to do with Tark: he's single. No wife, no kids, never married."

Eve sprayed a mouthful of coffee all over Lamn's kitchen window. Her cheeks burned a deep red as she grabbed napkins and began sopping up the dripping coffee on the window and on Lamn's shirt. Lamn threw his head back and laughed, he nearly fell out of his chair because he laughed so hard. Eve was deeply embarrassed, but within a few seconds couldn't help laughing at Lamn's laughter... within minutes they were both holding their middles with tears running down their face, laughing.

As they both started winding down and getting control of themselves Lamn looked over at Eve as he again moved a lock of her hair out of her eyes. "Whatever gave you the idea he was married?"

Eve felt her face turn full-on RED with embarrassment. Yet again she had misread the situation.

"Uh... well... sometimes 'obligations' is a code word for family... at least I thought it was. It made sense. When he distanced himself when we first got here, and then he didn't want to stay, and then he said he couldn't get away from me..."

"So you did hear him the other night?"

"Oh yeah, I heard."

"And you thought he wanted you for a mistress on the side? Did you think I would have given him a chance to talk to you if that's what I knew he was going to ask for?"

Eve stared at him blankly, because, yeah... that was what had gone through her mind. Suddenly she felt really shitty.

Lamn took one of her hands into his, sighing deeply. "Eve, this is all my fault. I got so caught up in finding you and getting to have you here with me, that I forget that this is all new to you.

"Not just me: Fae,... everything.

"It wasn't fair of me to just expect you to suddenly need a father, after living without one your entire life. It wasn't fair of me to expect you to trust me instantly, just because we're related. And it wasn't fair of me to expect you to be able to read our minds to understand how we are feeling or thinking when you don't even know what the social norms are yet. This is all my fault, and I'm sorry. I want to fix this.

"So first, let me ask you this: do you want the chance to be with Tark?"

She looked up at him, suddenly feeling like a little girl looking up at her daddy. "Yes, I really do." She held back the tears that wanted to blossom on her cheeks.

"OK, first things first. We have to go and pay him a visit before he's gone. Come on."

He swatted her on the leg playfully as he jumped out of his chair. She followed him through the halls until he came to his office door, and then she followed him inside wondering what he was getting. He went to the side of the room and opened a cabinet door, showing her that inside was a swirling vortex, a portal.

She groaned as he held her hand and pulled her inside with him.

38

Tark

The long walk home did nothing to calm Tark's inner turmoil. It was only made worse by the knowledge that it was all his own doing. He should have talked to her, at least let her know he wanted to know her better, instead of assuming what was best for her. He had no right to make that decision for her. Now, he had only himself to blame if she hated him.

Instead of heading home, he changed direction and headed for the garrison headquarters. He knew there was no sleep in store for him, so he might as well get ready for the mission. If he was lucky, he could just bury himself in the work, and maybe over time he would stop thinking about her.

Fat chance.

The garrison was always bustling with activity. He stopped in the office for a copy of the mission report and then went to the armory to grab any weapons or provisions they would need. There wasn't really a lot for him to do, but it was still better than sitting at home, lost in his misery.

As luck would have it, his group was already pulling together pro-visions to bring to the safe house they would work out of, so he lent a hand. Someone would call out an item, he would go to the shelf and pull it, call out the serial number, and then put it in the cases to take along. There was no time to see her eyes in his mind or hear her final verdict. Minutes became hours, as they worked through the night.

The sun wasn't up yet when the group leader indicated that the initial group should head out in advance, and set up the safe house for the arrival of the team. Tark volunteered to go ahead with them. He needed to get away from the Summer Court, and from his thoughts.

...And, from her.

Lamn

Lamn and Eve dropped into a small room, Eve literally so. Lamn picked her up and tried not to chuckle as she grumbled about portal travel. They walked into a hallway, where they were met by Tark's housekeeper Naya. She was a kind-looking woman with deep chocolate-colored eyes, and a friendly smile.

A quick conversation with her informed them that Tark had not returned to the house, but that he had sent word to have his travel bag delivered to the garrison late the night before.

Eve looked panic-stricken.

Lamn asked Naya to use Tark's calling glass, and Eve turned to him with an eyebrow raised. As Naya walked into the next room, Lamn placed his hand on the small of Eve's back (*Just like Tark*) and they followed behind. Naya left, asking Lamn to let her know if there was anything else she could do for him.

Lamn walked to the small table in the middle of the room with a mirror on it and sat at the chair in front of it. Eve just looked on, confused.

"We don't have cell phones here," Lamn explained, as he waved his hand over the front of the glass as if he was cleaning it.

A face appeared in the glass: a male fae in a uniform.

"Garrison Headquarters, 3QR. Quor speaking."

"Quor, This is Lord Vassal. I'm looking for Tark, he was due to leave for a mission to Earth today."

Quor looked through his manifests and finally seemed to find what he was looking for.

"Ah yes, Tark was scheduled to go with the first wave this morning–"

"OH THANK GOD!" Eve breathed beside him.

"But he chose to leave with the prep group last night, instead."

Eve dropped her head into her hands. But Lamn continued.

"Quor, can I ask you to take a message for me? It's very important. Can you ask Tark to get in touch with me as soon as he possibly can? Give it to his team leader to bring with the first wave?"

"Yes, my Lordship."

And the conversation was over. The mirror was just a mirror.

Eve

Eve really wanted to have a conversation with Lamn about why he had never told her they had the equivalent of videophones, but the huge hole she felt in her heart at knowing that Tark was gone, and probably hated her now, took all of her attention.

"There's nothing else we can do," Lamn said and took Eve home again. She was miserable and was sure Tark was too.

Eve hid in her room most of the day, to be alone with her thoughts, but Lamn managed to lure her out at dinnertime. Eve's face dropped when she saw the table in the Greenhouse set for two, clearly remembering their meal for three the previous night, but she carried on with grace and sat. Lamn had cooked a few more local dishes for her to try and he laid out his plan. He wanted to educate her about Fae, and what she could expect if she stayed.

Eve looked up from her plate in shock. It was the first time Lamn had said "if" she stayed. His eyes met hers, confused as to what he had said to upset her, but instead of telling him, she pushed her chair back and rounded the table to hug his shoulders.

Leaning over his shoulder she said, "I'm not going anywhere." His hands came up to cover hers over his chest.

"I'm glad."

In her heart, she had finally found family... even if she and Tark were still in question.

The lessons began with cuisine.

Two days later Eve was reading through some of the books Lamn had provided her for research material. Most of his books were in native Faeish, but he did have a selection that had been translated into several Earth, or other, languages. She was learning about their history when the door opened and Lamn strolled in.

"Have you got a minute?"

When she nodded he continued, "Our 'guest,' Vane, is requesting an audience with me, so I'm going to see what it is he wants. Then I thought you might be interested in seeing that Symphony we discussed the other night?"

Eve knew he was talking about the one he mentioned when Tark was having dinner with them, and her stomach flopped, but there was nothing she could do about that now, except try to make the best of it. Maybe the music would take her mind off of things?

In the meantime, what the hell did Vane want?

She smiled appreciatively and nodded at Lamn, and he turned and left the room.

Lamn

As Lamn climbed down the stairs into the cellar where his 'guests' were being held, he could hear singing as he approached. It had to be Richard. Vane would never sing that badly, in public.

He approached Vane's cell, noting the comforts afforded him in soft carpets and nice bed linens. Although he was locked up, he was far from suffering the elements.

Vane stood immediately to meet him at the barred doors.

"Finally! Can you do NOTHING about this incessant caterwauling? Or is this just one of the tortures I am to endure in your care?"

"I heard that," Was a meek reply from a few cells down.

"Good!" Vane and Lamn replied in unison.

"What is it you want?" Lamn asked, getting straight to the point.

"I wish to bargain with you." Vane had his head held high, arrogantly examining his fingernails, which was truly humorous considering he was standing in a jail cell, nude.

Lamn indicated his naked state. "Just what do you think you have to offer?"

Vane brought his face up to the bars immediately and hissed quietly, "Information, of course. You don't get to be a Lord in the Winter Court without learning a thing or two..."

"And what would you require?"

"Well, my freedom, of course."

"That option is not on the table, I don't even know if your information has any value."

"I wouldn't bring it up if it did not. I do not enjoy these accommodations, and would like to improve my situation, preferably away from the 'howling human.'"

"Then we are at an impasse." Lamn turned to leave.

"WAIT. Wait. Perhaps a... show of faith... as they say? Hmmm?" Vane was reaching through the bars as if he could entice Lamn to return.

Lamn turned but did not walk back. "Go on..."

"Well..." Vane began dramatically, "I know a place on the Earth Plane where there are several hybrids kept for entertainment. You collect them, don't you? This would be many at once, save you several trips..."

Lamn was distrustful. "Why would I believe that? Fae have always brought hybrids back to the Courts. Why would they keep them on the Earth Plane instead?"

Vane nodded. "It's true, in the past we always dutifully brought the hybrids back to the Courts, so that the nobility could take them. But what was in it for us? We did all the hard work. We found them, gathered them, and delivered them. And for our trouble, we were sent for more.

"We never got a pick of the new hybrids until they were used and sullied: all of the fight beaten out of them. Some of us agreed that perhaps WE would take our pick of the best hybrids and keep them for ourselves, a small percentage, only, so that our Lords would never guess. But I know where they are kept. I would show you. For a price."

"No, you would tell us."

"No deal. Either I go, or you'll never find them."

"The ONLY way I would even CONSIDER taking you to the Earth Plane is under compulsion."

"And I would rather rot here next to 'Richard the Limp' than agree to THAT."

Richard's whine floated to them "That's NOT true! I have a medical condition!"

Lamn started walking toward the stairs. "Suit yourself."

Vane stuttered and called out behind him, but Lamn wanted to let him sweat for a while.

If what Vane said was true, and they did have a stronghold of hybrids, the garrison would want to know. But no reasonable fae, in his right mind, would voluntarily give his true name and allow himself to be compelled. And there was no way he was letting that rat of a fae out of that cell without an airtight leash.

39

Lamn

The afternoon continued without incident. Lamn checked in with the garrison, to be sure there was no word from Tark, just in case, and when he was sure there wasn't, he prepared to take Eve to the symphony as promised. He would have loved to have shown her this experience under better circumstances when she was happy and curious. He knew she would be blown away.

But, perhaps there was value in this experience serving as a distraction. It might lift her spirits.

After a quick dinner, Lamn and Eve took the carriage to the arena where the symphony would play. It was a large oval marble building, several stories high, with arches and columns ringing the outside at each level, resembling the Roman Colosseum of the Earth. The structure itself was massive and impressive.

Inside, there was riser seating, so that each tier had a good view of the stage. The stage itself was at one end, and had a fabric awning built over it which resembled a clamshell, to enhance the acoustics. As Fae used no technology, the awning was spelled to multiply and distribute the sound effect to everyone present.

Eve

Dusk was quickly approaching, and torches lit around the walkways blazed. Eve and Lamn took their seats near the stage in a private box, as the musicians were tuning their instruments. Most of the instruments Eve recognized, even if she didn't know their names, but there were a handful that looked alien to her. She pointed and asked Lamn about each one until finally, the conductor walked onto the middle of the stage. The applause was instantaneous and filled the packed arena.

Eve sat on the edge of her seat, filled with excited anticipation, as the first few notes rose through the air, only to be followed by a fuller, deeper sound as more instruments joined in. The conductor flourished his baton in steady rhythmic flows, and the sounds wound through the air like a draft of fresh-scented wind, curling and tickling the crowd as it went.

At first, Eve thought she was imagining the sensations, but as the sound grew deeper and richer, she had to admit that it seemed to move through her, and pull her along for a sensory journey. She was smelling fragrant blossoms and then feeling the tiny silky petals as they slid past her cheeks and lips. The percussion lent an earthy feel of trees splitting under pressure, the concussive force moving her back into her seat. She smelt the fresh forest after rain, and felt the humidity on her skin, as the music wove its tale. In the air there was the faintest hint of color, light, sparkle, dark, and movement: all of it in time with the chords and harmony of the music as it played through the crowd like a summer breeze through the long grass, carrying every last body along with it. It was incredible!

Eve turned to Lamn to find him watching her with a smile, instead of the wonder that was playing out before them. Her heart was full of gratitude, and she couldn't stop the gentle tears of happy overwhelm as they rose to her eyes. He squeezed her hand, and they both returned to watching and experiencing the miracle that was fae music at its best for the remainder of the evening.

Mornings were getting easier for Eve, she no longer woke with a start wondering where she was. She was really starting to feel like she was finally home. That conscious thought was quickly followed by a squeezing in her heart as she realized that Tark was still away, but she was determined that she was going to do her best to be happy.

This is only temporary. He will be back, and we will work this out.

This was her new mantra. She wanted to start her new life without fear and depression.

After her morning hygiene ritual, she met Lamn in his usual spot by the kitchen window, coffee cup in hand. They exchanged a smile and a nod and sat peacefully drinking their coffee for a few moments of peace.

Then Eve remembered her question from the day before.

"What did Vane want?"

Lamn

Lamn turned to her, "What anyone in his position wants: his freedom. I told him that wasn't on the table."

Eve considered this for a moment before adding, "And what was he willing to offer in exchange?"

Lamn smiled proudly and noted to himself that his daughter was already wise to some of the ways of the fae.

"He claims to have the location of a stronghold on Earth, where several hybrids are being held. He claims he will lead us there."

"But not simply tell us." It was stated, not asked. Again, Lamn smiled proudly.

"Correct."

"And you said?..."

"No."

With that, they both got lost in their thoughts and coffee for several moments, until Lamn began to work through his mental process verbally.

"I will have to notify the garrison. I am worried that they will not have the same motivation to keep Vane secured when facing the potential for several hybrids in one mission, the more hybrids, the greater the chance they would be willing to risk it, I suppose."

"And you wouldn't?"

"No. It's shortsighted. We could get a thousand hybrids in this trip, and he would have gathered a thousand more, left to his own devices.

I'd want him compelled before I even let him out of that cell, but I don't have his true name, and, regardless, it may not be up to me."

At this Eve turned to face Lamn. "Is THAT why they always stated my full name when they tried to compel me?" This was news to her.

Lamn looked horrified but quickly recovered. He didn't relish considering all of the ways she may have been abused while in the Winter Court. He quickly picked up on her statement.

"*Tried* to compel you?"

"Yeah, compulsions don't work on me, remember? At the diner, I saw through your glamor, and didn't do what you wanted me to do."

Lamn stared at her, shocked. At the diner, they had set up a low-level compulsion, which would work on most hybrids, as they didn't have any defense against it. He would never attempt a compulsion on a full fae without the true name to make it binding, otherwise, they could simply refuse to comply if they were of any power at all. And he had never heard of anyone, hybrid or fae, who had been able to simply ignore a true name compulsion.

Until now.

"May... may I try? I've never seen it done." He asked her tentatively, not wanting to scare her.

"Yeah, go ahead. It won't work."

"*Eve Sherman, you will fetch me another cup of coffee.*"

The air grew dense, and the oxygen-sucking feeling gripped her, but Eve did nothing but smirk.

"Get your own damn coffee. And while you're up, get me one too?" At this, she laughed.

Lamn's jaw dropped. In all of his centuries, he had never heard of a fae being able to disregard a true name compulsion. He had a new appreciation for just how powerful Eve must truly be.

He suddenly remembered the last time he had heard her play the piano, and a thought occurred to him.

"Eve, would you be willing to play the piano for me?"

She turned to him, her eyebrow raised in question. "Right now?"

"If you don't mind, yes. I'd like to... check something."

"And you need me to play to check it?" She looked like she didn't have a clue what he was looking for. She nodded, and they both got up with their coffees still in hand and made their way to the music room.

Once there, Eve made herself comfortable on the bench, and Lamn took a seat nearby.

"Do you need sheet music?" He was getting ready to get up and get some for her, when she shook her head, no.

"I mean, I can read it, but I just like to let whatever music wants to come out of me work its way out." She suddenly looked self-conscious.

He simply nodded to her and sat back, and Eve closed her eyes and took a cleansing breath to get out of her own head.

She put her fingers on the keys, turning inward, perhaps to see which emotion wanted to speak to her through the music today, and then seemed to find something waiting to be explored.

Her fingers flew over the keys. Notes rang in the air like twinkling stars, seeming to laugh and play. They dipped and swayed, and rolled around one another fondly.

Lamn's gasp startled her eyes open, and she saw the gentle lights frolicking in the air before they dissipated with the ending of her playing. She pulled her hands back from the piano in alarm.

"It's ok, Eve," Lamn encouraged her. He seemed awestruck and delighted, his smile taking his whole face. He shook his head at himself.

He should have known. He should have recognized it before, the last time he heard her play.

Eve didn't move, just looked at him with worried eyes. She had never seen anything like this happen when she played before.

He spoke to her gently, seeming to understand her fear.

"Eve, you are in the Summer Court now. You are at the source of the power that is imbued in all fae, in your own blood. Your body heals faster here. And your natural gifts of the elements will start presenting themselves.

"I remember the last time I heard you play, the violence of the music seemed to affect the room and the atmosphere; I just didn't put it together. I should have realized that being a hybrid, you would have the element of Spirit. Spirit affects the arts. Spirit Hybrids tend to make the best artists: whether music, painting, writing..."

His eyes sparkled with adoration for her. She just sat mutely, waiting for him to break it down for her. Lamn sat back in his chair.

"I see another lesson is in order."

40

Eve

Lamn brought Eve into one of the many comfortable parlors and grabbed a few books from the library on the way in. Eve's reading list was growing exponentially, but she was eager to learn. She felt like she had a lifetime of learning to catch up on, and she wanted to be knowledgeable about her new world when Tark finally returned. She didn't want to be naive or misunderstand. Lamn sat in a comfortable chair to the left whereas Eve sat on a long sofa with her feet curled under her.

Lamn cleared his throat and opened a page in one of his books to begin.

"Our history begins in mythology, much as it does on Earth. Our gods came from the stars to settle on the Earth Plane: at that time all creatures lived together and shared one space.

"Each of the Gods represented an element. There was Serp of Matter, Lis of Air, Frek of Fire, Nix of Ether, and Sobon of Water: they were all the children of Sopha, goddess of Spirit. Each God was free to create his own beings of his own element: for instance, the trolls were of Matter; pixies were of the air; salamanders were of Fire; and kelpies were of Water. I'm using your English or Earth names for these creatures so you will recognize them. There are many, many more."

Eve cut in, "Like Armoniel. Hey, which god created Faeries?"

"I'm getting to that.

"All of these elemental creatures lived in harmony, killing only to survive, or for territory, but otherwise just coexisting.

"The elemental gods got bored with these creatures, they wanted something more. They wanted to create something more magnificent, but not as strong as they were, as Sopha had done; and so they got together and created the Fae.

"The Fae were different, in that they were imbued with the power of five elements, instead of just one, so they had more power. But Serp secretly held back with his gift to the fae, leaving them vulnerable to certain minerals, like iron, which is a poison to them.

"Instead, Serp wanted more power for himself, and decided that he wanted a race all of his own to set himself apart as a god, and perhaps set him higher than his brothers and sisters. So he created a race and imbued it with the power of Matter... but because he did so alone, he also dipped into the power of the planet itself, tying the creatures to it. His creatures were humans.

"Humans were crafty, but they lacked the power to manifest what you would call magic, the way the Fae do because they lacked multiple elemental power sources. If you look in your mythos, you will see the snake represented in all of the old legends. That was Serp.

"Like Serp, humans hungered for power, but with no natural weapons or magics, they instead manifested technology. Where some fae may have horns or claws, others may have spells. Humans had spears, then swords, and ultimately guns. Where we use elemental power to get things done, humans have technological machines."

Eve interjected, "So what does this have to do with music?"

"Patience...

"Sopha was very troubled when she saw what Serp had done. He had created a race that would follow in his footsteps, and shed blood in their quest for power and domination over all things, killing needlessly.

"As a mercy to these new creatures, she imbued them with her own power, the power of Spirit, so that they could decide to reach beyond their violent blueprints of life to a higher source of power and compassion, and with these, came the arts and the love of all beauty. Your mythological images of winged beings of light represent Sopha.

"To a lesser degree, all fae have some trace element of Spirit and Sopha, because she was the mother of the gods who created us. The reason our art and music is so multidimensional, compared to that of humans who have a stronger connection to that element, is that we can combine it with the other five elements. Our music is multisensory.

"Don't get me wrong: there is a lot of amazing human music and art. However, when performed by a fae, it evolves into so much more!"

"But this is all just myth, right?" Eve cast a doubtful look at Lamn.

"Well, all myth has its roots in truth, does it not?"

Eve considered this for a few moments.

It did make sense. It explained why everything in Fae was so 'extra.'

She looked to Lamn again, her hand raised as if to hold her thought. "So, why are there two Planes now? You said we shared the planet."

"Ah, yes, I did. At first, Fae and Humans lived together, with all other creatures. But the fae quickly learned from the humans how to desire: more control, more power, and more material things. Wars followed, and Sopha was distraught at the destruction the races leveled on one another, and any innocent creature that got in the way. She tore the dimension in half and decreed that the Fae would live on one side, and the Humans would live on the other.

"The elemental gods were not happy, and felt that they were being micromanaged, and so all but Serp created portals in secret, to allow visitation. The portals were never big, nor strong enough to allow for an army to invade; just enough to give the fae an upper hand. This was their revenge on Serp for overstepping in his quest for power."

"So you're saying I have matter and spirit elements?"

"No, I'm saying you have all six. But it's not just what elements you have, it's how strongly you can access them. Most fae, in theory, have all six, but matter and spirit are weak at best, and they may not be able to utilize the other four to their full potential.

"You have an extraordinarily strong tie to your Spirit power. We have yet to ascertain how strongly you connect to the other five."

Eve felt a shock of excitement shoot through her.

I mean, who didn't want to be told that they may be able to do magic? Let the experiments begin!

Eve got to see firsthand how the fae used their elements in daily practical ways. Ama, one of the housekeepers, demonstrated how she used her gift of matter and water to spell palm-sized stones so that when they were dropped into tubs of water they would convulse like an earthquake. Add laundry and soap, and voila! Instant washing machine!

So why the fuck were they having ME wash by hand in the Winter Court?!

Similar combinations of air and fire were used to dry the laundry quickly.

Ama walked Eve through the house, pointing out all of the ways the elements were combined to make life easier. She also pointed out that it wasn't an endless supply of energy, every use of power came with a price. It took a toll on the user. They had to manage their time and power to complete tasks and not leave themselves depleted, or they could get very sick. Eve remembered how tired she felt, after she had played the piano, and made a mental note to work on her endurance.

Eve was finally coming to understand the intricacies of this new world she lived in. At first, it had seemed so primitive, devoid of technology. But now, she saw the brilliance with which they had created their own 'devices.' She was eager to learn where her own strengths lay.

Tark

Tark squatted near the base of a tree, watching the house from his hidden position in the undergrowth. He had been there for hours, in the pouring rain, and tropical heat. He was soaked and pissed off.

Who's fucking idea was it to join this mission, anyway?! Oh yeah, it was MINE. Add that to the long list of things I have recently fucked up.

He hadn't been sleeping well, and he didn't seem to have an appetite. He tried hard to get posted in places where there was a lot of action or a lot of things to do. A stakeout in a torrential downpour was exactly NOT what he wanted.

But there he was, expected to sit perfectly still with his thoughts and just watch, NOT think about Eve, NOT remember her smile, NOT remember how his heart beat out of his chest when Armoniel brought her back alive, NOT remember her begging eyes when she asked him to stay... and definitely NOT think about the night she said no, and walked out of his life. He was trying so hard to move forward or at least stay busy. It didn't help that the team leader who arrived with the first wave had given him a message to contact Lamn.

As if I didn't have enough going through my mind already! Lamn knew it would be almost impossible for me to get a message back, and even if I did, it would be one-sided. I would have to wait for a reply to THAT. To keep the portals secure, back-and-forth communication is a serious no-no. So now I have plenty of time to obsess over what the hell Lamn would want to talk to him about. Was he pissed at me too? Was something wrong back home?

Tark just wanted to scream and tear his hair out, but he WAS still on a stakeout... and would be for the foreseeable future.

Fuck.My.Life.

41

Eve

Eve was surprised not to see Lamn in his usual morning spot by the kitchen window; however, his coffee was there, untouched. She had just finished making her own cup when Lamn walked in, clearly flustered and running his hand through his dark green locks.

"Trouble in paradise?" She asked, before sitting down and sipping her coffee.

Lamn sighed deeply. He did that a lot these days.

"Fucking Vane again. He's trying anything and everything he can think of to try to get me to release him. It's only a matter of time before I have to go to the garrison about him anyway, I guess."

"How did you get him to stop today?" Eve looked over her coffee at him.

"I threatened to give Richard a guitar to accompany his singing."

Eve, again, spit a mouthful of coffee all over the kitchen window, this time laughing uncontrollably. When she had finished cleaning up her mess, and gone to get another cup, she voiced her thoughts to Lamn.

"So he claims to know some secret hiding location for hybrids, right?"

Lamn just nodded.

"What if that was what he was talking to Rodolfo about when he had me locked in the cottage?"

Lamn perked up immediately. He hadn't even remembered about Rodolfo.

"I mean, if you could get your hands on Rodolfo, you might not even need Vane, and Rodolfo seemed a lot less willing to go along with the plan in the first place."

Lamn jumped from his chair and strode to where Eve stood in a few quick steps, before hugging her and lifting her off of the ground, almost spilling her coffee all over himself.

"Eve, you are a genius! I need to go! I have some contacts to make!"

And with that Lamn rushed out of the room so quickly that he didn't realize he had, again, left his full cup of coffee sitting by the window.

Eve took her fresh cup and was about to sit down with it when Ama stepped into the kitchen and announced she had a visitor. Eve just stared at her blankly.

Who the hell knows I'm here? Well, only one way to find out...

When Eve rounded the corner and saw Armoniel she broke into a run and threw herself at him squealing. He caught her in a tight embrace, that she refused to let go of, even when he seemed ready. When she finally let him go he held her at arms' length.

"I hope I am not arriving at an inopportune time?"

Eve didn't say a word, just smiled broadly and grabbed his arm to drag him into the house where they could talk. She hadn't realized how much she missed Armoniel. They settled into the greenhouse, and Armoniel looked Eve over.

"You are settling in well here? Are you enjoying it? Are the fae treating you well? You know you could tell me if anything was wrong..."

He seemed very concerned for her welfare and her safety, and she found that very touching. She had her very own guardian angel.

"Everything is fine, Armoniel... well, not everything... I mean, Tark and I had a misunderstanding, but other than that, YES. I am loving my new life here! Lamn is very good to me and... Oh, I should tell you,... he's my father." She seemed to cover the gamut of emotions from disappointed, to happy, to serious in one breath.

Armoniel nodded at her, "Yes, I am aware of your paternity." He stated it as a fact.

Eve stopped with the shock of it.

"YOU KNEW?! And you didn't TELL me?!"

Armoniel froze with terror. He hadn't predicted she would react that way.

Lamn

Lamn walked in at just that moment and had to smother a laugh. He was looking at one of the most powerful beings in the Universe squirming like a teenage boy. Eve clearly had him wrapped around her little finger. Armoniel looked at Lamn imploringly, and Lamn spoke up to get him off the hook.

"Eve, Armoniel is a Grigori, a Watcher. He knew before I did, but he did me the courtesy of not saying anything until I could introduce myself, and tell you myself. It was for my sake."

Armoniel sent him a huge thank you with only his facial expression, before turning back to Eve. "And I have my own admission, which I have withheld from you until you had a chance to reunite with your sire."

His eyes were downcast, and Lamn felt for him. Having seen how she reacted to the previous information he had omitted, he was sure there was going to be an explosion with what he revealed next. Lamn prepared himself as well.

Hadn't he felt just the same way when he had his 'chat' with her?

Eve's posture let them know she was livid, her arms were crossed over her chest, and she was staring daggers at Armoniel. Lamn stood beside him in support, as Armoniel confessed his truth.

"Eve, (sigh) There is no easy way to say this, other than to just state it. I am your grandsire. Ruth was my daughter."

At first, Eve's jaw dropped and her eyes opened wide, and then she threw back her head and howled with laughter. Armoniel and Lamn just looked at each other in shock, until Lamn finally said, "Apparently, this is how she takes this kind of news."

In between guffaws, Eve managed to squeak out, "You... You... and ... NANCY?!" And then she was howling with laughter again.

Lamn stepped back as he felt the anger and the energy rising in Armoniel in response. Even Eve seemed to notice the shift in the atmosphere.

"YOU WILL NOT DISRESPECT NANCY!"

Now it was Eve and Lamn looking at each other, stunned.

Armoniel composed himself and continued. "Eve, I know your opinion of Nancy is low, and I understand why. But please remember that she is a beautiful child of Spirit too; at least, at one point in her life, she was good and innocent. She has suffered great cruelty to become the person you know her to be today. Please do not judge her harshly, you do not know what she has endured. And yes, Nancy and I sired Ruth.

"I watched over Ruth all of her life, sharing my celestial protections with her, even though I had to remain invisible, out of respect for Nancy... I did the same for you."

Before Eve could even speak Lamn was already asking Armoniel, "What sort of celestial protections?"

Armoniel turned to him and answered, "My gift from Sopha was protection from enchantments, and that is what I shared with my line."

Lamn's eyes lit up. "Enchantments: like compulsion, and glamors?"

"Yes, those would fall under enchantments, I suppose."

An awkward silence fell in the room as Lamn looked between Eve and Armoniel, Armoniel couldn't meet anyone's eyes, and Eve seemed fit to be tied.

Eve

Eve looked between her father and, apparently, her grandfather. She was filled to overflowing with so many emotions, but the betrayal of being the last one to know something SO personal, and so vital to her, made it hard for her to move past it.

I know I'm being petty. I know I should just be happy to have found out. I mean, he DID save me. But if he's really a 'Watcher' then he knows... he

KNOWS how hard I've struggled without family. All this time... all this time... he was RIGHT there, and never said a word!

The tears flowed down Eve's cheeks, which only aggravated her more. She didn't want to look helpless now. Not after they had withheld her family from her.

Lamn spoke quietly, calmly. "Eve, please understand that the Grigori are bound by rules. While on Earth they are not allowed to interfere with humans. Sopha created them to keep watch, to help maintain the balance: she didn't want them to become a weapon to be used against humanity, so she forbade them from interacting. He could not have told you."

"But he COULD have sex with Nancy?!" She bit out bitterly through her tears.

Armoniel looked anguished as he hissed in pain between his teeth.

"No. I broke the commandment for a tormented human girl who had suffered her entire life. I selfishly granted her the one request she asked of me. And Eve, I have suffered for it. Everyone has suffered for it. Were it not for the fact that you are in the Summer Court, even now, I would not be able to make this confession to you.

"Eve, if the other Grigori knew about you and your mother, they would take steps to eliminate you. I could not bear the thought of any harm coming to either of you, and so my own punishment was to watch over you both, your whole lives, and never be able to get to know you or have a relationship with you. I had to watch you assume I was an irresponsible human who had abandoned you both.

"Please forgive me, Eve. I was selfish, and that was not your fault. I am sorry that you have had to suffer because of it. Please know that I have always loved you, and I have never stopped trying to be a part of your life, no matter how distant or how small." His voice cracked with emotion, so at odds with the image of the imperial angel he normally presented.

Eve walked to Armoniel and wrapped him in a big hug, even as her crying grew to become body spasms and sobbing into his robe. She couldn't hold her grudge against the power of his words. It was all that she had ever wanted, for the men in her life to come back, to claim her and take responsibility for their roles. It was even better that they had come back with only love for her; there were no excuses, no evading or gaslighting. He was accepting responsibility, he was validating her.

Armoniel had never abandoned her, he had endangered himself just to try to protect her and her mother. He had done it out of love.

Was it shitty? Yes, it was.

But it was done for the right reasons, and right now, she just wanted her family. Armoniel froze for a moment, unclear if she was still angry with him, or accepting of him: but as she tightened her hug around him he seemed to relax, and reciprocate. He had his own tears in his eyes.

42

Eve

Eve, the fae, and the angel made the oddest-looking family that Eve could possibly imagine, and despite her misgivings about how she had discovered her heritage, she sat with them in a parlor by the fireplace, and just basked in the unconditional love of family.

This.

This is what she had always wanted; what she felt was missing from her life. She suddenly wondered how Nancy was. She suddenly wondered what could have possibly happened to her to twist her mind the way it had. And she felt just a little bit of guilt for how she treated Nancy, and for leaving her alone.

Armoniel interrupted her thoughts to ask about the troubles with Tark she had mentioned, and Lamn helped to fill him in on the misunderstandings between them. Eve just wrung her hands as her cheeks flamed warmer and warmer. She felt so foolish. Armoniel nodded in understanding; clearly, the Watcher had seen similar voids in communication between humans.

"Perhaps this is one thing I can assist with?" He looked at Eve for her reaction.

It was immediate. Eve lit up like a Christmas tree.

"I could find him, maybe pass along a message for you?"

She threw her arms around him, ready to start crying all over again.

Eve was not used to having people who cared about her and who were willing to help without expecting something from her in return.

She didn't know how she could repay the kindness she was receiving. While it wasn't expected, she knew she would find a way.

Ama stepped into the room to inform Lamn that he had a message and then excused herself. As Lamn got up to receive it, Armoniel rose too.

"I should take my leave, I still have my duties to attend to. But I will stop and deliver your message."

At that Lamn turned to him and said, "Walk me to my office, I can give you their location."

Eve stood and gave Armoniel one last long hug. "You'll visit, right?"

She felt needy, but with the joy of finding family was the fear that they could be ripped away again. She wasn't holding back anymore, she would be sure to express her feelings.

Armoniel smiled down warmly at her. "Granddaughter, you could not keep me away." He placed a gentle kiss on her forehead.

After she released Armoniel from his hug, Lamn led him out the door, and Eve had renewed hope that things would only keep getting better from here.

Lamn

Lamn watched Armoniel dissipate in the air and then went to his mirror. Melrick's face was waiting in the glass, patiently.

"Melrick," Lamn began.

"Lamn. I have news. I have not been able to locate the one called Rodolfo, but my people continue searching for him discreetly. However, I may have better news for you. As I delivered 'Vane's' remains with the 'hybrid's' to Lord Jeffers, he saw fit to transfer his estate to me. I am in the process of searching for any sign of his true name, in the event that we cannot find Rodolfo. I also have discrete inquiries in the courts for that information, as well, though I don't hold much hope we would recover it there."

Lamn nodded and replied, "Your having inherited Vane's estate was a great stroke of luck for me, and I'm sure it's a great boon to you. Congratulations. The rest of the information is much as I would have expected. Again, I cannot tell you how much I appreciate your continued assistance. If we can infiltrate this group of rogue fae from the Winter Court, I will, of course, turn them over to you, to use for whatever leverage you wish."

"And that is greatly appreciated," Melrick responded. "It will take only a few more grand acts of loyalty, I think, to elevate my status to a much more comfortable level. Once there, I can leave all of this nasty business of hunting hybrids behind. I will send word, once I have more to offer."

It was short and sweet, and Lamn could only hope that Melrick would come through for him again.

Tark

Tark was heading back through the swampy woodlands when he became aware that he wasn't alone. He easily pulled the bowie knife from its sheath at his belt in a fluid movement and breathed in the scents around him. The telltale scent of ozone had him replacing his knife, and looking for Armoniel.

In a split-second Armoniel appeared in front of him, confirming his senses. Tark knew they were alone, as he was on his way back to the safehouse through the uninhabited Everglade swamps. He reached out his forearm in greeting, but instead of clasping his arm back, Armoniel pulled him in for a tight hug.

Okay... that was uncharacteristic of the Grigori.

"Tark, my friend... er... may I call you my friend?" Tark smiled at his awkwardness and nodded in the affirmative.

"Armoniel," he greeted, with a laugh.

"I have just come from a visit with my granddaughter, and she tells me that there is some miscommunication between you. I thought I would help by relaying a message." He smiled warmly at Tark, whose brows rose in confusion.

"Wait, I'm sorry. Armoniel, did you say your granddaughter– You have a granddaughter? Do *I* know your granddaughter?"

Since when did Grigori have families?!

"Yes, Tark, I believe you know her well. But not well enough, I'm afraid. Eve. Eve is my granddaughter."

Tark's eyes flashed with surprise, and his jaw dropped, despite all of his training. In a fraction of a second, his mind was going back over every moment they had ever spent together, looking for clues to her relationship with Armoniel. Lamn had told them she was nephila, he had just never put it together... it was obvious now.

Had Lamn known?

"Eve is your granddaughter?" he asked, swallowing a lump in his throat, suddenly feeling very nervous about this visit.

If Eve was unhappy with him, this Grigori could wipe him from existence. Is that what Lamn had been trying to get in touch with him about?! To warn him?

Armoniel chuckled at seeing Tark's suddenly terrified expression.

"Tark, I am here as a friend. I have come to let you know that Eve has asked me to express her regret in her handling of your conversation before you left. She admits that she acted hastily and based on mis-information." At this he leaned in and spoke near his ear conspiratori-ally, "She was under the impression you were married with a family and wished to keep her as a mistress."

All color drained from Tark's face. He could not imagine where she would have gotten that impression: first, that he was married and dis-loyal; second, that he would ever hold her in such low-esteem that he would consider keeping her for entertainment and nothing more. He was both mortified and enraged simultaneously.

Armoniel continued merrily on, completely missing Tark's facial cues that his world had just been turned sideways.

"She does, in fact, have a deep fondness for you, and expressed how pained she was at sending you away. She does not want you to 'hate her,' in her own words. And she is hopeful that if the two of you were able to meet face to face, at some point in time in the future, you would give her the opportunity to express her apology herself."

Armoniel seemed very happy with himself for having been able to help in this way, and he quickly followed it with this:

"Now, speaking as her grandfather, if I should ever discover that you would, in fact, be disloyal or disrespectful to her, or hurt her in any way, I would end your existence without an ounce of remorse. Are we clearly understood?"

He was dead serious.

Tark just stood in shock, and could only nod, dumbfounded, his jaw again hanging open.

"Very well!"

Back was the smiling friendly Armoniel, his serial killer doppelganger, momentarily forgotten. "It has been a pleasure speaking with you again, my friend. I wish you good tidings for your mission here on Earth."

And just like that, he was gone, fading into the air.

Tark just stared for several long moments at the air where the Grigori had been standing before finally coming to a mental conclusion about what had just transpired.

Holy fuck.

Eve

The next few days were uneventful, and maybe even a little boring for Eve. She had found a comfortable chair in the library and had made a study nest there. On the table next to her were thirteen books about various aspects of fae life: culture, history, clothing, government, mythology...

She spent most of every day in her chair, wrapped in a soft comforter, with a book split open in her lap. When she tired of one subject, she would mark the page and open another that had already been marked where she stopped previously. She had been rotating books for hours. Her eyes were starting to cross from so much reading.

The doorbell sounded downstairs, and Eve decided that she needed a break anyway, so she would go investigate and see who was calling. She marked her page, threw the comforter off, and quickly headed for the door. By the time she got downstairs, Lamn was standing in the entryway reading a parchment. Next to him stood a buxom fae woman with brown curls gently spilling from her cap, the kind of cap they made the servants wear in the Winter Court.

Eve stopped dead in her tracks.

Lamn turned and, seeing her at the stairwell, called her over. She cautiously made her way to Lamn, watching the female with curiosity. Lamn filled Eve in quickly.

"Eve, this is Sera. She was formerly employed by Vane and has come to the Summer Court seeking asylum, courtesy of Melrick. She graciously agreed to bring me some information to help us in our mission." He held the parchment up victoriously, "Vane's true name!"

Eve's eyes lit up, and a huge smile replaced the unsure frown she had been wearing. She wanted to do a happy dance but managed to squelch the urge.

Sera meekly spoke up, her voice just above a whisper.

"My Lord, I know that it is not my place, but Master Melrick has assured me that you are a most kind fae, and I would like to ask a small favor, if I may?" She seemed to shrink back defensively. Her eyes were wide as she spoke, and there was a small tremor in her voice. It was clear that she was afraid to death to even speak to a fae.

Lamn spoke with the same soothing calm voice he used with Eve when she was fearful. "Of course, Sera! If it is in my power, I would be happy to repay the favor you have done me in delivering this wonderful news."

Sera looked uncertainly at Eve, and then back to Lamn. "Could I be there, My Lord? Could I be present when you compel him? When he wonders who it was who delivered him into your hands?"

Again, she made herself as small as possible, but there was a fire in her eyes that Eve recognized. Eve smiled broadly in understanding and didn't wait for Lamn to answer.

"Of course!" Eve volunteered, looking to Lamn for approval, which he gave with a nod and a smirk.

Not wanting to waste a moment, Lamn looked between the ladies. "Shall we?" He asked with a quirk of an eyebrow and a wave of his arm to indicate the way, and this time, even Sera smiled.

43

Armoniel

Armoniel continued on, as he always had. His Watcher power gave him a broad view over the Earth plane, and with only a thought he could zoom in within his mind's eye, and see specific happenings more clearly. He was in his non-corporeal form, more a being of light than a being of matter, and he existed in an energetic realm that had no space or time. It simply 'was.'

Truthfully, there was much that he simply 'knew,' without needing to watch it, another power he had. But it was the watching, the 'witnessing' that fulfilled his obligation and was the basis of his purpose for existence.

He was always made aware when non-human creatures entered the plane. He had watched with sadness as his beloved humans, as he saw them, were lured away by fae trickery to leave the Earth Plane, and his watchful eye. He was also aware when the elemental creatures managed to cross the threshold, he would watch with great interest. If they simply existed without interference, he would let them be. If they created too much attention or destruction, he would remove them from the Earth Plane. They were not meant to exist there.

He continued his existence, living his purpose. Night became day, day became night.

His dalliance with Nancy had made him understand the human emotion of longing, and as a result of many years living with that emotion, he had come to understand another: futility. Before finding Nancy, he did not understand boredom. He was passionate about his purpose and devoted to Sopha and the humans. But after only a few short human generations, HIS descendants' generations, he now felt something new.

Dissatisfaction.

Watching was no longer enough.

He was still devoted to Sopha, and even more devoted to humanity, but he longed to do more than just watch what happened to them. He wanted to act. He wanted to protect them. And these new feelings brought in him a great sadness, knowing he could not.

So he continued to watch, impotently.

Armoniel became aware of another presence, and soon felt the energy of Samyaza, his leader approaching. He felt blessed to be visited by such a high-ranking Watcher. Samyaza was the first, under Sopha herself. At the same time, he felt the smallest bit of fear in the back of his heart.

What if his disloyalty to his duty was known?

It was not himself he worried about: it was Ruth and Eve. Always, it was Ruth and Eve.

Samyaza took form near him and greeted him in their native fashion, mind to mind, with the holy words of praise for Sopha and the Infinite Intelligence, and words for a welcomed reunion with one another. The Watchers were very childlike in their formation, treachery, and deception were not in their makeup. And their communication reflected this, with no flowery small talk.

Armoniel waited until Samyaza stated his reasons for his visit, and he wasn't kept waiting. "Armoniel, Her Most Compassionate Sopha has asked me to pay you a visit, and to relieve your heart of heaviness."

Armoniel would have frozen if he had a corporeal body at that moment. He knew which "heaviness" Samyaza referred to, so he didn't ask, and instead waited to see what would happen.

Samyaza continued his voice directly within the mind of Armoniel.

"Armoniel, I must confess to you that I am deeply saddened that you did not feel that you could come to me to confess your lapse in discretion. I would not have treated you or your offspring with cruelty. But that is for us.

"My business is on behalf of Her Great Compassion, and she has asked me to relay to you that she gives you, and your line, her blessing. She has seen the great strain it has taken upon your heart to continue to provide for them in secret, and she wishes to have this information be open, that you may suffer no longer. Your line is under her care, and no harm may befall them at the hand of any being of her making. Further, she has given you dispensation, that you may visit and be among them, and know them as your family, as it should be."

Armoniel was overwhelmed with the warmth and love of the message, and what it would mean for Ruth and Eve, and he felt unworthy to be given such an amazing gift, from Sopha herself, for what was ultimately a betrayal on his part.

"And what of my duties? I do not understand, Samyaza. I have broken the commandment of our kind, and I expected to be punished." Armoniel was making himself as humble before his leader as he could.

"Armoniel, do you think you are the only Watcher to know love? It would be different if Sopha knew that you simply enjoyed the pleasure of a human body for lustful reasons, but she has shown me how she has watched you care for your offspring. She knows your heart. No, Armoniel, you will not be punished. You have already suffered a torment greater than Sopha would have wished."

Armoniel had spent his existence believing that what he wanted, what he did, was wrong. That he was wrong. He just couldn't seem to wrap his understanding around what he was now hearing. This was deemed wrong for his entire existence.

"I... I am eternally grateful to Her Great Compassion for this blessing, for which I know I am unworthy. But... I cannot understand. ... Why?"

Armoniel heard the chuckle and felt a small wave of amusement float from Samyaza as he answered. "Armoniel, we are tasked to watch so that we may understand Love. We see the great evils that humans are capable of, and yet we do not grow to hate them, we grow to love them more. We uphold the balance through Love, and it is the greatest expression of Sopha, herself. She will not see it wasted here when it can be expressed so fully to those young ones, who now carry your understanding of Love into the human realm. You should be with them, to guide them in that power, yourself."

In a lifetime of seeing everything, of knowing what may happen next, Armoniel was shocked by this turn of events. He had always assumed that one day his secret would be revealed, as all truths are eventually revealed, and that he would willingly suffer the consequences. If need be, he would beg for mercy for his child and grandchild, who were without fault. But for himself, he understood what would probably happen.

To suddenly be told that he was free of his obligations, of his guilt, and of his constraints that kept him from the women he loved... His energy rang out like a blast in all directions, unstable and intense. The gratitude and the love that poured from him shone like the sun. He was reduced to the very core of his energy, with no thought, no word. He was the expression of Love.

A great sense of pride radiated from Samyaza as he existed within the space with Armoniel. He emitted pleasure that one of his Watchers had truly expanded beyond the purpose they had been given, as Sopha had always hoped they would. But Samyaza still had more to share, before Armoniel returned to his family.

"Armoniel, there is more you should know. Uriel has visited Sopha for guidance, his gift of Prophecy has given him knowledge that troubled him greatly, and Sopha has asked that I share this with you. She would like for you to act on her behalf in this matter, and perhaps to avoid a brutal conflict that might arise if the current patterns and intentions go otherwise unchecked."

Armoniel drew himself back into conscious awareness and gave all of his attention to Samyaza as he continued.

"Uriel has seen the patterns below. There is a wave of darkness in the form of the Winter which moves against humanity and the children of both worlds. For years the Winter has claimed that they have rights to claim the children of both, and we have not interfered as they took them from the Earth Plane.

But now they cross a boundary. They are imprisoning the children of both and claiming rights to them, while still on the Earth Plane where they have no jurisdiction.

"Sopha is aware of your allegiances with the Summer, and that they are planning to move against the Winter to recover the children of both. She would like for you to involve yourself in this, on behalf of the Watchers and their mission to keep the balance. She would like for you to try to avoid the war that is coming, as it would devastate Winter, Summer, and humankind alike."

Armoniel started to speak his acceptance of his role, but Samyaza cut him off.

"Before you agree, you must know one more thing, and you must agree that you will not let it sway you from your mission of peace. Ruth is among the children of both, being held by the Winter."

Armoniel felt his overflowing heart suddenly crack and explode.

44

Lamn

Lamn warned Eve and Sera, as they approached the door to the basement, about the trace amounts of iron in the bars of the cells. There was not enough to physically hurt the captives, just enough to weaken them. However, it could also do the same for them. He wasn't sure how the metals would affect hybrids.

Lamn made his way down the staircase, and he could hear Richard's voice in the background, still singing loudly to while away his time. Eve made a sour face, as the memories of so many of his songs sprang to her mind. Sera made a face like she had smelled something rotten, but said nothing.

They continued down the long staircase, then a hallway, before Lamn motioned them behind him and made the approach to the cell holding Vane. He was immediately on his feet, springing to the bars. With a quick glance, he saw Eve behind Lamn, and a cruel smirk lit his lips.

"Reconsidered then, have you?" His smug air of arrogance was back, and Eve couldn't help herself. She burst out laughing at the sight of the nude fae attempting to pass as royalty. Lamn kept his face composed, perhaps showing just a little annoyance, as he closed in on the bars.

"So it would seem." Lamn reached into a bag, and carefully pulled out a pair of handcuffs. "You will put these on before we release you from the cell."

Vane looked outraged. "You will put me in IRON?"

"We will put you in diluted iron, enough to be sure you can't act against us without you under compulsion." Lamn stood his ground. "Or, you could just stay in the cell and enjoy Richard's concert."

"Hey!" Came the weak response from down the corridor.

Vane was reaching through the bars quickly. "Give those here!" And without further prompt, he quickly snapped them onto his own wrists and then demonstrated that they were on securely.

When Lamn was satisfied that he wouldn't be able to act out magically, he produced the keystone he had removed from Vane's clothing. It seemed a good time to test his theory. And he was rewarded when the cell door clicked and then swung open. Lamn made sure he was in between Vane and the ladies. He ushered Vane ahead of him down a hallway, to a room at the end.

Vane entered cautiously, and finding that it was just a sitting room, proceeded to make himself comfortable in a chair. Lamn followed him in, with Eve right behind. Sera stayed at the doorway, just out of sight. Eve couldn't tell if she was afraid to be seen by Vane, or just waiting for the right time to make her appearance.

Eve turned to Lamn with a smirk on her face. "Dear God. Now that he's had his junk all over that chair, we'll probably need to burn it."

Vane shot her a dirty look, and then seemed to deign her beneath him or his attention.

"Do we need the slaves present for this?" He asked snidely and looked pointedly at Eve.

Lamn was on top of him before Eve could even exhale. "If you EVER speak about my daughter like that again, I shall carve your tongue out with a dull knife."

Eve had never seen Lamn that violent. He was perfectly in control, but his rage filled the room like the smoke from a fire. Vane swallowed hard, still trying to appear in control of the conversation, but he cast unsure glances Eve's way.

"NOW..." Lamn began, taking a step back, "You will tell me where the hybrids are being held."

Lamn pulled out a piece of paper and a pen and put them on the table beside Vane, who rolled his eyes and dropped his hands into his lap with a plop as flesh met flesh.

"I have told you, I will not disclose the location without going there myself."

Eve wandered closer to them. "Is that your final answer?" she asked with a smirk.

"I-.." Vane stopped whatever retort he was going to give Eve, and looked at Lamn warily, before starting again. "I refuse to give you the location without being present at the site myself. That is my final decision." He shot Eve a side-eye and a sneer before returning his attention to Lamn.

Lamn sighed. "Well, that is unfortunate, Vane."

"Yes, cry me a river, and all that. Why have you brought me here, if not to comply with my bargain?"

Lamn paused for effect, looking like he was trying to decide how to deliver some news, knowing it was provoking Vane. And it worked.

"WELL?!" Vane demanded.

Lamn turned to him slowly, almost bored. "Vane, I really tire of you and your attitude. Your version of a bargain really doesn't provide anything for me if you know you can try to escape. While there are others who might not care whether you get out of this or not, I can guarantee you that I have a vested interest in being sure you never get to walk free again. So here's what's going to happen, you are going to tell me the location where the hybrids are being held."

Vane laughed, not a real laugh, a snooty arrogant laugh that he put on for dramatic show. "And when I DON'T?" he asked, airily.

"Oh, but you WILL. *Crank Vane Devons I compel you to divulge the location where the hybrids are being held. At no time will you in any way harm or act against me or anyone with me.*"

Eve started howling with laughter. "CRANK?!!! His true name is CRANK?!" Within seconds she was doubled over laughing, tears rolling down her cheeks.

At the same time, Vane was sputtering and seething with rage.

"HOW?! HOW did you get my true name?!" He was turning purple he was so outraged.

Sera moved into the room and passed Eve, still lost to fits of giggles. She came to stand right in front of Vane, and she saw the exact moment when he realized that she had something to do with the Summer Court getting his name. He didn't know how she had found it, but the look in her eyes said everything.

Vane stared at Sera, unbelieving. He jumped out of his chair, and raised his arms to grab her and throttle her, but his arms just hung frozen in mid-air, the compulsion holding him. He never took his eyes away from hers as he launched into his thoughts on the turn of events.

"YOU... You horrid, ungrateful little bitch! I overlooked your filthy origins! I gave you everything! A job! Attention! I let you service me! I treated you better than you ever deserved, and THIS is how you repay me?!" His eyes were alight with rage, his face contorted, and spittle flew from his lips.

Sera stood her ground. She answered quietly, but firmly. "No, *My Lord*, THIS is how I repay you." She quickly drew her leg back stiffly and then swung it forward with as much force as her fae genetics would lend her, straight into Vane's naked groin. The impact sounded like a ripe melon hitting the hard ground. As Vane fell over with a screech, his eyes bulging, and his body curling in on itself, Eve couldn't help but notice that even Lamn winced and moved his body protectively as well.

Lamn walked to where Vane was curled on the floor whimpering and moaning. "The location," was all he said.

Vane began to cry openly, at first a few tears of pain, but soon he was wailing like a newborn baby.

Lamn was not at all impressed. "THE LOCATION." He demanded more forcefully.

"I...I don't know it!" Vane wailed between sobs.

Eve's eyes widened in fear as she and Lamn shared a look.

"You SAID you knew where it was, and you would take us there. You cannot lie. Explain yourself!" Lamn demanded.

Vane was choking on air, he was crying so hard, and his high-pitched wails were grating on Eve's nerves.

"I… I know how to get there from our drop-off point. (SOB)… So I wasn't lying… (SOB)… If you could get me to the drop-off point, I would have shown you…(whimper, whimper, whimper)… but I don't know where that is either! (SOB)"

Lamn pushed himself to stand, disgusted. He realized Vane had every intention of leading them straight into an ambush and freeing himself. They were no closer to finding the imprisoned hybrids.

"You won't kill me, will you?! I swear that's the truth! (SOB)" Vane was attempting to climb to his knees and pull on Lamn's pant leg while he begged for mercy. Mercy he'd never shown for anyone else.

An idea began to form in Lamn's mind. "Sera, might you have use for a servant when you settle in here?"

Sera's eyes lit up again, and the corner of her mouth quirked upwards into a small smile.

Vane let go of Lamn's pant leg and stared in horror at Lamn, and then at Sera. He tried to crawl backward on his knees as if he could somehow escape his fate.

"No…. No… NO!!!"

"*Crank Vane Devons, you will serve Sera as her personal slave and servant. You will follow any command or instruction without delay, backtalk, or retaliation. You will not try to escape your servitude. You will never act in any way against Sera, any of her friends or associates, or other staff members, in word or in deed. You will never insult or demean her again, privately or publicly. In fact, any time you attempt to insult her, you will instead insult yourself with the same words.*"

Vane flopped on the floor and began sobbing and wailing again. Sera turned to Lamn with large eyes. She had just wanted the opportunity to rid herself of the fear of Vane. She had never anticipated an act of revenge so deserved for him. She nodded her head in gratitude to Lamn, and he reciprocated. It was an unspoken understanding.

As they turned to leave the room a quiet broken voice sounded from the floor behind them, "I am such a cocksucking bitch! I hate myself so fucking much!"

This led to uncontrollable laughter as they stepped into the hallway.

45

Eve

Eve was disappointed that Vane had led them on a wild goose chase for the hybrids, but even that couldn't spoil her excitement. She climbed out of bed, stretching. She clumsily dropped her robe from her trembling fingers. She was nervous, very nervous, even though Lamn had promised her that her meeting with the High Council was only a formality. Today was the day that she would become an official citizen of the Summer Court. She would officially be recognized as Lamn's daughter and heiress.

What made it even more exciting was that her girlfriends, the refugee slaves Lis, Dzhen, and Fhik, were meeting at the same time. They could all emerge as citizens together! Her friends had adjusted amazingly in the Summer Court and had even lined up jobs and a place to live. They had chosen to share a house and stay together. Considering their history with the fae in the Winter Court, Eve understood safety in numbers.

Lamn had tried to add Sera to the roster but was unable to get confirmation, so they were bringing her along as well, in hopes she would be heard. If not, she would have to wait for a future date. It was just a matter of time, Lamn assured her. Eve couldn't wait until Sera was a citizen, then she could take her first servant out of Lamn's holding cell and to her own new home. It still made Eve chuckle.

She rushed through her morning routine, and then picked an outfit that she felt made her look the most fae. She knew no one else might see that, but for her, it was the feel. She was downstairs and pouring coffee in no time flat. As she fixed her coffee, she suddenly wished Tark was here to share her moment with her. She wondered how he was doing, if he thought of her, if he was ok... She stared into her cup as if she would find the answers.

Lamn appeared behind her and placed a kiss on the back of her head.

"You will do great today. Try not to worry." She turned to see his reassuring smile. She didn't want to share what was really bothering her. They both had enough going on, and there seemed to be no need to worry about things that they could not change.

She had barely drunk any of her coffee before Ama was bringing her girlfriends in. They squealed like school girls and hugged with excitement. Minutes later Sera was introduced, and the foursome became a fivesome.

Poor Lamn! Eve thought with a chuckle.

After a short carriage ride, the group all descended upon the Hall of the High Council. The building was magnificent, reminiscent of Rome at its height. White marble and large thick columns dominated the architecture. The ladies all became subdued when they faced the building and remained in quiet awe as they were led down corridors and to the main chamber where their status would be determined.

Inside was equally impressive, with more marble, high vaulted ceilings, and arches everywhere. There were gold accents tastefully adorning the edges of surfaces, like a modest display of sanctity around the otherwise booming display of power.

Once in the main hall, they were all seated on a bench, while Lamn went to find an official and see about adding Sera to the roster. The ladies waited in anxious silence, sharing nervous glances. Lamn returned with a smile, mission accomplished!

There were many benches in the hall, facing a raised semi-circular dais with seven seats. The center seat was slightly higher than the other six. A man at the side of the room made an announcement in Faeish and everyone stood. The ladies all rushed to get on their feet as well. Seven fae walked in through a door behind the dais, and each moved to a seat. The fae at the center stood looking over the room. His eyes moved over Eve, and she was reminded of courts back home; she suddenly felt like she was on trial. But the fae finally took their seats, and everyone in the room followed suit.

Eve sat and watched as name after name was called, and that individual would get up and go to stand in front of the Council. Some had another person with them, some went alone. Sometimes they talked in Faeish, other times in English, and once Eve heard Spanish.

It was about half an hour before Eve's name was called, and she jumped up nervously. Lamn also got up and escorted her to the Council floor. The man in the center said something in Faeish, to which Lamn replied. Then in English, the Counselor addressed Eve.

"And what business brings you before the Council today, My Lady?" Eve looked nervously at Lamn and he just nodded proudly at her.

"I wish to become a citizen of the Summer Court. I wish to stay here with my family."

"And this Lord, he is your family?"

"Yes, Sir, he is my father." She smiled as she said it, and Lamn looked so damn proud.

"I see here that you have been studying our ways, our culture, and our language, is that correct?"

"Yes, Sir. My father has been helping me."

The Counselor then turned his attention to Lamn. "You will vouch for her? You will ensure that she has the means to provide for herself, and a place to live if she stays?"

"Yes, Sir, I will." Lamn reached for her hand and held it in his own like she was still a small child. Eve let him because at that moment she was savoring the feeling of her family claiming her, being proud of her, and wanting her to do well. Tears threatened to leak out of the corners of her eyes. No one had ever volunteered to take care of her.

The center Counselor turned to his fellows and spoke a few words in Faeish, and after a very quick deliberation, Eve was awarded her citizenship.

This process continued several more times, and Eve was delighted when Lamn went up with each of her friends and vouched for them. More than that, he put himself down on record as being responsible for them. It would be up to him to make sure each of them had whatever they needed to start a new life, and he was more than willing.

Once the last of them had been seen, Lamn herded them back outside the building, where they promptly made a scene, squealing and jumping up and down with excitement. Lamn was laughing along with them when a male approached the group from the carriage lane. He called over to Lamn, who turned and smiled broadly at the man.

Forearms were grasped, and greetings exchanged before Lamn introduced the gaggle of ladies to his friend Behn. Behn was similar to all fae in that he had strikingly good looks, and an amazing body that was evident even covered in clothing. His hair was like metallic silver, and it flowed like liquid metal as the wind caught his long tresses. He had mischief in his gray eyes as he took each lady's hand in his gently and kissed the back of it respectfully with a slight bow.

When Lamn introduced his daughter, Behn's shock was evident. Lamn chuckled as he relayed how he had just recovered her from Earth, and Behn made sure to take an extra moment to connect with her eyes as he told her how delighted he was that Lamn's jewel had been returned to the Summer Court. He bowed deeply before taking her hand and leaving the most gentle of kisses on her knuckles. Eve blushed crimson at all of the attention, and the other ladies giggled and nudged her with elbows and winks.

Lamn took Behn aside, and the two spoke briefly. It was obvious to Eve that they were good friends, as they laughed and clapped each other on the arm. Lamn made his apologies to Behn, as he had the ladies' celebration to attend, but he did ask Behn to visit one night so that they might catch up and talk further. Ben smiled broadly and said he would, his eyes flicked to Eve. He looked to each of the ladies to extend his farewell and congratulatory wishes, stopping on Eve again.

As the ladies all turned to get into the carriage, Eve caught Ben looking at her, only her, with a warm smile. She returned the smile, and as Lamn prepared to help her inside the carriage Behn nodded his head in acknowledgment that he had to let her go. He seemed reluctant.

As the carriage pulled away, Eve's friends were all talking excitedly about what they would do now that they were citizens. They could work, have homes of their own, and pursue their own desires. This was all new to the rest of the ladies who had been slaves since childhood. They had never been given a choice in anything, and now their lives were their own. They were overwhelmed with the possibilities.

Eve knew she was lucky. She had choices in her life. Even if she made bad choices, they were hers. And even she was being given a clean slate, a chance to start new. Again, she wished Tark was here to share this moment with her. And Armoniel. It was the only thing that would have made it perfect.

The carriage stopped at the estate and the rustle of the ladies' silk dresses spilled out onto the walk and rushed up the stairs with hoots of joy. This was a day of celebration! Eve followed behind and when she reached the door she smelled the ozone that always preceded Armoniel.

She stopped and he materialized beside her. She threw her arms around him. "You came! We were just about to celebrate! I-"

She stopped short when she saw the look on his face. Yes, there was love for her, but there was also something tragic happening in his eyes. She grabbed his hand and dragged him back to the carriage.

"LAMN!" She called loudly. He stepped out from behind the carriage, where he had been talking to a stable hand. His eyes reflected the joy of seeing Armoniel and quickly shifted to worry as he took in Armoniel's features.

"Armoniel, what has happened?"

Eve and Lamn could both feel the apprehension in the air. Before Armoniel could speak, Lamn ushered him and Eve into the house and into his private study. Armoniel took a seat, his elbows on his lap, holding his head in his hands. Eve knelt beside him and put a hand on his arm reassuringly.

"What's wrong? What happened?"

Armoniel seemed to pull himself together, and looked between Eve and Lamn as if he didn't know where to start. "I have been given a new mission. This is very uncommon for a Watcher. I have been asked to come and assist the Summer Fae as they work to recover the hybrids that the Winter Fae are holding prisoner."

Lamn gasped a breath in shock. He had told no one, not even the garrison, Vane's story about hybrids being held. If Armoniel knew about it, that meant that something had happened on the Earth Plane. It was pointless to ask how he knew, they were Watchers, they watched.

Eve was confused. "But, that's a good thing, right? You get to spend time with us and help us."

Armoniel sighed deeply. "There is more. You may both want to sit down to hear this."

Eve was already kneeling on the floor, and Lamn leaned to sit on the edge of his desk.

"I have been told that Ruth is among the hybrids being held."

It was as if a bottle rocket had gone off in the office as Eve and Lamn both shot to standing, arms flailing, screaming, "WHAT?" in unison.

Eve watched as Lamn, her calm and trusted Lamn, lost his ever-loving mind. He seemed frantic, shooting questions at Armoniel. Eve could see the way the muscle in his body tensed, he was preparing for action.

Several minutes later, Eve had gotten Lamn calmed down and stopped him from storming the Earth Plane to recover Ruth, with Armoniel in tow. She left them to their strategic planning while she returned to her celebration party. Her heart wasn't in it anymore, but she couldn't abandon her girls on their big day. Still, her eyes lingered on the study door a little longer, before she turned and headed for the ballroom.

46

Tark

The overall attitude in the safehouse was frustration. These were fae who were seasoned in the field. They had all done extraction missions, many times over. Sometimes there were setbacks, or things didn't go as planned. This was one of those missions.

It's taking too long. We should have been back by now.

Tark thought the words but didn't share them out loud. Morale was already low, with the continued setbacks they had been encountering. Even with the higher stakes of more Winter Fae in the mix, they should have been able to wrap this up by now.

They had been watching what they assumed was an enemy safehouse, but it was clear that something was off. Fae would arrive but never leave. And ten days later another fae would leave that no one had seen enter. Either there was another entrance, or the building was much bigger on the inside than it was on the outside. They knew there was no other entrance. The small crappy wooden hovel had only one door. And as it was built in the swamp, it was highly unlikely that there were hidden rooms underneath it. Clearly, however, something was going on.

Without going inside they would never know. And they couldn't just rush inside without knowing if there was a group of enemy fae somehow hidden away inside. While the latter seemed highly unlikely, they still couldn't explain the comings and goings enough to deem it safe to raid.

And so the mission lingered.

Tark just wanted to get back. He wanted to know how Eve was doing. He wanted to sleep in his own bed and get out of the wet and insect-infested swamp.

The team leader came into the common room where the fae were sitting around and wasting time until their next duty hours came up. Several other fae filed in behind him, and Tark saw the makings of an impromptu meeting.

Sure enough, the team leader whistled for everyone's attention. The television was turned off, which elicited a groan. The cards were put down. All eyes and ears were on the team leader as he began.

"We have just received an update on the mission. We have reliable intel that tells us that this is a much bigger issue than we had previously thought. I'm expecting a new wave of officers from garrison tomorrow, and we will brief you on the nature of the changes after I have had a chance to talk with them. Until that time, rotations remain the same. The mission remains the same. I expect you all to watch and gather as much intel on the target as you can *without* engaging. Am I understood?"

The responding noise included groans, yeses, and hoots.

The team leader released them to resume their activities, turned on his heel, and left the room. Tark was on his feet in a flash, hurrying after the team leader. He called out to him, and halfway down the hall, the fae stopped to wait for him to catch up.

"Sir, with new troops coming in, I was wondering if there was any way I could be temporarily rotated out. I have some urgent business with Lord Vassel." Tark was crossing his fingers behind his back and hoping against hope.

"Well then troop, you're in luck. Lord Vassel is one of the officers slated to arrive tomorrow, you can take care of your business then." He was already walking away from Tark as he finished.

Well shit. That backfired spectacularly.

Eve

It was late in the evening, and the other girls had taken their party on the road to continue the celebration. Eve stayed behind and helped in any way she could. Lamn had called the garrison on his mirror and informed them of the new situation. That, in turn, had led to some big mucky muck from garrison stopping by the house to speak to Armoniel in person. Once 'Big Mucky-muck' was satisfied that the information was valid, they immediately made plans to put fae on the ground and be ready to extract the hybrids by any means possible.

Having a Grigori on the team was a huge boost for them. They had not been honored with assistance from the Watchers in over a thousand years. The garrison was making a huge deal about it, and they were taking far longer than Armoniel was able to sit patiently and wait. Finally, Lamn stepped in with some suggestions to get the ball rolling, before he and Armoniel just went rogue and invaded by themselves.

The plan was set.

Lamn, Armoniel, and a few bigwigs from garrison would leave in the morning to outline the new parameters to the troops already in place. The location was originally thought to be a black market hub for the Winter Court, but they had never suspected that there was hybrid sex trafficking going on, and certainly not under the jurisdiction of the Earth Plane. Precautions would have to be put in place to protect the hybrids, and to capture as many of the Winter Fae as possible, to stop their future trafficking.

Eve knew it was almost pointless. For every Winter Fae they captured or killed, there would be another boot licker eagerly pushing his body aside to take his place. She wondered if this problem could ever truly be solved.

When everything had been talked out as much as anything can be talked out, Lamn retired to pack. He offered Armoniel a room to stay for the night, and Armoniel accepted the invitation, even though Watchers don't sleep. He wanted one night to be in the same house with his family, an entirely new experience for him. As he was as old as time itself, THAT was saying something.

Eve fought the urge to go to bed. When Lamn left to pack, she stayed and chatted with Armoniel. She found him incredibly intelligent, (*DUH!*) but strangely naive in so many ways. She wondered if it had to do with the fact that while he saw much, he didn't get to discuss anything. Eventually, fatigue got the better of her and she had to admit that she needed sleep. Her grandfather kissed her on the head and she stumbled to her room in the wee morning hours.

The morning sun was deceptively bright and peaceful. Eve could hear the clamoring of movement throughout the house. She rushed to make herself presentable and headed downstairs. The kitchen was already filled with men in uniform, Lamn among them, and of course Armoniel. They were enjoying coffee and chatting as other men were loading carriages with gear to take to the portal.

Lamn pulled away from his conversation to wrap Eve in a strong hug. "I don't know how long we will be gone, but Ama knows how to run the household. If you need anything, let her know." He smiled warmly and brushed a lock of her indigo hair out of her eyes.

Eve was trying hard to push down the crushing weight of fear as it rose in her throat. Here it was, the chance for her family to be taken away from her after she had only just found them. It felt like watching the other shoe drop in slow motion.

No. She would not succumb to fear. Not in this new life.

She smiled back, or at least she tried to. He seemed to feel her inner turmoil and pulled her in for another hug.

"I am going to be fine, Eve. We all will. Armoniel will make sure of that. It turns out this was the mission Tark was on, so I'll be with him too. You know there's nothing the three of us can't accomplish, never mind all these other fae." He smiled at her through the bravado, and she cracked a smile back. This time a real one.

Time was moving too quickly, and soon the fae were all filing out the door, chatter forgotten, focused on their mission. Eve stood back and watched them all go. Lamn and Armoniel gave her last hugs before they too joined the others.

And then the door was closed. They were gone.

47

Tark

The rain drove down in sheets as the jeep left the road and took the fae further into the wilds of the Everglades. Here there was still a dirt path they could follow, but before long it would only be possible to continue on foot. The terrain here was treacherous at best, and that was without the snakes, alligators, and various other murderous fauna.

When the Jeep could go no further it stopped and allowed the troops to get out, grabbing their gear and provisions as they went. This was only the first Jeep of many, the others were close behind, and it had to turn and move, or risk being blocked in.

The rain never stopped its assault as the fae marched single file through the underbrush and around mangroves and cypress trees. Their clothing and gear became heavier as they got soaked, and their boots sank into the muddy soil. Other than the occasional command or check-in, not a word was spoken. The only sound was the relentless drumming of the rain and the 'THUCK' noise of boots being pulled out of the vacuum of the mud. It was miserable all around.

When they finally arrived at the safe house, which was really more of a warehouse by appearance, they were all just happy to be out of the rain and away from the alligators and biting insects. The team leader and a few of his group leaders were there to meet the arriving officers, and Tark was among them. All eyes opened wide in shock as Armoniel walked in with the group, and as Armoniel's eyes caught Tark's, he waved in greeting. All eyes then turned to look at Tark, who said nothing and just waved back.

The new team was assigned their quarters, so that they could change and refresh themselves, before debriefing the team leader. Lamn made eye contact with Tark and jerked his head to indicate that he should follow. Tark side-stepped the gaggle of people and worked his way over to Lamn and Armoniel. Tark picked up Lamn's bag and they headed for his room.

After a very brief shower, and a dry change of clothing, Lamn and Armoniel finally got a chance to check in with Tark. As they wouldn't have very long, Lamn gave Tark the abbreviated version of the goings on back home: namely that Eve was a citizen, as were her girlfriends. He also gave him the condensed version of Vane's story and its outcome. That brought them to their current situation, and Armoniel filled him in.

Tark seemed distracted. "I wish I could have been there for her hearing."

Lamn stopped short. "ALL of that, and all you heard was Eve became a citizen?!"

Tark's face flushed red, starting from his neck and building quickly up his cheeks. "No! No, I heard it all..."

Lamn just laughed outright. "We need to get this business over with so I can get my mate back, and YOU can finally make my daughter happy for a change."

Tark continued to sputter and blush, but Lamn simply pulled him into the hall by his arm, and soon they were walking to the conference room, with Armoniel behind them.

Eve

Eve snuggled into her study nest. She couldn't work on learning Faeish without Lamn's help, so she instead went back to studying governance. She had heard talk about the nobles, and lesser nobles, and had pretty much figured out the feudal system. She wanted to know who ruled above them.

The doorbell rang downstairs, and as Eve knew no one, and wasn't expecting her girlfriends, she let Ama answer it and continued working. A few moments later she heard footsteps approaching, and soon Ama appeared at the door announcing Behn's arrival.

Eve dropped her book with a thump as Behn stepped into the room. She was eternally grateful that she had taken the time to put herself together that morning, against her own argument that there was no need to dress up with no one home. She stood, and offered her forearm as she had seen Lamn and the others do. Behn's eyes crinkled with mirth, as he took her hand instead, and kissed her knuckles respectfully.

Eve was in uncharted territory here, without Lamn to guide her in the proper ways to be a good fae hostess, so she fell back on what worked on Earth.

"Good to see you again, Behn. I'm sorry, but if you're here for Lamn, he was called to Earth for a mission." She felt awkward but put on her best warm welcome.

Behn didn't seem to notice her discomfort, or if he did, he politely didn't say so.

"Yes, Ama was just telling me. That's a shame. I thought that, as I am already here, perhaps I would take the time to get to know you, if you're not too busy? I admit, I was intrigued to find out that Lamn has a daughter."

Eve blushed but offered him a seat, then she asked Ama if she would bring up coffee for Behn. When Ama excused herself, Behn resumed the conversation.

"Those are a lot of books. Are you studying?"

Eve immediately felt insecure. "Uh, yes. I am trying to learn how to fit in better. To be honest, some days I feel like a fish out of water. Everything here is so familiar, and at the same time it is completely different."

Behn nodded. "I know how you feel. My first few visits to Earth had me gaping like a tourist every time we entered a city. I felt like I was learning a whole new form of magic."

Eve nodded eagerly. She could relate to that as well.

"So, what are you learning about today?"

"Well, I was going to work on my Faeish, but without Lamn I'm finding it impossible. So instead I went back to governance."

Ama reappeared with a tray and two cups of coffee and all of the fixings, as well as a plate of finger sandwiches. Eve gave her an appreciative look and thanked her before Ama put the tray down on the table between them and excused herself.

"I can see where Faeish would be difficult without a partner. I could help if you'd like. I used to tutor when I was an adolescent."

Again, Eve could feel the blush burning in her cheeks. She wasn't sure if she would be considered rude if she rejected his offer of help, and she would honestly rather work on language than politics any day. Behn leaned over and traced the spines of the books until he found the volume on language.

"Where did you leave off?"

He smiled warmly at her. He was very disarming. She found it easy to talk with him, so she decided to just go with it.

They spent the next two hours working on basic phrases for general conversation. Eve found it much easier to understand the language the way Behn explained it, and in no time at all, she had basic, rudimentary conversation skills. Eve was enjoying her time learning with Behn so much that she was startled when Ama asked if Behn would be joining them for dinner. She looked to Behn, the question on her tongue, when he smiled and said, "I'd love to. Thank you."

They continued their lessons until it was time to eat, and then Behn took the book down to the greenhouse, Eve's favorite place to eat, so that they could continue learning over dinner.

It was late that evening when Behn finally took his leave, and Eve was sad to see him go, even if her head was full to overflowing with everything she had learned that day. At the door he took her hand again, pressing a respectful kiss to the back of her knuckles, and asked, "If you'd like, I would love to help you with the language again. You are a quick learner."

Again, Eve's cheeks burned pink, and she found herself saying, "Yes, I'd like that," in a way that was just a little too breathy.

Behn rewarded her with a smile that flashed his perfect teeth, as he stepped back toward the stairs. As he was leaving he promised that he would come by the next day if she was available, so that they could continue her lessons. And then he was in his carriage and rolling away into the darkness.

Eve felt a little bit giddy. Behn was kind and respectful, *and let's not forget hot!* No, he was no Tark, but it was nice to have other male friends.

Is that what Tark is, a friend? She frowned at her own internal dialog.

Closing the door she dissected her relationship and her feelings for Tark. No matter which way she looked at it, *yes, he was a friend. But only because she never had a chance to explore making it more.* But she desperately wanted it to be more.

48

Lamn

The team and officers were all seated around the conference room table, with styrofoam cups filled with terrible coffee in front of them. Lamn had filled the team leader in with their new information, and all that was left to do was to fill in the rest of the team.

One of the officers got up and turned on the overhead projector. On the screen was an overhead map of the area with an 'X' and arrows showing ingress and egress. The team leader went over the new information, that the site they were monitoring was somehow connected to an Earth-based brothel and hybrid sex ring for fae. It still wasn't understood how the tiny decrepit pile dwelling could possibly house anything of size, but the comings and goings left no doubt *something* was going on.

An underling expressed his concern about not knowing what was inside and the danger of simply raiding it sight unseen. Lamn turned to look at Armoniel, with an eyebrow cocked in question. Armoniel then spoke up and offered to scout the building, as he had the protection of invisibility. It wouldn't preclude them from knowing he was there at all, but they wouldn't be able to see him.

There was silence in the room as the fae all stared at Armoniel, and Lamn chuckled to himself. The fae were unused to having these 'superpowers' at their disposal. Still, Lamn was unwilling to jeopardize the whole operation if Armoniel was discovered. He instead suggested that Armoniel simply follow someone when they walked inside, rather than just transporting himself into the building. This seemed agreeable to everyone.

The plan was then set. When the next change of watch took place, Armoniel would accompany them. They would simply have to wait for the next time an enemy fae approached the building for him to slip in behind them. It would be up to him to find a way back out and to report back what he had found inside the shack. They would base their next steps on that information.

The meeting was adjourned, and everyone returned to their quarters or duty station.

Eve

Eve finished her morning coffee and considered what she wanted to do next. She would be studying with Behn later, so she wasn't eager to hit the books just yet. She rinsed out her coffee cup and left it in the sink with the rest of the dishes, and just allowed herself to walk around the mansion. She still couldn't bring herself to call it a house.

She wandered by the music room, but she wasn't really in the mood to play. She passed the Library. She was bored, and couldn't seem to find anything that attracted her attention. As she went down one corridor she saw the door leading to the basement. She could faintly hear Richard singing.

Richard... Ugh.

They still hadn't done anything about him, so he still sat in a cell downstairs. Really, it was more like a room that had a bay window with bars in it, but it was still a cell. She suddenly felt a pang of guilt. Sure, he was a douche canoe, but they couldn't just leave him down there forever. A part of her felt that she should check on him, while a larger part of her argued that he was getting what he deserved and she should just forget about him.

In the end, her humanity, or faedom, won out.

The door was unlocked, and she proceeded down the long staircase.

The music got louder as she got closer. It was only a few moments before she reached the cell floor and started for his cell.

Of course, Vane was on his feet in an instant.

"I demand that you release me at once!" She could hear his sneer even before she saw it.

"Not today, Satan, not today." She continued walking.

Behind her, Vane tried again.

"Eve Sherman, you WILL release me immediately and assist me in leaving the Summer Court. You will come with me to the Winter Court where you will be my plaything without refusal."

Eve stopped walking, just a step beyond Vane's cell. She felt the magic as it coalesced around her form, invisible... and then fell away harmlessly.

He doesn't know...

She took two wooden steps backward to stand right at Vane's door. His eyes were gleeful and his smug smile triumphant.

He really did look like a cartoon villain, all he needed was a thin handlebar mustache.

She pretended to have the faraway look she had seen on Becky as she looked in his general direction with a small smile on her face. Vane did the fae equivalent of a happy dance, rubbing his hands together enthusiastically, and Eve swore to herself she would need bleach to clean out the mental image of his junk swaying in the breeze while he pranced in victory.

She walked to his door and put her hand in her pocket as if reaching for a key. She fished around for a while and finally pulled her hand back out with a piece of candy. She slowly unwrapped the candy and popped it into her mouth, all the while appearing dazed.

Vane stopped dancing. He looked completely befuddled.

Eve slooooowly panned her gaze, until she was looking Vane in the eye.

"No. I don't think I will Shrinkydink. But I will pass on this info to your new Mistress when I see her." She winked at Vane as she continued her walk down the hall.

She could no longer see Vane, but she could hear him choking on his confusion, stammering, and stuttering, obviously wondering HOW she had refused his compulsion. She had never let him in on the fact that she had faked it for him before.

And that, folks, is why guys should never want their girls to fake it. Am I right?

Richard had stopped singing so he could eavesdrop, and as Eve approached his cell he looked up in surprise.

Eve was equally surprised. Richard was sitting in his cell in nothing but his tidy whities.

"Richard?! What happened to your clothes?" Eve averted her gaze. Yes, she had already seen him before, but after all of the hot fae around it was his bloated pink body that had her looking elsewhere.

"I'm doing a nude strike in solidarity with my friend Vane." Richard smiled up at her and sat up straighter as if to showcase the goods.

"Leave me out of this, you wretch!" Shot down the hall from Vane's cell.

Eve lowered her voice as she continued. "But Richard, he can't see you, and besides, you still have your underwear on."

"Yeah, well, like you said, he can't see me, so he'd never know!" He beamed at her like he was a genius, and Eve just shook her head.

Some things never changed.

She suddenly realized she really didn't have anything to say to him. Clearly, he was still delusional and enjoying his stay. She was about to turn around and leave when Richard got up and approached the barred window.

"Look, Eve, I know this has been hard on you. But I just want you to know that I forgive you for everything. We can still be friends." He was serious.

HE forgives ME?!!!

Now she had something to talk to him about.

And then it hit her. She wasn't sure it would work, but she was part fae, so there was no harm in trying...

"Richard Royce, you will tell me the truth about how you felt about me

during our relationship, and why you ended it." She felt the magic swirling. It wasn't as strong as when the fae did it, but she could definitely feel it.

Richard stopped like he was in a trance. He cocked his head to the side in thought, his eyebrows scrunched in concentration. When he spoke, he was still staring off into the distance.

"If I'm honest, I thought you were too good for me. You were really smart, and you always called me on my bullshit. It excited me but pissed me off at the same time. I love a challenge, but I hated that you were always right. I hated that you were smarter than me, really. You were much more sexy when you just agreed with me.

"I also thought you were too good-looking for me. You were super hot, with a smokin' body. I can't tell you how often I jacked off to pictures of you. I couldn't tell you I have E.D. I didn't want you to leave me. So I drank too much so I could blame it on the booze. I knew if I pissed you off enough, you wouldn't come looking for the dick, so I had that going for me.

"I know what I look like. I know I'm not super smart. Don't tell anyone, but I'm a mediocre musician. But I saw all the guys that just acted like they were 'all that' getting the girls, so I thought 'why not me?'

"My relationships don't usually last long, my girlfriends usually figure me out within six months or so; so I make it a habit to start looking for a new one within four to five months. That way I get to be the one who dumps the girlfriend before she can dump me. It keeps things exciting and keeps me from getting dumped.

"It's a lot of work you know, finding someone who doesn't already know you, or about you. Thank God for the internet. I had one prospect fall through before I found my next girlfriend. I'd message them when you weren't around, get all excited, and then get to fuck you if you were over. It was kind of a win/win for me. I got to have the fantasy relationship and the fantasy body... just not with the same person. It worked for a little while.

"I thought Sou was perfect. She was my solution. She was young and had never been to the US. She hardly spoke English. She thought I was amazing. She thought everything about me was amazing, probably because she didn't really understand half of it, but whatever. It didn't matter. If I brought her over, and she married me, she really wouldn't be able to leave me, would she? Even if she figured me out, she'd be stuck with me, right? But in the end, even she was miserable with me. Truth be told, I'm pretty miserable with myself most days. I'll never admit it, but there it is."

Richard blinked a few times like he was coming to and then smiled at Eve like he hadn't said anything.

Eve turned on her heel and ran for the stairs.

Never ask the question if you don't want the answer.

49

Tark

Tark and Lamn were hidden behind the foliage, binoculars in hand, watching the shack in the swamp. Armoniel just stood where he was comfortable, as he was invisible. They volunteered to take the shift which would most likely see action, as they had worked with Armoniel before. Professionals or not, everyone else seemed pretty freaked out by him.

They had already been waiting an hour and a half when suddenly there was movement on the west side of the clearing. Two male fae were lumbering for the shack, and they were carrying what looked like a bodybag between them.

One guess what's in there. Tark looked up at Armoniel to nod. It was go time.

Armoniel evaporated and almost instantaneously reappeared directly behind the last male fae. They must have been expected, because as they approached the door opened, and someone propped it to stay open while they hauled in the large bag. Armoniel didn't have to walk behind them, he walked in ahead of them while they shifted the weight of the bag to carry it up the stairs.

He was in! Now they had to wait.

Eve

Eve ran a cold face cloth over her face to try to hide the bags under her eyes and the blotchy skin from crying.

Damn Richard!

No, this wasn't Richard's fault. She should never have asked. Because really, what difference would it have made if his answer was anything else. Why couldn't she just let it go and forgive him for being a prick, and move on with her life? What did his opinion matter, anyway?

It was just so tragic that he didn't love himself, when she had cared for him so much. It hadn't been enough.

She heard the doorbell ring and cursed, as she tried to fix her makeup to cover the evidence, before heading downstairs.

Behn stood in the hallway, all smiles, until he saw her face. For just a moment a wave of concern washed over his features, before he expertly schooled them back into a pleasant smile. Eve was grateful for social protocols at that moment. She really didn't want to have to explain why she was upset. While her eyes may be puffy, her smile was genuine as she met him at the bottom of the stairs.

As always, Behn lifted her hand gently, and respectfully placed an austere kiss on the back of her knuckles like she was royalty. It did give her butterflies, but she ignored them. At least, she told herself she did. Once they were at her study nest the work began in earnest. Behn first quizzed her on the information she had learned the day before. He confided he was shocked at her recall, as she missed only one phrase. He had never had a student who seemed to absorb language so quickly and completely.

They laid out a plan of what to learn and in what order: conversation, directions, rooms and furniture, etc. He would give her a list of all of the nouns (plates, cups, bowls, forks) as well as a list of verbs (drinking, eating, setting, clearing, washing) so that with each topic she learned she would be able to use them conversationally. Once basics were covered, she would move on to more specific topics: like medicine, philosophy, theology, etc.

Since she had a good handle on common etiquette and conversation, they moved on to giving and getting directions, as well as commonly visited places. This way, she would never be lost.

Eve had never enjoyed learning so much. Behn was a great teacher. He was entertaining, but also kept her on task. He was funny and genuinely nice. When they took breaks they would have coffee or chat, and he was really interesting. He was the kind of person she wanted to hang around, he made it easy for her to be herself. Gone was any facade of propriety. They were both just comfortable being who they were together.

The hours flew by as she parroted the phrases he taught her. He insisted her pronunciation was amazing, and he only had to correct her a few times. She was a natural.

Must be in my blood!

They were both surprised by how fast the afternoon slipped away when Ama appeared at the door to ask about Behn staying for dinner. Eve didn't miss a beat. She told Ama in perfect faeish that, "Yes, Behn would be joining her for dinner." Behn's smile dazzled her. Ama smiled broadly as well and responded in faeish, "Very well, I will take care of it," as she excused herself.

They were both laughing as Behn hugged Eve off the ground and then put her back down. Eve looked up at Behn suddenly as a thought occurred to her.

"How do you say I love you?" she asked.

"You.. you want to learn to say 'I love you?'" Behn's cheeks blushed a little.

"Yes!" She answered with a big smile. "I want to say 'I love you' to my father, I want to say it in faeish!" Her smile lit up her face.

Behn laughed at his own internal dialog and then focused on her. He said the phrase slowly.

Eve tried to mimic it. "Eehk maloosh."

Behn smiled and corrected her encouragingly.

"This is a tough one for English speakers. It's EeHH. You need to make the hhhhh sound with the tongue in the back of your mouth. There's no hard K sound. Don't close your teeth. Same for the shhhh sound at the end, don't close your teeth. They are very soft, made with the tongue."

She tried it one more time, and that time said it perfectly.

Eve squealed and jumped up and down, and then jumped to give Behn a tight hug.

She looked up at him and his head came down to hers, suddenly his mouth was on hers, warm and comforting. His lips were gentle and loving, and yet firm. She felt passion rolling off of Behn in waves so thick that it was as if he had a strong cologne that acted like an aphrodisiac. It almost had a *smell,* and it was thick in her nostrils and lungs. Her chest gulped it in. She was completely sucked into the experience like they formed an electric charge, her arms around him, his arms around her. There was nothing except the warmth of their bodies pressed together and the fervor and hunger of their lips as they tangled and danced. A moan left her throat.

Tark.

The spell was broken.

She launched herself out of his arms, eyes wide, heaving in breaths, trying to get clear air, trying to regain her composure.

Behn seemed equally bewildered, staggering back, his breathing was shallow, and he ran his hands through his silky silver hair. He turned and walked a step or two away, to put some distance between them, before he finally turned to face her. He stood behind a chair as if having a piece of furniture between them was somehow safer.

For a second they just stared at each other, stunned. Behn was the first to snap out of it.

"Eve... I am ... I am so sorry... I ... I don't know..."

"No, Behn... I..."

"No, Eve, I have to apologize. That was wrong of me. That was very wrong of me. I had no right to do that, to take advantage of your kindness to me. Please forgive me."

He looked distraught. Eve understood wanting to apologize, but his reaction seemed a bit over the top, and she wondered if she wasn't missing some other fae rule of protocol or etiquette. Even after apologizing, she could see beads of sweat forming on his forehead.

"Behn, there is no need to apologize. But if you feel you have to, fine. I forgive you. It's ok."

Behn shook his head, still looking uncomfortable.

"Eve, may I be perfectly honest with you?"

She immediately nodded yes.

"One of the things I like most about you is that I can be myself with you. It's so refreshing. With you, there's no pretense. I'm not expected to try to impress you with my station, and you're not trying to do the same with me. With most women, it's a competition for dominance. I adore that you are just who you are, always, regardless of company. You are a breath of fresh air. I enjoy your company more than you could know."

"So why are you so upset that you kissed me if I'm so wonderful?" She asked teasingly.

Behn looked at her with vulnerability, willing her to understand as he continued. "I should not have kissed you because I do not have a romantic interest in you. If I'm perfectly honest, I don't know what happened right there. It's as if being that close to you... this is going to sound crazy,... but it's as if I smelled a scent, an aphrodisiac. My body just reacted, I swear! It wasn't my intention. Something overpowering happened. You must believe me, Eve, I'm not making excuses. I claim full responsibility for my actions, and I will accept any consequences." His cheeks blazed with shame.

Eve's eyes grew wide.

"Behn, I felt that too. It wasn't just you feeling that. But I thought it was coming from you."

Eve's shock was reflected by Behn's, and for a moment they just stared at each other uncomfortably, neither wanting to move.

Finally, Eve asked quietly, "So you don't have a romantic interest in me, huh?" She quirked a small smile.

He smiled in return, somewhat sheepishly. "My Lady Eve, you are the most perfect and divine person I have ever had the pleasure to know. If only you were male, I would be courting your hand for marriage right this very moment. And I would die a thousand deaths if you denied me."

50

Lamn

It was another three hours before the door to the shack opened again. An enemy fae pushed through the door and clomped down the stairs. He was completely unaware that Armoniel was right behind him.

And then Armoniel was standing next to Tark, who made a motion for Lamn and Armoniel to head back with the information, and to radio for a replacement for himself. Lamn nodded as he and Armoniel headed carefully through the underbrush to put some distance between themselves and the shack. Once they deemed themselves far enough away, Armoniel ported them back to the safehouse, where they promptly gave everyone a heart attack by materializing in the conference room.

Officers were gathered quickly to hear about what Armoniel had learned.

"It's a portal," he began. "Although I have never seen the fae do this before, they have figured out a way to create a standing portal within a structure. Usually, the force of a portal left open will rip a structure apart, that is why you find their portals in the forests. They are clearly drawing on a great source of power for this.

"They have only two fae working within the structure. I looked at their guard roster, and it appears they change shift every twelve hours, at two thirty. Usually, the new guards arrive through the portal, but occasionally they come in from outside.

"The portal leads to the... *establishment*... they operate. I overheard conversations after they brought a new hybrid in today–"

"The bodybag?" Lamn inquired.

"Yes. They were upset that they can't just deliver the hybrids directly to the establishment, as it's not too far from here, and that they have to drag them all the way out here into the woods. One of the guards made it clear that their orders were that no one approaches the establishment directly."

"Well, that would explain why we haven't seen a lot of activity anywhere but this godforsaken swamp." A voice grumbled from the back.

"It must be heavily shielded inside so that high concentrations of fea aren't noticed by my kind or others." Armoniel finished.

"So NOW what?" One of the officers piped up.

Lamn smiled. "Now, we send someone through the portal. It just so happens, I have a volunteer!"

Eve

Eve was sitting at the table in the greenhouse with a map spread out in front of her. Her eyebrows were knitted in concentration as she ran her finger along a road on the map and recited the towns along the route. She had stopped when the name of a town had eluded her, and she was wracking her brains to remember what it was called. Behn leaned over her, his arm braced around her shoulders, as he looked to see which town was giving her trouble.

"New York!" She finally said, throwing up her hands and laughing. Behn laughed with her as he corrected her.

"I have seen New York. That is NOT New York!"

She looked up at him, still laughing, as he leaned over further and pointed to the town.

"Duursheng."

"That was my next guess!"

At that, they both burst into another fit of laughter.

Tark

Behind them Tark stood motionless at the door, watching them. He noticed Behn's arm around her, and the way she looked up at him adoringly. It destroyed him. His heart fell into his gut, and he quickly turned and left the room before he was seen.

Lamn

Eve and Behn continued their geography study until Lamn and Armoniel joined them in the greenhouse. Behn jumped back at the sight of Armoniel, shocked. He had never seen a Grigori in person and had only heard about them.

Eve lit up. "Father, Gramps! You're back!"

She rushed from her chair to give them both warm hugs.

"Not for long, I'm afraid, my dear. We've come to get Vane for a mission."

"VANE?!"

Now Eve looked shocked. Lamn gave a quick glance at Behn, nodding in acknowledgement before he continued.

"I'm afraid I cannot discuss the details here, only that we hope we will be back shortly for good."

Eve nodded, reluctantly, and Lamn and Armoniel headed for the basement to retrieve their latest recruit.

Lamn was angry at himself for not having pushed Vane for more information sooner. He compelled Vane, and then he and Armoniel questioned him as to his involvement with the stronghold. He had been one of the fae responsible for starting it with three others. They got the names of all involved, the staffing requirements, the layout with interior map, the security, etc. The only thing they could not get is the exterior location on the map, as Vane had never seen it from the outside: he had always portaled in.

Satisfied, Lamn got word to Melrick about their logistics and time-frame. He would honor his promise to turn over any Winter Fae.

It was hardly long at all before Lamn, Armoniel, and Tark were back at the safehouse with Vane in tow. Lamn had not bothered to give him the dialog beforehand and had simply compelled him to join them on the mission and to follow their orders as quickly as possible without hesitation or sabotage, and without making anyone aware that he was doing so, in any way. They even dressed him for the occasion. He was clearly pissed, but what could he do about it?

The officers eyed Vane with distrust but were satisfied that Lamn had him under control. The team leader pulled Lamn aside where they couldn't be heard.

"I don't like sending him in alone. What if he breaks the compulsion, or finds a way to stay there somehow? If he doesn't come back with intel, then we will have played our hand. He could blow this whole thing."

Lamn just smiled knowingly. "I don't trust him either, that's why I'm not relying on him coming back. I'm going to have him swallow a small tracker before he leaves, and I have a tracker sewn into his clothing. It helps having human allies with technology. Wherever he emerges, we will have it surrounded almost immediately. We'll have forces surrounding the shack, too, in case anyone tries to get away before we can disrupt the portal."

They spent the next several hours in preparation.

Lamn left to meet Melrick at a predestined location to explain what would happen. He gave Melrick a cell phone to use to keep in touch. Melrick had used one before, but he had never used a smartphone, so Lamn had to explain the few features that they could use to best communicate. When everyone was up to speed, Lamn returned to the safehouse.

The officers weren't thrilled with Winter Fae allies being on hand when the raid was made, but it had been a condition of Lamn's, and Armoniel's. They needed as much faepower as they could get, if they were going to be successful.

The hours waiting for darkness seemed to drag on, as if time itself was dragging its feet. Once the sun finally set, they were ready to move.

Lamn turned to Vane.

"Crank Vane Devons you will swallow this pill first, and then you will proceed to the shack which holds the portal to the hybrid stronghold when we

bring you there. You will act naturally, and give them a realistic excuse for wanting to go there if asked. At all times you will act as you would normally have acted when you visited that place in the past. You will discreetly find out how many fae are guarding and or working at the stronghold. You will find out where all of the hybrids are being kept. At no time will you indicate, by any means, that you are doing anything other than a routine visit. As soon as you have that information, you will return to us through the portal."

Vane clenched his jaw, and Lamn saw a vein throbbing in his neck. If looks could kill, Lamn would be dead where he stood. Fortunately, looks couldn't kill, and Vane couldn't do anything more than take the offered capsule, and a glass of water so that he could swallow it, as ordered.

The jeep rolled as quietly as possible to the drop-off point, and Lamn, Tark, and Armoniel hauled Vane out of the back so they could begin their trek to the shack. Once they had a visual on it, Vane seemed to snap out of his fit of rage. He seemed eager to get to the shack. Still wary of a trick, Lamn released his handcuffs but had Armoniel escort him, invisibly, to the door. Even Vane couldn't see him. For good measure, Armoniel would follow him inside as well, to be sure he followed orders.

The compulsion was working as planned. Vane hurried to the shack and threw the door open. Once inside, he became the arrogant prick he usually was. He immediately criticized one of the guards, looked over their paperwork for omissions or errors, and then headed for the portal like he owned the place. Armoniel watched him walk through.

He was about to settle in and wait for an opportunity to leave when the door opened again, and another fae was entering. Armoniel rushed to the other side of the room to take advantage of the open door, and papers flew off of a desk behind him. He didn't stop to worry about what the guards made of it.

With Armoniel safely back, Lamn messaged the safehouse to find out where the tracker was showing up on the map. They had a confirmed location. The old abandoned meat packing plant at the edge of the swampy forest, sat about five miles to the Northeast.

Lamn realized he was going to be deeply in debt to his human allies for all of the technology that they had utilized, but he was already grateful for the help it provided. He would have to petition the garrison to make this standard on the Earth Plane for future missions. With plenty of guards still surrounding the shack, as well as surveillance technology, Lamn, Tark, and Armoniel were free to head to the new location for the raid.

51

Lamn

The vehicles were all parked blocks away, and teams of two or three at a time were sent to carefully encircle the meat packing plant. If the Winter Fae were watching for an attack, they would easily pick up the number of fae in the immediate area. Vane had assured them that they didn't pay much attention to the neighborhood, only to the immediate vicinity. They had guards on the inside of all doors but none outside, as they didn't feel they were necessary. After all, no one knew they were there, except the fae already inside.

The plant had been abandoned for almost thirty years and had been for sale for twenty before that. It was a crumbling husk of a building that was slowly being reclaimed by the tropical flora over the years. A rusty fence still stood in some areas, with other areas completely enveloped in green groping vines.

Lamn had relied heavily on his human allies. He supplied them with the location and asked them to give him any relevant information they might need. The power had been shut off long ago, as had the security monitoring contract. This meant door alarms and fire alarms were disabled, as the older technology didn't have backups or were no longer supported.

From the fence line surrounding the building, Tark could see that there were lights on. A message from one of the other teams identified a generator on the other side of the building, a power source. Lamn's allies assured him that the security system was still disabled, with no company to monitor it.

They could follow Vane's movements through the building via his trackers. They knew he was making his way to the control area where he and his fae buddies had set up their own throne room to watch the festivities.

Lamn looked at his timekeeper. In one minute he would send the signal. Small teams would force the main entrance and the side entrance. Once those were cleared, the signal would be sent for remaining forces to sweep the building.

Lamn turned to Armoniel, one last time.

"Can you see *anything* in there?"

Armoniel just shook his head sadly. It was deeply concerning to him that there was a shield that could block out even his 'all-seeing' power. It did not bode well.

Time was up. The signal went out, and the first wave of fae moved to the doors. One opened without force, the other had to be physically removed. There was only a small skirmish at each door; apparently, there was only one guard at each, and neither had any technology for communicating with the rest of the building.

It seemed just a little too easy.

The "all clear" was sounded, and the second wave moved in. Lamn, Tark, and Armoniel were among them. They met with very little resistance in the hallways. The Winter Fae they encountered seemed to be patrons of the establishment and were unarmed and unprepared. As they were captured, or killed in a few cases, they were handed back out of the building to be handed over to Melrick.

Tark

At a large intersection, Lamn nodded to Tark. They would split up here. Tark and Armoniel would gather up the fae operating the building. Lamn and a few others would head for the holding cells for the hybrids and evacuate them. The rest of the force would clear the clients and hybrids on the entertainment floor. They each took off carefully in their respective directions.

As Tark reached the top of the staircase he saw Vane and a few other Winter Fae jump to their feet. Or, they tried to. It's hard to jump with your pants around your knees. They had been sitting in chairs and sofas, looking over the balcony to the floor below, where they could watch all of the rooms in which their customers were enjoying the hybrids. There were even a few hybrids on their knees here, now trembling in fear behind the furniture.

Tark launched at the nearest fae, who was trying to get his pants back up, Armoniel was right behind him. There were several more of the Summer Fae just reaching the top of the steps as the fighting began. The Winter Fae were enraged to have been infiltrated and bared their fangs and claw-like fingers. Knives were unsheathed with 'snicking' noises.

Vane just stood there in shock, as he had been compelled not to sabotage the mission until a Summer Fae knocked him out cold. There was chaos in the semi-darkness as punches were thrown and knives swung and stabbed. It took a few minutes, but the enemy fae were out-numbered. Tark and the others managed to subdue the males on the balcony. They were all secured and dragged out of the building.

Tark tried to tell the females they were there to help them, but the crashes, screams, and shouts from the floor below had them trying to squeeze themselves into small spaces and make themselves safe. They were absolutely terrified and shaking like trapped animals.

He could not afford to spend the time it would take to make them understand he was there to help them. In the end, he had no choice but to order his men to simply grab them as carefully as they could and carry them out to a waiting vehicle. The females put up a fight, but they were no match for the strength of the fae soldiers. One by one they were all carried out to safety.

Tark headed for the cells where the hybrids would be kept, while other soldiers cleared out all of the rooms which clients were using. Occasionally a hybrid would make a run down the hall for her life, and

Tark would have to snatch her and hand her off so she would get out of the building.

He was about to turn left to join Lamn when a glow appeared in the corner of his eye. He recognized the rippling waves of light caused by a portal and headed that way at full speed. Armoniel was right behind him.

The glow was shining through a doorway, and Tark rushed in and found two guards, probably just escaping from the shack. He took them down quickly, handcuffed them, and handed them off to a soldier. Then he turned his attention to the portal.

He knew he had to disable it, but it was somehow more complex than a normal fae portal. He felt for the power of it and was knocked backward. Armoniel reached for him to steady him.

"Tark, you won't be able to stop this. I think I will have to do this."

"Do what you have to do," was all Tark could say. He didn't care WHO took it down, as long as it stopped working.

"You may want to step out of the room," was the only warning Armoniel gave him before he spread his arms wide. His wings expanded behind him, and his glow expanded, brighter and brighter. Tark made it out into the hallway before he would have been blinded but still couldn't look in the direction of the door. Tark heard a deep booming voice, although he couldn't tell what was being said, just before the explosion picked him up and launched him thirty feet down the hall.

The walls shook, and the concrete building groaned and creaked with the impact of the force. Chunks of ceiling and dust were showering down, and walls and columns were randomly falling over. The building was no longer stable. They had to end this quickly.

Tark moved to get up, but he hurt literally everywhere. He could hear the shouts and screams, and he knew he had to move. Suddenly, Armoniel was there, lifting him and sending warm healing into his limbs. It wouldn't fully heal him, but it was enough to get him moving.

As quickly as his body would allow, he ran back to the holding cells, where Lamn was actively pulling hybrids out of their cells kicking and screaming for their lives.

"Ruth?!" Armoniel yelled in question.

"NO," was Lamn's answer, as he grabbed up another emaciated female who looked more like a feral cat than a person.

Armoniel ran deeper into the cell block, Tark behind him, until they reached the cell at the end. As the building crumbled slowly around them, the woman in the cell sat laughing. At first, she chuckled, but soon she threw her head back and laughed like she was deranged.

"RUTH!" Armoniel called to her.

She picked her head up suddenly, seeing Armoniel her eyes grew as big as saucers and she covered her mouth with her hands as she screamed.

Tark pulled the cell door off of its hinges and Armoniel ran into the cell. Ruth did not move to escape or to fight, she just kept screaming at the top of her voice. Armoniel gathered her gently, and when she didn't fight he carried her out of the room, dodging bits of falling ceiling and wall.

They got to Lamn as the rest of the team was reporting that all of the cells had been emptied, as they themselves headed out into the hallway. Bigger and heavier pieces of concrete were starting to fall around them as the building started to collapse in on itself. They turned to escape and found themselves blocked by a wall of heavy rubble. They were trapped.

Armoniel handed Ruth, who was now sobbing and wailing, to Lamn. Once she was safely in Lamn's arms, Armoniel created his own portal and took Lamn, Tark, and Ruth directly to the Summer Court. He would not sacrifice one more minute away from his family.

There was a slight whoosh as the portal disappeared after the team had all stepped into it, followed by a massive crash of tons of concrete as the ancient building structure finally gave way and caved in with a boom and a cloud of dust.

5 2

Eve

Eve paced. She thought, humorlessly, that she would wear a path in the carpet. She had been pacing for hours. Behn had stayed, and was a great calming force for her, but after hours and hours with no word... she was starting to lose her mind just a little.

Okay, a LOT.

Behn had just started to ask if there was anything that he could do, when Eve heard loud voices and commotion coming from the entry hallway. She jumped out of her chair and raced to the stairs. She almost cried for joy when she saw Lamn, Tark, and Armoniel, all back, all safe. She rushed down the stairs, Behn behind her.

Armoniel was carrying a wild looking woman. She was absolutely filthy, with mud brown hair that was matted and stuck out in all directions. Her clothing, if you could call it clothing, consisted of dirty tattered muslin, full of holes and threadbare. She wore no shoes. Eve noticed that the little finger on her right hand was missing.

Her eyes were wide, and she sniffled and whimpered as she clung to Armoniel's chest. He stroked her hair gently and cooed to her like a child as he carried her inside and headed for the stairs. He nodded to Eve as he passed her, and she saw the tears in his eyes slowly making their way down his cheeks.

She turned back to the entryway which was now empty. She could hear Lamn's voice in his office as he was suddenly shouting.

"THEN THEY CAN COME TO ME TO MEET. I WILL NOT LEAVE MY FAMILY AT THIS TIME!"

A few seconds later he threw his office door open and rushed into the entryway. He spotted Eve and raced to her, grabbing her up in a hug and lifting her off of the floor like he hadn't seen her in years. He was covered in dirt, dust, and blood, but Eve didn't care. She clung to him.

As he put her down gently she could see Tark behind Lamn, heading for the door quietly.

"And just where do you think YOU'RE going?" She called to him.

He stopped, shoulders hunched as if he had been caught being naughty by a parent. He turned to her with big sad eyes, which flicked briefly to Behn behind her, and then back to her. He too was filthy, and she really didn't give a shit.

Lamn placed a hand on her arm and told her he would be back soon, he had to go upstairs and make sure everyone was alright. Eve nodded at him and turned her attention right back to Tark.

"Tark, we need to talk."

He CRINGED. He visibly cringed.

Behn chose that moment to excuse himself, as even he could see they needed a moment alone. He gave her his usual respectful kiss on the back of her knuckles and then headed out the door.

Tark looked miserable, thoroughly miserable. He took a shuddering breath and then started to speak.

"Eve, I'm happy that–"

She cut him right off.

"Don't presume to know what I wanted to talk about."

"It's pretty obvious, Eve." His entire body shouted defeat.

Eve closed the space between them quickly and then punched Tark in the arm as hard as he could. He grabbed the arm with his other hand.

"OW! Hey, now–"

And then her mouth was on his. At first he tried to back away, but she threw her arms around his neck and hung on for dear life. His resistance died instantly, and his lips met hers passion for passion.

It was never a tentative, quiet, unassuming kiss. No. It was full of claiming, hunger, and longing. It was full of long hours of wondering, and of loss, and of being found again. It was full of promise, now and more.

His lips parted and hers parted with them. He stroked his tongue experimentally into her waiting lips and she thrust hers into his with force and clarity of intent. He wrapped his arms around her tightly as they feasted on each other's lips and breaths. She wrapped her legs around his waist, and they clung together for endless minutes.

She could sense the 'scent' again, the aphrodisiac that had caused her and Behn so much embarrassment. This time it was even stronger, heady, intoxicating. She knew she had to break the kiss or get sucked under. She forced herself back, even as his lips chased her, until he finally opened his heavy-lidded eyes to take her in.

He gently let her down so that she was standing on her own two feet, but he never released her from his arms. She slowly pulled away, even though she didn't want to. She couldn't talk while she was under the effects of... whatever it was. And it really took all of her willpower just to take that step away. He looked equally reluctant to let her go, and she had to shoo him back a few times until he finally stayed.

"I don't understand." He said to her. She could see hope in his eyes, as if she were the sun and the moon. As if she had the power to make him simply curl up and die at her feet.

"I know, Tark. That's the problem. Neither of us understands. But I want to. I want it so badly. I want to know you, all of you. I'm so sorry I was such an ass."

"Eve, HOW could you think I was already mated, and that I could ever disrespect you so much as to want to have you as well? I could never do that to anyone, but especially not to YOU."

"You said you had 'obligations.'"

"And I did. My estate, my business... but not a family, Eve. Not a mate. I live alone. VERY alone."

"You didn't want to stay here, with me, at first... I thought–"

"NO, because I was becoming attached to you!"

"And that's a bad thing?"

"I thought it was. I thought you deserve so much better than *just* me, Eve. You are Lamn's daughter, which makes you a high noble. You could have your pick of suitors. I'm a lesser noble. What will I ever have to offer you? I thought it was selfish of me to want to keep you when you hadn't even really seen your new life yet.

"But the more I tried to let you go, the more it haunted me. It was too late, Eve. I'm absolutely mad about you. I wake for you. I breathe for you. I live for you. I can no more stay away from you than I can the air I breathe, or the sun that lights my day.

"So there's my confession, Eve. I am the most selfish bastard of a fae. Because I want for you to be able to have the best, as you deserve, but I can't let you go to do so. I just can't."

His look was tortured. He had bared his soul, and was waiting on her verdict: live or die.

"I turned you down because It made sense to me that you might already have someone else. I never did think to ask when we met. I thought we had made connections, and then you would turn cold and leave.

"But Tark, even when I thought you had someone else, EVEN then I wanted you. I wanted to be with you. And I hated myself for being so weak that I would again allow myself to be less important just to feel wanted.

"It KILLED me to tell you 'no' that night at dinner. I felt like I ripped my own heart out. It was self preservation, but honestly, I died either way. Knowing you're single... I can't do this anymore, Tark. I can't dance this dance, two steps forward for one step back.

"So here's MY confession: I want to be with you, Tark. I want to learn about you, and your life, and all of the things that are important to you. I want to be important to you."

"What if you grow to resent me, when you realize you could have had more?"

"Honestly, Tark?! FUCK more. I've lived my entire life with little to nothing. Now I have a huge house, and all kinds of stuff. I have magic. I have a family. Know what I don't have? Love. A partner. A guy who respects me and appreciates me as much as I do him. A guy who is funny and appreciates my humor. A guy who cares about me and invests in me just as much as I do for him. I have NEVER had that, and I have always wanted it.

"Stuff can be replaced, but you're lucky if you ever find that one person that fits with your heart, and makes you feel like you're home. I can live without titles, or crazy mansions. I can't live without you."

Tark stared at the floor, toeing the tile with his shoe. "And uh... that guy you were with? Where does he fit into your heart?"

Eve realized the green-eyed monster was alive and well.

"Behn? Behn is one of my best friends. I can be myself with him. He helps me study and learn new things. I can relax with him; know why?"

His eyes came up to meet hers. "Why?" it was a squeak.

"Because he has zero romantic interest in me. He plays for the other team."

Tark just stared at her in confusion.

"He is attracted to males. I have the wrong equipment, we could never be a romantic couple."

"I beg to differ, I think you have all of the RIGHT equipment," Tark chuckled.

"Then we should be a romantic couple." It was a hopeful whisper, which Tark answered by sweeping her up into a strong embrace, and this time kissing her tenderly and reverently before putting her back onto her feet gently.

Lamn's voice wafted down from the top of the staircase.

"I'm glad you've finally got THAT all sorted out. Eve, would you like to come meet your mother?"

53

Eve

Eve stood just outside the doorway. She was terrified.

What if her mother didn't like her? What if she rejected her as Nancy did? I mean, she abandoned her at birth, right? She just didn't know if she could handle that rejection twice.

Lamn saw her hesitation and wrapped his arms around her. She wanted to cry, and she hadn't even met the woman yet.

Lamn whispered, "She's still in shock I think. We cleaned her up, but she's still pretty unstable. I'm hoping that seeing you will help to bring her back some, okay, so don't get your hopes too high."

Too high?! Eve was just hoping she didn't kick her out of the room!

Lamn had his hand at the small of Eve's back as he ushered her into the dimly lit room. Her mother was sitting in bed, sitting propped up against pillows. Armoniel was at her side, his hand on her arm, soothing her.

As Eve approached the side of the bed, Lamn sat next to her on her other side, taking her hand gently. Her eyes were still wild and she seemed skittish, but she was clean and her hair brushed, so that her natural strawberry blond color was evident. She looked like she was only a year or two older than Eve. And she was really very beautiful.

Eve took a moment to soak her in. *She really did have her mother's face.*

Her mother seemed to notice her then, and her eyes grew wide with terror.

"HOW did you get my FACE?! HOW?! You can't have him! You can't have him! He's MY mate!" She started sobbing and wailing again, clutching at Lamn with claw-like hands and holding him in a death grip. Armoniel placed another hand on her shoulder, and she suddenly calmed as if drowsy.

Eve was mortified.

She understood. Her mother didn't know her, had never even seen her. How could she understand? A thought bubbled into her consciousness, and she held her finger up to indicate she'd be back in a moment. She quickly excused herself from the room and ran down to the kitchen.

She returned ten minutes later with a cup in her hand of hot tea, her mother's favorite, Lamn had told her. She moved slowly as she approached her mother before speaking quietly and calmly.

"Ruth, I have brought you some tea. Your mate tells me it's your favorite. He talks about you all the time. I know he's missed you. I've missed you too."

Her mother looked at her, and then at the cup, before reaching out a hand to take the tea. She sipped it gently before closing her eyes, a little smile forming on her lips.

"I do love this tea."

Eve smiled. She didn't want to push her mother any further that night. Let her rest. They had the rest of their lives to get to know each other.

After too few hours of sleep, the household was up and bustling again. Eve woke late in the morning to the sound of voices downstairs. She was still exhausted, but she got up and made herself presentable to see what was going on. She made her way into the kitchen and the coffee maker. Lamn walked up behind her and gave her a big hug. She turned to look at him, and the adoration and pride in his eyes made her knees weak.

"You were amazing with her. I'm sorry we couldn't just have a happy reunion, but it's going to take some time for her to recover fully. I am so proud of the way you handled the situation. You are definitely her daughter!"

Eve had to choke back the tears. She hugged him back, and then turned to fix her coffee.

Male voices approached, so Eve stayed by the counter, out of the way. Two fae in uniforms came into the kitchen. As Lamn was offering them coffee, Eve was already pouring. They both greeted her politely as she served them their cups, and placed sugar and cream on the table in front of them.

One of the officers turned to Lamn.

"We believe we got all of the hybrids out. They are currently in the hospital, being treated, but I fear that the damage is far deeper than physical."

Lamn just nodded, his face was all business, but Eve knew him well enough to see the wince of pain that crossed his eyes.

"We got most of the Winter Fae as well. Those were turned over to your... ally. With the exception of Vane. We found a few more bodies in the rubble so far. Let us know where you want them."

"I will contact my ally and see what he wants done. I wish to fulfill my end of our bargain for the help that he rendered to us, at his own risk." He looked pointedly at the officer. There was no room for debate or argument.

"Very well, I will await your orders. Also, I received the final report from your human allies. Apparently the building was owned by a Rudolph Cavalieri, he purchased it ninety two years ago."

"That's an awfully long lifespan for a human."

"Indeed. That was the first point of interest. The second was that it was placed in a Trust for holding under the name of Serpent Enterprises about fifty years ago."

"You find that suspicious?"

"Well,... I may be stretching on this, but after reading Armoniel's statement there are several things here that are alarming. One, there was a standing portal INDOORS in two locations.

"Two, the portal was powered far beyond what our portals take to go from one plane to another. I asked Armoniel if he would look at one, to compare it, and he said ours are powered by a much smaller source. He said the portal to the stronghold was almost overpowered; it had far more power than it needed.

"Which brings me to point number three, Armoniel said the building was shielded so that even the Grigori could not see within it. Now, I have never heard of any place on Earth which the Grigori cannot see. That is the nature of their purpose, as it was made by Sopha. Simply creating such a thing is in direct defiance of Sopha herself. There is only one entity I know of who has ever dared to try to defy Sopha."

"Serp."

"Serp." The officer nodded solemnly.

Lamn seemed to think everything through before turning back to the officer. "I agree that these things are all unaccountable, but we have no proof that Serp is responsible for any of this. No one has heard from the Old Gods in a millennium. What gain could there possibly be?"

"That's not true." Eve interjected. All eyes swung to her, and she blushed instantly.

"What do you mean, Eve?" Lamn asked encouragingly.

"Well, Armoniel said he just recently got a message from Sopha. I mean, she didn't deliver it herself, but it was still from her. And she wanted Grigori involvement in this. Maybe they know more about this than we do?" She was blushing furiously as she finished. She suddenly felt very foolish and small.

"You make a good point." Lamn nodded at her.

"So what do we do next?" The officer asked to no one in particular.

Lamn stood. "I think we should see to the recovery of the hybrids. Maybe once some of them are more... stable... they may be able to tell us more about what happened there. Maybe they can shed some light on this. In the meantime, we still have Vane. We can question him now that we know what to ask. Beyond that, we watch and wait. Just like we always have."

The officers had left hours ago, and Lamn had retreated to his office to finalize paperwork. Tark was at garrison helping to break down all of the gear from the mission, and Behn was not available to help Eve study because he had distant family visiting. Eve sat in her study nest, processing everything that had happened.

She made her way down to Lamn's office and knocked quietly. When he called "Come in," she gently pushed the door open.

Lamn looked up and smiled warmly. "Eve! Have I been neglecting you?" he asked teasingly.

She chuckled. "No. I was just thinking about something, and I wanted to talk it over with you."

"Okay, what's on your mind?"

"Well, it's about Richard."

Lamn looked surprised.

Eve continued, "I mean, I know he's an ass, but he really doesn't belong here. What I mean to say is, I don't think it's right to keep him here, locked up. I think he should be returned to Earth." She eyed Lamn uncertainly.

"I'll be honest, I really hadn't thought too much about him, with everything else that's been going on. But I see your point. If it makes you feel better I have no problem dumping him back off on the Earth Plane."

Eve smiled genuinely. She felt it was the right thing to do.

Twenty minutes later Lamn and Eve were making their way into the basement and down the row of cells. Richards' voice rang out proudly as he belted out one of the songs from his second self-recorded album. Eve winced. When they got to the window Lamn immediately stepped in front of Eve, blocking her view.

"WHERE IS YOUR CLOTHING?" He demanded.

"Nude strike," was all Richard answered.

"But you're NOT nude," Eve called out from behind Lamn. She didn't need to see him to know.

"And HE wouldn't know that if you didn't keep announcing it! JEESH!"

Lamn shot a "What the hell is he talking about?!" look at Eve, and she just shook her head as if to answer, "Just let it go."

Lamn turned back to Richard. "Today is your lucky day! I'm taking you back to Earth!"

"WHOA, WAIT, WHAT?! NO! I don't want to go back!"

Lamn stopped short and then pinched the bridge of his nose between his thumb and forefinger.

"You don't want to go back to Earth." It was a statement, not a question.

"NO! Why would I go back?"

Lamn groaned and asked, "So... just where DO you want to go, then?"

"Well, I thought I'd stay HERE!" Richard said with a huge grin. "Well, I mean not HERE, here, like jail cell here, but here... wherever this place is!"

"Why don't you want to go back?" Eve asked, clearly ticked off that she thought she was doing him a favor, and he yet again spit it back at her.

"Why? Because there I'm ordinary. Just another human. Here, I'm different!" Again he grinned wide.

"And how would you survive here? Where would you work?" Lamn asked him dryly.

"Well, you know, I worked in electronics–"

"Don't use them here."

"And I did video and audio editing–"

"Don't do those here either."

"Well, I'm pretty useful with my hands, I mean I could do labor work–"

"We literally have magic for that."

Richard beamed as he said, "I'm a musician! I can play music!"

"What you do is an assault on the senses, and I could not see any way you could support yourself doing that."

"Betcha I COULD!"

Lamn looked at Eve, and she subtly shook her head no. Not because Richard could possibly win, but because it would create a shit show of drama for Lamn.

"I'll take that bet!"

Eve blew out a frustrated breath. This was far from over.

A half-hour later Lamn had set Richard up with a room at the local Inn. He had given him five days to report back that he had work that would support him. Eve and Lamn watched his carriage pull away.

Eve wished it was for good.

54

Eve

Eve was starting to get a rhythm. She had a morning routine, which included coffee with Lamn. She had a mid-morning routine, which included studying with Behn. And she had an afternoon routine that included talking and canoodling with Tark. The afternoon routine often spilled into her evening routine, which was normally spending time with Lamn, and maybe visiting with Ruth if she was up to it.

It had been two days since they set Richard free, and they hadn't heard a word back. For this, Eve was eternally grateful.

They had just finished dinner, and Tark and Lamn were joking around in the kitchen as they cleaned up. Eve watched them, laughing. It made her so happy to see the men in her life happy. She stepped away from the counter to give her father a hug, and then she gave Tark a quick kiss, as she announced she wanted to go up and visit with Ruth if Ruth was agreeable.

Lamn was always nervous about Ruth and her condition, but she had been getting more and more mellow as time went on. And the tea and Armoniel's calming touch had helped her as well. Lamn had confided in her that she had horrible nightmares that had her thrashing and screaming at night, but by day she was getting clearer and clearer.

Lamn spun the towel between two hands before releasing one end to snap Eve in the ass as she scooted by. The guys went back to their joking as Eve headed down the hallway toward the stairs.

Eve poked her head quietly into the bedroom. Ruth was sitting in a chair by an open window. The sun made her hair shine like spun gold, and a gentle breeze blew it away from her face. Ruth turned to see her and smiled shyly.

"Mind if I join you?" Eve asked timidly.

"I am fortunate you wish to join me. Please, come in." Ruth seemed very clear today, and it was obvious she understood the situation between them. She was still frail, but today her eyes showed a mind that was sharp as a tack, and a soul that was full of sadness and regret. Eve sat in the chair next to her but didn't say anything. After they both looked out the window for several long moments Ruth chuckled wistfully.

"You are so very like your father. He always knew to just be still and wait, and the matter would unfold itself. You certainly don't get your patience from me." Eve smiled broadly, but again, said nothing.

"I owe you many things." Ruth began. "But the first is an explanation.

"I love your father with all my heart. The day I found out we were expecting a baby was the happiest day of my life. I planned to tell him when he returned from a brief mission, no need to distract him. I went to the portal, as I had done so many times before. It was early, and there was no one around. I was content to wait. But the portal opened, and it wasn't your father or his men coming through, but one of the Winter Court. I didn't know what he was running from, but he wound up in Summer territory. I don't think he came here with any intention to take anyone; I was just in the wrong place at the wrong time.

"He grabbed me, and before I knew it we were in the Winter Court. When he first brought me there he was going to turn me over to his Lord, but after only a few days of travel, he decided to break the rules and keep me for himself. It was becoming harder and harder to keep picking up and moving. He was paranoid, looking over his shoulder constantly. I was panic-stricken, knowing your father would be looking for me. The fae who took me realized I was a hybrid, although neither of us knew what kind.

"I only just found that out from Armoniel. Apparently, my scent is different from that of human-fae hybrid. It affects fae like a strong sex spell, it overpowers them with lust.

"You can imagine my horror, knowing I was just barely pregnant, and having a fae holding me captive who only became more and more obsessed with me and lusted after me. The problem I encountered is that since I am mated, I have a very bad counter-scent which is only distinguishable when someone is skin-to-skin with me. So I was basically sending out a 'come get me' signal, only to make him want to vomit when he got close enough to touch me. You can imagine how angry this made him. But he was creative. He learned to use my hybrid scent to work himself into a frenzy, and then bring in other hybrids to satisfy himself. I became a living aphrodisiac if you will. I started to worry about what I would do when I started showing signs of motherhood, so I devised a plan: a terrible, evil, selfish plan to save my child.

"As I said, the fae was very obsessed with me, he acted like my scent was a drug, and he needed more and more sex and violence to satisfy him, so he needed more and more hybrids. Our group was growing larger and harder to keep out of sight. So one night, after he had gotten what he needed and was fairly satisfied, I spoke to him. At first, he punished me. But I made sure I planted the seeds. I told him that there was nowhere in the Winter Court that would be safe for him. It's a shame he couldn't just move to Earth, where his Lord would never think to look for him.

"I saw the idea take hold. And then it bore fruit. He gathered a few like-minded fae and convinced them to keep some hybrids for their own pleasure, and they should do it on Earth so no one would be the wiser. They would have their own rogue territory where they would be High Lords. I saw this as my opportunity to escape. I just had to bide my time and find a way.

"Soon enough my condition became apparent, and the fae were delighted. If it was a girl, she would have my scent and not have the scent of a mate. They were all giddy with the prospect of having my child, regardless of gender. Either way, they would take my child and raise it as a sex slave. They would lock me in a cage and have orgies all around me, where they could scent me. I cannot begin to tell you of their depravity.

"Finally as the time to deliver grew near, I knew I had to get out, so I spoke to one of the fae alone without the others knowing. My scent had affected them all, causing them to argue and bicker unless they were actively having sex. I think they forgot that hybrids can lie. I told him he was always my favorite, and it didn't seem fair that he did so much but still had to share. I told him that if he would take me away with him, he could start his own business with me and my offspring, and not need to share. He would have my child all for himself.

"He fell for it. Late one night, when the other two fae were back in the Winter Court, he released me. He put me in a car and told me to wait while he got supplies. They didn't know compulsions didn't work on me. I jumped right into the driver's seat and took off as fast as I could. I drove until I ran out of gas, and then I hitchhiked until I got back to Oklahoma and home. I was going to see Nancy, but you were determined to be born, so I went right to the hospital. The police called Nancy anyway. I got an earful from her, but right then I was so grateful to hear it. I had only just delivered you when I heard a voice in the hallway, one of the police officers. They were talking about the car I had stolen from the fae. They were putting together that I was the one who had stolen it. I couldn't take the chance that they would tell the fae where I was.

"I didn't want to lead them right to you, so I ran. I hot-wired a car in the parking lot and drove until I ran out of gas. Then I stole another one. I had planned to go back and get you from Nancy, once I was sure they didn't know where you were, but I never got the chance. One of them found me in Colorado. They brought me back and put me back in the cage. They cut off my finger as a reminder of how much they could hurt me, to keep me from running again. Not that they ever gave me the chance.

"I will forever regret not getting to hold you, not getting to see you take your first steps, not getting to raise you. I know you don't know me at all. But one thing you should know is that I love you. I left you so you could live, and I don't regret that you got to live a normal human life for as long as you did. It was the hardest thing I ever had to do. But I would do it again."

There were tears running down both of their faces.

55

Tark

Tark had planned a special day for Eve. He had asked her to clear her calendar so he could take her into town. He planned to do some shopping, have dinner with her, and then take her to see his estate. He knew his estate wasn't as big or as impressive as Lamn's, but he also knew it didn't matter to her. She was going to be the first female he ever asked to stay overnight with him there. He had already talked to Lamn about it, but he was still very nervous about how she would respond.

Eve came bouncing down the stairs in a beautiful jade-green silk dress, with a low-cut neckline, that hugged her figure nicely before flowing out at the bottom. Her long indigo locks swung from side to side with each step she took. She was an incredible vision. He was instantly aroused and had to do equations in his head to avoid embarrassing himself.

She knew just what effect she had on him as she stopped in front of him and spun slowly so he could take her all in. He groaned. She smiled broadly and kissed him deeply for his unspoken compliment. She was learning to read him so well.

Tark broke the kiss off sooner than he would have liked to, because he would never like to. But they had things to do. He offered his elbow, which she threaded her dainty arm through, and he walked her out to the waiting carriage.

He brought her to see several of the artisans in town, first they stopped at a painter's studio. They compared paintings and styles, and Tark bought a painting of a swan taking flight that Eve truly seemed to enjoy. Next he brought her to see a blacksmith, which confused her in her long gown. At a safe, and clean, distance she appreciated his works: swords, knives, and different practical metal pieces. The next stop was a bakery where Eve got to sample several different delicacies. Tark made sure to buy a dozen of the chocolate covered berry treats that she liked most. Next Tark took Eve to a jewelry maker, and she got to watch as they created rings, bangles and necklaces out of fine silver and gold metals and beautiful gems. While Eve was distracted talking to the jeweler, Tark made a very special purchase, and tucked it into his pocket for later.

Eve's head was spinning. She practiced her Faeish during their day, both with Tark and all of the artisans. It was getting easier for her, and she was really starting to feel like she belonged. They strolled quaint streets, looked in shop windows, and held hands like teenagers.

As they passed a bookstore, Eve heard music... it was familiar. As realization hit her, her stomach sank like a rock. She abruptly stopped walking, jerking Tark's hand as he was about to move forward. He turned to see what was going on, saw her staring across the street, and followed her line of sight.

There, on the street corner, sat Richard. He had a guitar case open on the ground in front of him, and he was belting out his music like he was on stage during a concert. He was in full performance mode. Eve ran her hand over her face as she blew out a groan.

This wasn't street performing, this was begging. And the citizens of Fae didn't know what to make of it. Eve and Tark watched; as people approached Richard they looked confused or disgusted, and crossed to the other side of the street.

Before she could do anything, Tark stepped into her line of sight.

"Today is for us. This can wait. Okay?" He looked into her eyes hopefully. With one last glance at Richard, she brought her full attention back to him and nodded with a smile. They hurried down the street, and away from the spectacle.

Tark brought her to a quaint restaurant at the edge of a lake, and their table was situated on a private balcony overlooking the water. After their day of shopping and discovering they were both exhausted and hungry. Tark explained all of the dishes to her, and Eve chose a meal made with a meat they didn't have on the Earth Plane, with some equally foreign vegetables. The wine she was familiar with.

They ate, talked, laughed, and drank until the sun started setting. Tark sat transfixed, staring at Eve with the lake and the sunset behind her. He was in awe. Her mouth was moving, she was talking, he just didn't hear a thing. He wished he could bottle this moment, seal it in time forever.

Does she even know how beautiful she is?

"TARK?" She laughed.

He shook out of his stupor, and grinned at her. He was busted.

The entire ride to his estate Tark bounced his knee with anxiety. Eve definitely noticed it, but didn't say anything. He hadn't told her yet where they were going. The carriage wound around the final corner and then drove up the long tree-lined drive to the large house at the end, just on the banks of a lake.

When it stopped, Tark rushed to help Eve out. She eyed the building with large eyes, seeming overwhelmed with the size of it, and for just a moment Tark felt pride in himself and his accomplishment.

"Where are we?" Eve asked quietly, still looking over all of the turrets and windows.

"You'll see!"

Tark placed his hand on her lower back and gently urged her forward, up the stairs, and to the massive double doors. A doorman appeared and pulled the doors open for them, and they walked inside.

It was a lot like Lamn's estate, only on a slightly smaller scale. Smaller, but still HUGE. The marble and the decor were a little more masculine, but it was all done very tastefully.

Tark stopped and took both of Eve's hands in his. "Welcome to my home. You are the only female I have ever brought to see it, I mean, other than family, of course." He blushed furiously.

She looked at him with surprise. Clearly, she had not expected to hear that from him.

"Let me give you the tour!" He chirped nervously, and Eve had to giggle a little at his discomfort.

He walked her around the first floor, his office, a parlor, a music room, the kitchen and dining rooms. Then he took her up the stairs and showed her several guest rooms, a library, and a parlor. Lastly he took her up to the third floor, which was primarily his quarters: a parlor, his bedroom, and his private bath.

He opened the doors and let her walk through. He watched her intently as she took in all of the details, from his books on the shelves, to his telescope, to his desk. In his bedroom she admired the color scheme, the arrangement, the size. She gravitated to the glass doors which led out onto the large deck, and when she stepped out she gasped in awe. The sight of the mists hanging low over the lake with the last red rays of the sun was incredible.

And the sight of her taking it in was more than Tark could put into words. He walked up and hugged her from behind. She twisted her head to give him a kiss.

"Do you like it?"

"LIKE IT?! What's not to like? It's huge, and beautiful, and I can smell you in every room!"

Tark had to pull away from her a little, lest he poke her in the ass, the way she was talking.

"Well, I'm glad you feel that way." He made his way around her so that he was standing in front of her again.

"And why's that?" she sassed.

"Because I have a problem," he teased back.

"You do?"

"Yes. My scent is in all of these rooms, as you have so aptly pointed out. That will never do. It's not nearly good enough. I should very much like to be able to smell YOU in every room."

"So what would you recommend," she teased back, "that I walk from room to room so you can sniff me in each?"

"Mmmmm... not quite what I had in mind," he answered with a smirk.

"OH! I know!" She grinned, "I can rub the curtains all over me in each room!" She laughed as she said it.

"OR..."

"Or?"

He was suddenly and adorably timid.

"Or... you could... come and stay here with me?" He still had a small smile on his face, but she saw right through it. He was scared shitless.

"Tark? Are you asking me to move in with you?!" She asked with mock offense.

"Not... exactly..." He slowly got down on one knee, holding her hand in one of his while he reached into his pocket with the other.

Eve froze with her jaw hanging open in complete and utter shock.

"Eve, I know I messed things up royally when we first met, and I know we have only known each other for a short while, but I meant it when I said that I couldn't let you go. I can't. I can't even imagine my life without you in it. So if you have it in your heart to forgive me a second time for being a selfish bastard, I would very much like to ask you to be my mate. Oh... and here... I know that on Earth they have a custom of presenting a ring when requesting a mate, I hope you like it."

And with that, he pulled out the ring. If Eve's jaw wasn't already hanging open, she would have dropped it at the sight of the ring. She couldn't even breathe. It was incredibly detailed with filigree work unlike anything she had ever seen, and the indigo stone in the center was ENORMOUS. Almost gaudy. Almost.

She was speechless. She couldn't get her mouth to close so she could form words.

Tark watched her, at first pleased that he had been able to surprise her, but the longer she stood and gawked at him, the more he started to feel like he must have done something horribly wrong.

"Eve? Say something."

She said the only thing she could.

"EeHH Malooshh"

Tark was up and dominating her mouth with his in a millisecond. He pulled her close and worshiped her mouth with his lips, then ran kisses across her jawline, and down her neck. She moaned softly as she tilted her head back to give him more access, and he greedily continued his feverish kisses downward, occasionally nipping or sucking gently on the tender skin of her neck.

Eve knew the moment the scent hit him. His fingers held her a little bit tighter, and his arms held her a little bit closer. His kisses became frenzied. He was gasping and moaning with each breath even as he moved one hand into her hair and the other smoothly floated down to cup her ass to him. She felt his very evident desire prodding her abdomen.

She was feeling the same intoxicating rush of desire flooding her body. She worked hard to try to pull back, to maintain some clarity, even though her body was on fire. The pulsing ache between her legs was like a black hole of desire, slowly pulling them both into its gravitational pull. While she wanted to rip the dress off over her head and climb him like a tree, she knew now was not the right time.

And so she fought with herself, to create some space. To clear her head. Even as she made space, he would follow her, step for step. She would remove one hand, he'd place it elsewhere. She would back up, he would surge forward. While she certainly was not concerned that he would force himself on her, she was finding it disconcerting that she couldn't seem to pull away from him. The fear of just losing herself altogether to this sensation was just too terrifying. She finally placed both of her hands on his shoulders and pushed, with a firm, "TARK, NO."

That seemed to cut through the fog of the drugged-like state he was in. He was still panting and obviously wanting, but he was also aware something had gone wrong. He stopped and shook his head, groggy in the euphoric haze. Eve walked to the edge of the railing to give them a little distance and breathing room. Tark seemed frozen in place, his eyebrows knitted in concern.

"Eve, did I do something wrong?"

"No, no, Tark, you didn't. I'm... I'm just not ready yet."

"Eve, Honey, we don't have to do anything you don't want to–"

"I mean about moving in, getting married... this is really sudden, and I just need a little time to think it all through. You know, process."

Tark did his best to look supportive, but Eve knew him too well. He was clearly devastated, and trying not to make things any worse. She walked over to him and looked him in the eye.

"Tark. Eehh Maloosh. This isn't a 'no'. This is 'I just need to process.'"

Tark looked up through his lashes sheepishly. "You promise this isn't a 'no?'"

He was so childlike in that raw moment. Eve laughed out loud.

"Do you trust me?" she asked him.

"With my life," he answered immediately.

"Then give me a little time to come to terms with the changes, ok?"

"OK... Does that mean no sleepover?" He stuck out his lower lip to pout dramatically. Eve burst into laughter, and he soon followed.

"No sleepover... but I could use a knight in shining armor to escort me to my father's home safely." She batted her eyelashes at him equally dramatically.

In one fluid motion, he wrapped an arm around her beneath her knees, with his other arm around her upper back, lifted her off of the ground like she was a princess, and proceeded to carry her all the way back out to the front.

While they waited for the carriage he looked into her eyes and whispered, "Eehh Maloosh eim Gaishh."

"What does the rest mean?"

"It means 'I love you, my Goddess.'"

He leaned down and kissed her reverently, with his hands cupping either side of her face gently. But he didn't linger too long, for fear he would want to ravage her like an animal in heat. Her flaring nostrils and dilated pupils told him she was feeling it as well. Tonight might not be the night, but by the Old Gods, when they finally did get together, she just might kill him.

He'd die happy.

56

Lamn

Lamn strolled into the kitchen at his usual early hour. He liked to get up before the rest of the household. So he was surprised when he smelled coffee and was even more surprised to find Eve sitting at her usual spot by the window. She was NOT an early riser.

She was wearing her 'worried face.' He noticed that when she faced a problem she couldn't work through logically, her eyes would take on a pained quality, and her lips would curl down into the slightest frown. But her eyebrows would lift in the middle, instead of curling downward, like when she was irritated.

He made his own coffee and took his seat beside her, looking out the window as she was. A half-hour of silence passed before she looked in his direction and he asked what she wanted to know.

"How did you know Mom was the one?"

He smiled at her gently. His memories of Ruth were one of his favorite subjects to discuss. "I don't know that I consciously 'knew' it. I felt it. We hadn't known each other long, and we were stuck on the Earth Plane while I recovered. I think it hit me when I thought of going back to Fae without her. I panicked. I completely lost it. There was some part of me that just refused to lose her. I knew then that I needed to make her my mate."

Eve smiled, but it didn't quite reach her eyes.

"But... how did you know it was love?... And not just... her scent?"

She was treading carefully, as this was very personal, but she really had to know. And she had to know from him.

He eyed her with a small smirk.

"Is THAT what this is about? Okay, your mother nursed me for a while when I was injured, we were together all the time, and yes, her scent drove me crazy, but I was injured and there wasn't a lot I could do about it. Then she started feeling too attached to me, she tried to put some distance between us. She asked others to check my bandages and make sure I was healing. She stopped coming by herself.

"I went crazy. I couldn't get her out of my system. I asked every day when she would be back. I thought maybe I had scared her away. I was terrified I'd never see her again. By the time she came to her senses, and realized that she was just as crazy about me as I was about her; the scent had long worn off. The feeling never did.

"Eve, the scent affects the body, it's like a stimulant. It is very primal, it makes you want to act on it. But it doesn't make you feel like you're in love or make you want to get married. Those are emotions of the heart, not the lust of the body.

"Oh, and Eve, he was in the field for quite a while, away from your scent, when he talked to me about how much he missed you and what he hoped for in the future. Please consider that before making any long-term decisions."

And then he winked at her. Before he leaned in and kissed her lovingly on her forehead.

It was early afternoon when Sera received her guests, Lamn, Eve, and Tark into the sitting room in her shared house. The other girls were out working their new jobs, but Sera had the day off, and had arranged the meeting when Lamn had called.

Eve noticed how confident she looked. Her cranberry silk dress flowed around her beautifully. But it wasn't just her clothing. She walked with poise and grace, as if she had been receiving guests all of her life, and not serving them. Gone was the timid mouse of a girl. She really was in her element.

She invited them to sit, as she called for coffee. "Vane."

The door flew open, and Vane scurried in, dressed... in a maid's uniform. He wore a small, low-cut blouse, and a very short black ruffled skirt with layers beneath it so it puffed out, and over that was a small frilly apron. His long hair had been pulled up into a ponytail with a ribbon tied in a bow around it in the back.

Everyone froze in shock, except Sera.

Vane broke the silence, staring at Sera and shouting bitterly, "I fucking hate myself so fucking much!"

At that, everyone, except Vane, fell into uncontrolled fits of laughter. Eve was doubled over, her arms around her middle, tears streaming down her face, fighting for air, laughing hard.

Vane just stood there, enraged.

Finally, Sera asked him to bring in a tray of coffee for their guests, and to be sure it was not tampered with in any way. He answered coldly, "I am a fucking bitch and I will suffer for this!" before he strode out of the room to follow the order.

Eve had fallen over, still laughing. Tark had to prop her back up as she gasped in lungfuls of air.

Lamn thanked Sera for receiving them, and explained that they had recently gone on a mission to the Earth Plane to free some captive hybrids. He asked her if she would allow him to question Vane further about his involvement with the hybrid traffickers.

As expected, she was absolutely fine with it.

When Vane reappeared moments later with the tray of coffee and finger sandwiches, she waited until they were all laid out before she ordered Vane to stand in the middle of the room and answer any questions her guests might have fully and honestly, and to help them in any way he knew to be possible.

She stood and turned to Lamn. "I assume this information is confidential, so I will be in the kitchen. Please just send Vane to let me know when you are done with him." She smiled warmly, took her coffee, and left the room.

The shade of furious never fluctuated on Vane's face. He was livid.

Lamn began the interrogation.

"Vane, tell me who is ultimately in charge of the brothel stronghold we just raided?"

"I have told you, myself and two other fae, whom I've named before."

"Is there someone who made it possible for you to create the establishment?"

"Someone?" He was evading.

"Was there any being, fae or otherwise, who made it possible for you to be able to create your establishment?"

"Yes."

"Who was that being? What was his/her name?"

"That I don't know. We worked through an intermediary, a Fallen Watcher."

Tark gasped in shock, and Eve looked at him with an obvious question in her eyes. He subtly nodded 'no', and she understood he would explain later.

"And what was that Fallen Watcher called?"

"Botis."

"How can we contact him?"

"You cannot. He can come to you, and only if he wants to. Are you quite finished yet?"

"Is Serp involved with these business dealings?"

"SERP?! As in the Old God, Serp? You really are losing your mind, aren't you?"

"Who created and powered the portal between the stronghold and the shack."

"I ... I'm not certain who created it or powered it. I had always assumed Botis did it, but I did not witness that."

"And who set up the protective field in the building?"

"Again, I assumed it was Botis. We could not create something so strong."

"And Botis never mentioned who he worked for?"

"No. He only called him his Lord."

"And you never thought to ask who it was you were dealing with?"

"Of course I thought to ask! I'm not a fool. But Botis was quite closed-lipped, and to be honest, he provided a lot more for us than we did for him, so I was getting the better end of the bargain, and didn't want to cock it all up."

"And just what did you provide for him?"

"We gave him a few hybrids, information about the Lords we serve in the Winter Court, and where he could find the portals. Useless information really, things he could have gotten from anyone."

Lamn's face drained of color. This was very, very bad.

57

Eve

Eve stood nervously at the railing of the patio, looking out over the water. The beauty and peace of the scene did nothing for her frayed nerves or butterflies. After their meeting at Sera's, she had asked Tark if they could go back to his estate, just the two of them. His smile had lit the room. Now she was rethinking her decision.

Chill out! For God's sake, it's not like you've never been alone with a guy at his place before! Calm down, already!

She'd been with guys before, it's true. But she had never had this 'scent' phenomenon before. Traditionally she was tender and romantic, unfortunately, none of the guys she had ever been with were. She found them grabby and needy, so she was used to having unsatisfying sex.

The whole 'scent' problem just threw her for a loop. Now she wasn't worried about being the one holding back. She worried she would lose herself like some crazed animal, and Tark would think less of her. She didn't want him to think she was some sex maniac, but when the energy started building last time... it had taken ALL of her self-control to just back away. She knew that men liked to be the aggressors, she didn't want to chase him away, not after everything they'd been through.

Tark walked up behind her, and seeing her frown, put his arms around her loosely to give her freedom to move.

"Change of heart?" He asked, genuinely caring.

"N...nooo."

She looked up nervously through her lashes. He chuckled down at her, then leaned down to whisper conspiratorially, "Okay, love of my heart, I will make a fae bargain with you: we have several different things we can do tonight, but you are in charge. I am your servant, here at your disposal, and I will do nothing without your command. Sound fair?"

"What kind of a bargain is that?! No," she answered, mortified. He couldn't expect HER to call the shots! She'd be tearing his clothes off in seconds.

"It is a bargain that I can live with. I don't want to push you into anything you may not be comfortable with, so you decide what we do. There are books, we could walk, we could take a bath, we could eat..."

"And then?" she asked, suddenly timid.

"And then nothing," he replied. "We can just go to sleep now if that's what you would like to do. I could sleep in a guest room if it would make you feel more comfortable. Eve, I expect nothing in particular. This night is your night."

"This is OUR night," she said, looking into his eyes.

"And I am happy to give this night to you, to be yours, for whatever you may desire." He smiled at her genuinely.

She blinked a few times in confusion. She wanted to jump him. SO BADLY. But she also didn't want to appear like the kind of girl who just asked him here for a booty call.

She had to find a way to get him to make the first move. Maybe she could distract him with a few other things, and then he'd just take over?! Seemed like a good plan!

Tark

"Okay, how about a snack first?"

She smiled up at him wickedly. He knew she was up to something, and he couldn't wait to see what it was. But he had been ready for this, himself. He ducked into the bedroom, and came right back, pushing a silver cart covered with pastries, cheeses, fruit, and the chocolate candies that Eve had liked so much. He walked her to the little table on the patio and pushed her chair in as she sat. He then transferred the many plates of edible delights to the table, before sitting, himself.

He poured them each a glass of wine, one he knew she liked. Holding the glass aloft, he made his toast to her, "To my beautiful bride-to-be: my heart knew I loved you long before my head caught up. I will be forever chasing you in my heart, and I hope that not a day goes by that I don't catch you again."

She raised her glass and added her own toast, "To my sexy husband-to-be: you challenge me in so many good ways, always opening me up to new experiences, always making me want more. I hope that not a day goes by that we don't experience having more, together." She smiled her wicked smile at him and proudly noticed that he had to subtly adjust in his chair.

They sipped their wine, and before he could take a bite of anything Eve was offering his lips a chocolate-covered berry with her fingers. He took the berry into his mouth, and eagerly returned the favor. She, however, brought her dainty hand up to hold his gently in place while she ran her warm soft lips over his fingertips, letting the tip of her tongue sneak out to take the berry as it stroked the underside of his fingers.

His eyes clamped shut and he groaned.

Game on!

They continued to hand-feed each other tasty morsels, savoring in the flavors and the stolen touches of fingers or flicks of tongues. At one point Eve leaned into him with a small bite of chocolate held between her teeth. He didn't know what it was about her baring her teeth at him that excited him so much, but he was instantly rock hard, and regretting letting her set the pace. He leaned in, taking the chocolate into his mouth, as she snaked her hand around his head firmly and kissed him deeply with the chocolate still between them. His tongue stroked hers, and the velvety sugar of the chocolate flavor stoked his inner fire even higher. A deeper groan rose from his chest.

Before he could abandon his senses, Eve pulled back gently, demurely. Her wicked smile was still in place. The only satisfaction he could take was that her own eyes were dilated as well, she may be playing coy, but her nipples announced she wanted him as much as the bulge in his trousers announced his interest.

He would play her game. And they both would win.

"What next, Eim Gaish?"

She looked around, considering. "A bubble bath?" She batted her eyes at him innocently.

He let out a gentle "oof" before smiling up at her. "Your wish is my command!"

With that, he hopped up quickly, hoping she didn't notice the tent of his pants he covered with a cloth napkin, as he jogged back into the bedroom and headed for the bathroom. He ran the hot water and pulled out some of the bath items he had purchased recently for Eve's visit. He wasn't really sure how to use them, so he poured the contents of a few bottles into the water, and hoped for the best. Almost instantly, a thick layer of bubbles formed on the top of the water as it continued rising. As the water continued to fill the tub, so did the iridescent bubbles. When the bubbles reached the very top of the tub, Tark stuck his hand in, to find the tub only half full of water; and half full of suds.

He tried scooping armfuls of suds out of the tub and running them over to the shower; which left him covered in bubbles from head to toe, with bubbles all over the floor. Realizing there was no undoing this mess, he instead embraced it, allowing the water to continue to rise, and the bubbles to overflow in a cascade. This gave the appearance of the tub sitting in the clouds.

He shook his head at his own ineptitude and hoped that Eve would find it charming... or at the very least funny. He strolled back out to the patio, and upon seeing him with clumps of bubbles stuck in his hair and all over his soaked clothing, she burst out laughing. He couldn't even be embarrassed. He loved to see her laugh.

He extended his hand, like a proper servant, and helped her up. He walked her through the bedroom, and into the waiting bathroom with the steaming tub of water sitting in its own cloud of bubbles, seeming to fill the room. She gasped and giggled.

Before he could turn to give her privacy, she whipped her shirt off and threw it over his face. He peeled it off and she was bent over in front of him, in the process of stepping out of her pants. The cheeks of her ass were practically pressed into his hardness, and he stifled a moan.

She walked quickly toward the tub, reaching behind her to unclasp her bra, and pulling it off of her shoulders she flung it carelessly. As she reached the edge of the tub she gave him one last wicked smile over her shoulder, before she again bent over, ass in the air, and stepped out of her panties, which remained lost in the cloud of bubbles.

He stood looking at her naked back like she was a work of art, his divine goddess. His mind was broken by the sight of it, he couldn't even move.

Eve gently stepped into the tub, first one leg, then the other, and slowly lowered herself down. A new cascade of bubbles overflowed around the edges, and she truly did look like an angel among the clouds. She turned her mischievous eyes on him, smiling seductively.

"Aren't you going to join me?" she asked all innocence.

Tark's hardness throbbed like a gong. There was NO way he'd be able to sit in that water with her and not touch her. That would lead to kissing her. That would lead to bending her over the edge of the tub and...

He turned away, blushing crimson, trying desperately to remember equations, inventory, or anything other than the previous line of thought. It took a few minutes, and a lot of mental acrobatics, but he finally felt like he had just a little control over himself. He turned back to see her pouting her lower lip out manipulatively.

"Eim Gaish... I would love the honor of washing you and relaxing you." He strode over to the tub, knowing this was a futile exercise, but determined to see it through. He had promised her. He could do this.

He pushed away as much of the bubbling mess as he could so that he sat right next to the tub. He pulled out a soft sponge he had bought just for her and submerged it in the steaming water.

Eve groaned quietly in pleasure, her eyes closed. Tark groaned inwardly, adjusting his pants. He soaped the sponge up until there was a good lather and then sent a prayer to the Old Gods before he gently pulled her shoulders forward to run the sponge all over her back, neck, and arms. Eve cooed and sighed with each movement. Tark couldn't see her body below the blanket of bubbles, but he knew she was aroused. He tried to keep his mind on his mission, and not think about the warm wet body just underneath the sponge in his hand. He could only feel her general shape. *He wanted to brush his fingers over every inch of her...*

FOCUS.

When he finished her back and anything he could reach, he gently pulled her back to sitting. He was trying to work up the courage to wash her front when she gathered her legs up and stood in the water facing him. Clumps of billowing bubbles drizzled down her body, drops forming from her breast and dripping back into the tub. She stood in front of him soapy, wet, and gloriously naked. Her little thatch of soft indigo curls, at the summit of her thighs, was right in front of his face.

"I thought it would be easier to wash my front this way..." She offered innocently, "Unless, you changed your mind and want to join me in the warm water?..."

And then she smiled.

She had won.

She knew it.

He knew it.

He ripped his clothing off, not bothering with buttons or ties, tearing the shirt down the middle, and pulled his pants right over his legs in one motion. He launched himself into the tub with her, and she lowered herself back down as well. He sat at the edge of the tub and gently pulled her over to sit between his legs, her back to his chest. Luckily, the sponge was still within arms reach, so he began to lather her chest, paying attention to each breast, moving down her ribs, over her abdomen and hips, down the outside of a thigh, and then back up the middle pausing at the apex, before resuming with the other thigh.

Eve wriggled in his lap, brushing her smooth wet ass against his obvious hardness. Tark's hands stopped where they were. He let out a hiss between closed teeth at the feel of her smooth body stroking him. He wrapped his arms around her in the water, pulling her closer, increasing the friction on his demanding stiffness. As if she were a sea creature, she spun fluidly within his hold, so that they were face to face, belly to belly. He could feel the silky bulbs of her breasts pressed into his chest, her tiny nipples prodding him. He could feel his cock breaching the soft thatch of her curls, directing itself to lodge in the wedge of her body, where it knew it needed to be.

Not yet...

He stood abruptly, much to Eve's surprise, pulling her with him. Stepping out of the tub briskly, he grabbed two large soft towels. He extended his hand to her to help her out. He wasn't quite sure what she was thinking, but he saw where this was heading, and he didn't want for their first time to be in a bathing room.

Eve

Eve took his hand gratefully and stepped carefully out into the cloud of bubbles still floating on the floor.

DAMN IT! I ALMOST had him!

She was dying to just grab him, take him, have her way with him. Why was he being so difficult?! Most guys would have been balls deep into her by now! The scent! Could she use that to her advantage? Get him to lose control first, so she wouldn't seem too eager?

Tark was toweling her off, and she sighed contentedly. She did love that he pampered her. No one had ever given her this much attention before. When she was dry, he went to work drying himself. Eve took the opportunity to get a really good look at him without his clothing on. He was very muscular, with that sexy cut of abs leading down to...

Holy Cow, he's HUGE!

Tark laughed, and Eve looked up to realize she had been caught staring at his dick. She blushed fiercely. She couldn't deny it. Hell, she could hardly keep herself from going right back to staring at it. Tark walked up to her, suddenly confident. She blushed even more, trying to find anywhere to look so that she wasn't embarrassing herself.

He stood right in front of her so that she could feel the heat of his body, but not his skin on hers. He gently took her hand in his, and placed her palm over his hard cock, gently. It jumped under her touch, straining and stiffening. With his other hand, he lifted her chin and turned her face gently until she met his eyes.

"Eve, I am yours. All of me. I would be delighted for the rest of my life if you would look at me like that, any and every time you want to. This..." His cock thickened in her hand, "is all yours. I expect you to take it whenever you want. It exists only to please you, to bring you to mindless ecstasy, and it is wasted otherwise. If you want it, you must take it. Promise me? Please don't make me beg you, Eve, because you know I will."

Her body moved without thought. She launched herself onto him, arms tightly around his neck, legs wrapped around his waist. She could feel his hard length pressed beneath her wet pussy, straining against her. Her mouth kissed his savagely with tongue and teeth bared. Her hands dug into his hair pulling his face into her kiss, closer, harder, deeper.

He met her savagery with his own. One of his hands massaged her ass firmly, while the other massaged the globe of her soft breast, reaching to pinch the taut pink nipple which had hardened into a pebble. She moaned deeply into his mouth. Her self-control was beginning to slip into a euphoric haze. She felt him react to the scent affecting him. His cock, impossibly, grew even harder, his body shuddered, and his breathing was ragged.

Holding her firmly in place, he marched them into the bedroom. When he stood over the bed, he pried her arms off of his neck, and let her drop onto the mattress behind her, her legs still entwined around his waist. She was panting and grinding her wetness against him. He leaned over her, one hand on either side of her head, suspended above her. His eyes were wild with need, and his breathing was strained.

"If you want this, you must order me. That's our bargain."

"Tark..." she whined.

He moved as if to stand back up, and she threw her arms around his neck to keep him in place.

"Make love to me?" She asked meekly.

He returned her wicked smile. "As you wish Eim Gaish..."

He gently lowered himself, and began kissing her throat slowly and softly. His hand gently kneaded her breast. His other hand trailed its fingertips over her torso, down her thighs. He moved with a languidness, a respectful gentleness.

Eve groaned in frustration.

"Is something not to your liking, Eim Gaish?" He kissed her jawline. Only his caged breathing gave away that he wanted more.

"It's just... ugh...."

He could see her struggling to say it, without saying it. He knew she was a strong fierce woman, and he didn't want to make her into a meek plaything for his pleasure. He wanted to fuck her as a tiger, not a lamb. He took her hand again and wrapped it around his cock again. This time she immediately squeezed, and stroked it, from base to tip. He moaned loudly as he looked her in the eye.

"Tell me Eim Gaish. Tell me what you want me to do with that cock. Tell me how to use it on you. Tell me how to make you scream in pleasure. I want to hear you scream my name as you ride that cock. Just tell me what you want."

"I WANT YOU TO FUCK ME, HARD!" She wasn't waiting any longer.

She managed to push him over onto the bed so that she was on top of him. Rather than jumping on his cock and riding him raw, like her body was begging her to do, she instead straddled his waist, plastering hungry kisses, nips, and flicks of her tongue down his neck, a little payback. He groaned, and let her take the lead.

Her fingernails raked him like claws over his pecs and ribs, and she latched her teeth onto one of his nipples and nipped it gently. He groaned and his body jumped at the sensation. She worked her way down his abdomen, trailing her tongue over his six-pack until finally reaching her desired destination.

She had never liked this with other guys. They were too forceful, too greedy. But she couldn't wait to try this with Tark. She wanted to make him lose control.

She shot him her wicked smile as he watched her intently. Grabbing his length in one hand she began to pump her hand up and down, base to tip, firmly. He threw his head back and moaned her name loudly, his body going tense. She brought her mouth down so that he could feel the heat of her breath against his most tender skin. Snaking her tongue out, she trailed it up the underside of his shaft, and then down again. Each touch had him groaning, calling her name, begging. His breaths were ragged, and his cock was like a rock wrapped in silk in her hand. She continued pumping him in her hand, letting her tongue swirl around the tip only. He begged her, calling her name over and over.

Experimentally she took him deep into her mouth, sucking gently. His body spasmed in reaction, his hand fisting in her hair gently. He wasn't holding or forcing her, he was guiding her, communicating with her. His hips rocked in time with her mouth. She had this power over him. She fucking loved it. She continued to suck him in as deeply as she could, her hand pumping furiously, and she reached between his thighs with her other hand to massage his balls.

He was up and over her with a loud roar.

She was on her back again, arching off of the bed, her legs spread wide, wanton and not caring.

He landed on top of her, devouring her mouth, one hand still fisted in her hair, his other hand behind her ass pulling her warm wet core against the throbbing ache of his cock. She knew he wasn't going to last.

He ripped himself away from their kiss, breathing heavily, chest heaving, and looked into her eyes. She realized he was looking for permission.

"Fuck me, Tark. Fuck me hard with that cock! That's an ORDER."

She reached down to move the head of his cock to her slick opening. He slid inside easily. He slowly stroked in and down, letting her adjust to him. He would slide in a little more, and then slide back. Slide in a little bit further, wait, slide back. Each time he got deeper. Each time Eve groaned, as he hit new heights of pleasure she had never experienced before, and he would groan with her.

The deeper he got, the louder Eve got, as she felt the most primitive pleasure she had ever experienced. She just wanted him seated all the way inside of her, she wanted to be full with him, the pleasure was building, and he was taking too long.

"NOW, Tark, HARDER!" She demanded.

She was wild, and out of control, the feelings so intense that she reacted purely on instinct. Her feet were behind him, her heels in his ass, encouraging his hips to push his cock all the way inside of her. Her fingers clawed at his back, leaving welts on his skin.

She threw her head back and screamed, "Faster, Tark! Harder! YES! YES!"

She was thrashing, clawing, scrambling... her pleasure built so high that she was euphoric, almost suspended in time. All that mattered was the friction of his massive cock pumping into her.

Tark

Tark rammed his cock into her body, hard and fast, his hips slamming hers roughly. He was beyond thought. He was an animal. He could feel her pelvic bone hitting his own and it only sent him higher. He cried out her name like a prayer, in between groans and primal grunts. His pleasure rose, the euphoria seeping into his body. He could not stop. All he knew was thrusting into her, feeling the muscles in her pussy squeezing his cock, harder. *HARDER. YES!!!!*

Her body suddenly went taut, her back arched, as she screamed through her endless release. On and on it continued, her body locked around his, convulsing. He let out a roar as her pussy clamped down around his cock, grabbing it inside her and milking him into her. His body shook violently, as it felt like his very life essence was being sucked out of him and into her body. It was the most amazing pleasure he had ever experienced. Her body went slack underneath him, falling onto the mattress, gasping for air, and he soon followed suit, completely spent and boneless as he fell in a puddle on top of her, heaving breaths.

The energy in the room seemed to vibrate and pulse, still very intense around them. Finally, the energy seemed to sizzle around them like an electric current. They both jumped with a scream, as a shock jolted through their bodies, and then the energy seemed to settle on their skin, enveloping them both like shrinkwrap, until it faded into them.

He moved beside her, his body completely soaked in sweat, and stroked her cheek with his thumb.

"What WAS that... shock?" she added on for clarity.

"THAT was our mate seal." He smiled at her with pride as he rubbed the end of his nose against hers.

"You knew that was going to happen, and you didn't warn me?" she laughed.

"To be fair, I only *hoped* it would happen. One never knows for sure."

"So does that mean we're married now?"

"It means we are natural mates, and that we are bonded to each other. But it is only between you and I. It is not recognized as a formal mating, or marriage, until you have the ceremony for that."

"Oh thank God!" she laughed.

He looked at her, incredulous. "What do you mean?! You would be unhappy being married to me?"

She could see his feelings were hurt. "NO. I'm just looking forward to the wedding night sex, that's all!" She smiled at him.

He pulled her in for another deep kiss, enjoying the taste of her on his mouth. She placed a hand on his cheek lovingly and looked deeply into his eyes.

"Tark"

"Yes Eim Gaish?"

"I order you to do that to me again!"

<h1 style="text-align:center">58</h1>

Armoniel

This was unprecedented for Armoniel. He had never imagined that his fallen brothers may be actively working *against* humanity. He knew of Botis, he remembered when some of his brothers had gathered in defiance of their purpose, left their roles as Watchers, chose to 'fall' to Earth. He even saw a few of them on the Earth Plane occasionally. They just seemed like purposeless souls. Yes, they had rebelled against protecting humanity, he had never thought they would take the further step of defying Sopha by working against them.

He directed his consciousness into the realm where his brothers stood watch, knowing he would find Samyaza there. He quickly felt Samyaza's presence, and he coalesced nearby. There was gladness at the reunion.

"Brother, I am surprised to see you back so soon! How is your family?"

"They are well, Samyaza, I thank you for inquiring about them. I have actually come to seek your guidance on an urgent matter."

"Tell me what troubles you, Armoniel."

"The recent assignment that Sopha requested of me, it was not just an Earth/Fae issue, I fear. I have discovered that Botis of the Fallen was assisting the Winter Fae in their deception and abuse, and he is not working alone. It would appear that he has changed allegiance."

"That is troubling news. I have seen Botis on the Earth Plane. He now takes the form of a viper, as if he could hide from our Sight. Do you suspect Botis now serves Serp? He is the only one of Sopha's children who would likely act in this way."

"That is what I fear."

"This is troubling indeed. The humans were Serp's own creation, and it is well within his character that he might seek to grow his dominion to include fae as well. Tell me all that you know, Brother, and I will call a council meeting."

Armoniel laid all of the facts out for Samyaza, what was known, and what was suspected. Almost instantly the atmosphere came to life with the presence of the most respected of Watchers.

Samyaza relayed what Armoniel had told him to the group, and then they were invited to share what they had witnessed from the Earth Plane. Armoniel's heart felt heavy, it did not look promising.

From what the Watchers pieced together, there was a much larger movement at play. One in which Serp was manipulating human, hybrid, and fae alike, and he was recruiting the dissatisfied Fallen Watchers to act as his agents. They could only hypothesize that his purpose was for more dominion and power, based on his history, but several things were very clear. There would be suffering among the creatures of the planes. And Sopha would NOT be pleased.

Eve

Eve looked around the table. Her mother and father, and she still couldn't believe that she could say that, sat next to each other giving each other adoring looks. Tark sat beside her, his hand resting on her knee. They enjoyed their first meal together as a proper family, with the tropical backdrop of the greenhouse behind them. Eve squeezed Tark's hand, as her heart just about burst with love.

Ruth was growing stronger everyday, and Eve really enjoyed her company. It was clear Ruth adored her, it was also clear that Ruth had the same stubborn streak that Eve had inherited. But there was nothing that could come between them again.

As the conversation wound down the group headed for a more

comfortable sitting room, and Eve helped Ama clear the table, it was just habit for her. She refused to be waited on like royalty. Tark hugged her from behind as she loaded dishes into the sink. He leaned down and whispered into her ear, "I noticed you are not wearing your ring. Should I be concerned?"

Eve rolled her eyes as she twisted in his arms to face him, and put her wet hands around his neck.

"Maybe I want to make a formal announcement, and I didn't want to ruin the surprise?" She teased.

She could feel a wave of relief roll off of him as he covered her mouth in kisses.

"That's enough, you two. Save it for later." Lamn teased as he walked by them to leave more dishes.

Tark tore his mouth away, reluctantly, but couldn't stop himself from staring into Eve's eyes. He was desperate for her to make her decision known and end his anxious suffering.

"Armoniel!"

From the kitchen, Eve heard Lamn's voice in the sitting room. She grabbed Tark's arm and pulled him with her to greet her grandfather. She could see Lamn and Armoniel standing by a sofa, and caught the last few words of their conversation, "... is being taken to the Archangels for further direction. There is nothing we can do now but wait, and disrupt his plans wherever we find them." Both of their eyes snapped to Eve and Tark as they walked in. Armoniel nodded at Lamn, their conversation closed for the moment, as he rushed to sweep Eve up in a hug.

When everyone was seated, and coffee was served, Eve took a moment to just bask in the love of her family. It was not that long ago that she thought she was just an outcast, a small-town girl, with a dead-end job, and dreams of being something more someday.

Today was someday.

She stood nervously, and Tark raised an eyebrow at her, his eyes hopeful. "Uh... Tark and I have an announcement to make."

Tark jumped to his feet beside her. All eyes were on them, Lamn had a knowing smirk.

Eve fidgeted with her hands, and Tark could see she was holding the ring.

He leaned in and whispered in her ear, so only she could hear. "This would be easier if I knew what your answer was."

She pushed the ring into his hands so no one else could see it. He froze in place, a devastated look of horror on his face.

Does he think I'm rejecting him in front of the whole family?

She leaned in close to him, so only he could hear, and whispered. "So you can put it on my finger with everyone present."

He reacted immediately, throwing his arms around her tightly and squeezing, the air whooshing out of his lungs loudly with relief.

"Can't... breathe..." She managed as she tapped her useless arms against his sides.

Tark chuckled self-consciously as he released Eve. She nodded to him, and he kneeled down, one knee on the carpet, reenacting the proposal scene for Eve's family. Ruth gasped, and tears spilled from her eyes in anticipation. Lamn looked on proudly, and Armoniel was openly weeping with delight. Tark wasn't sure what he was supposed to do, so he slid the ring onto her finger, and looked up for some direction as to what to do next.

Eve let him off the hook. "We're getting married!" She announced with a huge smile on her face.

Everyone was up, embracing the bride and groom-to-be. Tears were shed. Congratulations were offered. Eve looked from person to person: her mother, her father, her grandfather, her fiance... THIS. This was family. She was surrounded by people who accepted her, loved her, and supported her. She could share this life event with them, and have it mean something. She knew without a doubt they would always be there for her for the rest of their lives. And as fae, and Watchers, seemed to live endlessly, she could count on having them with her pretty much forever. She finally had the family she had always craved. She finally understood happiness.

THE END

Fay Smith is a military brat who moved much of her life. The constant upheaval led to a love for reading and eventually writing. There is always some piece of her in her writing. She writes several genres, including Science Fiction, Fantasy, Romance, and Erotica. She currently lives in New England, in the USA, with her husband, three dogs, and a cat. You can find her on Instagram, TikTok, and Facebook as FaySmithAuthor.